KALLIOPEE:

A WIFE'S SACRIFICE

BOOK TWO

KALLIOPEE: A WIFE'S SACRIFICE

Koko Nhan

El Paso, Texas
www.warmpublishing.com

Original title: *Kalliopée: Le tribu d'une épouse*
published by Black Ink Édition
La Jarne, France

Interior design by Warm Publishing
Cover design by Angela Haddon
Art by Scarlett Lovell
Translated from French by Iris Clark
Proofreading by Claire Ashgrove

ISBN: 978-1-958447-36-9

TRIGGER WARNINGS

Although Kalliopee is a romance please note that there are several themes within this book that may trigger those who have experienced similar trauma. If you are easily triggered by dark content like violence, sexual assault, grief, and other proceed with caution and at your own discretion.

♫ *Because novels are also entitled to their soundtrack, Kalliopee: A Wife's Sacrifice comes with a playlist that you'll find at the end of the book.* ♫

Prologue

Almost three thousand years ago, the world as it existed disappeared. The many conflicts between the ancient nations brought chaos to our planet. Men, too blinded by their desire to possess goods that didn't belong to them, ignored the signals that Earth was sending. They were blind to the diseases that decimated the majority of the population, to the climatic upheavals that made life hostile on ninety percent of the land. Worse, they tested the planet, throwing bombs on its farms, on its cities populated by innocents, which lit up the sky. When Humanity realized its mistake, it was too late. Cities were ravaged by fire, epidemics were uncontrollable, and foodstuffs were exhausted. From each continent, only a handful of men remained. They all left, searching for a place to live without fearing the worst.

However, refusing to admit their mistakes, the men blamed the women. After all, some of them ruled nations.

Someone had to be responsible, and it was out of the question to bear the burden of any guilt. As punishment, women were disenfranchised, scorned, and enslaved.

It was under these precepts that the Union of the Five was born several centuries later. Aquaria, people of fishermen and sailors, took advantage of the ocean in the northeast of the continent. Lapisia, a kingdom made rich by its minerals, established its citadel at the foot of the Rocky Mountains. Viridia, for its part, enjoyed green valleys and lakes. Its fertile lands allowed the whole Union to feed itself and provide for its health. Nivisia supplied the other four kingdoms with fine woods and game. And finally, there was Liberisia—where nomadic people settled according to the seasons. Its citizens were among the hardest workers. They provided an invaluable workforce.

But if Humanity learns from its mistakes, it ends up forgetting them. At the risk, one day, of repeating them…

CHAPTER 1

KALLIOPEE

I find it difficult to tear my eyes away from my reflection. The mirror shows me a woman so different that I barely recognize myself. The crown I wear today is about to return to its box, never to come out again. By tonight, mine will be just like Karel's.

A slight smile forms on my lips at the memory of our night together, but the next moment, fear twists in my stomach. Will I be up to the task? Will the promises we made yesterday be kept? Will we manage to stay united as we vowed when our bodies became one?

"You seem happy, Your Highness."

I turn to Sienna, swallowing my smile. A knock on my door prevents me from replying, and then a servant enters, bowing when I invite him in.

"Your Highness, His Majesty King Läven is here."

My eyes widen. I never thought he would make the trip here. Not even for my wedding. Since I left my homeland, I haven't received a single letter from him. Or perhaps they hadn't been given to me… As for me, I couldn't bring myself to write to him. What could I have said? Lies? Reproaches?

"He wishes to speak with you," the servant informs me.

I lower my head just long enough to gather my chaotic thoughts. I cling to the belt of my robe, hoping that fiddling with it will help me find a response. I inhale, exhale, and finally puff out my chest.

"Show him in," I command with confidence.

A single look at Sienna, and she understands my silent request, slipping away and leaving me alone. I take a step toward the closed door, swallow hard, and then fix my gaze on the handle as it turns.

The next second, the hinges creak, and my father appears.

I feel as if time stands still when his eyes fall on me. Emotion overwhelms me, and despite the reproaches I want to make, I throw myself into his arms like a child. I forget my questions and resentments because the little girl inside me rejoices at his presence. He doesn't push me away, and just like when I was knee-high, he gently strokes the back of my neck with his fingertips. This comfort fills my lungs with air. My heart beats so loudly that I have to close my eyes to calm it. I breathe in the scent I've missed so much, the warmth that has always soothed me, and the strength that made me feel like I would never be afraid of anything. In my ears, I hear the beats resonating in his chest.

"Father," I whisper, my throat tight as my fingers cling to his jacket as if to ensure he is really there.

"Let me look at you," he says, his voice hoarse.

I pull away and blink to make the tears disappear before they can fall and ruin my makeup.

"You still have the most beautiful eyes," he smiles nostalgically, caressing my cheek.

At his words, my lips stretch into a smile. When he steps away completely and his warm palm leaves my face, I feel the cold taking over my body; my smile fades. He turns around, stopping to look at the torn tapestry in amusement.

"I see you haven't lost your fiery spirit."

I study his slender silhouette, and pain discreetly seeps in. His crown, adorned with as many jewels as mine, rests on his head. His chestnut curls fall onto his neck, giving him a wild look. When he spins around, he offers me a perfect smile. His well-groomed beard, tinged with red, has started to gray in places. Yet, despite that, he retains an almost boyish expression. My eyes rise to meet his azure gaze. I didn't know if I'd ever see him again, but now that he's here, I'm torn between loving him and hating him.

"A lovely piece of work," he teases, giving me one of his famous winks.

Faced with the lightness of his words, I no longer feel like loving him. Does he have any idea what I've endured? Can he imagine how much I've suffered? No, or he pretends to be unaware to ease his conscience or his guilt. Either way, it hurts.

His smile fades as my silence screams my anger and resentment.

"Kalliopee," he calls softly.

"Did you know? About the queen and the princess? Were you aware?" I murmur, my voice pleading.

I hope he'll tell me he suspected nothing, that he sent me here thinking I'd be safe. Yet, the way his head turns away proves I hadn't imagined his knowing.

"Why?" I ask.

"For peace."

That single word makes me feel guilty for harboring this resentment. Because, like him, that was the goal I wanted to achieve. Once again, his gaze locks with mine, and I realize what sets us apart. I could never have sacrificed someone else to achieve my goals. However, if he had told me everything in detail, there's no doubt I would have come here anyway. I would have come here willingly, knowing what awaited. What I was risking.

"It was the only thing to do. You know that as well as I do," he says sternly.

"But what about me? You… As a father, you always said you'd kill anyone who threatened my life, and yet you sent me here, to this king, when… when…"

I lose my words, unable to gather my thoughts. As much as I hate King Xerios, he never hurt me as much as my own father. Today, I realize the people we love deeply are the only ones capable of wounding us so painfully.

"The queen and the princess were killed by Viridians. You must have known the king would want to make me pay for that, right?"

"They attacked you?" he asks, worried.

A sarcastic laugh escapes my lips. How can he care when he's the one who sent me here? How dare he be concerned about my fate now?

He scratches the space between his eyebrows, as he always does when he can't solve a thorny problem. And while this gesture once touched me, today, it tests my patience. I want to scream at him to hurry up and find his words, to command him to mend my wounded heart.

"It's not—"

His sentence dies as a new knock on the door sounds. Immediately, a flock of maids rush into my room, and a majestic dress is laid out on my bed. I realize it's time. I observe the fabric without blinking, not daring to look at my father. Yet, in the corner of my eye, I see him taking a step in my direction.

"I'll see you at the ceremony," I say in a tone meant to sound detached.

I feign this coldness that is so unlike me to mask the sorrow I feel. He adds nothing and, like a breeze, disappears. My heartbeat quickens, anxiety taking hold.

"Your Highness?" a maid calls.

My eyes follow the direction of her voice, and with a timid smile on her lips, she points to the dress. Mechanically, I slip off the robe covering my body while the servants place the dress in the center of the room. The dress is unique, not only because it's intended for a royal ceremony. No, it also represents an unprecedented alliance. Interracial marriages are forbidden, and those of mixed blood have as few rights as women. Yet, this morning, the Prince of Lapisia will marry the Princess of Viridia.

Exceptional event. Exceptional dress.

The lace top is a dark red, the color of the desert city. Thin straps, adorned with pearly beads, will hold it to my shoulders. While the fabric is fitted at the waist and perfectly hugs my chest, the bottom is made of tulle, giving it significant volume. It's a succession of layers of a paler red, while the train is emerald-green. *My color*. As if the fabric had brushed against a verdant surface. It's sublime. Yet, with a knot in my stomach, I slip one leg into it. Several adjustments had to be made in the past few days, and I fear it may need altering again.

Two maids stand on either side as I position myself in the center, and they lift the dress up along my body. My arms gently slip into the straps. When they reach my shoulders, I'm surprised. I expected to feel the weight of the garment, but on the contrary, it feels as if I'm wearing nothing at all. The two maids step back in unison, and then I feel cold fingers closing the buttons on my back. This chill is enough to restore my lost breath. Eyes closed, I wait. Finally, when the maid steps away, I open my eyes again, filled with a mix of fear and excitement.

"It suits you perfectly, Your Highness."

I smile at her, thrilled that no further adjustments are needed. The maids, beaming, eagerly gesture for me to look in the mirror. The two weeks of preparations have allowed me to reassure the staff about me, and now, they greet me, sometimes even smile at me. It's… *surprising*. But pleasant. I approach the mirror, and a sense of unease washes over me when, at last, I see myself. Although this marriage was planned, its imminence is frightening.

It's what I want, yes. I love Karel, and I'm convinced I can only be happy by his side, but apprehension grips me. In a few hours, I will be bound to him until our bodies return to dust.

CHAPTER 2

KALLIOPEE

Breathless, I wait in front of the temple doors. My ladies-in-waiting have left me, and now I'm alone on my father's arm. Both of us are nervous. Today, the weather is mild, and I hope it's a good omen, a sign my marriage won't suffer drought. Even though I know it's an illusion, especially these days.

I close my eyes, and the veil covering my face brushes against my skin. I feel my blood pulsing in my ears, and my carotid artery throbs powerfully in my neck. Although I harbor resentment toward my father, I cling to his jacket to keep myself from turning back because, suddenly, I'm terrified by the significance of the event. I scold myself inwardly. This marriage doesn't change how I feel; alongside Karel is where I want to spend my life. My father's warm palm brushes my fingers to stop their trembling. The gesture, though gentle, isn't enough to calm me.

With a thunderous rumble, the grand doors open, but my eyes remain closed. Inside, the whispers we could barely hear moments ago cease, and a sinister silence falls. My shaky legs refuse to move. My father whispers my name, and my eyelids lift heavily. My gaze slides down the main aisle. It seems so long that I fear I won't reach the end. But finally, I see *him*. His body is rigid, and I can barely make out his features, but I imagine he exudes, as always, a charismatic strength.

On their own, my legs start moving when the wedding march of Lapisia begins. A melody I've heard endlessly for days. I've been trained to move in rhythm; I mustn't go too fast or too slow. While the task seemed easy before, today I struggle to pace myself. The closer I get to him, the more his features become clear, and the stronger my urge to run to him grows. Even though the veil swaying against my face prevents me from seeing him clearly.

I inhale, close my eyes, and open them again immediately. Just a few moments to remember what I feel for Karel and for my people. A few moments to remind myself I don't want to be anywhere else. When my eyes lock onto Karel's again, my heart leaps fiercely, and my body straightens. With my back straight and my head held high, I walk down the aisle that leads to him. Him, so commanding in the jacket adorned with medals that showcase his bravery in battle. Him, so princely, with a crown that is raw and true to his nature. His sharp gaze fixes on me without blinking, a mix of tenderness and possessiveness that takes my breath away. When I see him like this, I sense no hesitation, no fear, just a perfect certainty. As I approach, I notice his ruby-red jacket is also trimmed with dark green.

As I pass, some murmur. Yet, when Karel's eyes catch mine again, with an intensity unique to him, I ignore what they might be saying about me. Only he matters. It has always been only him.

I feel my father's face turn toward me, and under my fingers, his arm tenses. Does he sense my heart now belongs solely to the man standing before us?

My breath quickens. Impatience overtakes me, and I have to force myself not to rush. Just ten more steps.

A slight smile tugs at the prince's lips. I return it, and my eyes grow moist. I've never been so terrified and excited in my entire life.

As the distance between us shrinks, a flood of memories overwhelms me. I remember the day I said goodbye to him because our destinies had to part. Returning to Viridia, I realized that love could hurt. The face of the young boy who gave me my first feelings overlaps with the man he has become. They are quite different, yet my feelings are unchanged.

No, I lie. They are even stronger than before. Today, I'm certain nothing will ever alter them. No one but him could ever make me love so deeply. Our reunion was intense and painful; I thought I could hate him, but even then, I desired him. Despite everything, especially myself.

When we reach the foot of the steps leading to the altar, my father squeezes my fingers firmly. Karel approaches us slowly, like the predator he is, with a restrained strength. Every step is calculated, and as always, his charm is effective. He turns his attention to my father, who greets him and hands him my hand. The absence of Karel's eyes as an anchor almost makes me falter, but fortunately, the warmth emanating from him the moment our palms meet is comforting and reassuring. Over time, it has become familiar and necessary to me. Karel takes his place by my side, and with a slight pressure on my fingers, he eradicates the remaining fear I had. I swallow hard as we climb the few steps that lead us to the master of ceremonies, before whom we kneel, heads bowed.

At that moment, Karel releases my hand, and the feeling of calm dissipates. I already want the ceremony to end so I can curl up in his arms.

The veil makes me hotter and hotter, and I'm dying to remove it so I no longer feel like I'm suffocating.

"Ladies and gentlemen, we are all gathered here today to witness the union of Karel Edark, Prince of Lapisia, son of Xerios Edark, and Kalliopee Talae, Princess of Viridia, daughter of Läven Talae."

He pauses before stepping behind a lectern while I hear the guests take their seats on the benches set up in the temple. During this welcome pause, I reflect that when I was a child, only the father's name was mentioned in a person's identity and it didn't bother me. Today, I wish the mother's name was also mentioned. By omitting it, it's as if she is stripped of her role.

"Across seas, deserts, forests, I swear fidelity to you," the celebrant's voice proclaims, making me start slightly. "In life, death, war, or peace, I dedicate my heart to you."

As the officiant pronounces these words, I focus on the vivid colors of the stained-glass windows reflecting at our knees. Despite the warmth outside, the atmosphere here suddenly makes me shiver. Without placing my hand on my chest, I can feel the power of my heartbeat. It's frightening because I feel like my heart will never slow down.

"Through the centuries, the world has changed, but not the love that unites two souls," he continues. "Love grows even in arid land. It doesn't need water to flourish. Love survives wars, diseases, tragedies. And today, under the eyes of our ancestors, we celebrate the love of a prince and a princess. The union of two Crowns."

Out of the corner of my eye, I watch Karel, who, despite his bowed head, remains straight and proud. Nothing happening here seems to affect him. In a way, I envy his composure, but I'm beginning to know him well enough to realize that most of the time he's playing a role. At least, I believe so.

"Your Highness," calls the officiant.

Immediately, Karel straightens and offers his hand to help me do the same. Together, we turn to face each other, and I have to lift my head to meet his gaze.

"Across seas, deserts, forests," Karel repeats in his deep voice, which, as always, makes me feel like I have a weight in my stomach. "I swear fidelity to you." He raises his hand, palm facing me, his bright eyes still locked on mine. "In life, death, war, or peace, I dedicate my heart to you." As he presents his left palm to me, I struggle to breathe. I know it's my turn to say these words, but I can barely swallow.

His eyebrows knit together, and I take a deep breath. "Across seas, deserts, forests," I repeat, my voice raspy. Sometimes I wish I could be like him. I wish I could keep my cool, not be so transparent. "I swear fidelity to you." My palm rises to meet his, without touching. "In life, death, war, or peace, I dedicate my heart to you."

During this exchange, neither of us blinks, making me almost feel like it's just the two of us, as if the room isn't filled with guests here to celebrate our union. Karel always has the ability to transport me to another universe, an alternate reality where we are alone in the world. Each time, it allows me to catch my breath.

A man approaches Karel, holding an open chest in his hands. On the reddish velvet lie two gold bracelets, resembling small cuffs or chains. They are thin, with a slight gap visible. I know that in a few moments, that gap will disappear, along with my freedom. The prince had managed to make me forget the stakes of this ceremony, but seeing the bracelets feels like a cold shower. I'm aware of what they symbolize: my belonging to this man. My enslavement. Although I'm certain Karel won't abuse his position, knowing I'll have to wear them frightens me. The vows we just exchanged and the officiant's introduction about love now seem completely hypocritical.

His fingers grasp the first bracelet, and an unpleasant warmth fills me. The veil clings to my damp forehead.

"Breathe," Karel whispers, so only I can hear.

Easier said than done… It's not him who's about to have shackles on his wrists. I shift my focus to his face. Taking his task to heart, he lowers my right arm and places the first bracelet on it with the utmost delicacy. I inhale, then struggle to swallow as a man approaches, holding a tisonnier that will lock the bracelet together forever. My throat is dry from anxiety, and Karel notices my change in demeanor. His eyes immediately lock onto mine, and his brows knit together. He turns his head and sees the metal rod, its tip glowing red from the flames. Without hesitation, he takes it, and I feel his fingers apply a gentle pressure on my wrist, which he still holds.

The tisonnier quickly meets the bracelet. Karel fastens the thin gold plate, then begins to solder the two parts together. Unconsciously, my body tenses, and I close my eyes. Even with my eyelids shut, I can sense everything: Karel's held breath, the temple's solemn silence, the glowing tip of the rod. Its heat radiates toward my skin without even touching it.

There's no need for words to accompany this symbolic ritual; that would push the hypocrisy to its peak. My eyes open again as a few drops of water trickle onto my wrists. Using a small cup, Karel extinguishes the incandescence of the band that will mark my belonging from this day forward. A slight smoke rises when the elements meet. In the following minutes, Karel does the same with the second bracelet. Despite my hatred for what is happening, I remain strangely mesmerized by his actions and to ward off the cold from taking over, I focus on his warm fingers brushing my skin now and then. When he finishes, he gently releases my arm, and our eyes meet.

The possessive glint in his eyes quickens my heartbeat. Now, I am his. I push back the significance of my enslavement and think only of what truly matters to me. After all, isn't this what I've always wanted? To unite my fate with his? In a moment that belongs only to us, isolating us in a bubble that nothing and no one can penetrate, he silently promises me something that makes me want to leap into his arms: *I will treat you as my equal.* I'm aware that, in our world, willpower and power don't always align—especially since I have many enemies, starting with his father—but I need to believe him.

I take a deep breath, and we once again face the officiant, kneeling. Lapisian chants rise in the nave, echoing in the temple. I can't find them beautiful, and though I'm usually curious and eager to discover new things, I can barely listen.

The ceremony continues, and the officiant gives a speech I don't even hear. When two men, dressed in robes bearing the colors of our kingdoms, position themselves before me, I know what's coming next. As expected, my head is relieved of my crown. It's quickly placed in its case. I watch it, unable to look away. It has always seemed heavy and uncomfortable, but it represented what was left of my heritage. When the case closes, I feel as if the first chapter of my life has definitively ended. Over my lashes, I glimpse the crown that will now adorn my head. It's an exact replica of the one resting on Karel's dark curls: raw, hammered, engraved metal. Once it crowns my head, I'm surprised. It feels as light as a feather.

I stare, unblinking, at the only weight I feel: the weight of the sealed bracelets on my wrists. Each second, they seem to grow heavier. Karel stands, and my breath catches. I've attended unions before, but I never realized how grueling it could be, how this symbolic ritual could inflict such a real wound. Though I love Karel, I hate what is happening today. The prince stands behind me, and my trembling arms rise above my head. He joins my wrists as the officiant approaches me.

"From this moment, Kalliopee Talae, Princess of Viridia, daughter of Läven Talae, you will be the wife of Karel Edark, Prince of Lapisia, son of Xerios Edark. Through this union, you relinquish your title to become a Princess of Lapisia. You relinquish your name. You relinquish your identity."

Despite my efforts, I can't stop my eyes from filling with tears.

"Through this union, you renounce your freedom."

I can't prevent the knot from forming in my stomach.

"Through this union, you agree to sacrifice your body, your soul, and your life to your husband."

A tear falls, and my hands, held by the prince, can't even wipe it away.

"Now, Karel Edark, Prince of Lapisia, son of Xerios Edark, you will have at your disposal your wife, Kalliopee Edark, Princess of Lapisia, daughter of Läven Talae, her body, her soul, her life, according to your desires."

My throat tightens as Karel's grip tightens. I try to regain my composure, but I fully realize what my life will be now. This ceremony symbolizes the end of my freedom. And though it was never complete, it will now be nonexistent.

The prince releases my hands, and I stand. I catch his profile as he takes his place beside me, then we face each other. He gently lifts the veil that partly obscured me from his view, and his brow furrows at the sight of the tears streaming down my face.

To seal our union, a kiss must be exchanged. It's a hypocritical way to ask for a woman's consent, but do we have a choice?

His lips touch mine. They are as cold and unyielding as marble, far from the gentle kisses he sometimes gives me, worlds away from the more forceful ones that sometimes take my breath away. This one is lifeless. Empty. Hollow. I would have resented him if he'd tried to soothe the invisible wound he unintentionally inflicted on me.. Around us, the guests rise, acclaiming the prince. Why would they acclaim me? I'm supposed to gain nothing, just give.

We turn to face the assembly, and then his breath brushes my cheek.

"One day, I will free you from these chains, *Shaadi*. You will be my wife, and free."

My face turns toward him, and I see he has abandoned his impassive mask. His eyes now reflect an unyielding hardness.

"I hate them as much as you do," he murmurs, staring at one of the bracelets now adorning my wrists.

Before I can find the right words, he presents his profile to me, then his arm, and together, we walk back up the aisle to leave the temple.

One day, I will be a free wife. I believe it, but I also know I will have to wait until he ascends the throne. I'm convinced of this bitter truth as my gaze meets the king's piercing stare.

Chapter 3

Kalliopee

"Their Royal Highnesses, the Prince and Princess of Lapisia," a herald announces as we enter the ballroom.

I hold my breath while Karel firmly grips my hand. I gaze around the room with a wonder I struggle to measure. The ruby-red of Lapisia blends with the emerald-green of Viridia. Everywhere. On the hanging tapestries, on the tablecloths, even the flower arrangements adorning the room intertwine our colors. I hadn't imagined they would marry so well, that the whole would be so harmonious. I glance up to observe the high ceiling and quickly lower my head, overcome with vertigo. My free hand grabs the top of my dress to avoid stepping on it. The guests part as we pass and bow respectfully. My fingers tighten around Karel's when I fear nervousness might overwhelm me. With the most graceful stride possible, we cross the room to the two seats on the dais. Karel shows no emotion. I wonder what he feels, and if, despite the ceremony's symbolism, he's happy to be united with me. He rarely speaks, and to claim that his difficulty in communicating doesn't, sometimes, plunge me into a sea of doubts would be a lie.

Finally, on the dais, we turn to face the guests and sit down. A man delivers a speech that I only partly listen to; I'm too preoccupied with the intensity of my father's stare. His jaw seems clenched, his body tense. I know him well enough to know he's angry with me, but whatever the reason, I don't believe he has the right.

I'm brought out of my thoughts by the applause of the audience watching us. The smiles from the guests puzzle me. I wonder which ones are genuine and which are feigned. I gradually realize that maybe my ability to discern between kind-hearted people and dishonest ones never existed.

"Are you okay?" Karel whispers once we no longer pique the assembly's curiosity.

I turn to him but only see his profile. His eyes are locked on the audience, as if I dreamed his question. Seeing that I don't respond, he turns to me. His brows furrow, and his gaze slides down to my lips, which curve into a smile that I try to make convincing.

"Would my daughter honor me with a dance?" my father asks, extending his hand.

I immediately focus on my father, placing my palm on his. I face Karel again, who with a barely perceptible nod encourages me to accept. I straighten, place my palm in my father's hand, and we make our way to the dance floor. Guests step aside, giving us the space to dance. He draws me closer, my hand resting on his shoulder: a ballet we've performed on numerous occasions, and my body moves by instinct, evidently haven't forgotten. In Viridia, he and I were accustomed to opening the ball. As soon as the music starts, we move in rhythm. The sweat on my skin causes my fingers to slide, prompting my father to tighten his grip. We turn and turn again.

"Did your trip go well?" I inquire, trying to make conversation.

"Quite well, considering the circumstances."

I let my gaze wander around the room and easily spot the Viridian soldiers tasked with ensuring their king's protection. My father has been cautious; they are numerous.

"I'm not taking any risks," he reassures me. "I'm leaving at dawn."

"Why so early?"

"I prefer not to overstay our welcome with the Lapisians. I'm not in danger, but I'm not exactly welcome here either."

I nod, aware he speaks the truth. Who knows if renegade Lapisians might seek revenge. The sooner he's back in Viridian territory, the safer he'll be. I take advantage of his presence to ask the questions that have been bothering me since I left.

"How is Viridia faring?"

A tender smile crosses his face at the mention of our kingdom. "Wonderful. Our men have returned home; for those who didn't return… their families can finally mourn without fear of losing another member. Life has resumed, and it will surely take time for the specter of war to no longer haunt us, but the future looks promising."

Relief washes over me at his words. For years, our daily lives had been under the shadow of a conflict that brought us no respite. While the battles were far from our kingdom, the wounded and the dead poured in every day.

"The palace seems quite empty without your presence," he murmurs thoughtfully.

"I'm sure your days are too busy for you to have time to miss me." I attempt to lighten the mood.

"Silas has been a great help; I'm not alone."

"He didn't come," I note.

Silas is one of the ten members of the royal council. Probably the most influential, but also the one I like the least. He's actually the one who pushed my father to propose this alliance.

"He doesn't like long journeys," he replies.

I simply nod.

"And Malo, how is she?" I ask, a hint of worry in my voice.

His gaze, directed toward the assembly, turns to me. His lips tighten, but in the next instant, he puts on a smile that doesn't reach his eyes. "She's now the wife of a respectable farmer."

My father has never been good at deceiving people. Me least of all.

"For whom is he respectable?" I dare, teeth clenched.

"Kalliopee…" He seems to be lecturing me.

He looks away and focuses on the dance. The atmosphere, tinged with reserve, suddenly thickens. Unsaid words weigh down our steps, slow our pace, stiffen our limbs. I know it's his way of avoiding a conversation that troubles him. I resent him for it, so I refuse to maintain the silence that suits him.

"Why have you never changed anything?"

He doesn't need me to be more explicit to understand my implication. His silence breaks my reserve, and I stop my steps, annoyed that he treats me like a child. With an authoritative gesture, he pulls me closer and invites me to continue, which I do reluctantly. The attention of the guests, focused on us, prevents me from causing a scene on my wedding day.

"Because that's how the Union of Five operates. We define the rules together," he reminds me condescendingly, as if I understand nothing at all.

I refuse to let him continue hiding behind the Union—which has ceased to exist since the war—to excuse his inaction.

"There's no Union of Five anymore, it's been over seven years," I counter, unable to hold back my thoughts.

"In that case, let's say I'm not that kind of king."

My brows furrow at this response, its meaning escaping me. When his eyes finally meet mine, I sense nothing but gentleness. I don't understand what he's implying, but I don't have time to dwell on it as he leads me onto a new subject.

"Are you happy with him?"

I tilt my head to see what he's staring at so seriously and notice Karel deeply engaged in conversation with his friends, including a man whose back is unfamiliar to me.

"I am," I affirm, locking my gaze with my husband's, who has felt my eyes on him. "And I will be even happier when he becomes king."

My heart swells at the intensity with which Karel examines me.

"I hope so for you, but don't forget where you come from," my father lectures, forcing me to face him.

I suppress a contemptuous laugh trying to escape my lips. No, I will never forget Viridia, nor the decisions and passivity of its king.

"I know where I come from, Father, but Karel is now my husband."

His hand grips my hip unkindly. He stares at me sternly, with a hint of severity, like when he caught me misbehaving as a child. "And I am your father," he scolds me in a whisper.

Emotion washes over me at his words. How can one love someone so deeply and yet despise them just as strongly?

"He's now my husband," I repeat, jaw clenched. "And if I were ever forced to choose between either of you, it would be him."

"How can you—"

"What?" I cut him off insolently. "Isn't that what these bracelets mean? If you had been that kind of king, I might have had the right to choose *you*, but today, I have lost my free will."

I lie when I say my marriage compels me to support Karel. It was my heart that chose him, at the expense of everything else. My father resents me for speaking these words, but I resent him just as much. Before leaving Viridia, I respected him. Today, I'm not sure if that's still the case. My father has come down from his pedestal. He doesn't seem as tall and strong as he once did. I don't understand why he never did anything to change the fate of women, if only for me. Isn't that what a father should do? Protect his child at the risk of his own life? Would Mom have approved of his passivity?

"I love you, Father," I soften. "But because you did nothing, I no longer admire you."

"I'm not that kind of king," he justifies himself once more.

"What are you talking about?" I ask, impatiently.

Our words are no longer harsh but only truthful. There's no more pride, no more dignity, only a king owning his weakness. I look at him differently now, noticing each wrinkle etched into his face over the years. The helplessness radiating from him is more disconcerting than I expected.

His cerulean eyes meet mine, and in a whisper, he admits his truth. "I'm not one of those destined to change the world. I'm not strong enough, Kalliopee."

Troubled, I look away and catch Karel's gaze again. He watches the scene intently, probably thinking my father and I are sharing a moment of tenderness and affection, but he seems to understand the turmoil that has taken hold of my heart.

"Neither is he," my father concludes.

"You're wrong. You don't know him!" I snap.

I pull away from my father and face him. My attitude barely hides the resentment I feel toward him, but before my words can outpace my thoughts, I decide to walk away. I've barely taken a step when he grabs my arm and slips a chain into my hand. I turn and open my palm to see what's inside. A small vial on a pendant.

"You might need this one day. You'll probably have many enemies," my father murmurs in a severe tone.

"Poison? Really?" I laugh, outraged.

"Take it, please."

I roll my eyes, and though he would probably like to scold me for my bad manners, he knows he no longer has the right. I decide to accept his gift, even though I never intend to use it. To hide it, I open the chain and fasten it around my neck, tucking the pendant under my collar.

I turn away from my father and walk off. A strange feeling overtakes me as the distance between us grows, as if everything has been said. As if this is the end of our father-daughter relationship. I pass Amadeus, who seems to be having a heated conversation with a man staring at me intently as I walk by. When I reach Karel, he still watches me with the same seriousness. I suppose his friend's presence prevents him from asking the questions burning on his lips. The young woman with short hair, standing between the guards Jonah and Zaïn, greets me.

"Let me introduce Lavia, Jonah's wife."

She gives me a smile and a curtsy before raising her wine glass to her lips. I immediately notice the bracelets around her wrists. It's surprising how I never paid attention to them before. Now that mine weigh on my arms, I seem to see them everywhere. All around us. No matter the colorful dresses or the jewelry adorning these women's necks, I only see their restraints.

"If you don't mind," Jonah interrupts my thoughts, "Lavia and I plan to dance all night. For once, we've managed to get rid of our girls."

"You're the one who insists they be home every night," Lavia replies.

"I don't want to miss another second," he answers, never taking his eyes off her.

Silently, without saying another word, they exchange a look. I suddenly feel like an intruder in this silent, truthful conversation. Jonah grabs Lavia's glass and, after congratulating us again, leads her to the dance floor. I smile, touched, as I watch her laugh into her husband's neck. I never suspected Jonah was capable of humor.

Watching them, I realize that no matter the sacrifices Karel and I must make, peace is worth it.

"Well, I have things to do," Zaïn says.

Karel laughs at Zaïn's words. "Enjoy your night!" says Karel.

"Like it's the last one," the soldier replies, winking to make his intentions clear.

As Zaïn walks away, I notice he's heading toward a group of young women, their bare arms signaling their single status. I turn to Karel and see that the man I had observed from behind is now watching me with curiosity that lacks hostility.

I'm surprised by how much he looks like my husband. Their eyes are almost identical, though the stranger's are lighter, less intense. His smile mirrors Karel's perfectly, though his jaw is less angular. If I had to summarize my first impression, I'd say this guest is a more refined version of Karel.

"Maybe I should have left you at the base of that cliff," the young man jokes, winking at me.

I cautiously smile at Karel, who is looking at the chain hidden under my dress. I expect him to ask about it, but he doesn't. Instead, he steps beside me.

"Kalliopee, this is Kaïs, my cousin."

Kaïs offers his hand and performs a courtly kiss once my fingers rest in his, never losing his playful demeanor. I'm unsure what to make of him. Strangely, he doesn't make me uncomfortable, but I also know I tend to trust too easily. When he finally lets go, I quickly pull my arm back, a gesture he notices but doesn't seem offended by.

He steps closer, scrutinizing my eyes curiously. Instinctively, I step back and bump into Karel's chest, who is now behind me. Karel's hands rest on my hips in a gesture that's both protective and possessive.

"Stop bothering her, will you?" Karel chides.

Kaïs steps back, still smiling. "I'm just teasing my lovely cousin-in-law. Did you know I could have been your husband? Admit it, you would have had a better deal. I'm… a bit more flexible than Karel, and I smile a lot more."

"The difference is obvious," I agree.

I instantly regret feeling so comfortable as to joke, but he takes it in stride and even throws a playful glance at Karel.

"But why could you have been my husband?" I dare to ask.

"He claims he saved my life," Karel grumbles.

"That's exactly what I did!" Kaïs replies.

"No… it was just a sprain," continues Karel.

Kaïs rolls his eyes and shakes his head. I feel strangely out of place in this duo, but I also feel I'm about to discover a side of Karel I don't know.

"If I hadn't taken you back to the palace, you would have died."

"You didn't take me back; my horse did. You just helped me get on it!" the prince protests.

The conversation, though lively, reveals the affection these two men share, and I sense Karel and his cousin have many memories together.

"We're going to have a lot of fun in the coming weeks. Be careful not to slip this time; I won't be there to rescue you," Kaïs concludes.

My eyebrows knit together at this announcement, which I don't understand.

"I'll be your guest for an indefinite period," he answers my unspoken question.

"It's definitely *definite*," Karel counters.

I smile, watching this unprecedented face-off. Indeed, we're going to have a lot of fun. The conversations promise to be lively, especially since I know Karel must like him a lot. Otherwise, he would have already ended the discussion.

"My uncle will be thrilled to have me stay," Kaïs continues.

"He hates you," Karel says.

"Does he like anyone on this earth?" Kaïs mocks.

I can't hold back my laugh, and at this sound, Kaïs's smile broadens.

"I like you!" he surprises me.

"If you don't mind, we'll leave you here. We have to give our guests a dance, then we'll go to bed. It's been a long day for Kalliopee."

I'm about to deny it and confess I'm just starting to have fun, but Karel doesn't give me the chance and pulls me away without any gentleness. I give a tight smile to the guests we pass to mask my annoyance at his behavior.

I straighten and tug sharply, but discreetly, on my arm to let him know I don't like how he's acting. Karel stops immediately and faces me. He notices me rubbing my wrist, and his gaze locks onto mine. My heart skips a beat when a flicker of guilt seems to cross his face. He didn't hurt me; I just wanted him to stop dragging me like a child. But I don't have time to tell him because he steps beside me and offers his hand, never taking his eyes off me.

"Would my wife care to grant me this dance?"

The way he says *wife* is both gentle and possessive. I feel important, loved, and more than anything, unique. Before I let myself be overwhelmed by emotion, I place my fingers in his and nod. This time, it's my stomach that tightens.

Chapter 4

Kalliopee

With hesitant steps, I follow Karel as he leads us through the labyrinth of palace corridors. The guests are still celebrating our wedding in the grand ballroom. We finally enjoyed the festivities to the fullest, but after numerous dances, I think we both wanted to be alone. I was excited when he suggested we retire, but now, with each step we take, my anxiety intensifies. Unlike usual, we're not heading to my room or his. From now on, we will have our own quarters in new apartments. Karel doesn't speak, and his silence only heightens my anxiety. I inhale nervously, catching his attention. His short brown curls, which I had been staring at incessantly, give way to his dark eyes as he glances back at me over his shoulder. Every time our eyes meet, I feel like I'm falling into a void.

"Is everything okay?" he murmurs.

The gentleness in his voice is particular to him. It's not pronounced, and I think anyone else might not detect it. I nod, unable to muster a smile. My chest rises a bit too quickly, which he notices. Yet, he says nothing and turns his head to continue our progress. My fingers grip my dress tightly as we finally reach the doors.

"I asked for the apartments not to be decorated," he tells me. "I thought you'd want them to reflect you."

He gestures for me to enter first, stepping aside. I face the door and, without further thought, lower the handle. The wooden door opens silently, revealing a large room. I expected to see a bed, but instead, we're greeted by a living room. Karel steps ahead and points to another door.

"My office is now here. And there," he adds, indicating the adjoining door, "you have your own library."

An irrepressible smile spreads across my lips at this announcement, and I'm already eager to explore the shelves.

I take a closer look at the room and notice the finely crafted armchairs arranged around a small table, then a much larger table that could serve breakfasts and lunches. My gaze stops on a bay window that seems to lead outside. I quickly approach it, and excitement fills me as I realize it's a terrace overlooking the garden I love to wander. I turn to Karel, a huge smile on my face.

"I won't see the tower anymore," I exclaim, delighted, unable to hold back my words.

"Welcome home," he whispers, his mouth curving into an almost imperceptible smile.

I've been here for several months, but the sincerity of his words fills my heart with joy and serenity.

I move away from the window and run my fingers over the fabric of the large sofa sitting in the middle of the living room. Just as he said, the room is devoid of any decoration. I can already picture making it reflect us—a blend of ruggedness and finesse. Strength against softness.

With his hands in his pockets, he stands by the entrance, never taking his eyes off me as I wander around. My steps lead me to what I assume is our bedroom. His body turns slightly toward me when I reach it.

"Is this our…?" I ask, unable to finish.

He nods, his eyes darkening.

My breath shortens because I know what awaits us beyond. I'm not afraid. This is what I want, too, but I can't help feeling anxious.

He must sense my hesitation because he crosses the space between us with slow steps. My stomach twists, and memories from yesterday flood back. It was perfect, just as I imagined. Yet, tonight feels like another first time, and the cuffs on my wrists make the anticipation bitter. I hate them for ruining this moment.

Karel notices my shift in mood, and his brows furrow when he reaches me. He's so close that our bodies brush against each other, and I have to tilt my head back.

Time freezes, our breaths matching in speed. I wonder if his heart is pounding as hard as mine. Our gazes lock, and I dive into his eyes, as always. I sense everything he's not saying, everything he's kept silent today. I swallow, my throat growing drier. I'm short of breath, and my thoughts become muddled. I can't think clearly or organize my ideas. A lock of hair crosses his forehead, which remains furrowed. A slight glint passes through his eyes, dilating them more each time our chests meet.

My eyes slide over his tense jaw, and then to his pursed lips. I watch them as if trying to enchant them to meet mine. This need is crucial, as if only they can keep me alive.

His hand grabs my neck suddenly, and he pushes me against the bedroom door. I stand on tiptoe to shorten the distance he has to cover. Our mouths meet, and immediately, my body ignites. I clutch his jacket, trying to deepen the kiss. I want more, so much more. I want everything—every breath, every rough touch. He handles my hips roughly, kneading them as if trying to imprint his fingers there. When he presses harder, I bite his lower lip, eliciting a moan to which I respond. His mouth attacks every bit of flesh leading to my neck. His breath grazes my ears harshly, and I think I hear him curse before his teeth sink into my skin. A cry escapes me. Everything is so intense, too intense for me to remain standing. My fingers climb his body to grip his hair, pulling mercilessly.

"Open the door," he orders, his breath ragged.

In my chest, it's euphoria. My heart pounds so hard against my ribcage that it's almost painful. I fumble for the handle and lower it as soon as I find it. My body moves back as the wooden surface no longer supports me, but Karel's arm firmly wraps around my back, preventing me from falling. He doesn't stop inflicting his wild delights on me.

He guides me inside by my hips and spins us so I'm once again pressed against the door. He breaks our embrace, but I struggle to open my eyes. My breath is gone, and I fight to regain it. When my eyelids finally lift, I meet his feverish gaze. His hair is tousled, and his lips are reddened from our intense kisses.

His palm rests on the surface of the door, and he lowers his head, depriving me of his eyes. "We should probably slow down," he manages to murmur, catching his breath.

I press myself more against the wood, searching for the reasons behind his sudden change. He straightens, looks at me, and seems to understand my confusion. He silences my questions by kissing me with a gentleness that isn't his usual. This time, each caress feels like a soft touch. Everything is more modest, more restrained. But that's not how I love Karel. No, I love him when he is himself, as harsh and brutal as the desert of Lapisia.

"No," I whisper against his lips.

He pauses, and then his eyes reveal his dilated pupils, not hiding his desire. I shake my head to emphasize my point. His hand gripping my hip tightens, and my pelvis moves toward him.

"*Shaadi*," he murmurs in a rough voice.

His grip tightens, stopping me from moving closer, and I feel my determination slipping away. I swallow and wait.

"Last night, it was—"

"It was perfect," I interrupt, convinced he's going to say otherwise. "I want you that way, Karel."

This time, I try to pull him toward me, gripping his hips, and it breaks his last bit of restraint. He gives in and kisses me with a power that makes my heart flutter and my mind spin. My vision blurs, and I close my eyes to let my other senses revel in the moment. His taste fills my mouth as our tongues entwine, my fingers feel the heat emanating from him despite the clothing separating us. Only our breaths and the creaking door, pressed by our bodies, break the silence of the room.

His hands slide up my back over the fabric, and just as I'm about to turn around for him to undo it, he tugs at the buttons, sending them flying. I take advantage of his distraction to tear off the pendant and toss it onto the rug by the bed. I don't want to answer his questions now.

His burning fingers touch my neck, then he lifts me to carry me to our bed. Just as eager as he is, I kneel on the mattress and help him remove his princely scarf, then his jacket. I don't waste time with his shirt, not sparing the buttons.

If my boldness initially surprises him, it soon quickens his movements as he works to free me from my dress. The second sleeve is caught by one of my bracelet's welds, forcing him to tug at it. He stares at it while my limbs stiffen. Then, instead of verbally apologizing for what the bracelet symbolizes, he does so with his kisses. His fingers grasp my exposed breast, and the roughness with which he kneads it draws a moan from me. His scent envelops me, making my head spin.

Desperate to touch him in return, I pull away so he can slide my dress over my hips. He doesn't hold back, and I hear the seams rip. He murmurs *I'm sorry*, making me smile, and then the cold rushes over me. My body is so hot that the room suddenly feels freezing. He's still standing, so I cautiously approach to help him slide the spoiled shirt from where it drapes off his shoulders.

When his torso is as bare as mine, my fingers trace his scars. I'm mesmerized by the stories they could tell. I've never dared ask him about them, not while we were unmarried. Now, I won't suppress my curiosity anymore.

Though I indulged in his embraces last night, these past two weeks away from him have left me thirsty, craving him. His hands encircle my hips while my lips kiss his neck, my teeth nibbling. He pulls me closer, and our skin ignites when they touch. I'm breathless from the intensity of the moment. My legs close, trying to soothe my eager desire for his presence. Is it possible to want someone so much? To the point where it feels like it's the only thing that matters? To the point where nothing else is important? Right now, I feel like I could kill anyone to avoid being separated from him. Realizing this, my heart leaps, and the fever overtakes me.

I cling to his body, eager for him to join me, and help him rid himself of his pants. He tears off my underwear and then forces me to lie down. He kisses me with renewed fervor, a heightened wildness. My temperature rises, and my urgent need for him escalates. Just when I expect him to settle between my legs, he covers my skin with burning kisses, divine bites. It's an avalanche of sensation that makes me feel on edge. I don't know how to contain this whirlwind of emotions. There are moments when what Karel makes me feel frightens me because I feel like I'm teetering on the brink of madness, of losing my mind. When I'm with him, I'm terrified by the intensity of my feelings. Just like the night before, a cold shiver runs through me from head to toe when he reaches my most intimate parts, but his face returns to mine, and he devours my mouth while his fingers slide along my hips.

"Are you in pain?" he manages to articulate between breathless kisses.

I whisper a faint, "No." In truth, my body is still a bit sore from our exploits yesterday, but I'm too afraid that if I tell him, he'll give me a watered-down version of the man he is.

Karel props himself up on his elbow and looks at me with such intensity that it heightens my desire. Then, his pupils dilate as his fingers, continuing their descent, slip between my wet lips. In that instant, all my traumas evaporate. I know it's him I'm facing and not a ghost.

"Are you sure?" he asks provocatively, brushing my sensitive spot.

This time, my *yes* is more assertive, more determined. Maybe also more vehement. The amused sigh he releases vanishes when I pull him to me, kissing him with a hunger.

He abruptly pulls away, his fingers leaving my intimate area, and I'm about to protest when his teeth graze the skin of my chest. He moves down, treating my stomach, and then my thighs, the same way. With an authoritative gesture, he spreads my legs and lifts my hips. My breathing is erratic. Though the position is a bit awkward, I know what he has in store for me is worth setting aside my modesty. His warm breath brushes my most intimate parts before he devours me hungrily. My limbs contract involuntarily, and my hands grip his curls tightly.

When I think the sensation can't be more overwhelming, his fingers penetrate me, and a moan escapes. My hips move freely, eager to bring about the release my body craves. The primal sounds Karel makes invigorate me, and I start trembling from the pit of my stomach to my toes as I reach the climax. It's brief, far too brief, but so powerful. My arched back collapses heavily onto the mattress, and I dare not open my eyes. Still, I feel Karel lightly touching my now-sensitive skin, and a blissful smile spreads across my lips.

It disappears when he forces me to sit up and wraps an arm around my hip, guiding me to straddle him.

I look at him and realize my body is not yet satisfied, as my core contracts at the hardness of his. He invites me to rise to my knees and, without breaking eye contact, slowly lowers me onto his member, taking my breath away. I cling to him as if that simple gesture could help me catch my breath. He fills me entirely, and I'm torn between delight and pain. He makes no further movements and seems to wait for me to adjust to his presence. Our eyes consume each other and communicate reverently. It's terrifying to read everything his eyes convey.

His thumb gently caresses the small of my back, then travels up my spine to rest on my neck. Our lips brush lightly. Seeing that he isn't initiating any further movement, I understand he's giving me control. Feeling a bit awkward, I slowly lift myself and lower again, and this time it's him who seems to lose his breath. His fingers tense at my neck as I repeat the motion. My breasts press against his chest, but he forces me to pull away when his fist grips my hair, pulling my head back. I continue my movements while he torments my breast with divine bites. Encouraged by his rough moans, I quicken my pace and deepen his intrusion. Sweat beads on my back, and my thighs grow tired, but I don't slow down, sensing that the climax is near.

"*Shaadi*," he murmurs against my skin.

That single word makes a small bubble burst in my lower abdomen, and my hunger intensifies. I want more than just a small bubble—I want *everything*. Lapisia, Viridia. I want him and his flaws. I want the possessive, angry Karel. The one who would be capable of burning down his city for me. In his arms, I feel more valuable than any treasure.

My hair sticks to my skin, and the friction of our bodies, combined with the burn his fingers inflict with their roughness, makes me explode into a million particles. I don't stifle the moan of pleasure that rises from my heart to my throat. My limbs are so weak he has to hold me to keep my rhythm, then he, too, is struck by orgasm. He fills me with a growl he doesn't try to contain, and it extends my own ecstasy. One final thrust, and he stills me. My head spins, and my hands cling to his neck. I struggle to catch my breath, but he gives it back to me with a kiss. His kiss is not gentle; it mirrors the intensity of the moment we just shared. And my heart roars even louder.

"I love you," I whisper, my voice hoarse.

I pull away and look into his eyes. He doesn't reply, but he doesn't need to. Words can deceive. Eyes cannot. And now, as his gaze pierces mine, I understand all he doesn't say.

CHAPTER 5

KALLIOPEE

When my eyelids lift, I'm surprised to find Karel beside me. I realize that from this day forward, he will always be the first thing I see when I wake up. Sprawled on his stomach, arms wrapped around the duvet, sleep doesn't rob him of his wary expression. As always, numerous furrows cross his forehead, making me smile.

I lie on my side, pulling the sheet up to my breast. Karel, however, shows no modesty. His naked body is exposed to me. My gaze lightly brushes over his tanned skin, tracing the contours of his muscular back, down to his divinely sculpted buttocks. I kneel, move closer to him, and let my fingers gently touch the scars that mark his skin. The contrast between his Lapisian complexion and these remnants of war is mesmerizing. When I worked at the dispensary in Viridia, I saw the ravages of combat. I helped many men heal or die. I can't help but feel my heart tighten when I imagine Karel in the thick of battle, when I think of the suffering he must have endured, when I remember his body, free of scars, the summer I met him. His skin was just as warm, but it wasn't streaked; it was smooth and uniform. Another sign the boy I once knew is gone, replaced by a valiant soldier.

Yet, a part of me swells with pride. Because he is still alive, because he survived those six bloody years. Because he didn't hesitate to risk his life to defend his kingdom, his people. He didn't stay behind; he was there with them during the darkest times in their history. That's likely why the Lapisians respect him so much. Because he was there, with them, during the darkest hours of their history.

Suddenly, he groans and stretches, rolling his shoulders. I hold my breath, only exhaling when I see he doesn't wake up. A silly smile spreads across my lips when I realize this man is my husband, and my heart swells with hope and happiness. I lie back down, facing him, and let his now-calm breathing lull me. Serenity washes over me, and I'm certain I could watch him for hours without growing tired.

However, feeling like I'm spying on him while he's most vulnerable, I turn my attention to the window. The day is just beginning to break, but I can tell that today, the ochre dust will cover the city's cobblestones. The wind blows in regular gusts, shaking the windowpanes. I sigh, realizing I likely won't be able to walk in the garden. Then I remember the room meant for me.

I turn to Karel who's still asleep and decide to take advantage of the moment to explore our quarters. I push back the sheet and, as quietly as possible, slip out of bed. Curious, I open a wardrobe and find his clothes hanging next to mine. A prideful smile forms on my lips. My fingers glide over his formal attire, then over the more casual clothes he wears in the evenings. Behind me, I hear him stir. When I turn around, I see he's only shifted position.

Continuing my exploration, I finally grab a silk robe. Using clips, I pin up my hair that's still damp from the shower we took last night. The memories make my cheeks warm. I had naively thought we would simply wash, but his fingers, intent on cleaning my skin, soon began to explore my body, reigniting my barely sated hunger. His chest pressed against my back, his member caressing my skin. My breath vanished, and I had only one need: for him to fill me again, to annihilate the emptiness I hadn't known existed before him. He didn't tease me for long. He took me, fully, his teeth sinking into my shoulders as he drove into me against the tiles. I was unsettled by not seeing his face but acutely aware of everything else: His breath in my ears, the rough sounds he made, the scent of lemon soap mingling with his natural musk, the coolness of the tiles against my breasts, and his burning fingers. The ache of not being able to kiss him as I wanted, and the void that shrank with each of his thrusts.

I have to force myself to pull away from memories of the night before and return to the present.

I tie the fabric around my hips and tiptoe out of the room, trying to make as little noise as possible. I only breathe again when

I reach the living room. I walk around it, observing each piece of furniture one by one. I feel less confined now that I know my private quarters won't just be a simple bedroom. Will I ever feel captive again, or will Karel maintain this illusion of freedom? I confess I don't know, but the feeling is so sweet that I allow myself time to savor it.

Like a child given a new toy, I settle into the armchair and bounce to test its comfort. Under my fingers, the red velvet darkens as I brush the nap the wrong way. I sketch out patterns, and then erase them.

Outside, the wind roars violently, causing me to look up. I leave the couch and approach the window. From here, I can see the desert and the small sand tornadoes forming on the horizon. It's frightening, eerie, yet hypnotic. The light, though early morning, dazzles me and forces me to turn away. A black spot blurs my vision, but I blink rapidly to make it disappear. I glance at the door leading to our bedroom and, before yielding to my childish need to wake him up, I head to the one leading to my library.

Timidly, I lower the handle and enter the room. Imposing furniture conceals the walls from floor to ceiling, and a large window lets in light. The scent in the air is pleasant, a mix of leather and old paper. In the center is a burgundy-red fainting couch, almost as wide as it is long. I close the door behind me and scan the shelves of the first bookcase, letting my gaze slide over the volumes. There are many authors whose names I don't recognize. Our ancestors did everything to make us forget our past and our mistakes, those that led us to lose all our progress. We kept some aspects of life from before, but many technologies have disappeared.

It seems that once, thousands of years ago, we could travel through the air and on machines that went fast. It also seems we could communicate across distances as easily as saying a simple hello. My father taught me, while we were planting the tree for my seventh birthday, that man, too eager for progress, had forgotten the earth was not inexhaustible. Supplies, even food, became scarce due to overconsumption and overpopulation… Now, all that remains of that past are a few books hidden from the common people.

I dreamily think about the lives of women before our condition changed. How free were they? Were they truly appreciated for their worth, as equals to men? Was there ever really a time, however brief, when a woman didn't fear being attacked simply because she was physically less capable of defending herself? A part of me wants to believe there was. The other, more skeptical part, doubts that ever happened. It's like war; I'm indeed an optimist, but I believe another conflict will emerge in a few years. Humans are perpetually dissatisfied and constantly covet their neighbor's possessions.

"Kalliopee?" growls a voice outside.

I jump and release the book I had unconsciously taken in my hands. I bend down, pick it up, and hastily place it back on the shelf. The door swings open and slams against the wall. Karel appears, disheveled. My eyes widen when I see he is still naked.

"Here you are!" He sighs, visibly angry.

I turn away, feeling embarrassed. "Where else would I be?" I ask after clearing my throat.

"I don't know. You're not usually an early bird," he scolds me.

My fingers play with the leather binding of a book worn by time. "I couldn't sleep anymore," I admit.

A knock at the entrance interrupts us. When I turn around, Karel motions for me to wait and disappears, closing the door behind him. I approach and discreetly crack it open to see who would come here so early. Karel stands with his back to me, still naked. However, he has the decency to cover his genitals with a cushion. This sight makes me stifle a laugh, which vanishes when his body tenses.

"What?!" he snaps.

"He was found hanging in his cell."

I think I recognize Vàli's voice, but I'm not certain.

"Zaïn was unconscious. If he went to such extremes, he was truly trying to protect the person we're looking for, Karel."

Karel's fist hits the door, making me jump and catching his attention. When my gaze meets his, I know I should have stifled my curiosity.

"*Riek*, Kalliopee! Close the door!" he orders angrily, swearing in the ancient Lapisian dialect.

I want to tell him off, to say that what concerns him concerns me, too, but I'm fully aware the Karel in front of me isn't the most patient. So, I obey, waiting for his conversation to end.

The raised voices reach me, and all I catch is that Vàli is tasked with investigating while we are in Aquaria. When I no longer hear any sound, I quickly move away from the door, pick up a book, and settle on the chaise longue. Long minutes pass before he finally joins me, dressed.

"I have to go," he announces harshly.

I lift my eyes from the book to meet his. I wait for him to tell me why he's so upset, to confide in me what's making him so nervous. I can see it clearly; his body is tense, his jaw clenched. He's on high alert, ready to eliminate any threat. I know Karel, and most of the time, he controls his reactions in front of others. The rare times I've seen Karel this enraged were when my safety was compromised. Is that the case now? What is he hiding from me?

"What did Vàli want?" I try.

"Nothing you need to know. I'll be gone for a few hours. Do you need anything before I leave?"

I bite back a sharp retort and turn away instead of letting my frustration take over. I hate it when he hides things from me, treating me as if I'm incapable of handling reality. I'm not fragile; he should know that.

Seeing that he gets no response, he quickly shuts the door behind him, not even trying to understand why I'm upset. He probably suspects. I grunt in annoyance and put the book away to avoid throwing it across the room. Unable to stay here while he's gone, I leave the library, cross the living room, and head to my bedroom.

I'll change, have breakfast, and take a walk around the palace. Staying in our quarters will only make me brood over my bitterness.

I jump when I enter the room and see Karel standing there with his arms crossed, facing me.

"Is something wrong?" he asks.

"No, why would there be?"

His eyelids close, and he takes a deep breath. He seems irritated, but I don't care. He doesn't move, while I pointedly ignore him and rummage through the closet for a comfortable outfit. Annoyed and uneasy by his presence, I go into the bathroom and lock myself in.

I stay there for a while and come out feeling somewhat calmer.

I put on a beige dress with a light drape that hides my stomach and ties at the neck. It's more like what I'm used to wearing, and I feel comfortable in it. Then, I braid my hair and lace up my shoes. A bit of powder on my face and some pearls for my ears complete my look. I bend down under the bed and, with my fingertips, search for the pendant that had slipped onto the rug beneath the heavy furniture. When I finally reach the chain, I grab it and stand. Kneeling, I keep staring at the vial. Why was my father so insistent that I take it? My heart races at the thought of ever having to use it.

"What is that?"

My husband's voice surprises me. His tone has lost its anger. I don't answer and keep my eyes on the greenish liquid in the small vial. The sound of his footsteps, muffled by the carpet, tells me he's approaching. I look over my shoulder and meet his gaze.

"So?" he insists gently.

"Poison, a gift from my father."

He laughs, and I smile. He doesn't know I'm not joking, and I realize telling him the truth only drives him further away. I stand, wrap the chain around my fingers, and walk to my vanity. "You didn't leave?" I ask, feigning calm.

He doesn't reply, and although I want to act indifferent, I can't help but watch him. My gaze slides from his black boots to his soldier's uniform. I guess he'll spend the day out in the field, whether in the city's streets or at the barracks.

"What are you going to do today?" he inquires.

I blink, then sigh. *What am I going to do?* It's not like I'm overwhelmed with activities. "I don't know."

"Do you want me to arrange some company? My cousin Kaïs could join you."

A shocked laugh escapes me.

"What?" he growls.

"The last lady-in-waiting you assigned to me fulfilled her role perfectly."

I wish I had kept quiet. I *should have* kept quiet. Unfortunately, the specter of Xintia still hovers between us. She's a topic we haven't discussed. An unspoken issue that sometimes chokes our words—my grievances, his apologies. I'm not one to harbor grudges; I usually forgive easily. But to do so, I need to unburden my heart, and when it comes to Karel, I'm unable to talk about her. About the woman who was his lover and who, out of jealousy, tried to take my life.

Karel's eyes avoid mine, while my eyes plead. I need to rid myself of these haunting ghosts: Xintia, those men. They're no longer here, but they still haunt my nights. I know I have no reason to fear what's gone, yet I'm convinced the danger isn't gone for good. It will return, someday, for different reasons and in new forms. I will never be safe, not with my status. My stomach churns, my throat tightens. Because even though I tried to show indifference to Xintia's hatred, the consequences were significant.

He's about to leave, aware we can't communicate. Suddenly, the thought of him leaving me alone here terrifies me. Is it due to the memories our conversation has stirred? I have no idea. Nevertheless, my impulsive request escapes my lips without pretense, just like that summer.

"Teach me how to defend myself."

He freezes in the doorway and turns to me, eyebrows furrowed. "What?"

"Teach me. Please."

Karel shakes his head, his expression remaining stern. I'm afraid he'll refuse, forbidding me any control over events. "Men are assigned to protect you."

"I know, but what if they're not enough, or one day I find myself alone and in trouble?"

I step around him to meet his eyes, to prevent him from fleeing again. I want him to see how vital this request is to me. Also, I hope to convince him. "I think maybe, on that day, I could have—"

"There were four of them," he interrupts.

"I would at least feel like I was doing everything to defend my life."

He shakes his head more vigorously and takes a step back. His refusal to let me fight only adds to how he tries to shield me from the truth.

"Refusing to see the danger doesn't make it go away, Karel. Keeping me in the dark doesn't protect me. Who hanged themselves?"

"It's none of your business."

"Yes, it is. Your reactions show that whoever it was had something to do with me. What are you hiding from me?"

"I stayed because I hoped we could part on better terms than a fight, but I think it's only getting worse."

He walks past me, not giving me a chance to catch up. When the door closes, I convince myself not to follow. I know I won't be able to change his mind or force him to talk to me.

Chapter 6

Karel

"Show me," I tell Vàli as soon as I join him in the dungeons.

He motions for me to follow and pushes open the door to the pawnbroker's cell. Weeks had passed with him saying nothing, resisting all our attempts. We had been quite creative in our efforts to extract information from him, but none had been successful. My men advised me to give up, but I refused. At first, I thought it was nothing more than an attempt to tarnish Kalliopee's reputation, but now I'm convinced something is going on, and this man was the only one who could have led us to a clue.

The prisoner hangs with his legs dangling in the air, held by a rope wrapped around the pulley we use to suspend detainees during our more forceful interrogations. His swollen face is unrecognizable, and his bloodshot eyes are glassy. I'm examining him from head to toe. His naked body is mottled with bruises of all shades. Then I look around the room. No furniture, nothing. Just a simple cell reeking of nauseating smells.

"What happened?" I ask.

"Zaïn was knocked out while guarding the cell. When he woke up, the door was ajar. He thought the guy had escaped, but instead…" he trails off, pointing to the body hanging in the air.

"Did he see who attacked him?" I inquire.

He shakes his head, and I hold back a curse.

"Why didn't he leave? And who could have helped him?"

My friend seems to have the same questions, and I sigh, exhausted.

"It must be related to his niece. She disappeared at the same time as those daggers. It has to be connected. Search the kingdom if you have to, Vàli, put your best spies on it, but find her!" I order.

"And you? What will you do in the meantime? We don't know the purpose of all this or the motives of whoever is behind it. We don't even know who the target is. You? The princess? This guy or his niece must have recognized her when she visited his shop, that's certain. It's no coincidence."

My thoughts are as scattered as his. I have many questions but no answers, and I think this is the first time events slipped so much out of my control. I'm torn between wanting to join him in his quest and the need to protect my wife by staying close to her.

Wife. That word resonates powerfully throughout my entire being. She's mine. And to think that two days ago she could have chosen to flee from me. That two days ago I could have lost the only thing that truly matters, the one person capable of healing my deepest wounds.

"I've moved up our trip to Aquaria. We leave tomorrow. I'd rather get her away, especially if there's an accomplice in the palace."

I feel a profound need to protect her, to keep her safe from danger, to take her far away from my city that hasn't spared her until now.

And I need to shield myself from the questions she might ask if I were to leave without her. I know her. When I caught her eavesdropping, I panicked. Kalliopee doesn't support my actions. How would she react if she knew I had tortured a man for weeks, hoping to extract information from him? The princess thinks only with her heart. She would have found mitigating circumstances for him or, worse, blamed me for his suicide. What she doesn't understand is that I will stop at nothing to eliminate any threat, to eliminate anyone who might endanger her life. She can accuse me of barbarism, but she can't fault my need to ensure her safety.

I sigh and leave the cell. Vàli closes the door, and we find ourselves in the corridor.

"What do we do with him?" he asks.

Leave him to rot. Feed him to the scavengers so his soul never finds peace. Dismember him and scatter his remains to the four corners of the kingdom so he never finds rest. I can't say what I feel, so instead I answer, "Have him buried in the common grave."

He stares at me for a few seconds before nodding. Yes, such

clemency is uncharacteristic of me, but I'm trying to improve. This man paid with his life for his silence. I have the strange feeling he wasn't silent for any cause but rather to protect someone. If, when the mystery is solved, I find I was wrong about his intentions, I won't hesitate to exhume him and let him rot in the sun.

"Will you be gone for long?" Vàli asks as I walk away.

"Probably about ten days."

It will take us three days to reach the ocean and the same to return. I don't think we will linger there. Just enough time to introduce my wife to King Nokken and negotiate the terms of our alliance. Then, I will bring her back home. As expected, my father decided not to join the festivities. It would have been surprising if he had left the comfortable walls of his home.

Moreover, I believe taking Kalliopee away from him can only be a good thing. She and I need to find each other away from the palace's animosity, away from the whispers and the king's hatred. He constantly reminds me of my duty, telling me I must keep my promises. Euphoria grips him, and I feel he will only pressure me more now that the princess and I are united. Inside, my emotions are chaos. My love for Kalliopee tries to suffocate my resentment and rage, which fight like furies. I thought I was ready to do anything to satisfy my vengeance, but now I'm not so sure. Just look at how I reacted this morning when I woke up. She wasn't there, and panic engulfed me. I felt like I was reliving her attack over and over again. And when I found her in the library, relief washed over me in waves. If Vàli hadn't knocked, I would have undoubtedly taken her to reassure myself.

I leave the dungeons and come face to face with Kaïs. His eternal cheerful smile snaps me out of my thoughts. My cousin is like that—playful, carefree. With him, everything is an excuse to have fun. We used to be very close, then our family lost two members, and I changed. So did he. He loved my mother a lot, and although she annoyed him by always being around, he appreciated my sister Maha just as much. When they disappeared, I became sullen while he became even more carefree. Very quickly, his parents left the city, and he was no longer part of my daily life. I know he's sometimes annoyed by my transformation, wishing to find in me the one who was his best friend, but that light-hearted boy no longer exists.

"I heard you're going on a trip," he announces cheerfully.

"The answer is no!"

"I haven't even asked you anything yet," he laughs.

"I'm anticipating. It saves time."

I walk past him and down the corridors. From the sound of his footsteps, I know he's following me, and I can't help but glance in his direction. With his nonchalant gait, he observes the outside. I could speed up, but I know it wouldn't stop him.

"You're exhausting yourself for nothing," I snap, annoyed.

"I'm going to exhaust you," he retorts with a mischievous tone.

I decide to ignore him, and we quickly reach the palace entrance. I cross the courtyard and then the tower, finally reaching the open doors leading to the citadel. The wind blows, and I have to pull up my scarf to avoid swallowing sand. The city is almost deserted. This week has been declared a holiday in honor of our marriage. My boots pound the cobblestones as I descend the main street. After a short while, I arrive in front of the barracks, Kaïs still on my heels.

When we enter the compound, I see my men training, regardless of the weather. Days like today are especially crucial as they teach us to fight with significantly reduced visibility. We must listen rather than see. It's a difficult exercise but essential when fighting in the desert.

Jonah drops his sword to the ground and heads toward us, a broad smile on his face. He gives my cousin a manly hug. "You stayed!"

"Finally, someone who isn't afraid to show enthusiasm!" Kaïs taunts me.

I let them chat for a few minutes and join Samael and Zaïn. The latter assures me he has nothing more than a bump and confirms he didn't see who knocked him out. Like us, he doesn't understand why the man hanged himself when he could have used the opportunity to escape.

"Your guy would have been spotted," Kaïs interrupts. "He would never have been able to leave the palace without getting caught. But… the person who gave him the rope definitely works here."

I shoot him an annoyed look but can't help but nod. I've come to the same conclusions. We decide to stop talking about it; we're just ruminating and need some distance to see things more clearly.

The intense way Samael is looking at me doesn't bode well, and I know from the smile forming on his lips that the matter of the hanged man will seem preferable to what he's about to bring up.

"So, how was the wedding night?" Samael asks, raising his eyebrows suggestively.

"Do you really think I'm going to share my intimate life with you?" I reply.

"Listen to him, *my intimate life*, he says," Jonah mocks to my right.

My elbow digs sharply into his ribs, but it doesn't wipe the smile from his face, and everyone starts laughing.

"So?" Samael insists.

The laughter dies down, and curious eyes scrutinize me, waiting for some juicy detail. Images from that night flood my mind. The intensity with which we made love, what I felt beyond anything I thought possible. Kalliopee often annoys me with her tenacity, but I must admit her strength of character is an advantage in our bed. She gives herself as she lives, with ferocity.

At this thought, I feel the need to be with her. I'm dependent on her, to the point where I'm certain I would succumb to madness if I lost her. She doesn't realize that while she may have shackles on her wrists, it's me who's enslaved. I feel like my life will now be dedicated to protecting hers. Her moans echo in my head, with a floating musicality. Her taste fills my mouth as if I were kissing her at this moment. I can even feel the softness of her skin under my rough fingers. Can love drive you mad? Yes, it can annihilate your existence, reducing you to a being begging for the slightest caress, the slightest breath, the slightest groan.

Lost in my thoughts, I don't notice Samael approaching. He grabs my chin and turns my face, his fingers gliding over the scratches my dear princess left. "A tigress? Lucky you!" he exclaims.

I push his hand away sharply and give him a threatening look. He should be careful not to cross the line.

"So, are you in the honeymoon phase? Everything's perfect, everything's rosy?" he continues.

A sarcastic laugh escapes my lips, and I immediately regret it when Jonah looks over at me.

"What did you do to her this time?" he asks.

I look up at the cloudy sky and sigh. What did *I* do? Nothing. I'm just married to a woman who never gives up. Teach her to fight? Absolutely not. I refuse to see her with a weapon in her hand; I refuse to consider the possibility she might one day need to use it.

Agitated by the reality she pointed out, I walk away from the group and leave them, stretching a bit off to the side. She's right, ignoring danger doesn't make it disappear, but right now, I need a break. Tomorrow, we leave for Aquaria. We'll talk about it when we get back.

My cousin seems to devour my friends' stories. No doubt he's thrilled to learn so much about Kalliopee and me. I am, after all, stingy with words.

Our eyes meet, and I nod for Kaïs to join me. He laughs and jogs over.

"You want to spar?" he teases.

I lace up my shoes and stretch my muscles before grabbing my sword. The characteristic sound of the blade leaving its sheath immediately invigorates me. My cousin steps away for a moment and grabs a spear. I raise my eyebrows as he returns, still smiling.

"A spear?" I mock.

"I'm the best in the kingdom."

I shake my head as I step into the training circle. Our friends fall silent and watch us intently. Like two predators, we circle each other. I'm taller and stronger than Kaïs, but his movements are more feline. They're silent, almost imperceptible to my ears. I tighten my grip on the hilt without taking my eyes off him. His gaze leaves mine for a split second. That's enough for me, and I lunge at him. Just when I think I've got him, he performs a backflip and lands gracefully on his feet.

We stop to size each other up. I'm surprised by how fluidly his body moves, as if it weighs nothing. Behind me, I hear the cheers of our friends.

With bent knees, Kaïs circles me with a speed I didn't know he had, as light as the wind. I must admit I'm stunned by his agility. Deciding to rely on my strength, I take a step forward, and with a leap, he retreats. Gravity seems to have no hold on him. As he lands, he kicks up a few grains of dust. The wind grows stronger with each passing second, and soon, the scene becomes hazy. Kaïs moves faster and faster, then the ocher fog gives way to clarity again. My cousin appears clearly, just a few steps away from me. My gaze drops to his spear, and the way he handles it's quite unusual. Holding it by the end, he spins on his heel, and the tip just barely grazes me. The dust swirls around him, and I no longer feel like an active participant in our exchange. I'm a spectator, admiring an astonishing display.

The laughter of my friends spurs me to take this fight seriously. My fingers tighten around the hilt of my sword, and this time, when his spear comes at me, I parry it with a backhanded stroke. Though his weapon doesn't break, the blow forces Kaïs to stop his spinning. He regains his balance, but my back foot gives me the momentum I need to attack. Instantly, my cousin leaps to the side, but I don't let him land on his feet to counterattack. I keep pressing with attempts while he keeps parrying. Just as he's nearly backed against a wall, he pivots, and with astonishing speed, pushes off it with his right foot. As if gravity has no effect on him, he continues ascending, running vertically. Before I can comprehend how, he vanishes from my sight, and I find myself face-to-face with the stone wall. His laughter reaches my ears from behind, but I don't have time to turn around; he pushes me and pins me down.

"So, cousin, getting soft?" he murmurs in my ear, a hint of pride in his voice.

He releases me, and I quickly turn to face him. When we were younger, he wasn't the most seasoned fighter—more frail, less brutal. But as I scrutinize him now, I realize he might be better than me.

"Is this sorcery?" I ask.

"Acrobatics," he replies, amused.

The guys join us, and I immediately notice Samael's envious look.

"I could help you protect the princess," my cousin declares solemnly.

Kaïs is like Samael, Jonah, and Zaïn—I trust him implicitly. Kalliopee seemed to like him yesterday, and I know she needs allies at the palace. We stare at each other for a few long seconds. He must see in me my desperate need to defend Kalliopee's life at all costs because his eyes narrow, and he silently communicates a promise that I feel deep within me.

I extend my hand to him, and he grips it confidently.

CHAPTER 7

KALLIOPEE

Standing in front of the palace, I wait for the horses to be harnessed. Back in Viridia, I would sometimes saddle Dark Horse myself, but here, that task is assigned to the stable staff. So all I have to do is wait is wait on my mount, Lune. Karel is next to me, reviewing the route we'll take with his men. He wanted me to travel by carriage, but I miss galloping too much and remember the chaotic journey to get here. He warned me, saying, "Don't come complaining," which made me grumble. Since our argument yesterday, we've hardly spoken, and dinner was kept lively only by Kaïs's jokes. I have to admit he's a charming man and lightens the tense atmosphere of the palace.

As I turn around, I notice Darkos, hidden in the shadows of the tower, watching me seriously. He gestures for me to join him before disappearing. I discreetly glance at Karel, who's deep in conversation with Samael, and walk up the steps inside, maintaining a false calm.

It only takes a few steps to see Darkos slipping into the staircase leading to the top of the tower. When I reach him, he glances furtively behind me before grabbing my wrist. My eyes widen as he hands me a small dagger. I try to pull away, but he tightens his grip and pulls me closer. "I won't be able to protect you there."

"I don't need you, Darkos. Karel's men are—"

"They're not from our *homeland*," he interrupts.

My breath catches as I stare at him. Did I hear that right? "Excuse me?" I ask.

"They're not from Viridia," he repeats.

I must have misheard… He can't be Viridian; it's impossible. He doesn't look like my people. My eyes slide over his skin, much darker than mine, but I also notice it's lighter than that of the Lapisians. Suddenly, what seemed like a trivial detail takes on a whole new meaning. These almost imperceptible differences. These nuances that blur ethnic boundaries.

"You're a mixed-blood," I guess.

He nods before moving away from me. I sense he's nervous, worried. Why? Is he afraid I'll reveal his true identity?

"What are you doing in Lapisia?" I ask.

"Did you really think King Läven wouldn't ensure your safety?"

His response surprises me. I hadn't considered for a moment that my father might be responsible for his presence at my side. Why didn't he tell me?

"I don't have time to explain, Princess. One day, I will, but please, take this blade."

I quickly decline. Karel refused my request, and accepting someone else's protection would feel like a betrayal. I already feel guilty about hiding Darkos's true status from him, and I can't take this weapon.

"Kalliopee," he says, impatiently.

I sense that calling me by my first name is a tactic to convince me.

"I can't!"

"It will protect you."

I inhale deeply, staring at the dagger that feels like it weighs a ton. Inside, a battle rages between my need to feel safe and my desire to earn my husband's trust. Unfortunately, I don't have the luxury of time and must make a quick decision.

"I'm sorry," I murmur, handing the weapon back to him. "I have to refuse."

He shakes his head as he takes the dagger. I hear someone calling for me, and Darkos, likely realizing he won't change my mind, disappears into the shadows. I wish I could thank him for wanting to protect me, but I turn away, still in turmoil. As I step out of the stairwell, I jump when I come face to face with Karel.

"What's going on?"

"I… I thought I heard something," I lie.

He looks intently past me as my breath catches, then fixes his gaze on mine. Since yesterday, our exchanges have been filled with sharp remarks or long silences. He steps closer, and I step back. His fingers wrap around my forearm, pulling me roughly toward him. My body collides with his, but he immobilizes me, forcing me to look at him by gripping my chin.

"Stop sulking."

"Stop giving me reasons to."

He closes his eyes for several long seconds, and I know him well enough to see he's trying to stay calm. I lower my head, feeling guilty. I'm aware of the efforts he makes for me, but I can't help always wanting more.

"Don't make me regret bringing you with me," he murmurs, his voice authoritative. "Behave like a wife."

Now the guilt fades, and I lift my head. A hypocritical smile spreads across my face. I probably should have taken that dagger after all. I'm tired of being told how to behave. Fine. If he wants a docile wife, he'll get one. "I'll be perfect; you won't regret this trip."

His eyebrows raise provocatively.

"We'll see if you like it," I add.

I pull my arm away and quietly join the others by the horses. He wants an obedient wife? He'll get one. Apparently, opposing him doesn't work. My only option now is to show him I'm the one he needs, and a watered-down version of myself won't do.

When I reach the bottom of the steps, Karel glares at me as he passes, and I give him a polite smile. My gesture makes him grunt and turn his head away.

A moment later, we leave the city. We are accompanied by Kaïs, Zaïn, Samael, and Jonah. From what I've heard, scouts have gone ahead to ensure we won't encounter any trouble on our journey. A scarf over my head protects me from the scorching heat and the sand whipped up by the wind. We spend long hours on horseback, and the arid plain gradually gives way to a landscape strewn with massive stones. Because our travel plans changed at the last minute, the palace tailors didn't have time to make me more suitable attire. So I'm forced to ride sidesaddle to keep my legs covered. It's uncomfortable, but I can't complain, not after insisting on riding. However, Karel did agree to lend me some of his shirts to protect my skin from the sun.

Here and there, numerous rocks, several feet high, break the straight line of the horizon. Kaïs rides beside me. He amuses me greatly, and the journey wouldn't be as pleasant without him. When he tells me one of his misadventures, I can't help but burst into laughter, which earns me a murderous look from the head of the procession: His Royal Highness, Karel. I can't help but sigh, feeling weary. Kaïs seems to have noticed the tension between us as he turns to me.

My fingers glide over the mane of my mount, Lune. I try to calm myself and avoid his remarks or questions.

"He wasn't like this before," he surprises me by saying.

My head turns instantly toward him, but his eyes remain on Karel.

"We used to be very much alike in every way," he continues.

I look back at Karel. From here, only his hair and neck are visible. No, he wasn't like this before. It's true. I had the chance to observe him in a group that summer. He was always at the center of discussions and debates. Sure, he and I only shared moments away from prying eyes, but that didn't stop me from watching him even when he didn't see me.

"But he's getting better," Kaïs interrupts my thoughts.

"Really?" I grumble.

"He would never have let me come before you intruded on his life," he replies, amused.

"It wasn't an intrusion…" I murmur to myself.

I was forced to marry him, and I didn't impose myself in his life by choice. We were both forced to make do. Well… it's true that at first, I was more than happy to take on this role, and despite our disagreements, I don't regret our union.

"Yes. He may have accepted the marriage, but marriage doesn't mean love. And he loves you."

I tense when Karel's mount turns around and comes back up the procession. My husband signals Kaïs to take his place, and he obeys, giving me a wink. I move forward so the others don't get too far ahead, and Karel positions himself beside me.

"Can you explain why, in of two days of marriage, we've spent half the time ignoring each other?"

"You're right, I'm sorry," I say softly, turning my head toward him.

He scrutinizes me, and I force a smile.

"You don't mean it, do you?"

No, not at all!

"Of course I do. I won't talk to you anymore about teaching me to fight or even about my rights."

"Still with that?"

Yes, still and always with that!

He grumbles before returning to the head of the procession. I can't help but revel in the thought that my behavior annoys him. It's childish, but Karel is childish most of the time, so I won't deprive myself. When Kaïs rejoins me, he makes a few comments about the necessity for a couple to learn to communicate. Alas, if he thinks the problem is only me, he's mistaken.

As the sentinels leave our campsite, I sit beside Jonah. He has been tasked with teaching me the ways of Aquarian life. The moon, high and round in the sky, lights our surroundings. We have stopped in a rocky valley sheltered from the wind. Zaïn and Samael will spend the night on higher ground, taking turns to ensure we are safe.

"Are you focused?" my instructor asks.

I listen as he explains the art of Aquarian nobility. It's surprising how customs can vary from one kingdom to another. In Aquaria, avoiding eye contact is considered arrogant. Kaïs, who is preparing the meal by the campfire, seems as attentive as I am. Jonah also teaches me a few words of the archipelago's dialect. I try to absorb every detail because, no matter how much Karel irritates me, I don't want diplomatic relations to suffer.

When the meal is ready, I stay back a bit to mentally review my recent lesson. Maintain eye contact. Decline all gifts. In their culture, accepting a present is rude, whereas I would be offended if someone refused a gift I had spent hours making.

"Can I sit here?" Karel interrupts, standing in front of me.

"Of course," I reply with a soft voice.

"Do you like the meal?" Karel asks.

It's terrible. Kaïs may be funny, but when it comes to his cooking skills, he should stay away from the pots and pans. True to my role, I say nothing.

"It's delicious."

"How long are you going to play this game?" Karel asks.

"I'm not playing any games," I counter.

"Yes, you are. This meal is awful! Kaïs is the worst cook I know."

I then realize that assigning this task to his cousin wasn't without ulterior motive.

"So? How long are you going to keep this up?" he asks.

"Forever, my dear husband." I lie; I'm already fed up.

"And what else do you have planned?"

If only he knew.

"To be cheerful, not to speak unless you permit, not to sit until you've taken your seat, to stay two steps behind you when you move," I list, not hiding my delight.

He's about to get up when I stop him by the arm.

"Forgive me, I don't remember all my tutor's lessons. Those are just the rules for our public outings. In private, I must support you no matter what, never contradict you, and in our bed, you can—"

My words trail off as I watch him walk away. I admit I'm proud of remembering to use formal language. As a child, I hated those lessons and never imagined they would one day help me annoy my husband.

Just when I think I have a moment of peace, Karel turns around and strides back to me. I shrink against the rock that serves as my backrest.

"Enough!" he exclaims. "Stop this charade!"

"Stay dignified, Karel," I provoke him with condescension. "You can tell me how much I irritate you when we're in private. No one should see what you're feeling, *haìzi*." My smile widens.

"*Haìzi*?" he sputters.

Yes, choke on it. *Shaadi* gave enough. Everyone gets their little nickname.

"What did you just call me?"

"I can't remember, Jonah taught me some Lapisian's words. It was a mix of child, idiot, dwarf, and other more colorful words. I must admit *haìzi* was the one that sounded best to me. What does it mean?" I ask innocently.

He snorts like an enraged bull. "It's used to describe a man who can't—" He closes his eyes and exhales again. "It's an insult implying a man's impotence."

"Oh!" I knew exactly what it meant.

"From what I recall, you were quite satisfied," he retorts arrogantly.

I smile at him, still as hypocritically as before. "Let's hope I didn't jinx you," I say.

My plate flies and lands a few steps away. My cry of surprise, tinged with fear, alerts Jonah and Kaïs, who immediately stop their conversation. I don't have time to complain as Karel forces me to stand up.

"What are you doing?" I ask.

"Ignoring each other doesn't work, and pretending doesn't either. We're going to find a place where I can, with dignity, express how much you irritate me."

He grips my wrist with his fingers and pulls me behind him. I struggle childishly, then hit his arm, but it doesn't seem to affect him. We go around a rocky peak, and out of sight, he pushes me against the surface, warmed by the sun all day.

"Speak!" Karel exclaims.

"No way, when I do, you blame me. I'm giving you another version of myself, Karel. No doubt you'll appreciate it!"

"So, what? Is this how it's going to be? Whatever I say, you're going to agree?"

"When I disagree with you, you get angry and slam doors, then look at me like you want to tear me apart. Don't be a hypocrite."

Because as much as his *"Behave like a wife"* deeply hurt me, it's nothing compared to how he dismisses my fears and my need to be able to defend my life. He steps back from me as if I burned him and seems to be holding himself back. I know because of the way his fingers grip his hips.

"Having secrets is one thing. But stopping me from defending myself is another."

"I'm not hiding anything from you," he whispers, turning away.

Does he think I'm a fool? Does he believe he can deceive me? He can't even lie to my face.

"Try again," I provoke him, "but look me in the eyes this time."

His eyes lock onto mine, and my pulse quickens. I exhale loudly, a sign that this conversation is affecting me more than I want to admit. I'm angry with him and his need to protect me from everything, but ignorance doesn't protect. I thought he had realized that, and I think that's what frustrates me most.

"The pawnbroker hanged himself in his cell," he announces.

He turns around, presenting his back to me but not leaving. My mind races, and panic floods me. I didn't even know he was in the palace dungeons.

"Why didn't you tell me?" I dare to ask.

"Because I blame myself."

My brows furrow as I sense his body tensing, even hidden beneath his white jacket.

"I feel weak because I can't protect you. Something is slipping through my fingers, and I've never been so scared in my life, Kalliopee," he finishes, facing me again.

The slight fragility in his voice alarms me immediately. It's unlike him. "Karel—"

"I'm supposed to protect you, but I feel like I'm failing. That day, I should have, too, but I didn't. I should have never told you to leave; I should have stayed with you."

"You can't always be there," I try to reassure him.

Some things are beyond control. It's impossible to have a grip on the world we live in. There will always be some event, no matter how insignificant, that disrupts everything.

He strides over to me, his rough fingers encircling my throat without squeezing. His eyes fix on mine as his hands slide to my neck, gripping it fiercely.

"I wish you didn't need to know how to fight," he murmurs with a rage that sends shivers down my spine. "I'm scared something will happen to you, but that's not the only thing that frightens me."

I stare at him intensely, trying to grasp the meaning of his words. I shake my head in utter confusion. A lump blocks my breath as I realize that whatever he's feeling, it's causing him pain.

"I'm afraid of who I'm becoming. The more time passes, the less I can control myself around those who wish you harm. You can't imagine the images that flash through my mind, *Shaadi*."

His warm breath caresses my skin, making it tingle. My eyes fill with tears as I see the fury clouding his gaze.

"Even the officiant, when he spoke those words, I wanted to eviscerate him. I hated myself for putting those bracelets on you, for holding your wrists as if you were nothing but a slave."

"But that's what I am," I say, my throat tight. No matter how my husband treats me, I am not free in the eyes of the world. I belong to him, and my voice will never matter. "But it's not your fault, Karel. You gave me the opportunity to leave; I chose to stay."

"I hate this," he whispers, his breath now mingling with mine. "I hate it so much, *Shaadi*."

My chest rises and falls more rapidly, then he kisses me, a kiss that reverberates through my entire body. It's an addictive delight, a sensation one would want to experience perpetually, even though the next kiss will never be as powerful. The kisses that signal a truce between two souls have a unique flavor. Their intensity surpasses reason. What they make us feel goes beyond love. They have a life-saving, vital taste.

Chapter 8

Kalliopee

A little way off, hidden by wild hedges surrounding us, we set up our bed. Since leaving the rocky Lapisian mountains, we've traded the desert for much greener landscapes and a less oppressive atmosphere. The scenery is breathtaking. Huge trees line the roads, providing travelers with a canopy that shields them from the sun's rays. The temperatures are mild, thanks to the breeze that likely comes from the ocean. After riding since dawn, we unsaddled our horses and shared a dinner around a campfire.

I lie down on the sheet covering the fresh grass and watch Karel as he takes off his boots. Since our reconciliation yesterday, since I sensed the threatening shadow hanging over him, I've been secretly observing him. *"You can't imagine the images that flash through my mind."* No, but I have a feeling they're murderous. Sometimes, when his ghosts haunt him, I feel a helplessness that eats at my core. And, just like him, I'm filled with a rage that's hard to control. I'm angry at our kingdoms and this war that has filled Karel's life with corpses that chase him.

"Is everything okay?" he asks when he realizes I'm lost in thought. I return to him and nod. "We'll reach Aquaria by midday," he reassures me.

He's always on alert, ready to counter any threat. If he knew I fear no danger when I'm by his side, he'd scold me for being so carefree. But I can't tell him that because it would force me to admit that it's him I worry about. I'm convinced he wouldn't like that.

He lies on his back, one hand behind his head, and I roll onto my side. I trace the lines of his profile with my eyes, drinking in the sight of the handsome man he is. He gazes at the starry sky, looking thoughtful. I sit up, lean over him, and see shadows still veil his eyes. I wish they would disappear, at least for a few hours.

"What—"

Before he can question my change in behavior, my lips press against his. The wine that accompanied our meal gives him a fruity taste that completes my intoxication. My chest presses against his as my tongue battles to breach the barrier of his teeth.

His fingers wrap around my arms, probably to stop me from going further. I might have given up if this gesture hadn't been contradicted by the relieved sigh he releases when his jaw relaxes. I hold my breath, listening for any sound from the camp. The lively flames crackle, and we hear the laughter of our travel companions. My eyelids lift, and I meet his gaze. Serenity washes over me as I realize his darkness is retreating.

Karel stares at me, and I can sense the battle raging within him. As I prepare to straddle him, his hand rests on my knee. We lock eyes, a silent challenge between us. I hold back my impatience, waiting for him to finally yield. He does, just as his fingers slide up my dress. I straddle him, picking up the kiss where we left off. A silent moan escapes me when his thumb reaches the edge of my underwear. My hands immediately go to his pants, and as soon as I grasp his proudly erect member, my fingers slide along it. Karel throws his head back, depriving me of his lips.

Time freezes; we both still, our gazes locking.

Then, goosebumps spread across my skin, my core tightens, and waves of desire wash over me as I feel him tear my underwear. The next moment, I brace myself on his chest and rise onto my thighs before guiding him inside me.

"Not a sound," he murmurs authoritatively.

My pulse pounds in my temples, my body tingles with impatience, and I lower myself. He fills me completely, and I have to fight not to moan. I adjust to his presence, relishing this addictive intrusion. My hips begin to undulate. Our lips meet. It's too much. And yet not enough. The friction of our bodies sends electric shocks through my lower abdomen, each one more intense than the last.

The risk of being discovered heightens the moment, making the sensations more divine and my body's reactions more uncontrollable.

As climax approaches, Karel flips us over. He presses his forehead to mine while one of his hands lifts my leg. He fills me even more, and before a cry can escape, his palm covers my mouth.

"One sound, Kalliopee, and it's over."

Rather than cooling my desire, his threat intensifies the heat coursing through my veins. I nod, then my eyelids close on their own as he begins to thrust. I feel like my blood is boiling, my flesh radiating. I'm immolating. It's painfully delicious.

His thrusts become more brutal, pushing me closer to the edge each time. I cling to his jacket, ignoring the rocks and sticks digging into my back.

Luckily, our clothes muffle the slapping of our bodies, and the laughter of the Lapisians grows louder, the alcohol even making them sing.

I breathe hard through my nose, feeling the storm brewing, and then my fingers dig into him as the orgasm hits me with full force. Violently. Crushingly.

As he commanded, I don't make a sound. I fight my body's urge to vocalize its release. My limbs stiffen, my toes curl. I arch, struggling to contain my pleasure. But a second wave overwhelms me, triggered by the friction on my clitoris. I dig my nails into his neck and moan against his hand. The sound is nearly silent, and I feel like I'm dying, yet certain that nothing will ever be as good as what we share when our bodies are one.

Before I can come back down to earth, Karel's head moves to my neck as he lifts my leg a bit more, and with one final thrust, he climaxes too. Silently. Without a breath. Only the increased pressure of his hand against my lips, almost as if his fingers are sinking into my skin, betrays his state. He releases my leg, pulls away, then devours my mouth with renewed hunger.

As we approach the coast, the ocean spray reaches us. The air is filled with a scent that's both sweet and salty. It's not unpleasant, but having never smelled it before, I can't quite describe it. The path we're on prevents us from seeing more than a few steps ahead due to the dense forest vegetation. We've dismounted our horses, guiding them by their reins along the trail. I watch where I step to avoid injury and not slow down the group. The air is cool, and a gentle breeze caresses my skin. It's soothing. For the first time in a long while, breathing doesn't feel like a punishment.

In the distance, we hear unfamiliar sounds. Unfortunately, I know nothing about the wildlife or flora of these exotic forests.

"We're not far now," Karel tells me.

I smile at him as he extends his hand to help me over a pile of stones blocking my path. When he lets go, I turn to Lune, who seems much more comfortable than I am. I click my tongue, and with a small leap, she clears the obstacle with ease. To avoid crowding each other, our group has split into pairs. Kaïs is at the front with Samael, while Jonah and Zaïn bring up the rear.

I follow Karel calmly, who is a few steps ahead of me. He regularly checks to make sure I'm keeping up without difficulty. The tensions of the past two days have completely dissipated, and he didn't even complain when I let slip, *"This trip is way too long."*

"Do you hear that?" Samael shouts from somewhere ahead, out of sight.

Karel signals me to stop, and I gently stroke Lune's mane to calm her. My eyelids lower as I listen. My eyes open wide, and an irrepressible smile spreads across my face. "The ocean?" I ask Karel.

With his perpetually stern expression, he nods, and impatience overtakes me. In my life, the only landscapes I've seen are those of Viridia and Lapisia. I've longed to explore the world, and now I can barely contain my excitement. With a nod, Karel invites me to follow, and I gesture for him to hurry. He raises his eyebrows, then finally, a smile appears on his handsome face.

"Come on," I urge him. "Let's not just stand here."

"Something tells me you'll be less excited when you meet the king."

But he continues to walk. For me to be disappointed, I'd have to not know the king. But that's not the case.

"I've seen him before, when I was a little girl," I tell Karel, paying close attention to his steps.

Where he places his feet, I follow. I don't trust myself, and unlike him, I'm not suited for the terrain. Karel seems comfortable wherever he is, his instincts guiding his steps.

"And?" he asks, climbing onto a large, flat rock.

"He's an arrogant man, and I don't think he cares about the fate of minorities. He's not a conqueror, but an opportunist. He's not someone I would trust."

Karel steps down, giving me a clear path, but still offers his hand to help me. "You would trust anyone," he counters as I place my foot on the flat stone.

My thighs ache with every step, and I silently curse at the thought that in a few days, we will have to make the return journey. "That's not true."

His raised eyebrows show his disagreement. He's right, yes… I do easily trust people, but it's because I refuse to believe everyone approaches me out of self-interest. I want to keep believing the world is good.

"He's the kind of person who switches sides depending on what benefits he can gain," I add, hoping he'll drop the subject of my inability to distinguish the good from the bad.

"That's what most people do," he defends.

"You're wrong. People rarely act against their convictions and values. He has none. This king would betray his own mother, I'm sure of it. He'd wipe out an entire people if it could secure him eternal power."

"You gathered all that from meeting him once?" he retorts.

"I'm an observer. My impressions used to be accurate."

"And today?" he asks with interest.

He glances over his shoulder, and for a brief moment, I think I see a rare softness in his eyes. It's too brief to be sure.

"I suppose isolation has clouded my judgment."

As a little girl, I didn't have as many restrictions. My father let me observe his diplomatic meetings from a distance. Unfortunately, my intelligence quickly became a hindrance, and I found myself sidelined. The Viridians liked me, I'm sure, but as I grew older and the age of marriage approached, I was avoided. People feared I might marry one of their sons and bring misfortune to their family. My royal rank made no difference. I was born motherless. With my birth, the Talae bid farewell to their hopes of an heir to the throne. That could have brought me many suitors. After all, if I bore a son, my husband would become king until our son was old enough to rule. But the opposite happened.

One day, I overheard a palace maid laughing: *"She'll die in childbirth, and the poor man will be left with a newborn with eyes like his mother's..."* Rumors assigned me many tragic fates. I grew up with these beliefs, this dark cloud over my head. I've always tried to ignore these unfounded predictions, but I must admit the idea of pregnancy terrifies me. I'm afraid I won't survive it and will leave behind an orphan. Wounds are painful and slow to heal without the soothing balm of a mother's love.

"How did you see me back then?" he asks after a long silence.

"It would please you too much if I confessed. Some things are better kept secret. Everyone has their garden of secrets, my dear husband," I tease.

The closer we get, the louder the sound of the waves becomes, drowning out our voices. He doesn't press the matter, and we continue our progress.

"Let's see if your judgment is really that clouded now. What did you think of Jonah when you arrived?"

"He didn't like me. He didn't scare me, but I could tell he didn't hold me in high regard."

"That's not wrong," he mocks.

Upset, I glare at the back of his neck as he walks ahead. His eyes meet mine, and he looks at me with amusement.

"And Samael?" he continues.

"He's different from you. Calmer. Not a brute. I don't think he enjoys playing fighting."

"Playing Fighting?"

"What? Is there another word for it?" I smile broadly, relishing the moment almost tinged with carefreeness. At the palace, we're always careful with our words, but here, in the middle of nowhere, we find the complicity we knew years ago.

"You're wrong about Samael. Don't be fooled by the ones who seem the calmest, *Shaadi*. Samael is calm, yes, but he's the most sadistic among us. He's patient, meticulous, and never leaves anything to chance. The enemy would rather face Jonah or me than him. Their death would be quick if it were me. With Samael, it would be long and much more painful."

A shiver runs down my spine at his words. I lean forward to see if the subject of our conversation can hear. I used to think he was almost cute; now, I'll see him differently.

"And me?" he asks proudly.

"Do you really want to know?" I tease.

"No," he concedes.

Feeling victorious, I can't hold back my laughter. I'm not sure he would like what I have to say. Beneath our feet, the greenery gradually gives way to crystalline sand. My feet sink in, and a few particles get into my shoes. The trees are increasingly sparse, as if they're opening the way, and a current of air fills my nostrils with a briny scent. At least, that's what I think it is. I suppose it's the smell described in the travel stories I devoured as a child.

Karel steps aside, and finally, the ocean comes into view. My breath catches at the sight. I let go of my horse, which Karel immediately holds, and move toward the vast blue expanse. The water is clear, almost transparent. The waves form foam that settles on the wet sand.

I take off my shoes, mesmerized by the scene before me. My eyelids close as my bare feet sink into the hot sand. The farther I go, the finer the sand becomes, eventually giving way to a more compact texture. It's different but not unpleasant. When my eyes open again, the water reaches my feet without touching them. As it recedes, I take a step forward, lift my dress slightly, and wait for the next wave. When it reaches me, I'm surprised by its warmth and the strength of the current. A cry escapes me as I lift my dress higher, fearing it will get wet. My bare arms are covered in goosebumps, but the sensation is invigorating and thrilling. I'd love to swim in it; I hope we have the chance before we leave.

I decide to end my experiment and turn around. All the men are staring at me. Kaïs and Zaïn with amusement. As for the others, I can't tell. I adjust my dress, lace up my shoes with some difficulty, and notice they're still watching me.

"What?" I dare as I rejoin them.

Karel gestures for me to follow him and moves aside a bit to keep curious ears from overhearing. "Could you try not to expose your rear to my men?"

I stiffen, then let out a nervous laugh. "I just exposed my calves," I correct him.

"Trust me, they saw more than just your legs…"

I can hear the irritation in his voice, but I can't bring myself to face him. Embarrassed, I glance at his men, then quickly look away when I realize they're laughing. "How mortifying," I whisper to myself.

"That's not the word I'd use, but try not to do it again and give me a reason to go after my men..."

I nod, my cheeks burning, and we resume our journey. For a long while, I stay away from the group, too embarrassed to join them. Karel is up front, talking to Samael, who he elbows hard enough to make him double over.

When we reach the end of the beach, an island comes into view. A majestic palace sits perched on the mountain there, overlooking a city below. As I look at the horizon, I realize it's actually an archipelago. The vegetation seems as dense as on the continent we're about to leave. I'm awestruck by the sight before us. While lost in my contemplation, I see three boats approaching the shore.

I'm eager to explore the inside of this castle and the city that seems straight out of a fairy tale.

Karel signals me to stand behind him as the boats dock.

"Your Highness," greets the Aquarian who joins us. "Your men informed us of your arrival. His Majesty is delighted to receive you."

I don't miss the hungry look the man gives me, and an unpleasant shiver runs down my spine as I clutch Karel's jacket.

The Aquarian turns away, but his gaze has left an imprint I can't shake. As we approach the boats, my eyes settle on the glass palace, and my impatience turns into apprehension. My heart leaps, and suddenly I'm certain our stay here won't be pleasant. This place is paradise in appearance only.

Chapter 9

Kalliopee

Sitting in the boat in front of Karel, I lean to the side to admire the island we're approaching.

"You're going to tip us over," my ever-alert husband scolds me.

I sigh and sit back in the center of my bench. We had to leave our mounts in the stable near the beach, as the island is too small for horses. Our boat leads the other two, and I know the prince isn't thrilled about it. He dislikes arriving alone in unknown territory, and I can feel the tension radiating from him behind me. The man who greeted us sits across from me and hasn't taken his eyes off me. I smile uncomfortably, not looking away. Relief washes over me when he finally breaks eye contact. I don't like the way he stares at me; it feels unhealthy.

I watch the almost translucent expanse of the ocean with barely contained curiosity. The water is clear, and the corals are visible. The colors are vivid, dazzling, and mesmerizing. I jump when a huge fish swims under our boat. The next moment, a colorful dance unfolds beneath the surface. The waves make the boat rock, but it stays on course. The spectacle is sublime.

"Could you stop staring at my wife like that? It's disrespectful," Karel growls behind me.

I turn pale as his anger penetrates my bones. If he decides to go after this Aquarian, we'll end up in the water. I focus on the man sitting across from me. His head tilted to the side, he watches me unabashedly with a hunger I struggle to understand. It feels like he's assessing me.

"I didn't mean any disrespect to you, Your Highness," our escort murmurs nasally, not taking his eyes off me.

The tension emanating from my husband sends a shiver up to my scalp, making the hairs on my neck stand on end.

"It's her you're disrespecting," Karel retorts, his voice vibrating with anger.

A grating laugh echoes in my ears.

"Do you have a problem?" Karel growls, threateningly.

"Are you possessive, Your Highness?" asks the Aquarian.

I swallow hard, praying Karel doesn't lose his temper. But if this Aquarian keeps provoking him, I'm not sure he won't end up in the water.

Luckily, my husband seems to realize the kind of man he's dealing with and stops playing into his game.

The rest of the trip is tense, and I barely refrain from sighing in relief when we finally reach land. As my feet touch the sand, I lose my balance for a moment, but my husband steadies me by the arm. Once I regain my footing, he doesn't let go, sliding his fingers down to my wrist and holding it firmly. Normally, I dislike his way of steering me, but I accept his need to protect me from the man escorting us.

The other two boats arrive, and the group is ready to head to King Nokken's palace.

"Keep an eye on this guy," Karel murmurs to Jonah, who nods immediately.

"You can count on it," Jonah assures him.

Jonah walks ahead, passing our guide and showing him the damaged side of his face. I would laugh at the man's reaction if he didn't frighten me so much. Karel watches me for a few seconds, then releases a reassuring "let's go," more for himself than for anyone else. I nod, and we join the group as they begin to enter the city.

The streets are open, and the cobblestones are hidden under fine sand, so we have to watch where we step. The houses have white facades, and their roofs are actually terraces. These small homes have openings without windows. It's unlike anything I've ever seen. The alleys are lined with tall palm trees that provide shade, and numerous potted plants decorate the front of the homes. Everywhere I look, I see green and white.

We pass children running and laughing and women weaving fishing nets. As I look up the main street, I freeze at the sight of the enormous palace. The towers are so tall they seem to touch the clouds, as if they're emerging from the mountain. We climb countless steps, their surface porous but immaculate white. I'm careful not to trip over the irregularities, and finally, we reach the doors. I'm dazzled by the splendor of the place. The walls are carved from gleaming marble, and massive windows let in the light.

"Prince Karel!" a warm voice exclaims as we enter the hall.

I nearly faint when I see the impressive height of the ceiling and the glass roof that reveals a blindingly blue sky. I lower my gaze to see the man approaching us, blinking several times to see him clearly. He wears loose pants and a flowing shirt-like garment, all in bright colors—vivid red and gold—perhaps too bright. His blond curls fall onto his shoulders as he walks toward us. He greets my husband, who responds with a simple nod, then turns to me.

"You must be my friend's wife."

I'm surprised by the term *friend* but don't comment. Everyone is a friend until a better opportunity comes along and requires betraying the one to whom loyalty was sworn.

"I'm Prince Alesso," he says, placing a hand on his chest. "Nerea!" he exclaims. "Come on, they won't bite."

At his words, which made me jump, a young woman, slightly younger than me, appears from behind a pillar and trots over. Her top reveals her navel, adorned with a jewel. Again, the colors she wears are vibrant—shades of red, orange, and yellow.

"This is Nerea, my younger sister."

"Your Highness," interrupts the man who escorted us, "your father—"

"Areg," the prince cuts him off abruptly. "I know what I'm doing. My father should have come to greet them himself. You can go back to him now; I'll take it from here." He doesn't even glance at him and keeps smiling.

"You must have made many people jealous," Prince Alesso continues, looking at me with curiosity.

"All right, I'm going," Areg interrupts again.

"Yes, Areg! Go on." Prince Alesso sighs, rolling his eyes.

I notice his sister examining me as intently as her brother, and I suddenly feel myself blushing. With Karel still holding my wrist, I can't join Kaïs and Jonah, who stayed back.

Prince Alesso steps toward me and takes my face in his hands. Immediately, Karel pulls me back and positions himself between the possible threat and me. Our companions have moved to his side, and our host starts to laugh.

"Do not touch her," Karel orders in a deep voice.

"I wouldn't harm her," the prince defends himself. "Rarities like her are precious and sacred."

I don't understand his implication, but I decide to satisfy my curiosity by looking over Karel's shoulder. "What are you talking about?" I dare to ask.

My husband turns to me with a murderous glance that I choose to ignore. I'm curious, and he knows it. He should have expected me to want to know more.

"Nerea, would you please escort the princess to her room? I will take the prince to father."

My human shield presses closer to me, still on guard.

"Kaïs, you stay with her," Karel announces in a tone that brooks no argument.

My cousin by marriage winks at me before joining me and offering his arm. I guess it's his way of easing the tension, but I'm as tense as a bowstring as we move away from the group of men. I notice they're all armed and on high alert. I give Karel a pleading look, and he reassures me with a discreet nod. The next moment, he disappears from my view as we turn a corner. Kaïs pats my hand to urge me to calm down. I pay close attention to the corridor we are walking through. It's very wide, lined with plants, making it hard to believe we're indoors. Our shoes click against the floor. The white marble is polished so highly that our reflections are clear. I can't help but admire the view whenever we pass a window. The ocean reflects the sunlight, making it look like it's covered in countless diamonds.

Princess Nerea frequently glances at me, and whenever I catch her, she looks away. Being watched isn't unusual for me, but usually, it's done with hostility. I don't know what to make of the way she looks at me. I'm not sure if the lack of animosity is a good or bad sign.

After a short while, we reach a large door. Nerea's long hair, as blond as her brother's, brushes against her lower back, revealing her golden skin with each step. Her complexion is very different from my husband's, who is much darker. It's as if star particles have settled on her skin. The sunlight makes her shimmer.

"The prince requested in his letter that you all be housed in the same quarters. We have therefore prepared the largest suite for you," she informs us, pushing open the massive door.

Inside, enormous windows are open, letting in the sea breeze. The curtains dance with the wind. The sitting room that welcomes us is furnished with pieces that seem to be made of driftwood. Kaïs cautiously steps away to inspect the rooms without losing sight of me for too long, for which I am grateful. While Nerea seems as gentle and fragile as a flower, I also know some plants are thorny, even poisonous.

"You must be idolized in your kingdom," she whispers, her blue eyes shining with curiosity.

I don't have time to react as Kaïs' laughter echoes off the walls. I'm too taken aback to find his amusement.

"Why would I be?" I ask, intrigued.

"Your eyes, of course!" she replies as if it were obvious.

She walks away slowly, heading toward the large terrace. I turn to Kaïs, wondering what we should do, but he looks as lost as I am. He decides to follow her and disappears behind the curtain. After taking a deep breath, I join them.

"Do you know the legend about the birth of the first king of Aquaria?" she asks without turning to face us.

"No," I admit.

The Aquarian princess stares at the horizon without blinking and tilts her head to the side. "He was born from the union of the land and the sea. His father was a fearsome pirate, the most ruthless and cruel of all," she begins her tale. "He pillaged, killed, and undoubtedly did many other unspeakable things. His mother, on the other hand, was a young girl from a good family, sweet and naive. Those two should never have loved each other, and yet…"

She pauses briefly, and I approach the railing as well.

"During a mutiny, the pirate was captured and imprisoned. For many long months, he remained locked up. The suffering caused by his incarceration was more gratifying to his jailers than a death by hanging. The ruler's daughter was naturally curious, and one evening, she ventured into the dungeons, illuminated only by the candle she had brought. It took just a few seconds for the heartless pirate to fall for the beautiful girl with oceanic eyes. She reminded him of what he loved most and what he was deprived of. In her eyes, he forgot he might never sail the world's seas again. Every night, the young girl visited him, refusing to see him for who he was and the horrors he was guilty of, and she listened to his tales of travel. She began to dream of leaving the continent herself."

The sea breeze sweeps my hair as my eyes scan the thousand sparkles created by the movement of the turquoise water.

"One night, she helped him escape and begged him to take her with him. He didn't hesitate because, against all odds, the bloodthirsty criminal was madly in love. The young woman quickly became pregnant. But despite the happiness she felt with him, she saw in her lover's eyes what she missed so much: her lands. They knew, however, there was no going back. If she returned home, she would likely be sentenced to death. He had no home other than his ship. So they settled on a small island, inhabited by only a few families. It was a semblance of a compromise. But while the pirate loved his wife, he lived only for the ocean. That was his reason for being. He also knew this life was too dangerous for her, especially with a child. Out of guilt, he decided to leave. One evening, he disappeared, leaving her only a hastily written note. He promised to return when their son was old enough to fight. He knew the life he could offer them would not be worthy of her… She gave birth to a boy with eyes between land and sea. Yes, like yours," she says, smiling at me.

"What happened to the pirate?" Kaïs asks, seeing that she doesn't continue.

"Probably dead," she adds sadly. "The child born of that union built Aquaria and raised tall, reflective towers in the hope his father would come back for him and his mother. That never happened. Generations passed, the power was overthrown, and my father's grandfather ascended the throne—"

"What my sister is trying to say," Prince Alesso interrupts, appearing behind the curtain, "is that here, you would be considered a direct descendant of the true first king."

My gaze searches the room for my husband. Kaïs steps in

front of me protectively. A smile appears on our host's face at this gesture.

"Though it's certainly false, my father wanted me to marry you to, let's say, restore his reputation. He isn't exactly popular with our subjects. Higher taxes, the right of the first night… many reasons make him a rather despised king."

"Why are you telling us this?" I ask.

"My father holds grudges. Yours refused this alliance, and then offered you to the Lapisian prince. You can imagine how that news affected him."

"Where's Karel?" Kaïs demands, threateningly.

"Don't worry, he's safe. I just wanted to warn you, Princess."

"And you? Don't you hold a grudge against my father?" I risk asking.

"You are very beautiful, and there's no doubt we wouldn't have been bored together, but I'll wait until I'm on the throne to marry. A woman I'll choose myself, preferably."

His head turns to his sister, who he looks at affectionately, then the Aquarian prince faces us again. "And I'll make sure the same goes for her."

With these words, he leads Nerea away, leaving Kaïs and me alone. We stare at each other for a long time, trying to read between the lines, then I turn toward the ocean. My cousin by marriage does the same, and I observe him covertly. His usually cheerful face is very serious.

"King Nokken is known for his oversized ego. He'll probably look for a way to get revenge," he murmurs.

Yes, I'm aware of that. The more leaders I meet, the more convinced I am that my husband would be much better in that role. My heart doesn't calm down. I wonder what Karel is doing and if he suspects something is up. I know him well enough to know that a simple ego issue could turn into a war if he understood what I'm risking.

"Don't tell Karel," I whisper to Kaïs.

At these words, Kaïs stops looking at the horizon and stares at me.

"As long as the king doesn't try anything, I'd rather he remain ignorant. King Nokken is known for his pride, but not for his bravery."

Kaïs nods, probably as aware as I am that Karel might attack preemptively while the king may do nothing. We've avoided one war; I don't want another to start right after our vows have exchanged.

Chapter 10

Karel

"Prince Karel!" the king exclaims as soon as his son ushers me into his office.

I briefly pay my respects without lowering myself, while his smile widens. He sizes me up from head to toe. I keep my gaze fixed on his ever-stretching lips. If I'm not known for my clemency or benevolence, this man is the king of opportunists. He has no merit except being in the right place at the right time. Kalliopee has him pegged well.

"I was eagerly awaiting your arrival," he declares, turning away. "However, I was surprised by your letter announcing that you would be accompanied by your wife, the Viridian princess. I thought the marriage had been canceled. My queen was saddened not to have been invited to the ceremony."

I say nothing, knowing I can't come up with any valid reason for why he wasn't invited. He moves toward the window as I scrutinize every corner of the room. I realize we're now alone. My men were asked to stay outside the royal quarters, and apparently, Prince Alesso has deserted the premises. I'm not worried, though; King Nokken is neither agile nor particularly muscular, making him an easy opponent to take down.

"How's your father?" he asks, facing me again. He approaches his desk, letting his fingers trace the light wood.

"He's still on the throne."

"Still beloved by his subjects?" he asks sarcastically.

"As much as you are," I retort in the same tone, not breaking eye contact.

He lifts his head, a proud glint in his eyes. King Nokken's reputation precedes him. His own people hate him, and I know his days are numbered. That's also why he's so nervous, so dangerous. A cornered man is capable of anything.

"Follow me," he instructs, approaching a piece of furniture that he rotates.

I follow him obediently, even though I'm itching to reunite with my wife. We pass through the opening, which leads us into a vast study. When my gaze falls on the table in the center and the reliefs it displays, I realize it's a model of our territories.

"We have few soldiers," he informs me. "As you know, our people are better sailors than fighters… and it's true that any land army could wipe us out, even with half the men, but given the plan, we'll be up to the task, I promise you."

I nod absentmindedly. Having this conversation with him now makes everything feel too real. He smiles at me while I only dream of gutting him, but I know my urge is tied to an overwhelming feeling unfamiliar to me. I'm lost, torn. I hate them, but I'm convinced that soon I'll hate myself even more.

Yet, I can't help it.

I have to live with it.

I owe it to *them.*

***

Father hasn't left his chambers in days, and I've been here, in my room, waiting for guidance, waiting for someone to tell me what to do. The kingdom has been searching for these men for three days now, and since then, time seems to have frozen here at the palace. How can I deal with these visions that jolt me awake at night? How am I supposed to overcome this emptiness that only grows as the silence stretches on in the room next door?

"Do you want to go to the dorms? We could find the boys."

I stop staring at the ceiling and look at Kaïs, who is lying on his stomach, looking as exhausted as I feel. The pity in his eyes forces me to look away. No matter how many times he tells me otherwise, I know it's all my fault. I couldn't protect them; I couldn't save them.

"Karel," he tries.

"Kaïs, please."

I don't want to hear his speech again, hoping it will soothe my pain or guilt. He doesn't say anything more, but I hear his sad sigh. The mattress shifts, the door opens. I'm alone. Immediately, my eyes fill with tears, but instead of crying like a coward, I curse those Viridians. I should have been more attentive; if I had observed them closely, if I had analyzed their behavior, I would have seen the crime they were about to commit. If I had been more focused, I could have anticipated it and saved them. They wouldn't have died, choking on their own blood. I could have prevented the tragedy that plunged our city into chaos.

The pain in my chest intensifies with each breath. Are my ancestors punishing me for still being here? Do they want me to suffer with every heartbeat? I should have protected them or died. But no, I'm still alive, and I'm in agony. Out of breath, I get up and head to my father's quarters.

In the corridors, darkness has taken over the walls; silence lingers. It feeds my pain, my resentment, my loneliness. I want to hear her laugh echo, her shrill voice call out to me. I want to hear Mother call her Shaadi *like when she catches her scheming for an extra piece of cake. I just want everything to go back to its place because without it, I don't know where mine is.*

I knock on the door under the sorrowful gaze of the palace guards. "Father?" I call through the door. I think my voice cracks, that it's only a whisper.

No response. Nothing. This silence, always and forever. Yet, he's there, behind this door. I feel... abandoned. He blames me, I know it. To him, I've been a bad son, a bad brother, a bad soldier. He screamed at me, "Where were you? What were you doing?" *I was just by their side. I didn't understand anything. We were laughing, and then everything changed. That sunny day ended in darkness.*

Hurried footsteps pull me out of my daze and stop me from beating myself up even more. I turn and see Amadeus running toward me.

"Your father?"

I step aside to let him know that Father is in his chambers. He doesn't even bother to knock before entering. Darkness greets us. The pain amplifies, but this time, it's bitter.

"They've been spotted, Your Highness!" the advisor exclaims as he enters the room.

"Where?" my father's voice immediately responds.

I listen to Amadeus detail the route taken by the Viridians. He begs the king to stay there, as his sleepless nights and days without food have weakened him. I look around, impatient, feverish. The rage seeps in with more power. It flows through my veins, poisoning my soul. If I right the wrongs, if I avenge them, maybe the pain will fade. Maybe the fog I wander in will lift. Maybe each breath won't feel so excruciating. My breath shortens, my heartbeat quickens.

My father appears in a robe, his hair disheveled. Grief marks his features and emaciates his frame. He refuses to see me, to give me his attention. It hurts my gut. I want to beg for his forgiveness, but I can't. So, I feel for my belt, and finding my sword missing, I move toward his, lying on one of the couches.

"Karel," Amadeus calls out.

I look up at him, hand on the hilt. It seems like he's pleading, but I refuse to respond.

"Where are you going?" he worries as I turn to leave.

My limbs tremble, tears gather, and a painful lump forms in my throat. I see them everywhere. I hear them agonize as they cough up blood. I can't take these memories haunting me at any moment, day or night.

"Karel," he insists as I prepare to cross the door.

There's only one way to exorcize this spreading evil within me.

"Don't spare them, son," my father orders.

Days since he last spoke to me, and finally, I breathe.

I turn to him, nod solemnly, then leave the chambers, closely followed by Amadeus.

Finding these men will grant me peace and my father's forgiveness. This time, I won't disappoint anyone.

***

Nokken sits down in his chair. With a gesture, he invites me to do the same, and though I would prefer to remain standing, I comply to avoid provoking him.

He opens a drawer and takes out a parchment, placing it before my eyes. "If your letter was, let's say… shocking, I was quite reassured by the one from your father."

Nervously, I grab the document and see it indeed bears his seal.

"I must say, you Lapisians hold grudges tenaciously and have no limits in satisfying them."

I observe him in silence. The wide-open window allows the sea air to perfume the room. I focus on that rather than this man whose smile won't fade.

"Don't be mistaken, Prince Karel," he continues, amused. "I don't judge you; I would probably have done the same."

I lower my eyes to read the lines, and panic floods me. My throat tightens as I decipher the words written by my father.

"Under these conditions, you can count on us," Nokken informs me solemnly.

At these words, a simmering anger takes hold of me. I shake my head, then my fingers curl and crumple the parchment. Slowly, I lift my gaze to the king. A silent battle ensues between us. My jaw tightens, and I glare at him, imagining slicing his skin to carve a permanent smile on his face. My mind distorts my vision, and somehow, it calms me.

"Forget what you've read," I order sharply.

His head tilts to the side, seemingly surprised by this turn of events. Nokken's help might be useful, but not under any condition. Not at this price. Regardless of what my father thinks. The fact that he acted without my consent, offering such a deal without even discussing it with me, stuns me. It's clear I would have said no, and I wouldn't have brought Kalliopee here if I had known.

"Xerios will compel you," he replies.

"I'd rather kill her than hand her over to you," I retort in a voice that comes from the depths of my soul.

My hands grip the armrests of my chair tightly as I stare at this man I want to rip apart.

"Then you'll have to kill her," he finishes.

He knows as well as I do that a woman can't be given away without her husband's consent, and there's no way I'll honor my father's promise. If it were up to me, I'd grab Nokken by the collar and give him a scar to remind him who I am. But letting my impulses dictate my actions would endanger Kalliopee, my friends, my people.

If he were anyone else, he'd already be dead.

"You won't be able to marry her anyway," I remind him.

"True. But she would make a lovely ornament during my official outings. My subjects will revere her, and they will adore me."

I can't help but laugh at this. "That will never happen."

"Of course it will. And you know what? Seeing you so determined to refuse, seeing you ready to sacrifice your need for vengeance for her, only confirms I need a jewel like her."

"If you'll excuse me," I cut in as I stand up, "I'm going to join my wife. The journey here must have tired her."

"Go ahead," he replies, a hypocritical smile on his lips as I tower over him.

He doesn't even seem afraid of the idea that I might attack him. I realize then that he's more dangerous than I imagined. He has nothing to lose.

When I meet my men, I tuck the letter I kept inside my jacket and then share the details of our meeting. Jonah looks at me with barely concealed anger. He has never approved of my choices, but this one even less than any other.

"Your lies will be your downfall," he mutters before walking away, leaving me alone with Zaïn and Samael.

My pride wants to tell him he has no right to speak to me that way or that he should remember his place, but I know everything he says is true. He stays a few steps ahead of us as we head to the entrance. We don't know where our rooms are, and impatience gnaws at me. I don't like knowing she's alone in this palace. Yes, she's with Kaïs, but… what if he isn't enough to protect her?

I realize then that she's right; I need to give her the chance to defend herself and stop relying on others. Especially since, without even knowing it, I've led her into new danger. A move or two could make all the difference. I turn around and signal my men to follow me as I remember the corridor she disappeared into. Although my body is stiff, my pace is measured, and my steps are powerful. They alone reveal my nervousness and urgency.

We stop when the prince and princess appear. The young girl blushes when they reach us. He looks at me with what seems to be amusement.

"I hope you enjoy your stay with us, Prince Karel," the prince says.

He gives me a slight nod and walks around me. My body pivots and I watch him until he disappears around the corner.

"You never should have brought her here," Jonah reprimands me. "It pains me to say it, but she would have been safer in Lapisia. But no, you think you're the only one who can protect her from danger, and you'd drag her into hell with you."

My muscles tense, and the angry look he gives me drains my patience. I rush at him and pin him against the wall, gripping his jacket tightly. I do it because I know myself, and I might hit him if I don't find something to hold on to.

Zaïn intervenes and pushes me away. He's mad at me, too; I can tell by the way he looks at me.

"Calm down, guys," Samael tries.

"Is that what you think, too?" I ask Zaïn, ignoring Samael's attempt to calm us.

He turns his head away, then turns around and walks off. That's how Zaïn is. I may not be as close to him as I am to Samael and Jonah, but we've been friends for too many years for me to stay silent. We trained together, fought side by side. The court members don't understand the familiarity between us, but we've been too close to death to care about etiquette.

"You never say what you think," I spit out, bitter.

He pauses without turning around. I see his shoulders rise and fall. "What I think from the beginning wouldn't please you," he admits before continuing on his way.

I stare intensely at the back of his neck as he walks away. Normally, I would have made him spill his thoughts, but today, I'm tired. I run a hand nervously through my hair, then let go of Jonah and turn around. My friends are still watching me. Samael looks bewildered, glancing between Jonah and me.

"Is what your father said in his letter true?" he asks.

"Yeah, that was the plan all along," Jonah answers for me.

I glance at the door that separates me from Kalliopee.

"Is it still current?" Samael asks impatiently.

I face him again and see that his body is tense. I can't say a word, and he curses.

"Karel is daddy's boy," Jonah adds bitterly. "You'll do it, obviously. You always do what he orders. How far are you willing to damn your soul for him, huh? Your father is mad! Hasn't she suffered enough since she arrived? Did you really think he didn't know about Xintia's plans? And you follow him blindly. Don't count on me to stay by your side if it goes that far," he finishes. "You'll be alone. I'll protect her."

He's right, I always do what my father asks. But I refuse to involve Aquaria in our plan, I refuse to give them Kalliopee. Still, I know my father, and he knows how to bend me to his will. For years, I've been looking for a way to repay my debt, to right my wrongs, to avenge them. But now, there is my wife. My wife and her ideals. My wife and the way she looks at me. My wife and her love for me. My wife and what I feel for her. Will I be able to hurt the only person who allows me to breathe without pain?

"With my life, if necessary," Jonah adds, seeing that I don't respond.

"Why would you do that?" Samael asks him.

That's true, why would he choose her?

"Because I promised her, and I keep my word."

I take a deep breath and stare at the door. I could give my life for her, I'm sure of it. Unable to catch my breath, I tug at my collar. What should I do? How could I achieve the much-desired goal without hurting her? Without losing her? Because I would lose her, that's certain. She would hate me. Even more than I hate her people.

I turn my attention back to my friends, hoping to find in them a solution, a way to save what remains to be saved. I'm a lost cause. I realize this as the vise around my chest tightens. I'm incapable of choosing between the promise made to my father and my wife. *Liar*, my conscience whispers. I clench my fists to hide the tremors that shake my body. *You're torn between your desires and your duties, but deep down, you already know what you want.*

Each passing day brings us closer to the deadline, to our ultimate goal. Yet I feel my allegiance to my king wavering.

I shake my head, exhausted, then decide to join the only person capable of ending, even briefly, the turmoil that assails me.

I pass by Samael and Jonah and enter our quarters. As I push the door open, Kaïs points to one of the rooms. As soon as I enter, I find Kalliopee lying on the bed. She's staring thoughtfully at the ceiling, then she seems to notice my presence because her eyes fall on me. She smiles at me in a strange way. As her mismatched eyes probe mine, I wonder if the power my father holds over me is as strong as I think or if she is the counter-spell.

Inside, I struggle. Part of me desires what I've sought for so many years, while the other part is soothed by those heterochromatic eyes that make me question everything.

"Is everything okay?" she asks as I join her.

Without a word, I lie down beside her and pull her close. I position her so her gaze can no longer affect me. Guilt overwhelms me as soon as I'm freed from her benevolence, but I accept my pain. I refuse to be healed by the love I see in her; I don't deserve it. I close my eyes, and the images of Kalliopee mingle with others I hope to one day erase.

"I love you," she whispers.

My eyelids tighten. My heart stops. I hate her for deepening my guilt with words like these, for trying to bring me back to her with incantations that are so sweet to my ears. She sighs in fatigue and relaxes, surely aware I'm not in a state to talk.

My love for her is strong—I have killed for her and would do it again, and again—but I don't forget everything else. I don't forget that before her, I lived. Painfully.

CHAPTER 11

KALLIOPEE

"Look, over there!" I shout to Karel, leaning over the edge of the boat.

He glances over, without much enthusiasm, and quickly returns to the center of his seat. Prince Alesso decided to show us around the nearby islands. Under the water, a firework display of colors unfolds, just like when we arrived yesterday. Schools of fish swim by in different shapes, sizes, and shades. Yellow, blue, pearly white, orange—none are missing. My eyes feast on the spectacle. Behind us, bursts of laughter grab our attention. Kaïs nervously clings to the edge of their boat while Jonah tries to tip it over. The atmosphere of their trip starkly contrasts with the seriousness that envelops Samael and Zaïn on a third boat. Since yesterday, tension has emanated from the group of men, and I suspect that if Kaïs and I were somewhat disturbed by our meeting with the prince, Karel's meeting with the monarch must have gone even worse.

Last night's dinner was rather peculiar. The atmosphere was heavy, suffocating. Fortunately, Nerea filled the silences by asking me a thousand and one questions about Viridia and Lapisia. The queen was there, too, but I didn't have the chance to hear her voice. She remained distant, and the way she looked at me made it clear she would have preferred to be anywhere else. The only topic King Nokken talked with me about was an ongoing case involving a woman who had tried to kill her husband. He spent a long time trying to get my opinion, but I bit my tongue to keep from sharing it. Undoubtedly, he wouldn't have liked it, and would have pushed me to provoke Karel. I didn't miss any of Karel's glances. I sometimes caught him looking at me with a pain that made my heart anxious. I wish he would talk to me, share his troubles, but I know him well enough to understand he will only do so when he's ready. And I know myself well enough to know my patience has limits, and if he doesn't come to me, I will go to him. For now, I give him time to sort out his thoughts, hoping they don't drown him.

A loud *splash* grabs my attention, and I laugh as I see Kaïs, Jonah, and their navigator emerging from the water. My eyes fall on my husband, who hasn't even turned around and maintains a grave expression. He realizes I'm watching him, and his eyes come back to life. He gives me a smile that seems forced, but instead of making a comment, I return it and turn my back to him, trying to forget my worries. The scenery no longer looks as beautiful since Karel doesn't share my enthusiasm. Our boat finally reaches the shore, and Prince Alesso extends his hand to help me out. I expect Karel to interfere, being the overprotective husband he is, but he doesn't. He remains silent, miles away from me. I accept the Aquarian prince's assistance and step onto the wet sand.

At first, I stay on the sidelines, struggling to enjoy the tour of the monuments Alesso is showing us. While I know the king isn't very well-loved, it's clear his son is quite the opposite. People speak to him with respect, and young women sigh as he passes by. He's very different from Karel, who inspires fear and a certain admiration. Alesso is like a charming prince. He's funny, cultured, and has a way with words. He does it so well that I quickly become interested in what he's saying. Still, I can't help but look back often. Karel isn't fulfilling his role as a guest, and while his attitude worried me at first, it eventually starts to annoy me. I keep my thoughts to myself and decide to enjoy the visit.

"Our educational system isn't the most modern, but my father insists on it," Alesso tells me as we enter the school.

I don't respond, but I'm shocked to learn only young boys receive an education. In Viridia, while women don't choose their professions, they still have access to education. Here, I notice they don't and are all forced to stay home to take care of children, fishing equipment, or household chores. The building housing the classrooms is open to the outside. There are no windows either, suggesting the region rarely experiences rain or cold. Desks are scattered around, and the young boys stand to respectfully greet the prince. The teacher smiles kindly at him before informing the students that we come from Lapisia. The questions are numerous, and I try to satisfy the curiosity of these blond-haired children. The audience looks surprised when I step forward to speak. Apparently, women aren't used to speaking publicly. After a while, Karel breaks out of his shell and starts answering questions as well. I step back, hoping his participation will lift his bad mood. I naïvely think he's done brooding, but I realize I'm wrong when he shuts down again as soon as we leave the classroom.

"When I become king, everyone will have access to education," Alesso confides, pulling me away from my frustration.

I smile at him, grateful. I'm glad to see I'm not the only one aspiring to change, that he also wants to rid us of ancient traditions.

"I didn't care until my father first mentioned Nerea's marriage," he adds thoughtfully.

We offered her the chance to join us, but she declined. I'm not naive; I think she's completely fond of my husband. Though he never speaks to her and mostly ignores her, I catch her sighing every time he moves. Every time it happens, I have to hold back from laughing to avoid embarrassing her. The prince speaks a bit about his sister, and the affection he has for her is evident in every word he says.

"You love her a lot," I murmur.

"It's hard not to love her. Without her, I would have fled Aquaria a long time ago."

"You didn't aspire to become king?" I ask, surprised by his confession.

"No, I wanted to explore the seas, like a pirate. Our people stopped sailing many years ago. I just wanted to nourish myself with the landscapes I could see. My only ambition was to be happy…"

He sighs, and his laugh seems full of affection. I guess he's amused by himself, by who he was, and by the ideals he had.

"But," he continues, "Nerea is my little sister, and if I can improve Aquaria for her, it would be selfish of me not to."

I listen thoughtfully to his words and begin to imagine the changes our world could undergo. If only two kingdoms initiated the emancipation of women, wouldn't that encourage others to follow this path toward a more just society?

We leave the school, the men following us, and reach the center of the island where a market is bustling. We stay silent as we walk through it; there's far too much commotion for us to have a proper conversation. Once we're a bit away from the crowd, I ask him how the king manages to rule his kingdom when the water separates him from it.

"Administrators appointed by the monarch himself. They're tasked with handling the day-to-day affairs of the archipelago. Each sends a regular report to my father."

I nod and notice a stall with strongly scented foods.

"Would you like to try some?" he offers.

I step back, eyeing the food warily. Is this considered a gift? Should I accept or decline?

"It's very salty and rather unique, but it's not bad. You just have to be adventurous enough to try it," he adds, amused.

I'm afraid of making a mistake. The prince raises his eyebrows, clearly waiting for my response, and I finally make a decision.

"I'm not sure I'm adventurous, but I don't want to die ignorant," I say with a smile.

As he heads toward the vendor, he's stopped by Karel, whose face is now a mask of worry. His gaze is dark and doesn't hide the anger that seems to have overtaken him.

"She's not tasting anything, understood?" Karel growls.

Alesso steps back, and although he's facing away, I can tell from my husband's even tenser stance that the Aquarian prince hasn't lost his smile.

"If we had wanted to poison her, we could have done it last night."

I freeze as I realize my curiosity has brought him back to the tragedy he experienced. I immediately feel guilty and try to soothe him with an apologetic look. However, instead of calming him, it seems to fuel his anger as he looks at me with palpable annoyance before turning back to Prince Alesso.

"You stay away, and there's no way she's trying your specialties," Karel adds.

I decide to step between them and grab Karel's arm to pull him away. He and I need to have a discussion. As I expected, he brusquely shakes off my hand and walks ahead of me, his pace quick. Once we're out of sight, I stare at him with all the anger he's made me feel since we left the palace.

"You're not tasting anything," he repeats.

"How dare you imply to our host that he's trying to poison me?"

He laughs with such arrogance that I want to hit him.

"You're so naive."

I swallow hard. His remark hurts; he knows it, but rather than making him feel guilty, this realization seems to please him as his detestable smile widens. At times, he becomes the person I once hated so much. I know it's just a facade, but it doesn't stop me from feeling hurt.

"He's manipulating you, telling you what you want to hear, and you—"

He laughs again, not finishing his sentence, but I understand what he left unsaid.

It's true that I trust Alesso based on everything he's revealed about his plans, but I refuse to believe he's manipulated me.

"You're just jealous," I sigh.

"Do you really think he shares *your* vision of the world?"

I know his emphasis on *your* is meant to imply that he doesn't share it either, but I also sense it's just provocation. I brought him here to scold him, not to face disillusionment. Let him keep his venom; I refuse to let it spread in my blood.

I pinch the bridge of my nose and sigh. "What's been going on with you since yesterday?" I dare to ask.

"It doesn't matter."

His evasive response irritates me to no end. His lack of effort even more so. I understand his fears, but the prince has done everything to be an excellent host since yesterday. Yet no matter what he does, Karel remains convinced the entire world is out to get us.

"I'm just trying to be a good guest. You should do the same. Your behavior isn't very diplomatic," I reproach him.

He seems surprised by my criticism. What did he expect? That I would approve of his behavior? How could I when he's been physically present but mentally elsewhere since yesterday?

"I don't trust him," he defends himself.

"You don't trust anyone!" I exclaim, at my wit's end.

His eyes darken with anger, and he turns away, perhaps tired of our fruitless verbal sparring.

"I have my reasons. You should be more like me. You should be wary of people, Kalliopee."

He's not wrong; my naivety puts me in danger. But his way of acting isn't any better. He distrusts everyone and is constantly on guard, not realizing it prevents him from enjoying what life has to offer.

"If I did that, you'd be the first on my list, Karel. You hide so many things that sometimes I wonder if I really know you. Sometimes I wonder if there's anything real about you!"

No sooner have I finished my tirade than guilt washes over me. I shouldn't have let him drag me into this territory of resentment, provocation, and manipulation. Hurting to avoid being hurt.

Staring off into the distance, he refuses to look at me. If I didn't know him, his apparent calm might deceive me. Despite his efforts to hide his irritation, I can sense it. His muscles are tense, almost imperceptibly. Outwardly, he exudes a certain coldness, but up close, I can detect the anger crackling in the air. I know it's not really directed at me, but I feel like I'm the only one who can exorcise it. I accept this burden, but having him open up to me would be compensation equal to the task. I stare at him, hoping his eyes will meet mine. Realizing my hope is in vain, I take a step back to put some distance between us.

"Let's go back, and please, try to be a bit more pleasant. Even if you have to fake it."

I'm about to rejoin the group when he grabs my arm.

"King Nokken, he—"

He can't continue, and I sense he doesn't want to worry me. I'm relieved he has caught wind of the king's resentment, and I understand this is what has been tormenting him since yesterday. I should have suspected when I asked Kaïs to keep this information quiet. It was obvious the king would mention it to Karel. I face him again, and his grip loosens but doesn't release me entirely.

"I know," I murmur, locking eyes with him.

His eyebrows knit together, and he tilts his head. "How do you know?" he asks, concerned.

His fingers tighten a bit more, but this time it feels like an involuntary gesture.

"The prince told me the king had proposed a union between he and I before my hand was promised to you. Knowing him, his ego must not have been able to handle it. I trust Alesso, but not his father. Believe me, I'm staying vigilant, but don't let him provoke you. Nokken will do anything to get to you one way or another. He resents you for winning me."

He says nothing and seems lost in thought again. I realize I don't know everything, but the fact that he's coming back to me a bit is enough for now. I just hope he doesn't isolate himself as he's been doing since yesterday.

His gaze remains fixed on me, and the veil over his eyes takes my breath away. He watches me as if I could disappear at any moment. That fear is normal; we always worry about those we love, but with him, I feel like my end could be imminent.

"I won't taste anything," I reassure him, brushing his cheek with my fingertips.

His hand covers mine, and he looks at me with an intensity that sets my heart on alert. I want to force the words out of him, to make him share what seems to torment him so much. Yet I stay silent and simply press my lips to his. Since yesterday, they've been carved from marble, cold and flavorless. I hold back the tears I want to shed from this growing distance that seems to widen by the hour. I miss him every second his mind drifts away from me. I wish I could melt into his arms, beg him to leave the darkness, but my request is more measured.

"I don't know where you've gone, Karel… but come back to me soon."

He doesn't respond, his gaze lost in the void, and I'm worried he might choose his darkness over me. I take a deep breath, retrieve my hand as he releases it without even trying to hold on, and then walk away from the alley where we found refuge.

I try to appear calm as I rejoin the group of men, but I can't help looking out for Karel's return. When he rejoins us, he plays his part. I should be content, feel reassured, but he maintains that distance that makes me feel like I'm suffocating. Throughout the rest of the excursion, I watch him secretly. Even when he was horrible to me, he never seemed as unreachable as he does today. I try to catch my breath as anxiety tightens its grip on my chest. What is he hiding from me? And why do I have the terrifying feeling his secrets could destroy us both?

Chapter 12

Karel

"I don't know where you've gone, Karel... but come back to me soon." The words haunt me all day, burrowing under my skin. I tried to ignore the sadness that filled her when she said them, but it infiltrates every cell of my being. I wish I could share my torments with her, but I'm incapable of doing so. Shame and fear hold me back. She would despise me…

No, worse, she would hate me with a visceral hatred. She would rather die than stay by my side, and I'm far too selfish to let her go. For her, I want to find the strength to give up. But this plan, it's the only thing that's kept us going every day without *them.* If I hadn't had the hope of paying my debt, of putting an end to this constant pain, of finally filling the gaping hole their disappearance left, I would have lost my mind.

The visit ends quickly, and when we return to our quarters, Kalliopee announces she's tired and retires to our room. I watch her until she closes the door. It was just an excuse, I know. All she wanted was an escape. I can't blame her. I wish I could turn back time, come here without her, not find myself mired in lies that suffocate me.

My men accept Alesso's invitation and decide to go train with him. Although exercise usually helps me interrupt the battle I fight within, I prefer to stay here. I'm too lost to be distracted by anything. I go out to the terrace and lean against the railing. Just when I think I'll be alone, I'm surprised when Zaïn joins me. He mimics my posture, and we both look out at the horizon.

"Have you decided to talk to me?" I ask, without turning to face him. It's easier than facing his disappointment.

"I told you, you wouldn't like it," he murmurs.

"Since when has that been a problem?" This time, I look at him.

His eyes slide over me until they lock onto mine. War has created a language that today requires no words. On the battlefield, it's often impossible to talk. The noises never cease. The screams of agony, the roars we let out to muster courage or intimidate, the clashing swords force us to communicate with just a glance. In the look Zaïn gives me, I read his disappointment.

Only Jonah was supposed to be in the know, but he caught us mid-conversation a few months ago. Jonah was trying once again to dissuade me, and Zaïn tried to do the same. I knew that, no matter what, Jonah would support me, even if he didn't approve; but Zaïn, I was so afraid he would turn his back on me that I lied to him. I pretended to have come to my senses because, yes, I fully understand what I'm planning is insane, crazy, but it's this madness that's kept me moving forward.

Seeing that he doesn't answer, I repeat my question, growing impatient. I'm ready to explode, anxious at the thought that our years of fighting side by side haven't made our friendship unbreakable.

"Because our disagreement has never been this deep."

He breaks eye contact and stares at the sky before taking a deep breath.

"That day, I followed you blindly. I understood your pain; I shared it. We all loved your sister, and your mother was good to all of us. I never had parents, you know that. And thanks to her, I felt like someone actually cared about me. I would have acted the same if I had the chance to face the men who killed my family. I thought it was necessary for you to… I don't know, but I didn't condemn your actions. On the contrary, I approved of them. But the guilty have paid, Karel. Don't let your father's madness infect you. It will consume you."

I lower my head and look at the rocks below. I remember what I felt that day and the rage that took over me, never letting go.

"The hate is still there," I admit, my throat tight. "No matter what I do, it refuses to leave. It disappears for a moment, but every time, it comes back stronger, hungrier."

"It doesn't have to devour you," he counters. "You're a soldier; do what you do best, fight! Don't let it win this battle, Karel.

Are you ready to lose Kalliopee? Because no matter what happens, if you and your father go through with this, she will never forgive you."

Thinking about it, it's not just that she might hate me and leave that scares me. There's also the fact that her heart would break. How can I claim to want to protect her when I'm ready to inflict the cruelest wound on her? The wound my actions would cause could never heal. I push away the fear that only grows and focus on the ocean's waves.

"You have the right to be happy, Karel. Don't ruin everything."

Then he disappears, just like that. After stirring up the battle raging inside me, he abandons me. I cling to the railing to stop myself from going to her, from holding her out of fear she'll see right through me. She always does too well.

The sea churns. I imagine falling, letting the waters take and engulf me. My eyes would close and my heart's frantic beating would finally cease. My fingers tighten their grip as the memories I try to suppress flood me. The wave hits me so hard I tremble. I can't breathe. I sink into the depths of my memory.

We gallop to the edge of the camp. Under my eyelids, Maha and my mother appear. The hate is visceral; it controls everything. Every breath, every heartbeat, every decision. The men gathered around the campfire rise as we arrive, and despite the darkness, I charge in. My horse rears and tramples the first one. It's exhilarating, and it only feeds my rage more.

I leap to the ground and attack the Viridian, already wounded by my horse's hooves. I land a blow so powerful he falls backward. My fingers grab my dagger, and I plunge it into his neck. Immediately, I exhale a deep, guttural sound. For days, I felt like I couldn't breathe. For days, they had taken my breath away when they lost theirs.

He struggles, and I pull the blade out, letting his blood spill. My crazed eyes scan the surroundings. The boys have followed me and hold the men at their feet. Amadeus steps in front of me and tries to dissuade me, but if I had to stop, I think I'd feel like dying. I shove him aside and glare at the criminals, one by one. I unleash my chains, the ones that held me to the loving and good son I had always been. "Learn mercy, my son. It's what your father often lacks." *I let out a painful laugh.* Mercy? *What good will it do me now? Did it save them?*

A lump forms in my throat. I approach the man Zaïn is holding and grab him by the collar. My anger knows no bounds now; it's broken free of its chains. I shove him to the ground and straddle him. I punch him relentlessly, and soon his face is unrecognizable. My knuckles burn, but I never stop. When he stops struggling, I release him and stab my dagger into his eye. I pause, feeling like I'm both there and a spectator of the scene. "Don't spare them, my son," *my father had begged when these men were found. The pain he harbored seemed to mirror mine.*

With shaky legs, I stand and turn around. Only two are left, but they won't be enough to extinguish my anger. The next one fights back more. He returns my blow, dazing me and making me stumble. My hands break my fall, the ground scraping my skin. This resistance fuels my rage more easily. As I start to turn, a pain seizes my neck. It's fleeting, but enough to make me nauseous. I touch the wound and am relieved to find it's just a superficial cut. Unsteady, I get up, then whirl around to find him holding a dagger. He glares at me, and though he tries to hide it, his fear is evident in every feature. I feed off it.

The Viridian lunges at me but doesn't get the chance to reach me because Jonah intervenes. He holds him back, but the man struggles so much that my friend falls too close to the fire. The flames lick his skin, and his scream is so painful that my enemy's weapon no longer worries me. With a kick, I send it flying and rush at him. My blade plunges into his throat with more determination, more violence, more hatred, more pain. The roar I let out is inhuman, tearing at my vocal cords, but it feels like it unleashes a new, destructive energy within me. I am their scourge.

I don't recognize myself, but after all, I died that day, and tonight, I am reborn. Stronger.

When I lift my eyes, I'm relieved to see Jonah freed from the flames and Samael leading him away. My hands ache and tremble, but they are determined to continue their task.

Breathing hard, I close the distance to the last one. Head down, he doesn't dare face me, and as I approach him and he tenses, I swallow the lump in my throat. My breathing grows more erratic, and my trembling intensifies. I grab him by the hair.

"I can explain everything," he tries.

"Filthy Viridian," I spit, slamming my knee into his nose.

The impact is so violent the man falls to the side. The sound of his fall chills me to the bone. I wait for him to get up, but he doesn't. When my boot nudges his side to roll him onto his back, I see life has left his body. I lift him by the collar and furiously eye the rock soaked in his blood, then my frightened eyes shift to the criminal's skull. I sit astride him and shake him.

"Wake up," I beg. "Wake up!" I scream. "Wake up!" I howl like a wounded animal.

But he doesn't respond. I turn my head, searching for a new target. My men back away, and I meet Amadeus's alarmed gaze. Despite the faint glow of the flames, I see his tear-filled eyes and the tears he's shed. The lump in my throat grows, descending to my heart, squeezing so hard I feel like it's suffocating.

Time freezes, my fingers still clutching the Viridian's jacket, tightening. Images flood in. "Karel, I don't feel well." *I see myself laughing and accusing her of snacking too much, then I see Mother, a few steps away, falling. My laughter silenced, my heart died. I should have protected them or died trying. Instead, I held Maha's body when she, too, collapsed. I didn't hear the agonized screams rising around us as other innocents suffered. I only heard my sister's faint attempts to say my name. I only saw her tear-filled eyes, the blood flowing from her mouth, her legs fighting against the poison consuming her from within, while her hands clung tightly to the bag containing all the silly things on her list.*

I come back here, in front of this campfire, and let the rage speak instead of the pain. I don't want the pain. It's much harder to deal with. I strike him even though he's already dead. And with each blow, I let out a cry from the depths of my heart.

"I hate you! You and your people! I'll kill you all! To the last one, do you hear me?"

I feel like a madman, but I scream everything I want to scream at his kind. And I hope his soul will carry the message before disappearing into hell.

When my fingers are aching and my blows are less determined, Amadeus grabs my chest. Despite everything, I try to keep hitting, but his grip tightens, and he pulls me away from the body. I want to struggle, but I think I've run out of strength. When he stands me up, I survey the scene. The corpses of the four men lie on the ground.

I close my eyes, trying to find some relief, but there's nothing. Nothing but this pain that won't go away. Nothing but this thirst for vengeance that doesn't weaken.

They're dead, but nothing has changed.

I push Amadeus away roughly. I can't face him. I take a step back, then another, and turn around. I run to my horse and, despite the fatigue, mount it. Kaïs joins me, shaking his head, eyes filled with tears, but I choose to ignore him, and with a press of my heels, I urge my steed to take me far from here.

I push my stallion to go faster, farther. When there's nothing around us but the desert, I can't hold back the sobs, and a scream of agony escapes into the night. I don't realize it comes from me until my throat burns. Grief overwhelms me, and instead of trying to suppress it, I let it crush me as I traverse the desolate landscapes of my kingdom.

Chapter 13

Kalliopee

When I wake up, I notice night is about to fall. Lying on my side, I stare at the outside. I let the curtain, moving with the breeze, lull me. My eyes focus so intensely they begin to water. Determined not to hide away here, I sit up. I'm surprised to find Karel sitting at the edge of the bed, his back to me. As has been the case since yesterday, I see he's lost in his thoughts since he hasn't noticed my movements. I approach slowly, my breath erratic with apprehension, then wrap my arms around him from behind. He tenses, and it feels like a punch to my heart.

Just as I'm about to let go, he holds me back. His fingers fiercely clutch my wrists. I know he doesn't do it on purpose, and that sometimes, when overwhelmed by his emotions, he feels the need to grip me tightly. What kind of person would I be if I pushed him away while hoping he would come back to me? I move closer to him and rest my forehead between his shoulder blades, accepting that he marks my skin with his fingers. I feel like I'm breathing again. Yet, this faint relief doesn't manage to chase away the questions racing through my mind. I want to ask him what torments him so much, what drives him so far away from me, from us.

"I love you," I whisper simply, hoping it will be enough.

And it is, as his grip loosens. I repeat it, over and over. With each repetition, his breathing calms, his body relaxes. We often underestimate the power of words. They can soothe even the most troubled souls. After a while, his claws turn into gentle caresses. I then pull away from him and get off the bed to stand in front of him. My fingers run through his hair as he lifts his head. My throat tightens when I realize what he's fighting against: himself. I believe it's the most exhausting of battles, the most frightening, too.

I push his shoulders to invite him to lean back. When he does so without any resistance, I understand he's reached the limits of what he can endure alone and that he's coming back to me. I straddle him and lock my gaze with his. For a long moment, we stay like this, without wanting or needing to say a word. My fingers trace his face, from the top of his forehead, sliding down the bridge of his nose, and finally to his chin. I repeat this gesture many times. It's what my nurse used to do when I was sad as a child. These simple caresses were enough to drive away my darkest thoughts.

"I'm sorry for leaving," he murmurs after a long while.

My fingers pause between his eyebrows. Deep down, I knew one of us would eventually break the silence, but I was certain it would be me. A slight smile forms on my lips, then I gaze at him tirelessly, resuming my caresses. I try to imagine the hostile lands he had wandered into. I want to have the courage to ask him, but the fear he will push me away keeps me from doing so.

"You came back, that's all that matters," I murmur simply.

"Sometimes… I feel like I'm disappointing you," he whispers.

My fingers stop and rest on my thighs. I lower my head, not responding… Yes, it's true. Sometimes he does disappoint me, but only because I wish he would trust me, accept my support, and find me worthy enough to share his thoughts, even the darkest ones. I want to help him bear his burdens. I don't like that he keeps me at a distance; I always feel powerless. But Karel is a warrior, and he insists on facing his battles alone, convinced he needs no one.

His hands move up my back to my hair. With a gentle pressure, he invites me closer and kisses my temple. His mouth lingers there as his voice breaks the silence of the room once more, "Sometimes, I hate Viridia so much that I hate you, too."

His words take my breath away, but he doesn't give me time to recover before continuing.

"And then, I hate myself for daring to feel that way."

My fingers wrap around his forearms as he pulls away. Nervous, I open my eyes. Karel has shed his mask, revealing his true self, as complex as it may be.

"Looking at you reminds me of them, and it becomes hard to breathe and to love. I wish I could be like you, have the ability to forgive, but I can't. Hatred is a second skin."

Before I can stop it, a tear slips down my cheek. Karel stares at me with an intensity that disarms me, his eyes sometimes revealing the darkness within him.

"I try to let go, but I can't. I constantly have images running through my mind. Some where I feel the need to burn the entire world to ashes in the hope that the pain will disappear with it, and others where I lose myself in you so deeply that I feel nothing else."

His fingers hold onto my neck, and instinctively, my hands rest on his cheeks. I wish so much that I could help him rid himself of this consuming hatred and pain.

"I'm tired of fighting you, *Shaadi*. Of fighting myself. All I can ask is that you forgive me for the words I might sometimes say and for the ones I might withhold. Forgive me for what I might feel despite myself and for everything you make me feel despite yourself."

I say nothing and absorb these words for the days he speaks of, for those times when his pain will be so overwhelming that it blinds him to his love for me. My heart memorizes them to remember and forgive him as he asks. I seal my promise with a kiss.

Yes, I wish I had the power to save him, but all I can do is vow to remain loyal to him, to support him no matter what. Whatever he does.

"Princess, did you enjoy your visit today?" the monarch asks as we sit at the table.

"Yes, Alesso is an excellent guide," I reply nervously.

Tonight, only Karel and I have been invited to dine with the king. His advisor is also present, and the way he stares at me is unsettling. I avert my eyes and focus on the dish placed before me. Upon entering the room, we discovered it would be just the four of us. I wanted to turn back and flee, my fear overwhelming, but Karel advanced with dignity, giving me enough courage to endure this meal.

"Very well," he responds simply.

A heavy silence envelops us again. I try to calm myself by remembering that by tomorrow, it will be over. We have decided to cut our stay short, and although Karel refused to explain the reasons for our early departure, I can't deny the relief I felt. Alesso and Nerea seemed disappointed, but the king showed no emotion.

I timidly pick up my spoon and gaze anxiously at the soup in my bowl. I involuntarily recall Karel's words and am no longer sure I want to eat what the king has offered us. When I see my husband eating, I am reassured and follow suit.

"Prince Karel, we heard about your terrible misadventure."

My attention turns to the advisor who spoke, and the anxiety I felt when I realized we would be dining alone intensifies more. I feel cornered, trapped.

"My terrible misadventure?" Karel asks, on alert.

"Yes, you know. Regarding your wife being defiled by others."

My spoon clatters loudly into my bowl as my breath catches. Nausea washes over me.

"You still took the risk of marrying her. Who knows what diseases she might have brought you," he adds.

"King Nokken," my husband growls, "teach your advisor to hold his tongue."

I can tell he's restraining his anger; his body shows it more than his voice, which remains firm but calm.

"Forgive him, it's true that Areg sometimes speaks too much."

I pick up my spoon again to regain my composure, but my eyelids tighten as the king clears his throat, indicating the topic is likely not closed.

I wait, breathless, for him to continue, to finish me off.

"Princess, know that I'm sorry for what happened to you."

Despite my fears, I lift my head. The king regards me with feigned sympathy; I'm not fooled. Though part of me wants to feign a headache to escape this meal, another part refuses to give him that satisfaction and wants to see how far he will go. My lips curl into a smile as I realize his words are only meant to soothe his ego, bruised by my father's refusal to marry me to his son.

"But isn't that the risk all women face in this world?" I dare with confidence.

The sneer that distorts his mouth reveals nothing of the

bitterness he feels toward me, nor does the flash of hatred in his pale blue eyes. I know my insolence displeases him. Yet, although I urged Karel to behave as an honorable guest, I can't play my role tonight. Not when he used my traumas to provoke my husband.

"Unfortunately, you're right. I've been told what was done to you; it must have been painful," king Nokken adds.

I swallow hard as he lifts his glass. What happened to me is personal, and I hate that this man knows every detail. I wonder who could have told him.

"Although it's regrettable, I don't think it excuses your behavior," he informs me in a low voice. "You should know your place."

"And what is that?" I retort, irritated.

I could have stayed silent.

I *should* have stayed silent.

"To provide an heir to the future king. Wouldn't that please you, Prince Karel? For your wife to give you a male descendant?"

The monarch turns his attention to my husband, and I can sense the satisfaction emanating from him as he speaks.

Karel abruptly stands and grabs my arm. I turn my face towards him and see how close he is to his breaking point. He glares at the king with palpable hatred. Knowing that staying would only worsen the situation, I stand as well.

"We will take our leave," he announces, bowing slightly—not enough to appear subservient, but sufficiently to avoid disrespect.

"No, I don't think so. Sit down. The princess and I have more to discuss."

"I think everything has been said," I counter, controlling myself as best I can.

He smiles again. A sense of foreboding washes over me as he straightens in his chair.

"Really? Everything? Do you know that your husband—"

Before I can process what's happening, Karel pushes me aside and lunges at the king. The glint of the dagger in his hand elicits a gasp from me, and in the next instant, the blade is poised at the king's lips.

"Say one more word, and I'll carve off that smile you try so hard to maintain, regardless of the circumstances."

The king signals to Areg, who was about to intervene, and he sits back down. The advisor looks at me with evident glee. Like his monarch, he seems steeped in a vice he doesn't bother to hide.

"Release me, and I assure you I won't say anything more."

With his back to me, Karel doesn't move, and I wait, my heart ready to explode, for him to let go. I wish I could catch his eye and give him the strength to let his hatred subside. I wish I could soothe his anger, but my feet remain rooted to the floor, incapable of any step.

To my surprise, Karel straightens, and the king comes into view. A drop of blood beads at the corner of his mouth, but his smile hasn't faltered. My husband turns around, and the darkness in his eyes frightens me. He grabs my wrist, controlling his strength, and stiff-backed, leads me toward the exit. As we reach the doors, a clap of hands halts our escape. Immediately, armed men enter the room, and the ensuing panic makes me stagger.

"What are you doing?" Karel growls.

"Areg, would you kindly explain?" the king says.

Karel remains facing the doors while I turn cautiously to meet the malevolent eyes of the sovereign.

"Of course, Your Majesty. According to the laws protecting the royal family, any injury inflicted upon one of its members is punishable by corporal punishment. Naturally, the higher the rank, the more severe the sentence."

Without breaking eye contact with me, Nokken touches the corner of his lips with his thumb before bringing it to his mouth. My eyebrows knit together at this announcement, and I stifle a derisive laugh. An injury? It's barely a scratch.

"Areg, what punishment is given to those who harm the king?"

"Ten salted wounds," the advisor murmurs, unable to hide his glee.

"The one who dares to harm me hasn't been born yet," Karel states calmly.

My eyes dart between him and the monarch. The latter seems irritated by the prince's turned back, then he starts to laugh heartily, and a knot forms in my throat. My eyes close as I realize what amuses him so much.

"You are so naive, so self-centered," the king exclaims gleefully.

Karel's grip tightens around my wrist because he must have understood, as I have, that it is I who will suffer this punishment.

"Out of the question!" he roars.

He pulls me along and pushes through the doors. The armed guards do not stop us.

As we reach the corridor, the king's voice booms, echoing off the walls. "If you do not accept your punishment, Prince Karel, it will be war! Surely you realize I won't let anyone tarnish my honor."

Karel doesn't stop, and as he drags me away, I glance over my shoulder. The king, still smiling, watches us until we turn a corner toward our quarters. My heart pounds, and the injustice of the situation robs me of any desire to struggle as my husband pulls me through the palace.

Chapter 14

Karel

Mad with rage, I pay no attention to anything until Kalliopee's hand touches mine, loosening my fingers. I finally release her and stop walking. I lean against the wall and look up at the ceiling, unable to face her. With a nervous gesture, I pull my hair and turn away. I can't confront her distress, not now, not when there's chaos inside me. My forehead rests against the marble, and I stare at it endlessly, imagining smashing my head against it as punishment. Instead of my head, it's my breath that hits the marble with each exhale. My body is so tense it hurts. I try to untangle my thoughts, but one surpasses all the others.

"He won't touch you. I promise," I murmur.

Behind me, I hear the rustle of her dress as she approaches. Her heels click on the floor, then silence envelops us once more.

"We should talk about this somewhere other than this hallway."

I don't like the tone in her voice. Since when has Kalliopee been resigned? There's no trace of fight in her. Maybe she's holding back from yelling at me about how irresponsible I am. I keep telling her she must control herself, never show anything to others, and I failed to follow my own advice. I wanted to protect myself from the truths Nokken was about to reveal, but by doing so, I put her in danger.

I turn around, and what I see in her eyes displeases me just as much. Her long, slender fingers wrap around my wrist, and this time, she guides me through the corridors. With my free hand, I make her let go, then pull her close as we head back to our quarters. The scent of her chestnut hair only reinforces my resolve.

He won't touch her. Never.

When we reach the doors, she pauses before opening them.

"How do you feel?" she asks.

Guilt washes over me when I realize that, as always, she worries more about me than herself.

"We'll solve this problem," I assure her.

This time, the look in her eyes is no longer resigned—it's frightened. She averts her gaze, nods, and then pushes the door open. As soon as we enter, Kaïs and Samael appear from behind the curtain that conceals the terrace.

"What happened?" Kaïs asks, concerned.

It's true, we've been gone too short a time for the dinner to have gone smoothly. I immediately tense, and fury takes hold of me again.

"He set a trap for us," Kalliopee says. "He wanted to push us to the edge… and he succeeded," she adds after a moment's hesitation.

Samael stares at me, and I can only nod in agreement with my wife's words. He sighs and takes a seat in one of the armchairs in the middle of the room. Kalliopee recounts the events while I remain silent. My muscles tighten when she gets to the part where everything fell apart, where I condemned the woman I love to pay for my mistakes.

"They can't do that," Samael protests.

"Yes, they can," Kaïs counters. "I don't think there's any diplomatic immunity in cases like this. I'm sorry," he adds, looking at Kalliopee.

She gives him one of her gentle smiles, the kind only she can, and we all fall back into our thoughts. The silence stretches on and on. Night falls, and despite the breeze, I'm too hot.

"I refuse to let her suffer because of me," I say.

"It's not your fault," Kalliopee counters.

I turn my attention to her and scrutinize her. I expected to see lies in her features or her demeanor, but no, I see nothing but sincerity, which touches and angers me. How can she think that? How can she still defend me?

"It's the fault of this world. I understand why you acted the way you did… It's not your fault. Don't blame yourself for a law you didn't make. Since we arrived, we knew the king was looking for a way to get to you. His passivity when we announced our departure was suspicious. This king is proud; his pride is unmatched. If you hadn't acted, I would have ended up stabbing him in the eye with my fork."

She said every word without hesitation, with confidence. Still, I can't shake my guilt. I should have anticipated the consequences of my actions, but no. All I saw was that smile I despise, and all I felt was the irrepressible need to disfigure him. I don't know by what miracle I managed to control myself. Probably because, even without seeing her, I sensed the anxiety emanating from Kalliopee.

"Lapisia will never survive another war," Samael murmurs worriedly, drawing my attention.

I tense immediately, then my friend finally faces me. He looks at me, apologetic, and then I laugh. Yes, I laugh. Because the possibility he's considering is absolutely unthinkable. No one will ever touch her! How can he believe I would sacrifice my wife for peace?

"If you'll excuse me, I'm going to my room," Kalliopee announces softly.

I want to follow her, but I'm not sure my words would be enough to redeem myself. When she disappears, I close the distance between Samael and me.

"It's out of the question. Let him inflict his ten salted wounds on me if he wants, but he won't touch a hair on my wife's head."

"She's right," Kaïs sighs. "He's proud; he won't let you take her place."

"She's the one who will suffer instead of me," I remind him.

The cruelty of our world becomes clear to me. I've never really felt concerned, and I regret it now, even though I know I couldn't have changed anything.

"That's true," he finally says. "But the laws are the laws, and Nokken acts like a child ready to break another's toy if he can't have it. He won't give up."

I let out a nervous laugh at this comparison.

"Let him try to approach her. If he does anything, it will be war," I whisper.

"Then it will be war," Samael repeats, resigned.

Kaïs stands up, leaves, and returns with a bottle of liquor and three glasses in hand. He places them on the small driftwood table and pours generously. I take mine, my fingers trembling, and stare at the amber liquid as I sit down.

"She's stronger than you think," my cousin surprises me by saying before downing his drink.

"I won't change my mind," I say, bringing the glass to my lips.

I tilt my head back, and the alcohol burns my esophagus immediately. I close my eyes, savoring the numbing sensation. The glass clinks against the table as I set it down. Kaïs refills them. Samael remains silent and doesn't touch his drink. I suppose he's thinking of a way to get us out of this mess, but there's only one: fleeing Aquaria.

"We'll ask Alesso to help us leave discreetly. I don't think he approves of the king's actions," Kaïs announces.

I look at him, surprised. The prince would never betray the monarch. It's impossible. Nokken is his father. I down my drink and stand. In the end, I can't leave her alone, stay away from her. She might reject me; I don't know. But I need her to understand the depth of my remorse.

When I reach the door, I hold my breath and turn the handle. I thought I'd find her in our bed, but she's sitting at the vanity, brushing her hair, visibly lost in thought. The key that I turn behind my back brings her back to the room with me. Our eyes meet in the mirror. She's dimly lit by the glow of a lamp, but I can feel her turmoil, the thousand questions she's asking, the thousand fears suffocating her. She's shed her evening attire and is wearing a nightgown held up by simple straps. Her hair is swept to the side, revealing her shoulder and neck.

As our eyes remain locked, I suddenly have the urge to possess her. I have this visceral need to be inside her so she forgets what's hanging over us, to make her understand I will never let anyone harm her again.

My jacket falls to my feet, her mouth opens slightly, and she holds the brush against her chest. I undo the buttons on my sleeves, and approaching her, unfasten my shirt one button at a time.

"What are you doing?" she asks, embarrassed.

Now, pressed against her back, she has to lift her head to keep her eyes on mine. I kneel behind the small bench she's sitting on and take the brush from her nervous grip. My hands settle on her nightgown. The fabric is rough, far from the silky texture of her skin, yet her warmth burns me from the inside. I catch my reflection in the mirror. The darkness in my eyes hides nothing of my intentions or determination, nor the madness that seems to possess me. My nose grazes her shoulder and moves up to her earlobe. My eyes close as I inhale her scent like a predator. The aroma that emanates from her is intoxicating and arousing, making me want to throw everything to the wind. I've never learned to control myself, yet I always do with her. I silence my urges, my deepest desires.

My tongue traces up her neck. She doesn't taste the same as usual. The sea breeze has given her a salty flavor that makes me even hungrier. My eyelids lift to watch her in the mirror's reflection. She seems to have lost her breath. As my hands slide down her stomach and fiercely grip her hips, my teeth sink into her skin, eliciting a moan from her as she furrows her brows and closes her eyes. The next moment, I kiss the spot, and her mismatched eyes reappear as my fingers release their hold. Her lost gaze doesn't leave me, but soon frustration seems to take over her. I don't know if it's because I stopped or because I dared to start.

Rather than asking her, I trail up her neck, paying close attention to each of her reactions. My fingers grip her waist, and her breath hitches. My teeth reveal themselves, and her pupils dilate. When I bite her again, the loud moan that escapes her chest makes something inside me explode. The barriers collapse. I no longer hold back my madness from her. My hands leave her hips, one moving up to her hair while the other slides down her thigh. My hot breath hits her skin, as scorching as the marks from my bites. And when I pull her head back, her body arches. My fingers force a path between her closed legs as I plant a light kiss before my teeth nibble her skin again. She moans, parting her thighs.

Despite the fabric, I can feel everything this moment makes her experience: raw, powerful, living desire. I press roughly against her sex, making mine swell. My pants are too tight, but if I don't keep them on, I risk taking everything without giving anything back. Now that her head rests docilely on my shoulder, I use my other hand to pull up her nightgown. When my fingers finally touch her skin, they dig into her inner thighs. My breath grows heavier. I don't know how much time has passed since I entered this room, but I've lost track. I feel both like only a few seconds have gone by and that it stretches on infinitely.

Her body collapses against my chest. With a sharp movement, I spread her thighs further and let my hand slip into her underwear. I inhale involuntarily when I feel how wet she is. She's going to be the death of me, that's for sure.

My other hand slips under the fabric to reach her breast, which I grasp fully. I alternate between firm and sensual squeezes, bites, and kisses, while my fingers move along her slit. My body rocks back and forth, a sign that it wants to claim its due and all the things my mind imagines.

"Karel," she breathes.

To silence her, my fingers slip inside her as my palm presses roughly against her clitoris. I pause to calm my urges, but I want so much more. She grabs my curls, forcing me to open my eyes, while her other hand grips my wrist.

"Don't hold back," she murmurs.

My eyelids lower, but again she tugs my hair, and I'm compelled to face her.

"Are you seeing images, too?" she asks.

"Yes," I confess in a hoarse voice.

"I give you everything."

I try to pull my hand away, to detach myself from her. I'm too close to the edge, flirting too dangerously with the limit.

"Take everything," she adds.

We remain motionless, only our heavy breaths showing that we're alive, then her fingers force mine deeper inside her. I feel her walls tighten around me, and at that moment, I destroy my last reservations.

My hand leaves her breast and settles on her stomach. I pull my fingers out, drawing her over the bench. Without thinking about her comfort or mine, I roll us over and find myself lying on top of her, on the bedroom floor. My chest presses against her back, my sex against her buttocks. I kiss her skin, trail down her spine, despite the fabric, then descend to the small of her back. When I reach her rump, I straighten up. My eyes graze her skin. She lifts her face as she props herself on her elbows. Her profile comes into view as she looks at me over her shoulder. In the blue of her iris, I see the desire that possesses her, but she tries to contain it by biting her lip. She's sublime, like those angelic creatures from our childhood stories. Unlike them, Kalliopee doesn't have tanned skin. Her complexion is divinely opalescent, pure. Like her soul—devoid of any darkness.

I slide her nightgown up along her body, revealing her two perfect globes. I remove her lingerie, and when her bare buttocks are shamelessly exposed to me, I discard my pants. My hand slips between her and the cold floor, the contrast making me burn even hotter. I force her to rise, my knees spreading her thighs. When the tip of my cock meets her wet flesh, I pause. Not to hold back, no, but to savor the moment when I finally enter her. And that's exactly what I do as I thrust into her in one motion, filling her completely. My lungs fill with air, and I feel whole, complete. It's as if, until now, a part of me has been missing. That part was Kalliopee. I needed to reconnect with her, to drink her in like a wolf thirsty for blood.

A rough moan escapes her as I begin to move, letting my body express my distress. One of my hands supports me on the tile so she isn't crushed under my weight, while the other grips her hip so I can drive deeper and deeper. *There's no way I'll let him touch her*. Every time our skin slaps together, I imagine her enduring his sentence, and I become more possessive. Her moans grow louder as the images in my head grow more violent.

My teeth sink into her salty skin. I feel her weaken, tremble, under the force of my thrusts. Yet she doesn't ask me to stop. On the contrary, she begs me to give her everything. And it hurts. It hurts to see her suffer without ever complaining, hurts to know that I'm not sparing her either. I want to protect her, I want her to have the power to save me from myself, but I fear I'm a lost cause, having gone too far to avoid any consequences.

A rough growl escapes from deep within my chest as I come inside her. This seems to trigger her orgasm as her scorching walls tighten around me, as if to keep me from leaving, from freeing her. She breathes my name with such emotion that I pull out and roughly turn her over. I need to see in her eyes that she feels as intensely as I do. Her tear-filled eyes search mine with worry.

"I love you, *Shaadi*."

She stops breathing, her eyes clouding over. Her lips tremble into a soft smile, and I have to swallow hard to keep from being overwhelmed by emotion.

Her gaze slides over my skin, her hands resting on my neck.

"Then love me all night," she whispers, her voice tight, wrapping her legs around my hips.

If she knew all the images constantly in my head, she would undoubtedly run from me. She wouldn't hold me close.

Chapter 15

Karel

Tense, we all wait in the large room. When I woke up, the bed was empty, and I thought my behavior had driven her away. I expected to find her in the living room, but only my friends were there. Samael then nervously told me that Kalliopee and Kaïs had gone to meet Prince Alesso. I wanted to go after her, to turn the palace upside down if necessary, but my men convinced me it was for the best. That Kalliopee knew what she was doing. Since then, I've been pacing like a caged lion, stewing and fuming. How can they all be so calm? I don't trust that man at all; he is the king's son.

Just as my impatience reaches its peak, the door opens, and my wife walks in. I cross the room to her immediately. As I approach, she tenses but doesn't resist when I pull her to me, placing her behind me in a protective gesture. My cousin enters next, followed by Princess Nerea and her brother. Seeing him, my body vibrates with barely contained anger.

"He wants to help us," Kaïs tries to reassure me.

I find that hard to believe. Kalliopee entwines her fingers with mine, and my fury and anxiety subside. *She's here, with me. She's safe.* Despite the calm returning to my once-clouded mind, I scrutinize the prince, whose expression remains composed. No animosity, no arrogance. Still, I stay on guard.

"And how does he plan to do that?" I ask, suspicious.

"We'll need to be discreet," the Aquarian prince interjects. "Our father has gone to resolve a dispute on a small island farther away. That should give you time to escape. By the time he returns, you'll be long gone."

I analyze every word, every intonation, looking for a clue to confirm my suspicions, but all I find is unwavering assurance.

"Nerea will pretend to show you around the area. Shortly after, I'll escort the princess to the mainland."

"She stays with me," I counter.

"I knew you'd say that," Kalliopee murmurs behind me.

Of course, I'd say that. I have to protect her.

"If you're together, they'll watch you, and escape will no longer be an option," the prince tries to convince me.

A slight laugh escapes me. Does he really think I'll let him take my wife? I'm no fool. I've seen how he looks at her, how he talks to her. Kalliopee might be too blind and too accustomed to malicious attention to realize that what she takes for friendliness is actually seduction, but I see through his game. I detest this prince and his ways almost as much as his father, and I don't like the way he stares at my wife. Maybe he's in on the scheme with our fathers? Maybe he even hopes to make Kalliopee his mistress? If he dares come near her, I'll know how to deal with him. I try to suppress my jealousy, not to be blinded by possessiveness, aware that the only thing that matters now is that we leave this island as soon as possible.

Kalliopee's fingers press against mine, likely urging me to be reasonable. I take a breath and scrutinize each person in the room. He's right, if we leave together, we'll arouse suspicion.

"Your sister will escort my wife. Jonah, you go with them. I'll follow you."

I feel Kalliopee tense at my order, but what did she think? That I would let her go with him? I don't know this man's combat skills, and I still don't trust his goodwill. I'll feel more at ease if she's with her younger sister. If my wife falls into a trap, the Aquarian girl would be easily subdued. She wouldn't stand a chance against Jonah. The latter nods. In my eyes, he's the most capable of protecting Kalliopee.

Alesso sighs, blowing a blond strand of hair back onto his face, but he agrees, nonetheless. Not that he has a choice.

"We should hurry. Pack your things, only the essentials, and the group will be ready to leave."

I turn to my wife and take her chin between my fingers. My heart pounds. Last night, I was selfish, but I'm relieved to see only love in her eyes.

"You'll leave first. We'll meet on the beach, the one where you went swimming. Do you remember?" I ask.

She nods immediately, but despite what she tries to make me believe, I feel her trembling with fear at the possibility of being caught.

"Everything will be fine," I promise her. "Jonah will be with you."

She wraps her fingers around my wrists, holding on to me as her anxiety suddenly paralyzes her. I shake off the déjà vu that grips me and add, "We'll meet you with the horses, and when the king realizes we're gone, we'll be too far for you to be at risk."

I need her to believe it as much as I do. Otherwise, I'm not sure I can let her go without me. If she asks me to stay with her, I will. Even if it means this palace becomes a bloody battleground.

"Okay," she murmurs.

I look into her mismatched eyes and feel like I could get lost in them. I caress her cheeks, dotted with blush, lingering longer than necessary. I soak in her scent, her warmth, knowing that the coming moment will feel interminable.

"Trust me, I'll join you."

Behind us, I hear the men moving about as Kalliopee still clings to my wrists.

"I love you," she whispers softly.

My throat tightens, but instead of heightening her fear by showing mine, I smile. "You say that like I'm not coming."

Her mouth forms a pout, and I press my lips to hers abruptly. This time, I breathe in her breath, because I know I'm going to need it.

It doesn't matter that we're not alone or that it's not proper. I want to erase the worry lines on her face and the anxiety that weighs down my stomach. If it were up to me, I'd pin her against this wall and drink her in until I was sated. But all I can give her is this kiss. Brief but intense. In a short moment, it conveys everything she makes me feel. A love that is unparalleled, unconditional, and irrevocable. I force myself to pull away from her, even as the taste of her lips invades my mouth and clouds my mind, but when I manage, my eyes lock onto hers again. I notice a new energy radiating from her. A determination tinged with bravery.

"Princess Kalliopee," Nerea calls gently.

My wife glances briefly over my shoulder before stiffening and looking back into my eyes. A thousand emotions fill her, but I can't distinguish them. She pulls her hand from my arm, and I release her chin. Kalliopee moves around me, my eyelids close. I inhale calmly as the hinges of the door creak behind me. My fists clench, my feet anchor to the floor. I have to contract my body to stop it from moving on its own, to prevent myself from holding her back.

The door slams, and fear courses through my veins. Unfortunately, this feeling is never alone. It's accompanied by fury. Fury, I know all too well and find preferable. It doesn't paralyze my limbs. I let it annihilate any form of anxiety, and as soon as I face the Aquarian, I see red. My cousin immediately steps between us, likely worried I'll attack our accomplice.

"If anything happens to her, you're a dead man," I threaten.

"Karel," Kaïs gently scolds me.

The prince stares at me with no fear in his blue eyes. I step back and brush off Kaïs's arm before heading to our room. I need to keep my mind occupied to avoid imagining the thousand dangers that could hinder Kalliopee's escape. Restless, I check the room to ensure we haven't left anything important. When I find my men, I interrupt their conversation with the Aquarian.

"We need to form groups."

"You, the prince, and me," Samael says. "Kaïs and Zaïn will follow."

I nod and head to the window. The anxiety is so overwhelming that I'm suffocating under my jacket.

"We can go now; they should have reached the beach by now," the Aquarian informs us after a moment that feels far too long.

I waste no time and grab my cousin's shoulder. "Don't delay," I urge.

He knows the thought of them being caught scares me. Normally, I'd prefer to be the last to leave the island to ensure everyone's safety on the mainland, but I need to reunite with Kalliopee as soon as possible. Kaïs pretends not to notice my worry and nods. I take a deep breath, and our guide opens the door. As we walk down the halls, he talks about the supposed tour with such enthusiasm that I could believe we're really going to do the things he describes. Occasionally, he points out something. I never take my eyes off our goal: straight ahead. Anyway, Samael plays along for both of us.

When we leave the palace, I exhale, and my steps quicken as we descend the stairs leading to the small town. Samael occasionally glances over his shoulder to ensure we're not being followed. Finally, we reach the dock. Today, instead of boarding one of the boats bearing the Aquarian house's colors, we get into a fisherman's skiff. The trip feels endless, and although I can see the mainland, it feels like we'll never reach it.

I bite my tongue, gripping the edge of the boat to keep myself from swimming to shore.

"Karel," my friend sighs behind me.

"Don't you dare tell me to calm down or try to reassure me," I growl. "A sadist wants to tear my wife's skin for a moment of anger. So yes, I'm terrified he got his hands on her while she was escaping, and I won't be calm until I'm certain she's safe and sound!" I snap.

The prince in front of me looks at me with a compassion I don't understand.

"Why are you helping us? Why choose our side instead of your father's?" I ask.

"Why not?"

I scowl and break eye contact to check how much farther we have to go before we reach the shore.

"I don't condone my father's actions, and I don't respect him," he continues more seriously. "I keep a low profile only for Nerea's sake. With a bit of luck, the war he'll declare on you will end my suffering, and he'll die with honor," he scoffs.

"I'll be happy to grant your wish when I meet him on the battlefield."

His eyes search mine, and his smile fades. We stare at each other for a long time.

"I know what you're thinking. You probably see me as a bad son, but it's not just bad sons. There are bad fathers, too. Sharing that man's blood doesn't mean I have to see things his way."

His words resonate with me. Maybe I misjudged him. He might be trustworthy. Regardless, he's braver than I am. I want to break my bonds, too, make my own choices, but my father is the only family I have left. He's my blood; I can't go against him. Especially when I'm the one who stoked the flames of his vengeance.

"And your mother? What does she think of your ambitions?" I ask.

"My mother?" he laughs. "She's old school. I think I hate her more than him. A woman can't wish upon her daughter what she endured herself. Yet she insists on marrying her off to anyone. I threatened my father to renounce my title if he sold her to anyone. Fortunately, he values the purity of the lineage. It's inconceivable for him that a stranger, even married to my sister, would succeed him. For now, it works, but no doubt one day, he'll get an offer enticing enough that my warnings won't matter, and his obsession with blood will become secondary."

During our conversation, I hadn't noticed we were nearing the beach. We're just a few steps away. I don't wait and jump overboard. The water comes up to my waist, making me grimace. Samael and the prince stay in the boat, waiting for it to reach the sand. The waves hit my back, pushing me forward while I struggle to keep the current from pulling me back. It's a tiring battle against two forces, and when the ocean's level drops, I feel freer to move. I finally reach the sand and don't wait for us to retrieve the horses before ensuring she's okay.

Sure, this little exchange allowed me to learn more about the prince, but that doesn't mean I trust him. When I reach the beach where we arrived, I freeze before rushing toward the vegetation. No sign of Kalliopee.

"Where is she?" I scream, coming back to the Aquarian.

My blood boils, my pulse races, and my breath shortens. I'm on the verge of breaking apart, exploding into a million pieces. I grab my dagger and move toward him. I knew he wasn't trustworthy, and everyone else was fooled. She was the first.

"Where is my wife?" I rage, out of control.

"It's not him," Samael informs me, catching my attention.

My eyes widen, and my heart takes a brutal hit.

"Peace depended on it," he adds, reaching for his sword, on the defensive.

I lower my head and realize I've drawn mine from its sheath

after throwing the dagger to the ground.

"You sold her," I gasp, out of breath.

I wanted to kill the prince. But Samael—I want to eviscerate him.

I stagger, my throat tight. No words come out of my mouth. I see her again, terrified. I should have held her back, stopped them from taking her away. I should have protected her, like that day. I always fail—my mother, Maha, Kalliopee. Yet, I never thought the threat would come from them. A painful laugh rises in my throat.

"Lapisia will never survive another war."

My gaze locks with Samael's. I would have trusted him with my life. I fully grasp the magnitude of this betrayal. My limbs tremble as I approach him. "You sold—"

I receive a violent blow to the head that prevents me from finishing my sentence, but not from moving forward. I take a step toward the one I thought was a friend, but before I can make another move, Samael kicks, sending the weapon I was holding flying. I don't even defend myself. Betrayal is the worst feeling. It strips away all strength and erases hope. It can do more damage than a blade and kill faster than war. They were the only ones I trusted blindly. I look up at the clenched fist of the one I considered a brother. I don't turn away, not even when his knuckles connect with my brow. I let my body collapse to the ground, my eyelids closing. I don't fight.

This isn't like me, but it seems that lately, I'm not quite myself anymore.

Chapter 16

Kalliopee

We leave the suite, and despite the worry that has taken hold of me, I do not waver. I focus on my lips marked by his rather than on our path. I imagine him kissing me again and again. Last night, what we experienced was powerful, brutal. As I had asked, he took everything, and without realizing it, he took away my fears.

Despite the intense way he possessed me, marking me with his fingers and his teeth, I never felt like I was enduring it. I savored every second, every bite, every thrust. On that cold tile, I felt strong. It might seem paradoxical or contradictory, but that's what I felt. He helped me let go, to surrender to him. It allowed me to forget, even if just for a moment, what awaited me today.

We reach a narrower, much darker corridor, and Jonah's steps slow as the princess leads us to an alcove. I dare a glance at my escort and see him frowning. He doesn't have time to question Nerea because we arrive at a small door. The young woman turns to me and smiles with a hint of apology in her demeanor. She doesn't need to feel sorry; she's not responsible for anything. My lips curl slightly to reassure her. She steps aside to let me pass, but before I can grasp the handle, my arm is held back by Jonah's firm hand. His fingers tighten. I feel his fears, which fuel my own. I lower my head, suddenly unsure of myself.

"Tell me I'm wrong," he murmurs severely.

I face him, and my eyes lock onto his. His face falls as he silently pleads with me to disprove his suspicions, then his brow furrows in disbelief. He lets out a bitter laugh that makes me regret that he was chosen to accompany me. Kaïs should have been with me, but if I had insisted on him escorting me, Karel would have had doubts.

I don't have time to respond; he pulls me away from the door. Determined, he marches back up the corridor. Despite my fears, I know we have no choice, that leaving would be selfish of me. I pull my arm free from his grip while my feet try to slow our progress.

"Let me go, Jonah!"

"He won't be able to handle it!" he exclaims, furious.

"It's not just about him!" I shout.

He spins around so abruptly that I crash into him, my wrist still trapped in his grip. Time stops. I stay pressed against him, clutching his jacket with my free hand. This is way too difficult. My body starts to tremble because I wish I had the selfishness to follow him, to accept that he's taking me away, but I don't have that right. I hold back my tears and catch my breath. I swallow the lump in my throat that's blocking my air.

His fingers release my wrist, and his hands gently rest on my shoulders. Our position is undoubtedly inappropriate. It could even seem ambiguous, but right now, I need his strength. I need the support of the man my husband trusts the most.

"No, Princess, it's about you! How can you ask this of me?"

I step back and lift my gaze to his face. I sense the turmoil taking hold of him, and I can see he's torn between his duty to Karel and reason.

"I promised to protect you, and I would fail if I let you enter that room."

"You won't fail," I counter with a little voice. "Protect me by protecting the peace."

His hands leave my shoulders, and his massive frame pulls away. He stares at me, then shakes his head. I see his features harden in disapproval. He turns his back and heads away from the door. I fear he'll go to Karel and jeopardize our only chance to save more innocents.

"Samael said it: Lapisia won't survive another war. Your men are exhausted, your troops have fewer soldiers than Aquaria's, and those who survived are too weak. We will lose the war that threatens us, and what do you think will happen then?"

He stops walking as my voice echoes off the walls of the dark, gray corridor. I push aside my need to escape these oppressive walls for the fresh air outside and focus on the Lapisian's back. He's about to resume walking when I voice our unspoken fears.

"Karel's head will be on a spike. Yours, too, then all your friends'. You will die in battle or be executed. And us women? What kind of treatment will we endure? What we suffer will be a thousand times worse. Your fate will seem enviable. Is that what you want for Lavia? For your daughters?"

He turns toward me, his body tense and his face filled with distress. He shakes his head furiously, and I understand why Karel would trust this man with his life.

"Karel will go mad," he murmurs softly.

Despite the weakness in his voice, his words hit me hard. My husband's reaction scares me, too. That's why I didn't tell him anything. I had to keep him in the dark; he wouldn't have accepted it. He would have blamed himself, and I refuse to let him think he's responsible for what's happening. His only fault was blindly defending my honor. I was honest when I said he was guilty of nothing and that the laws brought us here.

"He… He…" he tries, unable to finish his sentence.

"He will understand. He *has* to understand," I repeat.

"You can still back out; you owe nothing to Lapisia," he tries to convince me.

"Too many innocents have died, too many soldiers, too. Lapisia deserves peace. There is no way others will die because of me. We can't hope that King Nokken will regain his senses; it would be in vain, and I don't want to live in fear of an imminent war. I refuse to see Karel go to battle and risk his life when all I need to do is—"

"All you need to do is what?!" he interrupts, now furious. "Do you know what salted wounds are?"

I step back, surprised by the vehemence in his voice and by his body closing in on me.

"They cut your skin. Not enough for you to bleed out, but enough to cause pain. Then they plunge you into salt water, and for every wound, they do it again. Over and over. You'll feel like you're burning while you drown. The torture will be so unbearable that you'll prefer death."

With each of his steps, I step back. I swallow hard, a cold shiver running through me as he details what awaits me. Kaïs wanted to tell me, but I refused. Now I understand ignorance was necessary. If I had known, I would never have reached this door.

Short of breath, the warrior watches me, trying to succeed with his gaze where his words have failed. Despite the nausea caused by fear, I turn away. My heart pounds violently at the thought of the punishment I'm about to endure. It far surpasses any fault committed by Karel. I take a deep breath, bite my cheek, and join Nerea. This time, my smile is too weak to be convincing.

"Princess," Jonah murmurs in a final plea.

I hold back the painful sob that would release my tears if I let it escape and lower the handle. I find myself in a small room where half a dozen women wait for me. They must prepare me for the punitive ritual. The door slams behind me, silencing Jonah's curses. I push aside my apprehension and move to the center of the room.

One of the Aquarians approaches me cautiously. I let her undress me without resistance. For this ritual, the most intimate parts of my body will be simply covered with cloth. That's all I wanted to know. That, and whether there would be an audience. I was relieved to learn that only a few council members would be present, and the sentence wouldn't be carried out in public.

When I'm naked, a young girl approaches and wraps my hips before covering my lower back. Every time her skin brushes against mine, I swallow my bitterness and the sense of injustice trying to take over. I keep my head high, though I'd rather collapse and run to Karel and the refuge of his arms. But I stay here and spread my legs when she needs to wrap them, too, one by one. She continues with two more rolls. When the task is completed, the oldest woman, who must be the matron, asks me to lift my chin. With gentle hands, she braids my hair. Despite her kindness, I want to push her away, scream at her not to touch me, or at least not to do it as if I were her own daughter. I close my eyes and clench my fists. She arranges the braid into a crown, and I feel a pin prick when she accidentally pushes it in too hard. My heart jumps, fear intensifying with each moment that brings me closer to the end of my preparations. The young girl returns, two rolls in hand. My arms lift obediently, and I let her wrap my chest. She isn't responsible for my being here; she's just doing her job.

***

When my preparations are complete, I go back to Nerea and Jonah. He stiffens at the sight of me, and I lower my head in shame. He once again offers to help me escape, insisting I owe nothing to his people, but I follow the princess down the corridor. I focus on the cool tiles under my bare feet, the breeze on my skin, my breathing. I ignore my thoughts, pushing them away as soon as they arise.

Now, as I kneel before the king, without Jonah to protect me, fear turns to terror. I have to bite my cheek to avoid worsening the situation by rebelling. I alone made the decision to come here; no one forced me. So, I must face it.

If I had listened to Karel, if I had said yes to one of Jonah's many proposals, I wouldn't be here.

We're in a peculiar room. It contains little furniture: just a massive chair, a small table, and a large bath with a chair in front of it. Only the king, his advisor, the prince, and two other men are present.

"Prince Karel has been accused of attacking the royal figure of Aquaria," Areg declares. "Therefore, Princess Kalliopee, as his wife, you're condemned to serve his sentence. The punishment is set at twelve *salted wounds*."

My head snaps up at this number, and I lock eyes with the advisor, who is grinning widely. Once the initial shock passes, I mask my fear. Ten or twelve wounds—does it make a difference? I glance to the side and meet Alesso's gaze. His nod reassures me that Karel is safe on the continent. I stifle the sigh of relief trying to escape, then face the king. He sits on the chair and gestures for me to stand.

Meanwhile, Areg approaches the table and unrolls a cloth containing a scalpel. Once again, I lose my breath. Nausea overcomes me, and I turn away as he steps closer. I focus on the damp tiles of the room.

"Take your seat," the advisor invites, his voice dripping with satisfaction.

Despite my trembling limbs, I move to the wooden plank. I feel the weight of the small audience's attention on me. Still, I don't falter and sit down. When Areg stands before me, he looms over me with a superior look that both revolts and disgusts me. He kneels without breaking eye contact, and this time, I stare back with arrogance. It's foolish, but this surge of pride helps me maintain my composure. I may endure this sentence, but I refuse to let them break my spirit.

His smile widens, indicating my attitude amuses him. He roughly grabs one of my ankles and ties it to the chair leg. He does the same with the other, tightening the bindings with force. Even as the ties burn my ankles, I don't react. I channel all my hatred toward him. The monster looms over me again as he stands, waiting for an order that doesn't come. I hold my breath, praying for a miracle, hoping against hope that Jonah will burst into the room. I quickly dismiss these thoughts… it was the only thing to do.

"The shoulder blades," the king suddenly orders.

Areg grabs my braided crown and forces me to bend forward. I ignore the tug on my scalp because I know it's nothing compared to what's coming. My heart pounds as my nails dig into my knees.

"What a pity to have to mar such pretty skin," the advisor murmurs before cutting into my back.

The pain is searing, sharp. It makes bile rise in my throat and forces a grimace. Areg takes his time, drawing out the incision so that I feel every bit of it. I stifle the scream I want to let out, holding back the tears I want to shed. My nails dig so deeply into my thighs that a drop of blood appears. I focus on it rather than the cold blade still on my skin. When the metal finally pulls away, I catch my breath. I can endure this. *I will endure this!*

The advisor releases my hair and forces me to sit up. His smile is still present, and despite myself, I try to read him. Whenever I've encountered cruelty or injustice, I've tried to understand the reasons that drive people to commit such terrible acts. It's foolish, but I find it hard to believe that such acts are done without cause. I've always thought they must stem from deep-seated pain. But what I see in this Aquarian's eyes is nothing but sheer pleasure in inflicting pain. He revels in my fear and suffering. How can someone be so cruel?

I watch him as he takes a few steps back and approaches what looks like a pedal. I try to block out the burning pain in my back, knowing that if I can't overcome it, I won't survive what comes next. His boot hovers over the mechanism, and my eyes widen in shock as I realize its purpose.

"Now!" orders the king.

The advisor's foot presses down, and instantly, my chair tips backward. As soon as my skin contacts the salt-laden liquid, I scream and struggle. Unfortunately, my scream is trapped in my throat as water floods my mouth when I'm submerged. The pain is so intense it feels like my entire body is on fire. Despite the burning salt, my eyelids remain open, searching for an escape through the turbulence my thrashing creates. A figure appears, then hands grip my shoulders, and I'm pulled forward again. My mouth opens wide, gasping for the air I've been denied, then I start coughing. My lungs expel the liquid they've swallowed. When I catch my breath, I lift my head and, despite the haze that obscures my view, I recognize Prince Alesso. I let out a sob, the only one I allow myself, and wipe my eyes to lessen their burning. My eyes meet the prince's, which are wet with tears.

"I'm sorry," he murmurs softly.

I can feel the sincerity in his voice. But I don't reply. Not even to tell him it's not his fault either. Right now, the pain is too much for me to care about others and their feelings, no matter who they are. My body wants to express its agony through trembling, but I suppress it by contracting every muscle.

"Again," the king exclaims.

This time, the cut is more painful, probably because of the salt now covering my skin. I close my eyes as I hear the advisor's footsteps moving away. I inhale, preparing to hold my breath. I vow not to scream. Once again, my chair tips back. Despite my promises to keep my mouth shut, I scream as soon as the water touches my skin. My legs struggle to break free from their bonds, while my hands vainly search for something to hold onto. The torture is even worse this time, as it's magnified. My chest heaves when the air runs out.

Jonah was right; the pain is so intense that at this moment, I think I'd rather die than endure this over and over. When the prince pulls me out of the water again, I'm already too exhausted to fight my emotions. As I expel the liquid I've swallowed, I let out a sob. I can no longer face the king or his advisor. I wanted to show strength, but it seems that two wounds are enough to prove the opposite.

I decide to shut down my mind while Areg continues his cowardly task. My back receives numerous blows. Four new cuts. With each one, despite my attempts to imagine myself elsewhere, the pain brings me back to reality, crushing my determination and hopes. With each cut, my hatred grows. They take pleasure in carving symmetrical lines into my skin, and I can no longer hide my disgust or fear as the king names parts of my body.

"The stomach," commands the monarch.

"No," I murmur, pleading, my voice hoarse from screaming and the burn of the salt.

Not where I can see it, where I'll remember. I refuse to be marked in such a visible way.

But no one listens, and I'm no longer in a state to defend myself. Despite the irritation in my eyes, I force myself to watch the blade as it cuts into my flesh. I can only see the light reflecting off it and can't even perceive the blood flowing out. My body is completely drained of energy; I have no control over it or its distress signals. It shakes uncontrollably. My chest heaves, and bile rises. This time, I can't hold it back.

A mad laugh echoes in the room, and I realize, as my throat burns, that it's mine. For the first time in my life, I feel the urge to kill a man, to torture him, to make him suffer until he begs for mercy. I call upon my ancestors, pleading for vengeance. In the illusion I create, I ignore the advisor's pleas. Another laugh escapes when I imagine widening his smile with the same blade that's cutting into me. The sound is weak, maybe only I can hear it. My body tips backward again, and this time, darkness engulfs me. I let it take me, without fighting, praying it will end my suffering.

Unfortunately, the respite is short-lived as I come to again. Blinking rapidly, I make out two new wounds; I wasn't even aware they were being inflicted. When I realize what he has carved into my skin, I lose it. I struggle, fight. It must look pathetic from the outside, my movements heavy, slow, weak. My screams are silent. But the rage that fills me is powerful. It screams my anger, my pain, my fear. So this is hatred? This is what it feels like? It feels like it's consuming everything, even my values, annihilating the goodness within me, wrapping my humanity in a dark shroud. Darkness obscures everything.

I try to count my punishment. I don't know if I have three or four wounds left to endure, but even one more seems too much, insurmountable.

"The right eye."

My body draws on its last reserves to tense up. Areg's shadow looms larger as he approaches me, and I croak an inaudible plea.

"Father!" booms the prince's voice. "If you do this, it will be the end of you!"

The silence that follows Alesso's threat fills me with a hope I can barely contain.

"Your son speaks the truth," declares another voice I don't recognize.

I don't have the strength to turn and see who spoke.

"The council already disapproves of the treatment you are inflicting on the Prince of Lapisia's wife, but if you go this far, we will not tolerate it."

Words are exchanged, but I can't understand them. The shadow disappears from my view, and moments later, a door slams. Immediately, hands begin to free me from my restraints. I flinch, curl up, and let out a weak *no* that burns my throat.

"It's me, Princess."

A moan of relief escapes my lips despite the pain when I recognize Jonah's voice.

"It's over," he says, his voice rough. "I'm taking you to Karel. Put this on."

I don't understand what he's talking about until his warm hands grasp my ice-cold wrist. He wraps me in his jacket. My tears intensify as he closes it.

"She should be treated before leaving. In her condition—"

"No way she's spending another moment in this palace," growls the Lapisian man, placing his arm under my knees.

As if I weigh nothing, he stands up. My fingers weakly clutch his shirt as the tears sap the last of my strength.

"I'm sorry, Princess. They kept me from reaching you."

He tightens his hold on my limp body, and I let myself drift away. With the certainty that, this time, the ordeal is over.

Chapter 17

Karel

My eyelids flutter slowly as a piercing headache grips me. I try to touch my head to assess the damage but realize my hands are tied. A deep laugh bubbles up from my throat when I remember what happened before I was knocked out, then it transforms into a furious growl. I attempt to stand, to free myself from the restraints binding my arms to the tree trunk behind me. Understanding that I'll only exhaust myself, I stomp my foot in rage while hurling threats at Samael.

As I throw my head back, he appears, and I find myself facing three pairs of eyes. My cousin cautiously approaches me.

"Let me go," I growl.

He steps back, likely aware that, bound or not, if he comes within my reach, I'll find a way to get to him. Samael's palm presses against Kaïs's chest, urging him to move away from me, and I catch his sorry glance before he looks away.

"You don't even have the courage to look me in the eye?" I spit bitterly.

"It's not—"

"It was Kalliopee's idea," Kaïs interrupts. "It was *her* idea."

What does he think? That repeating it will help me accept or believe it? No, quite the opposite.

"And you let her do it?" I snap.

They both lower their heads, and I shift my attention to Zaïn, who stays in the background. "You were in on this, too?"

He turns away, and I close my eyes, trying to regain my composure. "So you all knew?"

"Jonah didn't," my cousin responds. "Kalliopee feared he'd tell you. She thought he'd be on your side."

Obviously, she was wrong. He didn't stop her when he must have figured it out.

"She was right, it was the only thing to do," he continues.

I laugh at the certainty in his voice. Everyone relies on her. Her father didn't hesitate to sell her to Lapisia to secure peace, my father and I don't hesitate to use her to fulfill our revenge, and now them… No matter the reasons. In the end, she's always the one sacrificed.

"You think Lapisia would have tolerated another war?" he scolds.

I try to calm my heart, filled with guilt and resentment. My hands pull at the bindings, and I feel like I'm suffocating, tied up like this.

"Karel," he calls out to me pleadingly, making me stop. "Our troops have been halved, our supplies are barely enough to keep us alive. We'd never have enough food for an entire army. So yes, it was the only thing to do."

Nausea overtakes me as I look at each of them in turn. None of them fought for her; none tried to find another solution. No one warned me. I resent them for their silence and passivity. They all took the easy way out, knowing it wouldn't be them getting hurt. How could they let her do this?

I curse and try to stand, but every time my rear lifts from the sand, the bindings burn my skin, preventing any movement, and I fall back. When I'm too exhausted to struggle, I close my eyes again and let my head rest against the tree bark.

"She knew you'd refuse," Samael murmurs.

My eyelids lift, and I glare at him with growing resentment. I can see the apologies in his eyes, but I prefer to reject them by breaking eye contact.

"Karel… you'd sacrifice everything for her."

I lower my head because he's right. I have no limits when it comes to her. I thought my duty as a son would surpass the love I have for my wife, but no. Since we arrived, I finally decided that I'd choose her, no matter what. No matter the enemies I'd make. No matter if my own father stabs me in the back to punish me. No matter if Maha and my mother feel betrayed, wherever they are. It will always be Kalliopee.

"You should have suspected," he continues, forcing me to face him again. "Kalliopee, she…"

It's not hard to read the meaning behind his silence. Kalliopee is my opposite. Why didn't I consider the possibility that she'd sacrifice herself again?

"Free me," I murmur weakly.

Kaïs and Samael exchange a glance, then the latter nods. My cousin approaches while I keep my eyes on my friend. Sure, Kalliopee made this decision alone, but I can't help feeling betrayed. He deceived me by bringing me here while she was taken to the king. I suppose Nokken never left for another island and was just waiting for her to come to him.

The bindings loosen, and I'm finally free. But I don't get up immediately. I massage my wrists, replaying the events of the day in my mind. I go back in time, recalling her looks, her gestures, searching for clues I might have missed. If I had turned around after kissing her, would I have seen her fears? If I had looked her in the eyes, would I have understood what her anxiety was hiding?

I stand, using the trunk for support, and pass Samael and Zaïn to reach the beach. My heart sinks when I see the palace in the distance. I try to erase the images threatening to overwhelm me.

"Karel," my cousin murmurs, grabbing my arm.

"Not now. Please," I plead, facing him.

He seems surprised that I'm not trying to hit him or vent my anger. I am, too. But this time, the emotions I feel are far from that; they make me apathetic and desperate.

I turn away, feeling a void in my chest, and head back to the beach. Time tortures me, stretching endlessly. My mind conjures up too many imaginary boats, giving my heart false hope that exhausts it.

I'm responsible for what happened. If I hadn't been so convinced I was the only one who could protect her, she'd be in Lapisia. I would have ordered my men to ensure her safety there, and she wouldn't be suffering a punishment meant for me alone. I provoked Nokken; I underestimated his ego. No matter how I look at it, I made all the wrong choices. None of my decisions were right.

My torment ends the moment I see the royal canoe gliding toward the shore. Unfortunately, the clearer the figures become, the tighter my chest feels. My heart pounds desperately as I notice the limp body in Jonah's arms. I want to swim to her, to reach her, to rescue her. I want to take her away from everyone using her to save themselves. Yet, I'm forced to wait for her to come to me. It's not the first time I've felt so powerless, but every time, it feels like I could die from it.

When the boat finally hits the sand, my feet sink into the water, and a plaintive whimper escapes me as I see the state she's in. She leaves Jonah's arms without resistance and clings to my neck. Her bloodshot eyes open slightly. Although her irises focus on me, she doesn't seem to see me.

"Karel?"

The sound that escapes her lips is broken, almost inaudible.

"It's me, *Shaadi*," I confirm, my throat tight.

I suppress a sob as my trembling limbs lift her, then tighten my hold, murmuring words to soothe her pain. In my arms, she's as limp as a rag doll, a far cry from the energetic and determined woman I'm bound to. My feet dig into the sand, but I don't stop. We pass my men, and I forbid myself from looking in their direction because if I see even a hint of remorse in their eyes, I might go mad. When we are far from any saltwater source, I lay her down and kneel beside her. The verdant ground cushions her body, which I scrutinize with care.

"This should help her heal."

I look up at the prince who had the audacity to escort her here. He offers me a flask of healing balm. Despite my hatred for him, she needs it, so I take it.

He salutes me before turning away.

"No matter what role you played, Alesso. Make sure never to cross my path again, or I swear I'll repay you a hundredfold for what your father did to her. I don't have my wife's mercy," I threaten in a whisper.

He continues without acknowledging my threats, without defending himself.

My trembling fingers undo the jacket she's wearing, and my vision blurs when I see the slashes on her abdomen. I let go and close my eyes. My hands dig into the ground to resist my impulsive urge. That madman branded her skin with an *N*. I stand up and step away. I need a moment, just enough time to calm my thoughts and regain my composure. I must act as I would in battle. Think as if in war. I mustn't let emotions overwhelm me, or they'll drown me, and I'll be of no help to her.

I return to her, kneel again, and examine her wounds. The bands covering her chest are now barely holding.

"Bring me fresh water, cloths, and clean clothes," I order my men.

No matter how long it takes for her to regain her strength, we will stay in this forest until she's fit to travel.

"Karel," Jonah calls out to me.

I observe my wife's sleeping face, the strands of hair stuck to her cheeks, and the irritation on her skin, and I stand. My eyes drift over her damaged stomach and her barely covered body. I try to ignore the madness spreading through my veins, but another attempt by Jonah destroys my efforts. I face my friend and rush at him, slamming him roughly against a tree trunk.

"I'm sorry," he says, his voice hoarse. "I didn't know."

"I don't care about your apologies; I don't have time for that!" I growl. "So do me a favor and stay away from me!"

"I tried to dissuade her."

I believe him, but it doesn't ease my pain. My arm presses harder against his throat, and I imagine inflicting a thousand sufferings on him to relieve my hatred. However, I release him and return to Kalliopee.

"You've lost my trust. All of you have."

He says nothing, and I order everyone to leave us when my cousin brings what I had requested.

I clean her, and though she's asleep, she grimaces as I cover her wounds with cream. After tending to the cuts on her stomach and arms, I turn her onto her side and, with disgust, see that the incisions on her back form angel wings. The blade had relentlessly sliced through the partially torn fabric bands. I swallow my bitterness, my desire for revenge, and focus on dressing her wounds, promising myself never to let her suffer any punishment because of me again. I manage to control my anger out of necessity. If I don't compartmentalize my emotions, Nokken will bathe in his blood, and I in mine.

The day drags on, and she occasionally wakes up. She's too exhausted to speak, and her voice is too broken for me to hear anything when she tries. I gently stroke her hair until sleep claims her again. At night, I stay by her side while my men set up camp a few steps away. Kaïs convinces me to rest, and I reluctantly agree. She needs me, and if I don't get some sleep, I won't be any help to her.

Still, I don't stray far. I stay close by. Sleep doesn't take me for long, just enough to regain some strength.

The following days pass similarly. Despite the discomfort of the forest, none of my men ask when we'll be ready to leave. In any case, there's no way I'll move her in her current state. By the next day, she's willing to eat the broth Zaïn makes from roots he finds in the woods. Her eyes are still irritated, but they've stopped tearing. As for her voice, speaking is still painful. She doesn't talk but smiles at me. It's faint, but enough to revive my heart. My own smiles don't convince her, and hers quickly fade. What can I do? Pretend to feel a lightness I don't? Act like seeing her this way doesn't break me?

After three days, we're ready to return to Lapisia. Kalliopee can now speak without excruciating pain. Her voice is weak, but it's progress. She saves her voice by mostly staying silent. I wonder if, deep down, it's because she fears I'll take the opportunity to question her.

My men bring our horses, and we're ready to leave the forest. I turn my back to Kalliopee and kneel so she can wrap her arms around my neck, then I lift her. She's as light as a feather, but I'm relieved to feel her muscles contract as she clings to me. She's regaining her strength. I support her thighs and hear her whimper. I lower my head, feeling powerless.

My feet tread on the uneven ground passing beneath my eyes, and I easily climb over the stones that occasionally block our path. Her breath gently brushes my neck, and I unconsciously tighten my grip. I don't speak to her, even when I feel my skin dampen from her tears and she clings to me more tightly.

For several days, I've been waiting for her to express her suffering. Whenever her emotions tried to escape, she would hold them back, imprisoning them. Her eyes would close, her body would tense. She fought it, I knew. She showed nothing except when sleep overtook her, and I wondered when she would finally break. As stupid as it may seem, I'm relieved she's doing it in my neck. She prevents the others from seeing her pain, but she lets me feel it; she shares it with me.

"I'm sorry," she whispers, her voice hoarse.

"It's nothing, *Shaadi*. Never apologize for showing me how you feel," I murmur, my throat tight.

Her body trembles harder as she releases her sobs. I continue on, leading the group, without holding back my own tears, which probably mix with hers on my neck.

Each step takes us farther from Aquaria, from Nokken and his torture. But more than anything, each step takes us farther from the loyal son I've always been.

From the one who would have died for his revenge.

Chapter 18

Karel

After ensuring that Mira will take good care of Kalliopee, I leave our quarters. The journey was long, but we're finally home. As soon as we passed through the gates of the citadel, I knew I couldn't wait any longer. I crumple the document in my hand as I walk through the halls. The household staff greet me, but I pay them no mind. During our trip, I kept my anger in check and focused it on him—the one without whom none of this would have happened. He made a promise to Nokken that I refused to honor, and that refusal is what fueled the Aquarian king's bitterness.

My body tenses as the door finally comes into view, and I place my free hand on the hilt of my sword. Let anyone dare to stand in my way. I will not be stopped.

The door opens to reveal Amadeus, who notices me immediately. He appears calm until he senses my agitation. Without hesitation, he steps in front of me, blocking my path. "What are you doing?" he murmurs.

"I need to see him."

"Not now."

"I need to see him," I repeat, emphasizing each syllable, the rage boiling inside me.

He shakes his head and places his hand over mine, which is still gripping the sword's hilt. His paternal gaze assesses me. He doesn't seem surprised by my demeanor. Was he aware of what was happening?

"Karel…" he seems to plead.

"I can't, Amadeus, it's too much to ask."

"You won't help anyone. Least of all her."

I stare at him, confused, my heart pounding erratically.

"Come with me," he says before turning away.

I gaze at the door that stands as the only barrier between my father and me. I want to go in right now, to end it all, but I also know Amadeus has always given me sound advice. If, after explaining my problem to him, his proposed solution doesn't satisfy me, he won't be able to stop me. Resigned, I turn away from my objective and follow him.

We walk through the palace to the library. His sanctuary. It's always deserted there; no one will be able to spy on us.

When the door closes, I lean against it as Amadeus takes a seat in one of the armchairs.

"I heard what happened," he informs me immediately. "I'm sorry."

I exhale and rub my scalp furiously. "Did you know?" I ask, throwing the now-crumpled letter at him.

Amadeus unfolds the letter, reads it carefully, and then looks up. "I didn't know."

I stare into his eyes, trying to detect any sign of deceit.

"I assure you," he adds.

The sincerity in his voice convinces me, and I feel a wave of relief. I'm not sure I could have handled knowing the man who has guided me for so many years had kept this from me.

"I don't want to continue, Amadeus."

He gazes at me, unsurprised by this sudden turn. He examines his nails, then massages his forehead. I wait for him to tell me how to break my betrayal to my father and how to protect Kalliopee from the fallout.

"Your father must have no doubts."

I stand up, incredulous, and move closer to the table.

"What do you think will happen when he finds out?" he continues as I'm about to respond. "She will no longer be useful to the king. Look at what she's already endured. What will you do when he realizes he'll get nothing from you?"

"I'll protect her," I growl.

"How? You'll run?" he asks, his tone dripping with sarcasm.

"Yes, I don't care about the Crown. I'll take her far away from here."

"He'll find you. He'll hunt you down until his last breath.

Is that what you want for yourselves? A life of hiding? Living in constant fear of being discovered? You'll be fugitives, traitors to the Crown."

I shake my head, laughing. A prince who renounces his throne can't be punished. That would be absurd.

"You're a soldier, Karel. You're a soldier!" he scolds.

I then understand how my father could punish us. Desertion is treason. No matter how I turn things in my head, the outcome is always death.

"I don't know what to do, but I can't lie to her anymore. I have to tell her. She needs to know."

"You will do no such thing. She must remain ignorant," he commands.

"She's my wife! I can't hide the truth from her to that extent!"

I shake my head. I can't. Not anymore. Ignorance doesn't protect; she's told me that so many times, and she was right. I refuse to let my lies put her in danger. I won't bear the responsibility of more harm coming to her.

"Keep the princess from the truth. If she learns it, you'll lose your only chance for happiness."

He's right. She would hate me. I'm torn between my need to protect her by revealing everything and the need to protect myself by keeping silent.

"She'll never know," he tries to reassure me. "Your father won't reveal anything to her, not even to hurt her. He'd lose too much. And if you truly want to protect her, stay here and change the world. Only in Lapisia will you have that power. And in any case, make sure your father doesn't find out. He already doubts your loyalty. He's watching you," he informs me. "If you show nothing, he'll lower his guard."

"How can he doubt me?" I protest, disappointed. "I've always been loyal to him. That only changed in Aquaria."

He lifts his head and smiles as if I'm naive. "No, it changed the day she arrived. You were the only one who didn't realize it."

It's true that ever since she reappeared in my life, I've been full of doubts, but our vengeance kept guiding my steps.

"If that weren't the case, you wouldn't have given her a chance to leave before your wedding."

"If that were the case, I wouldn't have married her. I shouldn't have. She would be safe, our marriage wouldn't—"

"Or she would be dead," he interrupts. "The moment she walked through the citadel gates, she had only two options: death."

I wait for him to continue, but he doesn't. "You mentioned two options."

"Two options, yes, but the same outcome."

I reject his words; my father would have spared her if I had asked him. I'm sure of it.

"Whatever you think," he continues, "your father won't allow any backtracking, and you will become a troublesome obstacle. You want to protect her? Then stay alive. That's all you need to do."

Would my father really kill me to satisfy his vengeance? A part of me rejects this possibility, but the painful twist in my gut tells me another part knows it's true. It's terrified at the thought that I mean so little to him. To drive away this fear, I let anger take over. "I won't hesitate to kill him to protect her."

Saying these words brings me relief. Isn't it a way of *curing evil with evil*? Replacing pain with bitterness. He's not here to hear my words, but I say them to him anyway. As if the idea that it might hurt him is enough to soothe my own wounds.

Amadeus says nothing more; he doesn't scold me, nor does he try to reassure me. Silence envelops us, and I sense that everything has been said.

"If you don't mind, I have hundreds of papers to read."

I understand this is his polite way of dismissing me.

"Unless you'd like to help?"

I decline with a smile. "I'd rather go back to her," I reply, retrieving the crumpled document.

He gestures for me to leave, and before I open the door, I share my final doubts. "Nokken will probably write to my father, demanding I fulfill my part of the contract. What will we do then?"

"I'll make sure to intercept the letter. You know I also act as the secretary. When your father has no leverage over you or her, Nokken can gather his army all he wants. And… if Aquaria's help is no longer useful to us, he'll have no reason to demand Kalliopee be handed over."

Though Amadeus has guided me since I was young, I thought

his duty as the king's advisor would surpass any affection he might have for me or Kalliopee. Knowing he supports us is reassuring.

I nod and leave the room, feeling a weight lift from my shoulders as I walk the distance to her. Yes, I still have secrets from Kalliopee, but I'm no longer lying to myself. I realize, with the lightness of my steps, that my choice was the right one.

Chapter 19

Kalliopee

I wake up in our bed, my stiff body covered by Karel's. I try to free myself from his grasp, and he makes me laugh when he growls, holding me tighter.

"Where are you going, Princess?" he murmurs in a husky voice, turning me around.

"It's been daylight for too long. Sienna might come in at any moment," I scold him gently.

He sighs but doesn't let go.

When we returned, Karel insisted that Sienna stay by my side. Now, my servant has been promoted and manages the staff assigned to our quarters. This was unexpected because such a role would normally go to a man.

"And so what? What would she see? A fabulous naked body?" he asks, burying his nose in my neck.

His fingers trace my back over my nightgown as I hold my breath. I try to break free, but he pulls me closer, pressing my head against his chest. His legs entwine with mine, preventing me from moving.

Our journey back from Aquaria was much longer than the trip there. I was too weak to ride my horse alone, so I traveled in Karel's arms. His stallion needed more rest, and I required regular care. By the time we reached Lapisia, I had recovered enough to enter the citadel on my own horse. However, the psychological scars remain. I had hoped that returning home would help me overcome the trauma I experienced in Aquaria, but I see it's far from the case. I hate being touched; I can't even bear to look at myself. Each time, my breathing becomes more erratic, and the pain in my stomach intensifies.

His breath grows heavier, harshly brushing against my skin. He lifts my head with his fingers, offering me his dark gaze. Something changed that day. I don't know exactly what it is, but I see in his eyes a mix of respect and a more intense feeling of betrayal. I don't understand how it's possible. I want him to help me decipher it, but Karel remains Karel. He prefers silence over revealing himself. We haven't discussed what I went through or the fact that I accepted the punishment without telling him. He hasn't blamed me, though I understand it has built a wall between us.

Sometimes, when we look at each other for a long time, I can sense him on the verge of speaking the words that seem to press at his lips, but the next moment, he regains his mask of impassivity. I wish I could find the courage to talk to him about it. Sometimes, the memories invade my dreams with such realism that it feels like they reopen the wounds, rekindling the pain. On those nights, when my body is drenched in sweat, I wish I could wake him up for reassurance, but I feel I've lost that right by acting behind his back. So, I leave the bed and go to my library. I try to lose myself in stories that belong to others, and for a moment, I can breathe again.

Since that day, the overwhelming emotion I feel is this sense of suffocation. The nights are getting shorter, and I can see fatigue marking my face and draining all my energy. I return to our marital bed just as the sun is about to rise and slip under the covers before he realizes I've been gone. Sometimes, I fall back asleep, like this morning, and other times, I wait for time to pass, watching him as he sleeps.

He grips my neck while his mouth tastes mine roughly. His hands slide over my legs, lifting my nightgown, but when his fingers reach my back, I tense and hold my breath. I pray for him to stop, for Sienna to interrupt us, no matter the embarrassment it might cause. I just want him to stop touching me.

He kisses my lips one last time, and I catch my breath as soon as his warmth leaves me. The next moment, despair floods in. Karel pulls away and turns around. The walls between us seem to grow higher. He shows no emotion. With one hand, he pushes off the sheet covering us both and gets out of bed. His naked body crosses the room without shame, while I still cover myself with the bed linen when I'm in the simplest attire. He disappears into the adjoining room, leaving me alone with my thoughts.

When he returns, his hair drips onto his neck. His tan skin is accentuated by the white towel wrapped around his hips. I watch him intently as he dresses, not missing a single detail of the show he's putting on. His muscles flex as he pulls on his pants. He glances over his shoulder and catches me staring, forcing me to tear my gaze away. I get out of bed and escape. I close the door as soon as I find refuge in the bathroom. My robe falls to my feet before I slip into the shower.

As soon as the water hits my skin, Karel appears. My back presses against the ceramic wall, and my hand instinctively covers my stomach. Through the glass, my eyes meet his. His dark irises refuse to let me go. My breath catches, and I panic at the thought of him joining me. For a brief moment, I sense the pain my gesture causes him, but I can't help it. The first time I saw my back and realized the extent of the damage, I cried for hours. My stomach constantly reminds me that someone else marked me, as if by inflicting those three cuts, he claimed me as his. I hate them even more than the ones on my back.

Since then, I refuse to let Karel see me naked. To avoid any awkward situations, I pretend to be asleep when he joins me, I feign not feeling his hands as they brush against me, I act as if I don't feel the kisses he places on my neck or lips. He never insists and always ends up holding me with a sigh. Most of the time, I have to hold back my tears so he doesn't sense the sadness overwhelming me. He surely knows his proximity scares me and his caresses remind me of what I endured because his attempts to get closer have become less frequent. He holds me, yes, but it's not like it used to be.

He steps back, and without taking what he came for, he leaves. My heart is sucked into an enormous void, and I try to forget him by focusing on my shower.

When I leave the bathroom, I find the bedroom empty. I brush my hair, braid it, shed my robe, and put on a dress. The cream-colored dress hides my scars. This time, when I look at myself in the mirror, I don't feel any shame. I twirl, brush the fabric on my shoulder, and move around to make sure the sleeves don't reveal my skin. Reassured, I head to our large living room, expecting to find

Karel so we can share breakfast before he goes to the barracks. The empty cup in front of his chair tells me he's already gone. Lately, we only cross paths, but that's Karel. For him, the best way to make a problem disappear is to ignore it. Usually, I'm more confrontational; I would have done anything to get him to talk to me, but it seems that for once, his blinders suit me.

Sienna arrives shortly after, dispelling the sadness caused by Karel's absence. Her commands crackle in the air as she assigns tasks to three other maids. When we're finally alone, she serves my breakfast and asks if the prince will be joining me.

"He had a lot to do," I lie.

She watches me, her expression concerned. "Princess, I know I ask you this every day, but are you sure you're getting enough sleep?"

"Do I look that terrible to you?"

"No, of course not," she counters, laughing along with me. "You just look exhausted."

I smile at her, grateful, but I reassure her.

"What would you like to do this morning?" she inquires.

I pretend to think, even though there aren't many activities to choose from.

"Can you arrange a meeting with Amadeus?" I ask her.

She looks surprised by my request but agrees, nonetheless. She leaves my chambers immediately, and a servant clears the table once I've finished my breakfast. Instead of pacing, I head to my library and pick up the book I started last night. The morning passes slowly, marked by the turning of pages, one after another. Karel doesn't return to the palace, not even for lunch. I tell Sienna I'm not hungry, and though she says nothing, I can see the disapproval in her eyes. I return to my book, and just as I begin to doze off on the chaise, a knock on the door forces me to sit up. Sienna enters, followed by Amadeus, whom I greet with a broad smile.

"Princess," he says, joining me. "I was surprised you requested my presence."

Sienna leaves the room, allowing me a private conversation with the advisor. I invite him to sit, and he curiously examines the book I'm still holding, then the shelves around us.

"I was wondering why so many books had disappeared from

the royal library."

My eyes widen, and shame fills me at the thought that Karel might have deprived him of his reading material.

"Don't worry, I've read almost all of them already," he reassures me, amused. "But I suppose it's not to discuss history or literature that you called for me, am I wrong?"

I clutch the book to my chest and meet his gaze. "I wanted to know if the king had received a letter from Aquaria," I deflect. The truth is, I fear Nokken hasn't kept his promise.

"Are you wondering if any declaration of war has come from Aquaria?"

My face must betray my emotions because Amadeus's palm gently presses down on my hand, which has tightened around the book. "He kept his promise, Princess. Don't worry."

I sigh with relief, then turn my head toward the window. I stand, still holding the book close to my heart, and walk toward it.

"Lapisia will be eternally grateful for your sacrifice," Amadeus says from behind me.

I gaze at the botanical garden for a long time, searching for the right words. I thought the sacrifice would only be physical, but it feels like these wounds have reached my soul, tearing it apart. I no longer dare to open up to Karel; I refuse to let him touch me. I've been through worse and never pushed him away, but this time, I can't let him get close. I try to find an explanation for my behavior while feeling Amadeus approach from behind.

"I'm worried about the prince," he admits.

I don't turn around, focusing intently on the garden below. I'm too afraid of seeing judgment in his eyes. After all, I'm just a woman and should never have acted without my husband's consent, especially since I involved his men.

"He's isolated himself. He's shutting down. Princess…" he murmurs when I don't respond.

I face him, unable to hide the pain his words cause me. Since our return, Karel has kept his distance. Jonah, Zaïn, and Samael have been sent on missions, and Kaïs… he barely speaks to him.

"I betrayed him, they betrayed him. He resents me, but he'd rather endure it than admit it, Amadeus. I'm not the best person to get him to talk; I've lost his trust. And when he tries to get close, I push him away. Because even though I acted knowingly, this ordeal has left painful scars. I want to open up to him, ask for his support, but I'm too afraid he'll blame me for my recklessness. We're at an impasse."

I give him a weak smile and, to calm myself, I return the book to its shelf. "Karel doesn't easily trust people, and despite what he says, I've lost his trust. I don't think he'll ever forgive me."

"Prove him wrong. Don't give up."

"I'm not giving up; I'm just being realistic. He needs time, and I'm giving it to him."

A knock at the door draws our attention, and Kaïs enters, breathless. "He's gone," he announces immediately. "I just saw him leaving his father's office. Jonah returned alone from his mission; apparently, it was urgent."

His words sink in one by one, and I realize he left the citadel without telling me. A lump forms in my throat as a suspicion tries to take root. "Did he ask you to inform me?" I hope.

Embarrassed, my cousin by marriage lowers his head. "No, I thought you'd want to know."

At these words, something inside me breaks. I nod nonetheless, and Kaïs disappears. I turn to Amadeus, who watches me with concern.

"He'll forgive you, Princess. You'll regain his trust."

"Karel is inflexible. I think you're deluding yourself, Amadeus. He might forgive me, but as for his trust, I'll never regain it."

CHAPTER 20

KAREL

A scarf covering my mouth, I traverse the distances without stopping, Jonah on my heels. The hooves of our horses pound the ground relentlessly. My horse tires, but I push him, exhausting him. Since we left the palace yesterday, I've been feverish. Just a few words—*we found her*—were enough to spur me into action, and I informed my father I had to leave for a few days. I pretended to need to handle a group of rebels and had my horse saddled. We only stopped for a few hours to let our horses rest and to get some sleep. We're now only half a day from our destination, but I can tell my stallion is wearing out.

What makes me so impatient? The hope of eliminating one of our many problems. I feel like they're coming from all sides, cornering us, never giving us a break. As soon as one enemy is defeated, a new one appears.

A small town appears in the distance, and a single glance at Jonah is enough to communicate that we're going to take a break. Since yesterday, we've exchanged no words, merely ignoring each other when possible. I'm still too angry with him. I slow my horse's gallop, then he returns to a trot as we enter the streets. The people don't pay us any attention; none recognize me, hidden as I am under the fabric. Besides, I'm wearing common clothes. Our mission requires a level of discretion that our military uniforms wouldn't allow.

We pass an inn but continue on until we spot a stableman. For a pouch of coins, he agrees to take care of our horses for the night. We don't linger and head to the lodging in front of which there's a crowd. Paying no attention to it, we enter. The interior isn't luxurious, but it will do for a few hours. I hate having to stop, but continuing would risk our horses collapsing in the middle of the desert. Jonah heads to the counter and drops a few coins onto the wood.

The innkeeper immediately looks up and gives him a toothless smile before turning his attention to me. I move away, skirting the room, not inclined to befriend anyone. Since yesterday, guilt has plagued me. I left without telling her anything, but I was still too trapped in my own turmoil. It grips my chest, silences my mouth. How many times have I tried to tell her I'm angry she's turned away from me? She rejects me as if I'm responsible for her scars, deprives me of her body as if she's punishing me. When I joined her in the bathroom and saw how she hid from me, I felt such a surge of rage that I had to flee to avoid breaking everything around us. I wanted to find her under that cascade of water and scream at her to spit out those words she feels so strongly.

Upon our return, I naively thought things would go back to normal, but the trauma from Aquaria followed us to Lapisia. Seeing her withdraw only isolated me further, and I preferred to send my friends to Vàli rather than confront them. None protested. They must have realized, too, that distance was necessary.

"There's only one room left; a group of travelers arrived this morning," Jonah informs me as he stands beside me.

I don't respond and signal for him to go ahead. Out of the corner of my eye, I see him shake his head, but he says nothing more and follows the innkeeper, who leads us upstairs. As we cross the threshold of the room, the rancid smell hits me in the throat. The innkeeper rushes to open the windows. I remove my shoes while he apologizes to Jonah for the state of the room. A woman enters with fresh linens, and suddenly, I feel out of place. I watch my friend trying to be as pleasant as possible, though it's not like him, and I clench my fists.

I cross the room to the window, take a deep breath, and rub my eyelids. Why are we here waiting? Every day away from her is a day she's in danger. I shouldn't have left her alone with Kaïs; I should have brought her with me. I laugh, realizing Jonah was right. Too scared something might happen to her, I'd be ready to take her to the most dangerous places, convinced I'm the only one who can protect her.

The door closes behind me, and Jonah approaches. "We need to talk one day," he says, his voice weary.

I turn to face him, and my glare doesn't seem to discourage him. Still, I convey my anger and all the horrible things I'd like to do to him.

"Hit me, go ahead!" he surprises me.

I mask my astonishment with a disdainful smile and turn away. Outside, night is falling. We'll sleep for a few hours, meet up with the rest of the men, and tomorrow, at dawn, we'll catch *her* in her sleep.

When I tire of the view, I turn back and barely take a step toward one of the beds when Jonah's fist comes out of nowhere. My teeth snap together as pain shoots through my jaw. The uppercut, combined with surprise, sends me crashing to the floor. I groan, dazed, and try to get up. I stand and push Jonah's body away as he comes closer.

"That's not like you to just take it," my friend spits as I distance myself from him.

Without facing him, I notice the provocation in his voice. I blink, my breathing quickens, and a charge runs through my limbs. I clench my fists to keep from unleashing the storm.

"Why won't you hit me?!" he yells. "Why won't you punish me, damn it?!"

His arms push against my chest, trying to provoke me. I grab him by the collar and, driven by a surge of fury, slam him against the wall. With one hand outstretched between us, I forbid him from approaching. My body trembles, and madness blinds me.

"Why?!" he growls.

"Because if I start, I'm afraid I won't be able to stop!" I scream, losing control.

He freezes and lowers his head. We've had our share of quarrels, but never have they distanced us as much as today.

"If I hit you, Jonah, I'll kill you," I murmur.

We've always had a habit of reconciling by exchanging blows, a manly and often stupid way of smoothing things over. But yes, for the first time, I know it won't be enough and, on the contrary, it will only make things worse.

"It's that bad?" he asks, full of bitterness.

Yes, it's that bad. My father, Nokken… I never trusted them, but the trust I had in Jonah was boundless.

"You were supposed to protect her."

"I told you, I didn't know anything!" he snaps.

"I know." I believed him when he assured me the first time, but I wished he had fought for her in my place.

"But you'd rather blame me than her or yourself," he adds.

I blink, stunned by his assumptions.

"I didn't make that decision, Karel. She did, and for *good* reasons, but you resent her for not trusting you and you blame yourself because none of this would have happened without all your schemes. So go ahead! Blame me! Accuse me of not being able to fix the messes you were solely responsible for!"

He shakes his head and leaves the room. He's right. I'd rather hate my brothers-in-arms and blame them for Kalliopee's choice than blame her. Because I'd be a monster to do that after all the suffering she's endured. It's not her decision I condemn, but the fact that she made it without seeking my support. I resent her for scheming behind my back. And as for myself… if I let the guilt consume me, it would devour me.

After that, I joined Jonah downstairs. Neither of us said a word. We stared at each other for a long time, then he ordered a round, and we ate. When we went to bed, the atmosphere was still heavy with our resentments, but it was no longer explosive.

The sun had not yet risen when we left the inn. As soon as we were on our horses, we galloped across the desert under the pale moonlight. By morning, we reached my men's hideout. Zaïn was on guard while Samael and Vàli slept.

Now, we're hiding not far from the isolated house where the pawnbroker's niece was spotted.

"Her name is Navii; she lives with her grandfather," Vàli whispers to me. "He's a reclusive old man, but we haven't seen him in a few days. She's alone."

"You're sure it's her?"

"We asked the closest neighbors. She's kept a low profile, but in a place like this, everything gets noticed. She should have stayed hidden in Lapisia."

We need to hurry; the day is breaking, and soon the streets will be busy. This hamlet isn't very big, but that doesn't stop people from gathering.

I leave the cover of my rock and walk determinedly toward the traitor's house. We decided on a dramatic entrance, and that's what happens when my foot slams into the door, knocking it off its hinges. I put all the rage I've been accumulating into that kick. A frightened scream comes from an adjacent room, and I rush in.

A young woman with tangled hair curls up on the bed. Her eyes widen when she recognizes me, and she pushes the sheet aside to escape. Unfortunately for her, I am much faster and grab her ankle before she can leave the mattress. She struggles, her free foot trying to kick me, but I turn and drag her behind me. Her body hits the floor hard as I continue forward. In the small kitchen with rustic furniture, my men are waiting for us. I release her, letting her leg fall, and the room is silent except for her panicked breathing.

Samael grabs her under her shoulders and forces her up, roughly placing her in a chair. Terrified, she looks at each of us in turn. I pull up a chair and drag it across the worn wooden floor. She watches my every move, tensing when I sit down calmly. Time seems to stand still. I close my eyes, focusing on her erratic breathing, her nervous movements, her trembling leg. As scared as she is, I doubt she'll hold out for long. She'll reveal everything she knows without much persuasion.

"I'll try to be as concise as possible," I begin, pretending to be calm. "I'm going to lay out the facts. Then, if you deny them or refuse to cooperate to help me solve my problem, I'll let Samael handle the rest of the interrogation," I state coldly, gesturing to the man on my left. "What do you say?"

She swallows hard when her eyes meet Samael's, likely imagining something far worse than reality. Unfortunately for her, Samael doesn't resort to brute violence. He manipulates minds, driving them to madness until they beg for mercy or prefer death. It can take days, months, but as he likes to call it, white torture is his art.

"My wife sold the daggers I gave her to your uncle. When I tried to retrieve them, they had disappeared. It could have been just a sale on the black market, but your uncle's stubborn silence made us suspicious. Something is going on, and I think he was protecting you since you disappeared shortly after our visit to the shop. A few weeks ago, one of my men was attacked, and your uncle saw his suffering cut short."

"My uncle is dead?"

"Where are they?"

"He's dead," she says, this time to herself.

"Where are they?" I repeat, pulling my dagger from its sheath.

I thought the sight of the dagger would scare her, but instead of cowering, she straightens in her chair, staring at me. "You're too late. They're already at your place," she declares, a sly smile on her lips. "*He* has them."

Her announcement surprises and terrifies me, but I try to hide it.

"Who?"

She looks at me, then clears her throat. There is no longer any trace of panic in her demeanor.

"Many people hate you and the king. We are not what you imagine. We're not part of any organization, nor are we trying to overthrow the power. We just want to avenge the people we love. That makes us more dangerous, more elusive. Our motivations can't be bought, and our confessions can't be forced out of us."

My eyebrows knit together at the calm tone she uses.

"To be honest, there is one thing I can admit to you. I stole those daggers from my uncle without him knowing. I just wanted to make a little money. That was… That was all it was."

Her smile fades, and her eyes glaze over. "But you came to the shop, you vandalized it… When my uncle realized it was me, I thought he would turn me in, but he sent me here. He promised… He promised he would join me. He was supposed to come back…"

Vàli and I exchange a look. He had suggested this theory, this idea that maybe it was nothing, just a mistake covered by someone who cared. But I refused to believe it, convinced our lives were in danger. I was relentless, and a man died.

"And one day, this man knocked on my door. I was certain it

was the end for me, that they had come for me. But he told me my uncle had been held prisoner for weeks and his chances of survival were slim. If it wasn't my fault, he—" She chokes on her sobs, her shoulders shaking.

"Navii," I try.

At the sound of her name, her downcast face lifts. All traces of pain vanish, leaving only rage. A rage I know all too well, one I know is impossible to control. "You're attacking your own people for a Viridian," she spits.

"Who has them?" I ask evenly.

Her smile turns into a deranged grin. "Do you honestly think I'll tell you when our desire for revenge is about to be fulfilled?"

"Who is it?" I shout this time.

"Why would I tell you? What would I gain?" she asks, a bitter laugh in her voice. "Nothing. Absolutely nothing. We didn't come this far to give up. Do you think my survival matters more to me? Vengeance is all I have left! I just wanted to make some money, that's all. I didn't know, but look: everything the Viridian touches spreads blood."

"Samael," I call my soldier.

He steps forward, and the young woman's body stiffens as her eyes land on him. Yet when she locks her gaze with mine, I see she hasn't lost any of her determination.

"Your man doesn't scare me. Do you know what one can endure to fulfill their desire for vengeance? I admired you, Your Highness. As a child, I was one of those fools who imagined being united with you. I thought we were alike."

I laugh at these words. She and I? Alike?

"Our mothers were taken from us by the war. The only chance yours had was not being defiled by the Viridian soldiers. In Lapisia, you were spared, but do you know what the villagers on the path of their army went through? And you dare to marry one of them? Have you forgotten what they did to us? Did her witch's gaze enchant you to the point of turning your back on your own?"

With every word, she roars, cries. Each sound from her mouth edges me closer to a madness that makes me want to slit her throat. I just want her to be quiet.

"How can you forget what they did to our queen?"

"She is not them!" I thunder back.

I immediately regret losing my temper, but the hatred in her voice unleashed my own.

"Is that what your conscience whispers to help you sleep beside her? The only regret I have is that I won't be there when she disappears. Because the man who wants her dead is even more determined than I am! Then again… I don't know if it's you or her he's after. I imagine he plans to kill you both, one way or another."

"Your cause is futile. Your mother is dead, your uncle is dead. Isn't that enough? If you continue down this path, you will die, too. Tell me, what will you gain? Whoever he is, he will fail. I will ascend to the throne, and she will rule alongside me. We will govern a united people, without war. Is it worth losing everything you have left, only for the outcome to remain unchanged?"

Our eyes lock, and her insane smile stays fixed. Suddenly, she lunges at me, catching me off guard, and grabs the dagger I was holding. I immediately stand, causing her to fall. My men surround her, but she holds the blade to her neck. I signal them to stop, knowing that if she cuts her throat, the only sound will be her gurgling.

"I wish I could be there the day she proves me right. She will always be a Viridian. You will always come after her people."

I see acceptance in her eyes, and in the next moment, all hope of discovering the truth disappears in a river of crimson.

"No, no, no!" I cry out, rushing to the young woman on the ground.

I press my fingers around her neck, trying to stop the bleeding.

"Tell me his name! What has he planned?" I shout, desperate.

Despite my efforts to compress the wound, the blood flows too heavily for me to stop it. Her limbs go still. Her chest stops moving. Her eyes, though open, are empty.

I look down at my blood-soaked hands and laugh, just as mad as the woman lying next to me. What have I done? Fear makes me nervous, and I stand and step away from the gruesome scene.

"Karel," Vàli calls, joining me.

"We're heading back. All five of us. She's alone at the palace. If what this woman said is true…"

"We're going with you," Jonah replies, understanding.

I nod and turn away. I haven't forgiven my brothers yet, but for now, they are the only ones I can rely on.

CHAPTER 21

KALLIOPEE

Night has fallen long ago. The servants have left my quarters, and since then, I've been pacing. The dinner with the king went smoothly, thanks to Kaïs, who kept the conversation going. I was far too shaken by Karel's sudden departure. Why was it so urgent? What's happening? Does it have to do with the revelations he made to me on our journey to Aquaria?

I can't stand idly by, waiting for danger to catch me off guard. I need to be prepared; I have to be. I don't want to feel this constant fear gripping my chest anymore.

Holding my cloak, I watch the sky from my window. The moon bathes the desert in an orange light, highlighting the distant silhouette of the mountains. I sigh, resigned. *He probably won't come...* When Kaïs told me Karel had left, I ran through the halls hoping to catch him, but I was too late. I feared he'd never return and that our farewell would be a scene full of unspoken words in a bathroom.

His absence made me realize the danger I was in and the fear I felt whenever he was away. I don't want to have to hide behind his frame; I need to be able to defend myself if my life is threatened. So, when I saw the one person who would help me, I couldn't help but make my request. He didn't say no, but he didn't agree either. He turned away, and I left before anyone could see us.

I'm about to go to bed when a light knock at the door makes my heart race. I rush to the entrance and, without catching my breath, open it. My eyes travel from his boots up to meet his gaze. I recall the last words we exchanged before today. Is Darkos really here to protect me? Did my father ensure someone would watch over me, even from afar?

I blink and step aside to let him in. He stares at me as my fingers grip the small bag he hands me, just like when I first arrived here. I rush to my bedroom after whispering my thanks. I don't dare speak louder, not out of fear of being caught, but afraid he might change his mind. I discard my dress and pull out the completely black outfit Darkos had placed in the bag. I quickly put on the pants. The length is perfect, but they're a bit loose. I borrow one of Karel's many belts, and as soon as it's fastened, the pants no longer slide off my hips. I then put on the shirt, rolling up the sleeves on my forearms. The fabric is loose and light. Very light. When the last button is fastened, I quickly slip on the pair of boots, similar to the ones Karel always wears. They surprisingly fit well and are very comfortable.

Once ready, I walk to the full-length mirror. My reflection makes me smile. I lack credibility dressed like this. Yet, as foolish as it may seem, seeing myself in training clothes strengthens my courage and determination. I braid my hair and swallow hard. The risk of getting caught is significant, but so is the risk of being targeted by a madman again. I glance at the bed where I'll sleep alone until Karel returns. His absence is more painful than I'll admit. Perhaps that's why I'm driven to disobey him. I turn away, drape the cloak over my shoulders, and pull up the hood.

When I return to the big living room, Darkos is standing by the window. Without a sound, I join him. He seems lost in thought, and though I'm eager to leave the palace, I, too, gaze at the horizon.

"Do you miss Viridia?" he murmurs thoughtfully.

At the mention of my kingdom, I can't help but feel a pang in my heart. "When I think about it, yes. It was my home. And you?"

"It was never my home. People like me wander without ever finding their place."

I feel a surge of compassion, imagining what it's like never to have found one's place. I understand a little. He was rejected because of his blood, and I because of my appearance. Neither of us is guilty of anything. We're just different. However, I can't compare our situations. I have an identity. The mixed-blooded don't exist in any records. They're unprotected. How can you condemn the murder of a ghost? They are often hunted like beasts. Their life expectancy is short, as is that of their mothers, who are deemed guilty of giving birth to aberrations by consorting with foreigners.

"Let's go," he says, turning away.

I want to know more about him, to get to know him better, to show him he's no longer alone, but his tone leaves no room for further conversation. The discussion is closed.

I follow him immediately, and he tells me to wait as he leaves my quarters. Anxiety twists my stomach, but I'm convinced I'm doing the right thing. And this time, I'm acting for myself, not for others. From the end of the corridor, a slight whistle can be heard, and I silently close the door before trotting toward him. This is how we navigate the hallways. At times, he stops, and we wait for the sound of boots to fade before continuing our path.

"Darkos?" suddenly calls a voice behind me.

The soldier grabs my wrist, and we start running. Despite his build, he's quieter than I am. I try to lighten my steps so the man who called out to him doesn't follow us. Darkos takes a few detours, but luckily, we don't encounter anyone else, and he only releases me when we're behind the tapestry that leads to the underground passages. I'm surprised it hasn't been sealed off as Karel had said. I suppose once I agreed to stay willingly, he no longer saw a need to wall it off.

We move through the dark corridors. The humidity of the night and our running cause sweat to bead at my hairline. I watch Darkos ahead of me, wondering about his life and how he, a mixed-blood, managed to join the army. I know the condition of such individuals is no better than that of women. They are considered outcasts, even more so since the war began. I never understood what people found so repulsive about mixed blood until I realized the kingdoms have always wanted division. Each controls its subjects. Mixing races would create confusion. To which people do the mixed-blooded belong? I suppose the Viridians resented Darkos for his Lapisian origins, and the Lapisians would act similarly if they knew Viridian blood flowed in his veins. Karel's and my future children might change the condition of people like Darkos. At least, I hope so.

When we reach the storage room I used to frequent not long ago, Darkos turns to me. He pulls the hood over my head and looks at me for a long moment. I think in many ways, he and I are alike.

"How did you meet my father?" I ask, intrigued. I know this isn't the place or the time, but I need to satisfy my curiosity.

The laugh that escapes his throat sounds sad and weighs down my heart even more.

"There are things a princess is better off not knowing."

My eyebrows furrow as he tries to evade me, but I grab his arm to stop him. "Why?"

"The world is cruel. Protect your soul from all that is vile."

The dryness of his voice could have fooled me. His condescending tone, too, as if he wanted to convince me he didn't think I could handle the truth. But the fact he is here with me tonight proves otherwise.

"I didn't need you to figure that out. I've never claimed the world was beautiful, even if not long ago, I needed to believe it. I just wonder how a king could entrust my life to a mixed-blood." There's no discrimination in my words; they simply state reality.

"Maybe he wanted to right a wrong."

"By using you?" I say sarcastically.

He frees himself from my grasp and turns away. I understand I won't learn any more. I watch his brown hair fall onto his neck as he opens the door. Head down, I follow him outside. Staring at his boots, I can't help but think. His stride is determined as he leads me to the barracks. The streets are nearly deserted, though a few solitary souls still wander. He slows his pace and walks beside me. I sneak glances at the citizens we pass, remembering the last time I walked these streets. It was my wedding day.

"What happened to you in Aquaria has spread throughout the city," he murmurs.

I lift my head, but Darkos is looking straight ahead, and I hide under my hood again.

"They respect you now."

"Why? Because I suffered?" I ask bitterly.

"Because your sacrifice spared them."

The conversation ends as we reach the wooden gates of the barracks. Until now, I've never seen what lies behind them.

"There won't be anyone here," he assures before pushing the door open.

The hinges creak loudly. I tense, holding my breath, then

enter as soon as the gap is wide enough. Darkos follows and closes the door while I walk to the center of the courtyard. The ground is covered with sand, and various training stations are scattered around. I untie my cloak and drape it over what seems to be a dummy made of cushions, straw, and wood.

"What do we start with?" I ask eagerly.

I eye a punching bag, then some targets, stretching—or at least trying to. Darkos's laugh surprises me, making me turn to face him.

"Learn to walk first. Warm-up," he adds in response to my questioning look.

With a wave of his hand, he invites me to follow him to the center of the track. He stretches his muscles, and I imitate him, not missing a single move, eager to be a good student.

"We need to wake up the muscles before pushing them. If you skip this step, you risk injury," he informs me.

I nod in agreement, and we continue our stretches. Just when I think we can get started, he begins jogging in slow circles. I follow him immediately, and it takes less than one lap for me to start sweating and feeling breathless.

"This is to gradually raise your heart rate and body temperature."

"Is this really necessary?" I ask, placing my hand on my side.

The gesture doesn't escape him, and he laughs, which irritates me. I've never been a fan of physical activities, not because I didn't want to, but because it wasn't considered dignified for a princess, or even a woman. After three laps, just when I'm about to beg for mercy, Darkos stops and stretches again. I can't miss his satisfied smile as I do the same.

"Does this amuse you?"

"When you ascend the throne, I'll remember this day," he replies, his smile widening.

"You're more naive than I am if you think the throne is within my reach," I tease him.

He shakes his head and looks at me with a seriousness that makes me stop moving. But he doesn't say anything more and returns to the center of the track.

"We'll start by teaching you how to defend yourself without

a weapon. If someone wants to take you somewhere, they'll just grab you by the arm," he says, demonstrating as he speaks. "Go on, break free."

My eyebrows knit together, but I comply. I try to free myself from his grip, but my efforts are in vain. I try a different approach, attempting to pry his fingers loose with my free hand, but I fail again.

He releases me, a smirk on his lips. "You really think you can use your other hand?"

"Why not?" I provoke him.

At my words, he grabs my wrist again, this time pulling me behind him. My feet try to slow our progress, and my free hand only manages to touch his to help me keep my balance. Realizing he's right, I can't help but growl in frustration. That's enough to make him stop. He turns without letting go and faces me.

"If someone tries to grab you like this," he says, indicating our joined arms, "bend your arm, elbow up."

He demonstrates immediately. I wait eagerly for his next instruction.

"Then, pull it inward and hit with your elbow."

My eyebrows shoot up.

"Do it," he commands.

I follow through. My free hand rests on my clenched fist to help add force, and my elbow strikes his arm. Still, I remain skeptical. I'm not stupid; my attacker would have to be a child for me to break free so easily.

"That's the gentle method," he informs me.

I roll my eyes as he positions himself in front of me again.

"Now, if your attacker is more like me, you'll need to strike. You have options: a hit to the ear can disorient them enough to let go. Otherwise, you can aim for the knees. They'll expect you to strike—"

I see him hesitate, and I blush as I guess what he's implying.

"Oh!" That's all I manage to say.

"Right… He'll be so busy protecting his… parts," he adds with a throat-clearing, "that he… well, you get it."

I nod, regaining my composure. I'm taking this too seriously to let embarrassment distract me. "I'll never hit hard enough," I emphasize.

"It doesn't matter. He'll be surprised enough to let go of your hand, and that'll give you a chance to escape."

He shows me the places to strike and how to do it. He demonstrates that even if my arm is held, I can still use the rest of my body. For a good part of the night, he goes over different ways I might be attacked and how to free myself: opposite arm grabs, attacks from behind, everything. Even being grabbed by the hair, which cruelly reminds me of what I went through in the citadel. My only consolation is knowing that even if I had known these techniques before, my attackers were four strong, and I would never have escaped.

When Darkos finally says the session is over, I'm drenched in sweat and utterly exhausted. Every muscle aches, making me wince whenever I move.

"You learn quickly," he praises me as we leave the barracks.

Hood over my head, I glance at him briefly before focusing on our path. "I'll never be strong enough to defend my life."

"This is just the beginning. For now, you need to learn to flee, not to fight."

"Karel taught me some moves when we were young, but without practice, I've forgotten them all."

His lips press together as he continues walking.

"You don't like him, do you?" I dare to ask.

"Your father tasked me with keeping an eye on you, and everything that's happened to you since you got here was his fault, so no, not really."

"He protects me," I can't help but defend him.

"Look where it's gotten you. Your body has been defiled and scarred."

My steps halt at his words, and my gaze turns icy as it locks with his. "He's my husband, Darkos. I appreciate your help, but don't speak of him that way."

"You asked me a question, Your Highness," he taunts. "I merely answered it."

We quickly reach the storage room, and I sigh in exasperation as the door closes behind me. Darkos turns to face me, towering over me.

"I apologize, but I've watched him for the past five years, and I know the prince is impulsive and selfish. He acts without regard for the consequences. You can't blame me for my opinion when those consequences fall on you, Princess. Now, if this topic is off-limits, we won't speak of it again."

With that, he heads down the hallway, and we return to the palace. This time, we don't encounter anyone until we reach my quarters. The journey is heavy with unspoken words. I think I might not get another chance to train with him, but he surprises me by placing his hand on the door as I start to close it, after saying goodbye.

"From what I've gathered, your husband will be away for a few more days. That'll give us time to deepen your training. Be ready. We'll start again tomorrow."

Relief washes over me, and a smile spreads across my lips as I thank him, though he doesn't return it.

Until early morning, I replay the moves he taught me over and over in my mind, mentally practicing them. My training is still minimal, but I feel safer than I did when I woke up this morning. Filled with hope, I sink into a deep sleep.

Chapter 22

Karel

Seated in the armchair, I wait for my dear wife in a relaxed posture, which is the exact opposite of how I feel inside. My blood is boiling with impatience. I resist the urge to pace the palace corridors and fetch her myself. At this hour, she is probably dining with Kaïs and my father, and I doubt the king would appreciate me barging in the way I am now.

Imagine my surprise when I learned that my sweet princess has been sneaking out to the citadel at night during my absence! I don't know what angers me more—this or the identity of her companion. I close my eyes and take a deep breath. This isn't how I envisioned my return. I thought I could rest from my journey, savor our reunion, and apologize for my abrupt departure, which had been weighing on my conscience.

What was I thinking, detouring to the barracks? Now I have a headache reminiscent of my worst hangovers, and on top of that, I've got some nice scrapes on my hands. Lucky for me, my men were there to stop me, or I swear the kid who provocatively spilled the beans would be six feet under.

The door creaks open, and my eyelids lift. I turn my head to the right and see my stunning wife enter. I give her my most strained smile, which she doesn't return.

"You're back?" she squeaks.

Guilt radiates from her. Or maybe my grimace didn't fool her and scared her instead. Probably a bit of both. She steps forward, giving me a grin as forced as mine.

"Is this how you welcome your husband?"

My cold tone doesn't really surprise her, and as she approaches a bit closer, she frowns.

"My husband would have gotten a better welcome if he hadn't left like a brute," she retorts.

A laugh escapes from deep in my throat. I'll give her that. Kalliopee is now just a few steps away from me. She doesn't come any closer and eyes me suspiciously.

"You didn't get too bored while I was gone?" I ask, feigning casualness.

She blinks slowly, gripping the back of the chair facing mine. I release the armrests of my chair and lean forward, not taking my eyes off her. When I notice her tense fingers, my fists clench. I hoped the rumors were false, but from her behavior, I can tell the young apprentice was telling the truth.

"Is everything okay?" she dares to ask.

"What do you think? Do I look okay?"

"No worse than usual. You're not exactly the cheeriest person," she taunts.

She's amused, but if she knew, I think her smile would disappear. And soon, it will.

"I'd be better if I hadn't been told that my wife leaves the palace every night with another man," I say.

There it is, the moment her smile fades. I relish this sight, as much as it sickens me. While I'm satisfied to see her caught, I would have preferred this rumor to be false and for her to deny it vehemently. She steps back as I stand. I think it wiser to put some distance between us and stand behind my own chair. There can never be too many obstacles between her and me, especially when my nerves are this frayed.

"It's not what you think," she defends anxiously.

"And what do I think?"

"I don't know what you've heard or who told you, but I'm not seeing another man. He and I aren't in that kind of relationship, it's not—"

"Kalliopee," I cut her off, bitterness clear in my voice. "Believe me, if that's what I thought, you wouldn't even have the chance to say it. You and he would be lying in pools of your own blood right now."

She calms down immediately, though not without swallowing hard, and then looks at me hesitantly. "That would be… extreme."

Yes, it's obvious I could never go that far. It would break my heart, tear my soul apart, but it would destroy me even more to harm her in any way.

"You had me watched?" she suddenly snaps.

"I don't think you're in a position to accuse me of anything, but no, I didn't have you watched. I was just ensuring your safety. I didn't think it would be necessary even at night."

"Then how did you know if you weren't watching my every move?"

I sigh, irritated. It's true that Kaïs was keeping an eye on her, but unlike what she seems to imagine, it wasn't because I didn't trust her, but because I feared others might harm her. Absent from the palace, I could no longer protect her.

"Someone happened to see you one night leaving the barracks. Was it him who sneaked you out to the dispensary?" I ask, doubtful.

"No," she replies.

Relief washes over me, until she turns her head away. She's lying.

"He only showed me the city once. At that time," she continues, seeing my features tighten, "you were unbearable, making my life miserable, and any distraction was welcome. For the rest, I'm not stupid; I memorized the route so I could go back."

She doesn't add more as I struggle to digest the information. I don't know him. My father always arranges it so that his men have almost no contact with me before joining his escort. Why is he interested in her? Is this another move by the king? Although I disapprove of this guard being so close to my wife, I don't suspect him of being the one Navii spoke of. He would have acted by now, taken advantage of my absence to get to Kalliopee, I'm strangely certain of that.

"Why did you leave? Did your mission go well?" she asks, trying to change the subject.

"Are you interested?" I inform her rhetorically before she can pry further. I don't wait for an answer. "Now, if you'll excuse me, I'm tired. I'm going to take a shower and go to bed. As for your nightly outings, you know they're over."

I turn and head toward our bedroom, unbuttoning my jacket while massaging my neck.

"Karel, I need it."

"You're wrong, it's me you need!" I shout, turning to face her again. "I forbid you from approaching that soldier, from talking to him. You know what? Even worse, I forbid you from speaking to any other man but me."

She lets out a laugh but quickly swallows it when she realizes I'm serious. "You're joking!"

"Do I look like I'm joking, *Shaadi*?" I snap. "I'm gone for six days, and when I come back, I find out that every night my wife is learning to fight with another man. What kind of rumors do you think are spreading?"

"I'll talk to whoever I want," she retorts, storming off to hide in her library.

I cross the room and open the door where she's taken refuge. Jealousy consumes me, knowing she's been close to another man, enough to trust him, makes me furious. "You will not speak to any other man but me. Is that clear?"

"And by what right?" she screams.

"By the right of our marriage. '*By this union, you forfeit your freedom*,'" I recite.

Her eyes fill with tears as she takes a step back. "No," she whispers. "You promised me—"

"I would have kept my word if you'd given me a reason to."

She tugs at her bracelets in a vain attempt to remove them, and I look at her with disdain.

"I hate you and I hate this marriage!" she spits.

I don't take my eyes off her as she furiously tries to take off her bangles. "You're wasting your energy; you're chained to me."

She stops immediately, breathing heavily, and the hatred she directs at me makes me feel justified in my own anger. Then a veil of sadness crosses her eyes. Guilt washes over me, but I prefer to suppress it.

"Are you punishing me?"

I don't answer because I don't need to.

"I don't regret my actions, Karel. If I had to do it again, I would, no matter how painful it was."

I freeze when I realize she's not talking about her nightly excursions but about what happened in Aquaria.

"Punishing you?" I laugh bitterly.

Before she can respond, there's a knock at the door. Kalliopee, standing on the threshold of the library, nervously watches the main door. I gesture for her to stay where she is. I think she understands the extent of my anger since she doesn't make a move to join me.

I open the door and take a deep breath when the man who's been sneaking my wife out crosses my gaze. His eyebrows furrow, and he takes a step back.

"Yeah, I'm back!" I exclaim.

"I was just teaching her—"

I grab him by the collar and shove him against the opposite wall, preventing him from finishing his sentence. "You don't approach her. You don't talk to her, and most importantly, you don't touch her!" I order.

I glare at him with undisguised hatred. Despite the threat I pose, I don't see any fear in him. On the contrary, I can feel his body trembling as if he's holding back from fighting back or even hitting me.

"Do I make myself clear?"

"Karel," Kalliopee says anxiously, joining me.

She tries to push me away, but I tighten my grip, waiting for Darkos to confirm.

"Yes, Your Highness," he replies reluctantly.

I release him, and he glares at me as he smooths out his jacket. Then, the bold man turns his attention back to my wife.

"Move."

My rough tone is unmistakable. If he doesn't leave this second, I swear I'll tear his head off. I clench my fists, trying to control the jealousy that's eating me up inside and could drive me to do something unforgivable. I believe Kalliopee when she assures me nothing happened between them, but I can't stand the way he looks at her. Like he wants her. Without another word, he leaves. I then turn to Kalliopee, who watches him until he's out of sight. I hate the affection I see in her eyes and what it stirs in me. It doesn't make me angry; it terrifies me.

Preferring to ignore the lump in my throat, I return to our quarters and stop in the middle of the living room.

"I'm not punishing you for what you did; you're punishing me," I murmur. "You don't let me see you, touch you. I've tried to make amends, but every time I get close, you push me away. I deserve it; I know that. If I were more restrained, you'd never have had to endure this punishment, but you thwart every attempt I make, and I don't know what to do anymore."

"I'm not punishing you," she counters, her voice raw.

"Oh no? Then what are you doing? Do you think I don't feel your body tense every time I touch you? You curl up so much it's like you want to disappear completely."

I wait for her to respond, but she just stares at me, tears in her eyes. I hoped voicing my despair would bring me some relief, but the opposite happens as her silence drags on. Without another word, I head to the bathroom. I strip off my dust-covered clothes and step into the shower. I tilt my head back, trying to drown my thoughts under the cascading water.

"I'm not punishing you," she surprises me from behind. "I don't know why I act this way, but every time you touch me, I feel like telling you how ugly I feel."

I turn around to find her standing in the center of the room. Vulnerable.

"Yet, after your assault here, you didn't—"

"I wasn't responsible," she interrupts. "I didn't ask for it. But this time, it's different. I feared you'd hurt me by refusing to dry my tears, that you'd tell me I had no right to cry over something I agreed to endure. You've been so distant since we returned, Karel."

My heart is pounding furiously. If I had known, if I had understood… I thought she needed space, not that she was afraid of my reaction. I would never have pushed her away. It's true I was upset with her for acting behind my back, with the complicity of my men, but I would have been incapable of rejecting her.

I try to find the right words as I look at her. I know sometimes I choose the wrong ones and often end up hurting her, but tonight, I can't rush things. Not now that we're starting to talk again. Not now that the silence between us is about to break.

She faces me, her eyes pleading.

There are so many emotions swirling inside me that I feel dizzy. Regret mingles with the disgust I feel toward Nokken. Then there's this love that seems unreasonable at times, and this fear. The fear everything will collapse. The fear Kalliopee will slip away from me or be taken from me. I love her in a way that's almost insane, and I'm fully aware of it, but I don't know how to love differently. It grips me to my core. Does she feel it? This instability that threatens to drag me into hell?

I close my eyes, just long enough to sort my thoughts, and her voice, with a hint of weariness, sounds again.

"I think we'd better each take some time to think on our own."

When my eyelids lift, I see her disappear. I leave the shower, grab a towel, and when I enter the bedroom, I notice she's gone, taking her pillow with her. There's no way I'm letting the unspoken words keep us apart any longer. I open the closet to get dressed and notice clothes that don't belong to her. When I unfold them, I realize they're training clothes. I throw them on the floor, get dressed, and head to the library. She's sitting on the chaise longue, seemingly daydreaming. The clothes I throw at her snap her out of her reverie, and she looks at me, puzzled.

"I planned to teach you some things when I got back," I inform her. "But you're always too impatient."

She stands up and examines the clothes she's holding before facing me. "If you had told me sooner, I would have waited. But you always think I can guess what you don't say."

That's our problem, both of us. We spend our time interpreting each other's silences.

"Are you coming or not?" I ask impatiently.

She immediately gets up, walks past me, and disappears into our bedroom. When she reappears, she's wearing my training clothes and her cape. The sadness in her eyes hasn't dissipated, but unfortunately, I'm not the kind of person who can chase away doubts with pretty words.

For now, I'll give her what she's asking for. But I'm not going to go easy on her.

She's going to regret seeking help from someone else.

***

Facing me, she stretches without needing me to tell her what to do. I'm torn between pride and annoyance. My body, used to enduring, doesn't require as much warming up as hers, so I let her continue her exercises and retrieve some bandages from an old wooden cabinet under the porch. Tonight, the wind is blowing quite hard, but even though the conditions aren't ideal, they shouldn't stop us from training.

I join her as she's doing a split. I help her up and keep holding on to her as I wrap her hands. She watches my every move, and a vicious thought crosses my mind. Did he touch her like this? I look at her and notice her cheeks are flushed.

"What have you already learned?"

"I… I learned how to block an attack and get out of a hold. I still need more practice, but I think it will become instinctive soon. Darkos says I think too much, and it puts me in danger."

"Darkos, huh?"

"What should I call him?" she snaps.

I shrug. "Not calling him at all would be perfect."

She gives me a wry smile, and before she can say anything, I press my mouth to hers. It's brief but enough to feel the softness of her lips against mine. Just enough to feel like I'm catching my breath.

"You're so immature," she whispers when I pull away, a deeper blush on her cheeks.

I shake my head, smiling, and start wrapping her other hand.

"What are you going to teach me?" she asks.

"How to punch."

Sometimes, you need more than just to run away. You need to hit hard and where it hurts. I wish she didn't need to know so much, but with what the pawnbroker's niece revealed, I can't play ostrich anymore. I won't always be with her, and there's no way I'm letting my pride put her in danger.

"Why are you wrapping my hands?"

"To keep you from getting hurt," I reply, teasing.

Unfortunately, my joke falls flat, and sadness fills her eyes. I know it only reminds her of what she endured in Aquaria and the marks the salt wounds left on her. I hate her scars as much as she does, but not because they're ugly. It's because they're a testament to what a madman made her endure out of pride.

I finish wrapping her second hand, let go of her, then step back and look into her eyes. “You need to learn how to hit hard, but properly.”

I raise my palms to chest level and lift my eyebrows. She positions herself, fists in front of her face, and her right hand weakly hits my palm.

“You have to use your whole body weight to give your punches more force.”

She nods and tries again. This time, the impact is a bit stronger, but still far from sufficient in case of an attack.

“Still not good. Not like that either. Again. Pivot. Get some momentum. No. Keep going. Harder.”

I can tell that with each punch, with each command, she’s getting more impatient.

“Why didn’t you tell me what was on your mind?” I suddenly ask as she catches her breath.

She freezes, looks at me, then hits my palms again when I present them. “Because sometimes you can be insensitive.”

I take the hit with difficulty. Instead of protecting my ego, I decide to use this exercise to let her vent, to pour out her anger.

“Why did you act without talking to me about it?”

“Because you would have said no. You would have rushed in headfirst, and right now, we would be at war again,” she admits before hitting me.

“I could have been there for you,” I say softly.

“No, Karel. I believe you when you say I’m the only person who matters to you, I believe you when you say you could sacrifice your people just for me. And that’s what you would have done. I wanted to be able to count on your support, but you’re incapable of that.”

She hits me again, and I don’t know if it’s her words that have stunned me, but I step back from the impact. This time, she lowers her hands, as if she no longer wishes to fight, as if she’s laying down her arms.

“You’re right,” I admit. “I can’t stand to see anyone inflict pain on you. It’s beyond my strength. And right now, we would be at war, and I would feel no remorse. Even less now that I know the consequences of the punishment you had to endure. I'd rather go back to six more years of combat than endure this distance you keep between us. I've told you, I'm neither stupid nor blind. I wanted to join you when you left the bedroom to lock yourself in the library, but as soon as I heard your sobs, I found myself unable to open that door. Because I was terrified of facing your reproaches, of you rejecting me. You've never taken such distances with me. You've always let me see your anger and dry your tears. But I accept that you're angry with me, because this time, I was directly responsible for what happened to you."

I'm not used to pouring out my feelings, but sharing my remorse with her brings more relief than I expected.

"For the first time, I regretted this marriage," I admit to her. "I should have been the one to suffer that punishment, *Shaadi*, not you."

A cool palm rests on my cheek, forcing me to lift my head. My eyes meet her tearful ones. A few salty drops fall from her special gaze, and I wonder how many more she'll have to shed because of me.

"I'm not angry with you," she says so softly I can barely hear her. "Stop blaming yourself."

I dry her tears and take her face in my hands to kiss her with all the gentleness I can muster. As I breathe in, she stiffens, and I lose my breath. I find myself on the ground. The pain is so intense I feel like I'm dying. The air no longer fills my lungs as she bends down to my level.

"Never use the vows I was forced to make against me again! Got it?"

I would laugh if my crotch didn't hurt so much. "You just killed our future children," I manage to say in a high-pitched voice.

"And you killed a part of me tonight."

I realize the seriousness of her reproach and the wound I've inflicted on her. She helps me up, which I do while holding my breath as the pain persists.

"You see, he taught me a lot of things," she taunts as she walks away.

Chapter 23

Kalliopee

I smile as I walk away from him. I needed to make him understand his argument had hurt me. He always said he wouldn't force me to do anything, but after just one argument he invoked the loss of my freedom. I felt betrayed. Despite our disagreements and his constant need to control everything, I naively thought I wasn't chained. I believed that he wouldn't try to subdue *me*.

He stays with his back to me for a few minutes, and I can't suppress the satisfied smile stretching across my lips. I force myself to adopt a neutral expression when he joins me.

"I see his help has been useful to you," he complains, jealousy evident in his tone.

My smile returns, and I feel a strange sense of victory that doesn't escape him. He positions himself in front of me and starts naming techniques. For each one, I tell him Darkos has already shown it to me. I had told him I needed to perfect my skills, but he's determined to find a technique I don't know. I let him continue, aware it's an ego issue. The wind blows hard, and when a gust sweeps across the courtyard, I have to squint to keep the sand from getting into my eyes. With a swift move, he grabs my wrist, but I apply what Darkos taught me. I raise my elbow upward, place my hand on the one that's trapped, and pull them toward me. Stunned, he lets go as my elbow hits his arm.

"He taught me that, too," I provoke.

He nervously runs a hand over the bridge of his nose, then surprises me by grabbing my hair. He doesn't do it hard, but I still feel a tug at my scalp. I place my fingers on his and my right foot braces back before aiming for his lower abdomen. My heart speeds up, and even though it's just a game, the adrenaline gives more power and speed to my movements. Unfortunately, he anticipates my move and grabs my ankle to stop me from hitting him, making me fall back and land heavily on the ground. The impact knocks the wind out of me, but before I can get up, Karel lies down between my legs.

"And this? Did he teach you this?" he asks, his voice rough.

My eyelids lift. Karel is just a few inches away from me, our breaths mingling, and the playful atmosphere has completely vanished.

"And this?" he asks again, pressing his hips against mine.

His erect member presses against my leg, activating my nerve endings. I shake my head, unable to say a word. His gaze, which was merely possessive, now darkens even more. The game has given way to passion, and I believe he didn't intend to provoke me this much, but now that I've confessed what my behavior was hiding when I was avoiding him, I need to be certain he desires me despite my scars.

I swallow, staring at his lips with longing, and as he pushes up on his arms to rise, I grab him by the neck and capture them. His three-day stubble irritates my skin, but the return of the velvety warmth of his mouth stokes the flames burning inside me.

Since our return from Aquaria, it's the first time I've deepened a kiss, sliding my tongue between his teeth. He takes a deep breath, and I can tell he's trying to hold back, but after so long, after finally telling him what's been on my mind, I no longer want this distance that has come between us. His scent fills my mouth, making me sigh and intensifying my desire for him. These last few nights, whether I've spent them with or without him, have been painfully lonely, and I realize just how sad I felt when my heart pounds in my chest. I ignore the feeling and focus instead on his taste, on the smell of his skin—a mix that evokes the desert, brutality, and power. I don't think Karel is aware of everything he exudes and what he stirs in me. I cling to his hair in the hope of convincing him to stay, but the texture of his lips disappears as he pulls away, leaving me lying there, and breathless.

"If you start kissing me like that, I won't be able to hold back," he informs me gently.

"Who says I want it to stop?" I ask, shamelessly.

He seems to study me, then looks around before his gaze returns to me. "You deserve better than a barracks, better than the ground, no matter how clean it is."

I realize he's referring to the last time our bodies came together. In Aquaria. It feels like it was so long ago.

"You deserve to be respected," he adds.

My eyes lock on the moon illuminating the training arena. I don't dare face him, afraid he'll judge my desires and make my discomfort grow.

"You respect me, so I don't care about the place," I admit, this time with a hint of shame in my voice.

The truth is, I'm not sure I can wait until we're home. I'm afraid my apprehensions will take hold of me again and make me run away once more. When he helps me to my feet, I expect him to tell me I'm being unreasonable, but he surprises me by lifting me. He holds me close, kissing me as he crosses the courtyard. I don't know where he's taking us, but I don't care. Between my legs, I feel like the void is only growing, that I'm incomplete. His lips pull away, and my eyelids lift. I see he's set me on a table, sheltered by the overhang.

"No one will see us," he whispers, as if to reassure me.

His hands knead my hips with fervor as our gazes lock. The moment feels crucial. He draws our bodies closer, and my breath hitches, waiting for him to give me his. He flits over my lips, first gently, then with undisguised hunger. He drinks me in, and I return the fervor, burning with desire.

Our kisses become more invasive, hungrier, as he works to remove my shoes. His mouth trails down to my neck, paralyzing my thoughts. His trembling hands slide my top up, exposing my chest. He helps me sit up, then his fingers trace along my spine. A gust lifts the sand, which sticks to my damp skin. The hot air makes me feel like I'm suffocating, but I find my breath again through Karel's. Hungry, I pull his body closer, wrapping my legs around his hips. But his hands brush against my scars, and everything stops. My breathing. His movements. Our lips. Time is suspended.

Unable to shake the images of that bleeding, of that water drowning me, of those orders cracking, I open my eyes. When his eyelids reveal his distress, a lump forms in my chest. My fingers, tangled in his brown curls, release. I start to pull my top down, but he stops me. Without breaking eye contact, he moves my body to the edge of the table. I have to lift my head to keep from breaking this connection, my only anchor to reality. The moon casts shadows on his face, making him look sterner than he is. His hand moves between us, brushing my belly as he presses his forehead to mine.

"He will pay. One day… he will pay for what he did to you."

I believe the promise in his voice, but I don't want it. I thought I wanted this revenge myself, but I realize I just want to put an end to this king and his vices.

"Let's forget about that man. Let's not let him win, Karel, and that's what will happen if we feed the hate we have for him."

He's about to argue, but I stop him by capturing his lips. I feel him struggle with his emotions. So, I beg him to come back to me. To stay with me. He surrenders, deepening the kiss. The intensity of his caresses drives Aquaria out of my mind. His fingers work to undo the button holding my pants. With a practiced move, he lifts me, lowers my pants along with my underwear, and then abruptly places me back on the table.

The warm breeze brushes my skin, but the bite he inflicts on my neck the next moment sends a cold shiver through my body. My breath stops only to come back stronger. His palm rests on my chest, forcing me to lie down. Then his hands take hold of my knees, inviting me to wrap my legs around his hips.

Time suspends again, stretching infinitely, but this time in a delicious way. My hunger makes me impatient. I open my eyes when nothing happens. The sight before me is paralyzing, suffocating. His eyes pull me far away. They reveal everything Karel feels: unconditional love. Though I don't condone his barbaric aspects, I know this is who he is, and his actions are proof of his absolute love.

His forearm presses close to my head while his other hand tightens its grip on my thigh. I sense he's lowered his pants when I feel his sex at the entrance of mine. Without breaking eye contact, he penetrates me, leaving me unable to breathe or even think. My eyelids flutter, and a moan escapes me. The next moment, his palm covers my mouth as he pulls out to thrust back in, deeper. His forehead rests against mine, and I cling more firmly to his neck. The fabric still covering our chests makes me hot. Yet, I wouldn't want this exquisite torture to end for anything in the world. The thrusts grow even more powerful, and his hand presses harder against my lips to muffle my increasingly loud moans. The table beneath us is battered. Its creaks are as loud as the sound of our bodies slapping together. I wonder how it can bear the weight and ferocity of our bodies.

"I love you," he whispers against my ear.

Those words make my heart explode and heighten my desire to reach the peak. I never doubt his love for me, but Karel isn't one for sentimentality. His words are never sugar-coated; they are powerfully true and authentic. If I don't always feel the need for him to say those words, it's because I see it in the way he touches me, looks at me, treats me. So yes, I know that with him, I will never have a charming prince for a husband like those in many legends I've heard, but no one else could ever make me feel so alive.

He frees my mouth and buries his head in my neck. My lips press against his shoulder to muffle my escaping moans. My breath catches as I finally reach the peak. My body tenses, my teeth sink into his skin despite the fabric covering it, and I savor the sensation, wishing it would last. Karel follows with a deep, guttural sound that extends my orgasm.

As we gently come down, he doesn't pull away. He stays nestled inside me, wrapping me in his arms. I take a deep breath and enjoy the calm. I feel like it's only temporary. Despite all our efforts, the elements constantly batter us. But I'd be ready to endure it, over and over again. For him. Because he may not be a charming prince, but he makes me feel alive.

Chapter 24

Kalliopee

Five Months Later

Days pass by, taking weeks and then months with them. Almost two seasons have gone by, but the sky in Lapisia never changes. Here, time seems to stretch on endlessly. The ground remains relentlessly covered in sand, devoid of green or white. I stare at the horizon, watching the distant desert that sometimes makes me feel like I'm suffocating. In Lapisia, I constantly feel like I'm living in a bubble I can't escape. There aren't many activities, and friends are few. Fortunately, I have Karel, and our relationship has settled into a pleasant routine that rarely changes and eases my sense of being trapped in this city. Sometimes we argue, but he hasn't mentioned my restraints again—not even out of simple provocation. I no longer need to threaten his lineage. At that thought, I glance down at my still-flat stomach. Anxiety tightens in my stomach. Though Karel never brings it up, the lack of changes to my body doesn't escape the king, who reminds me of my role: to provide an heir. Strangely, each month when I bleed, I'm torn between disappointment and relief. The reality is that I'm terrified of bearing a child and risking my life, like my mother did when she gave birth to me.

"What are you doing?" Karel asks as he steps out of his office.

I turn to him and watch as he leans against the door. "I was just thinking," I reply.

He nods, without approaching, and I turn my head back to the view outside. I miss Viridia more each day. This winter, I imagined its plains covered in a white blanket and tried to remember what it feels like to be so cold that the snow burns your fingers to the point where you think they might fall off. Now, I try to recall the lush valleys, the coolness of the lake, and the scents of late summer.

In the reflection of the window, Karel's silhouette grows larger. He positions himself behind me, without touching me, and I lean back against his chest, seeking some of his comfort. Without a word, he wraps his arms around me. We sigh in unison, and it makes me smile.

"I still have a bit of work to do, but if you want, we can go out of the palace later," he offers.

I can tell he's noticed my gloomy mood and is trying to cheer me up. Karel now takes me out once a week to refine my self-defense techniques. We always go to the barracks at night when the streets are almost deserted. Karel isn't ready to let me mingle with the crowd yet. I am, but I understand his reservations and can't fault him for them. Of course, the lack of external contact is hard for me, but I console myself by spending my days with Sienna or Kaïs. My husband's cousin hasn't planned to leave the palace, and although his presence displeases the king, Karel insisted his stay be extended.

Tensions between Karel and his friends have eased. Sometimes, I catch them deep in conversation, and the atmosphere immediately becomes charged with anxiety. I've asked Karel to tell me what's worrying him so much, but I only get reassuring words or his lips pressed against mine. I've noticed other men have been assigned to our security. If he thinks he's fooled me, he's wrong. I understand the primary goal of these affectionate gestures is to keep me quiet.

Darkos remains as taciturn as ever, but occasionally, we talk about Viridia. These moments are rare, though, because Karel seems to appear whenever I run into the guard by chance, as if he has a sixth sense about it. Although the soldier has assured me he never felt at home in Viridia, I sense he misses it, or at least I suspect he does. I know nothing of the tragedies that have marked the life of this mixed-blood, but from the bits of information he has let slip, I've gathered his mother was Viridian and that she has passed away. I haven't tried to learn more. My curiosity stops where others' pain begins.

Karel places a kiss on my head and tightens his hold before releasing me. I watch him walk away and lower my gaze to my stomach once more.

"Kalliopee?" he calls out as I thought he had left.

I look up and turn toward him.

"This—"

I see his eyes are fixed on the place that now occupies all my thoughts.

"Don't pay attention to what my father says."

My heart skips a beat when he gives me a gentle smile. It's always unusual with him, but I savor it hungrily each time, perhaps because the rarity of his smiles makes them precious to me.

"I'm not in a hurry to share you with another human being," he adds. "It will give us more time to do what we need to do."

An irrepressible smile spreads across my lips at his suggestion, but also because, in his own way, he reassures me. I nod, and with a blink of an eye, he's disappeared behind his office door.

Instead of waiting for him in our room, I head to the library and retrieve the book I was reading yesterday from a shelf. Comfortably sprawled on the chaise longue, the pages turn without me even noticing. Some pages detach from the aging leather, while others are stained, indicating it's one of the oldest books in the royal library. I'll take it to Amadeus once I've finished. I always do. He loves books and takes great care of them. It would be unfair to deprive him of this one.

When my eyelids grow heavy, I realize that once again tonight, we won't be going out. Sometimes, Karel is so exhausted he falls asleep in his chair, and I have to wake him so he doesn't wake up sore the next morning.

I get up and return the book to its place before leaving the library. As the door creaks, I hear a noise: a muffled sound coming from Karel's carpeted office. I head there, push the slightly open door, and freeze in horror. I stand motionless as I see a man next to my sleeping husband. My eyes are drawn to the dagger in his hand while he calmly stares back at me. Terror paralyzes me, and I am unable to scream for help.

The intruder's black-clad arm makes a swift movement, then he steps away from Karel, who wakes up with a groan of pain that splits my heart and shatters my soul. I back away as the assailant, who seems vaguely familiar, approaches me. A crazed grin distorts his face, and the glint of the knife in his hand awakens my survival instinct.

I take another step back, not daring to blink for fear of losing sight of him. Urgency grips me as he comes so close I can hear his heavy breathing. He reaches out to me, but by some miracle, I manage to counter his strike with one of the moves Karel had persistently taught me. My limbs move on their own.

I'm not stupid; the element of surprise is in my favor. If I were a man, he would have tightened his grip on the knife handle to ensure it didn't fall. He would have been more vigilant and attacked more directly. For the first time in my life, my gender might save me. He underestimated me, and that's to my advantage.

"Help!" I scream, knowing that now disarmed, he has no choice but to flee.

The intruder pushes me, and I fall heavily against the small table in our living room. The corner digs into my leg, making me whimper, and then I hit the floor. I hear the front door slam violently as my eyes fall on the knife he threw to the ground. It's covered in a scarlet liquid I hadn't even noticed.

Recognizing the ruby-adorned handle, I realize it's one of the daggers I sold shortly after my arrival. I grab it and painfully stand to turn around. My body moves as if on autopilot, and I cross the threshold of the office. My legs carry me, albeit weakly, as the adrenaline ebbs away. I let out a sigh of relief when I see Karel is standing.

"Are you okay?" he murmurs, leaning on the imposing desk.

"Yes," I reassure him, my throat tight.

He rounds the desk, gripping it with increasing difficulty, and I panic as I notice he's as pale as a sheet. The adrenaline leaves my body, replaced by a crushing anxiety. One I've never felt, not even for my own life. As I take a step toward him to support him, he drops to his knees, letting out a bitter laugh.

"I spared his life, and this is how he thanks me."

"Karel," I worry as he collapses.

He falls onto his back, and I see the red stain soaking his white jacket. It never occurred to me it could be his blood. It's foolish, considering it was just us and the intruder. I had convinced myself so thoroughly that Karel was invincible that I came to believe it. Nausea washes over me, but I ignore it, refusing to be overwhelmed. I press my palms over the wound, trying to lock my eyes onto his, which have turned glassy.

"Karel, look at me," I command when his eyelids grow heavy.

He obeys, but even with his eyes open, he doesn't see me. I can't breathe, the urgency of the situation stealing my air. I press harder on his wound, never taking my gaze off my husband. Seconds tick by, and his complexion pales, his features relax. I look around the room nervously, hating the oppressive silence that is deafening.

I call for help. Once. Twice. Three times. But when Karel's eyelids finally give up the fight to stay open, I no longer hold back my tears. I beg, as his hands, which tried to cling to me, weaken and fall limply.

"Karel, please, Karel."

"I'm here."

Yet his voice is so faint I know he won't stay awake much longer.

"Look at me," I order him again.

His eyelids remain closed, and I think he's gone until his Adam's apple moves up and down with difficulty.

"I see you, even when my eyes are closed, *Shaadi*. We'll go back to the clearing when we leave Lapisia. We should leave," he rambles.

His body trembles and sweats, and I place my blood-stained hands on his cheeks to force him to look at me.

"Do you want to? Start over somewhere else? A new life?" he continues, his voice fragmented.

"Yes, we'll go wherever you want when you're healed."

"Is there a place you love more than any other at home?"

He's out of breath, his voice dying. And I am breaking.

"The weeping willow by the lake, I'll take you there," I answer.

Fear chokes my words. I hate everything this conversation implies. Since when does Karel indulge in sentimentality and nostalgia? Yet, because the present terrifies me, I envision a future we may never know.

My eyes well up, and I desperately turn toward the door, praying for someone to appear.

"Kalliopee," he calls.

"Yes?"

His eyelids lift, and I let out a sigh of relief. Unfortunately, the feeling is brief.

"It's going to be okay."

I nod, tears blurring my vision.

"Whatever happens, it's going to be okay."

This time, I shake my head from side to side. I forbid him from imagining the worst; I refuse to let him accept the idea of losing the battle. Karel is a soldier, one of the best, and he doesn't fear death. When his irises disappear again, I don't just crack; I shatter. It's violent.

"Karel," I scold, fear gripping my stomach, "you didn't bring me here to abandon me! I forbid it! You don't have the right!"

Around me, I hear footsteps and then shouts. The world stirs while I remain still. My fingers try to stem the blood flowing from his wound, and I lock my gaze on his closed eyes, despite the tears blurring mine. The sobs I hold back make me hiccup, but I fight to suppress them. They would seem premature and pessimistic. I refuse to do as he does, to admit defeat. Not now, not after all we've endured.

Suddenly, strong arms encircle me, and despite my screams and protests, they lift me, forcing me out of the room as someone retrieves the dagger I had placed on my lap. Karel disappears from my view as I struggle. We pass Kaïs, who looks on the verge of collapse, and then I find myself in my room. The door slams, depriving me of sight, of sound. I must stay by his side, not here. My feet touch the ground again, and the grip loosens without letting me go.

"Are you hurt?"

Until I heard his voice, I didn't care who had brought me here, but now I need his help. I turn around and see Jonah watching me, his eyebrows furrowed. I realize I haven't answered him.

"I'm fine," I say.

"What happened?" he asks just as Samael and Kaïs join us.

"They took him to the royal physician. That's all we know," Kaïs tells me, looking me in the eyes.

"I need to be with him," I scream, rushing toward the door.

"Tell us what happened first," Jonah demands, stopping me from reaching the door.

I try to explain, but everything happened so quickly that my account only takes a few seconds. With each detail, my voice breaks.

"I recognized the man," I inform them finally. "I had seen him before. He was part of your faction when I arrived."

Samael's eyebrows furrow, and he exchanges a worried look with Jonah. "Are you sure?"

"Yes, I wasn't sure where I'd seen him before, but Karel confirmed my suspicions."

"What did he say?"

"I think he implied this was how he was thanked for sparing a life."

"Hrim," both soldiers say in unison.

"Hrim? Hrim?" Kaïs repeats, bewildered.

"We'll explain later," Samael replies.

"Why would he want to hurt Karel? If Karel spared him, why seek revenge?" I ask naively.

"Maybe he loved Xintia more than we thought," Jonah speculates. "We don't know. He's lost everything. For some men, death is less dishonorable. We'll search every corner of the palace, the city. We'll find him."

I nod vigorously, then plead with Jonah with my eyes to let me pass, desperate to get to Karel.

"I'll go with you," Kaïs offers.

"Please, yes," I agree.

Jonah relents and steps away from the door, then opens it. The four of us leave the room and cross the living area. I stumble when I see the blood now soaking the carpet in his office. I turn my head away just as Samael reaches the entrance.

I follow closely, eager to find Karel, but I'm forced to stop when Samael halts. I don't have time to react or even see what caused the pause, because Kaïs and Jonah step in front of me protectively.

"Your Highness," announces an unfamiliar voice. "We are arresting you for attempted murder."

My blood turns cold and drains from my body. Then an involuntary laugh escapes me at the absurdity of the statement. Kaïs and Jonah step aside slightly, and I pale when I meet the stern gaze of the man. He's not joking. Terrified, I back away.

"What kind of bullshit is this?" Jonah spits.

"She was found alone beside the prince, in possession of the dagger used to stab him. A dagger that belongs to her. The testimonies from the guards who arrived first on the scene are clear. You, put the chains on her. We're taking her to the dungeon."

"Don't you dare touch her," Jonah yells, stepping back to protect me.

"Jonah, calm down," Amadeus says, attempting to soothe him. I hadn't realized he was there.

Aware the situation could escalate, I place my fingers on Jonah's arm to get his attention. He looks at me over his shoulder, his mouth tightening into a thin line when I shake my head, signaling resistance is futile. I make him let me through and find myself facing the king's advisor.

"It wasn't me, Amadeus, I can explain—"

"Unfortunately," the man next to him interrupts, the one whose voice I didn't recognize, "I'm the one in charge of this case. As you know, you're not allowed to defend yourself. The facts reported by the soldiers are clear."

At these words, two guards move toward me but stop when Jonah draws his sword. Immediately, Samael does the same. Kaïs pulls out a dagger hidden by his jacket. The men facing us mirror their actions. Only Amadeus and I are unarmed.

Time freezes, my heart races. I'm torn between defending my honor, even if it means a bloodbath right here, and accepting my fate. I used to act only for others, but as months pass and events unfold, my principles fade. Before coming to Lapisia, provoking a conflict would have been unthinkable. Now, it seems like the better option. Yet, when I see Amadeus's pleading eyes, I clench my fists and stifle the rebellion within me.

"I'll go with them."

"No, you won't, Princess," Jonah growls.

"Yes, I will," I say, turning to him. "They're right. No matter what I say, they won't listen to me. The testimonies of these men are the only ones that matter. At least until Karel can speak for himself."

"We should have been the first ones there," he snaps.

"Karel will wake up and support your claims. In the meantime, we'll find Hrim," Samael reassures, sheathing his sword. "We believe you."

I stare at him for a long moment, and as strange as it seems, knowing they don't think I'm guilty slightly eases my sense of injustice. Not everyone condemns me.

"I'm sorry, Princess," Amadeus whispers as I pass by and they put the chains on me.

I know he is, I can feel it, but I can't ease his guilt.

"I just want to make sure Karel is okay."

"Move," one of the guards growls.

"Don't touch her!" threats Jonah.

"I just want to see my husband," I plead, struggling, "he needs me!"

"He's safe, you're forbidden from approaching him."

At these words, something snaps. The atmosphere turns electric, tempers flare. The reasonable Kalliopee vanishes.

"You're not helping him, Jonah!" Amadeus exclaims as I continue to struggle.

I strike at the guards, clawing at them even with my arms bound, yelling furiously. It's not the prospect of imprisonment that drives my rebellion; it's the prohibition against being by the side of the man I love, the inability to support him.

"Princess," Amadeus calls out, stepping in front of me.

The tone of his voice, filled with pity, makes me realize the struggle is futile. I stop thinking, breathing, resisting. I lower my head to my bare feet, and my surrender breaks a dam—the one I had been holding up with my determination to fight. A torrent of emotions overwhelms me: terror, despair, injustice, rage. But more than anything, helplessness. Helplessness in the face of my situation, helplessness regarding Karel's condition.

The guards understand I will not fight anymore, so they drag me out of our quarters. I hear Samael curse, a glass shatter, my soul splinter.

As we leave the hallway, I'm buried under the stares of the staff. Guards, chambermaids. It seems the palace has awakened to witness my arrest. For the first time since my arrival, I don't walk with my head held high. I can't bear the weight of their judging eyes, condemning me without the right to defend myself. I can't stand the hatred they feel towards me. I think only of Karel and pray for his survival.

When we reach the dungeons, the smell of confinement and dampness grabs at my throat. I stare at my dress, stained with blood. They free me from my chains, then the heavy door closes. The darkness engulfs me, and it's in this moment I finally allow the sobs to consume me, the fear to possess me. I don't care about my sentence or how long it will take for him to wake up. I will endure until he returns to me. Because if he were to die, life would no longer matter.

This is where I am. I allow myself this weakness, the thought that if Karel were to disappear, the death penalty would be a release rather than a punishment.

CHAPTER 25

KALLIOPEE

Curled up in a corner of the room, I spent the first hours of my detention brooding over the events. When helplessness chains us, the mind has a tendency to try to change the impossible. It stubbornly rewrites history, imagines what could have been altered, and the scenarios that would have followed.

If I had insisted on going out.

If I had been less absorbed in my reading.

If I had arrived earlier.

It's a way to escape reality, to refuse it. But as soon as I remember where I am, fear overwhelms me. And I start over. It's a vicious cycle. My heart hasn't slowed its pace, and the anxiety hasn't loosened its grip on my chest. I close my eyes and take a deep breath, immediately regretting it. The smell is so acrid that my stomach churns with disgust. I pass a hand over my mouth, and this time, a gasp of terror escapes me when my lips touch Karel's blood. I pull my hand away and rub it against my dress. Despite the darkness, I stubbornly try to wipe away the dry flakes. When my skin starts to burn, I stop and let my head fall against the stone wall.

I don't know how long I've been here; I've lost track of time. Despite the absence of light, I haven't been able to close my eyes, too scared of the place I'm in, but I feel like I'm running on my last reserves. My eyelids flutter heavily. My stomach growls, reminding me I've been imprisoned here for quite some time. To avoid sinking into despair, I push myself up using the damp wall. The heat is stifling, and I struggle to stand, my body too sore from hours spent in the same position.

I immediately regret it. Taking a few steps gives me an idea of the room's narrowness. The darkness had at least kept my mind from realizing this. It only takes five small steps to walk its length and one less for its width. I move blindly, feeling my way along the walls until I find myself in front of the door. Since they locked me in here, I've tried to maintain my dignity. I haven't knocked, screamed, or begged. But the longer I'm here, the more willing I am to trample my pride. I need to know that he's alive and well.

I reach the wooden door just as it suddenly swings open, causing me to fall. My body hits the ground hard, and I try to catch myself. My wrist twists from the impact, and I exhale loudly. I bite my lip to stifle the pain, but a whimper escapes despite my efforts. I have to blink to adjust to the light coming from the hallway.

A figure approaches, but the backlighting prevents me from seeing who it is. Then the figure kneels. An overwhelming relief washes over me as I begin to make out the features. The feeling is short-lived, and tears well up in my eyes when I realize it's Kaïs, not Karel.

My cousin by marriage gives me a sad smile, and my heart splits in two. It tears apart from the inside.

"How is he?"

The lack of water makes my voice rough, but Kaïs still understands me.

"He hasn't woken up," he tells me, lowering his head. "He… It's…"

"Speak!" I urge, impatient.

"The doctors are doing everything they can."

My gaze drifts to the side. I feel empty, as if hope has left me, taking with it my determination and will to live. Kaïs places his hands on either side of my face, his thumbs moving back and forth under my eyes. I realize then that I'm crying.

"Why are you here?" I ask. I'm not fooled; I sense he's hiding something from me.

"My uncle questioned the first guards who arrived. He—"

I could defend myself again, assert that there was a man there, beg Kaïs to find him, but Jonah and Samael have already promised to do that. I know Kaïs is in a delicate position and that his relation to the king prevents him from taking my side, so I just nod to show I understand what he can't tell me.

"When will my sentence be announced?"

A few seconds pass, allowing me to hear the sound of his

breath. He sighs, resigned, before letting go of my face. "Tomorrow at dawn. The execution of the punishment will follow immediately after. I'm trying to buy time, but my uncle is determined."

"How long have I been here?"

"More than a day. Night has fallen some time ago… I waited until the palace was asleep to bring you this," he says, placing a fruit in my palm.

He takes more food from his pocket and sets it in front of me. "You should eat a little…"

I shake my head.

"Kalliopee…" he says, concerned.

I'm suddenly weary of this life that never grants me rest. Constantly fighting is exhausting. All of a sudden, I feel the weight of this past year, of everything I've had to endure. Like Karel, whom I had defended against giving up, I let go. It's sudden, as if seeing the light again illuminated my mind.

"I know the sentence; it will be quicker if I don't eat."

He closes his eyes, aware I speak nothing but the truth, then stands. I'm too tired to lift my head as he takes a single step that places him behind the doorframe.

"Don't lose hope, Kalliopee."

I can't reply, and the door closes. The loud creak of the hinges covers the shattering of my heart and my barely suppressed sobs. Kneeling, I bend forward and curl into a ball. I've tried to avoid thinking about the worst every second. I've tried not to think about him because it inevitably led me to thoughts of his death. But now, hope has vanished, and I allow him into my thoughts.

"I see you, even when my eyes are closed."

Me too, my love.

Despite my eyelids squeezing shut at the painful sight, I see him. The images clash, and with all the facets that make up Karel, it's ironic the ones he shows me the least often are the ones trying to stick. Behind my closed eyes, he smiles. And then, I cry. The scream I want to release doesn't come out. My throat, parched from dehydration, can only produce a pathetic sound. I can't even scream my sorrow.

***

The door opens, but I don't flinch, too lost in my thoughts. I've spent the night in the corner of the room, without eating or sleeping. I find myself devoid of strength and fight. Despite everything that has happened to me here, I've never given up, but it seems the harm done to Karel has brought me down.

I lift my head toward the newcomer. Although I can't make out his features, I guess he's a guard of the king. He approaches me and helps me stand. Surprised by his gentleness, I blink to adjust to the light. Gradually, Darkos's face comes into focus.

"Hold on, tonight we'll leave Lapisia," he whispers.

I shake my head slowly, my stiff neck preventing me from giving more force to my gesture. "There will be war."

"There will be war regardless," he counters. "Your father will be enraged if you're executed. Stop thinking about others for once!"

I don't tell him I'm actually only thinking about myself, that war is the least of my worries, that I'm simply resigned. I pull my arm from his grasp and move towards the exit.

"Kalliopee," he calls softly.

But I've already joined the second guard, giving him no chance to convince me. I could leave, start my life over in Viridia, but my heart is broken. Karel likely will never wake up, and I'm too tired to fight. No matter my end, I'm bound to his. I just hope Jonah and Samael will avenge Karel properly.

We climb the stairs to the surface. I look down at my clothes and can only see the dirt covering my body and the dried blood staining my dress.

When we reach the throne room, I'm forced to kneel. It only takes a light pressure on my shoulders for my legs to give way. I listen to them state false facts, and my heart sinks when I learn Karel's condition is critical. An organ might have been pierced, and he's lost a lot of blood. So, I escape, I disappear. I imagine a life where the tragedies never happened, where we were spared. A world without war and grudges. It's beautiful, certainly utopian, but it's enough for me. I console myself by believing I'll find him there and we'll finally be free to be ourselves. Far from the dictates of the monarchy and society. My rebellious spirit will flourish, and his fractured soul will forget its traumas.

"Kalliopee, wife of Karel Edark, Prince of Lapisia, son of Xerios, you are accused of attempted murder. According to the law, any woman who attempts to take the life of her husband is sentenced to death. Kalliopee, you will be exposed to the public, without water or food. Time will take its toll, and when you breathe your last breath, your body will have the desert as a tomb. Thus, you will not only atone for your sins in life but also in death. You will never find rest and will eternally pay for your crime."

In the fog of my thoughts, these words seep into me. I force myself to look up. Seated on his throne, the king stares at me intensely, snapping me out of my apathy.

"Do you have so little faith in your son?" I spit out. "Or are you rushing to punish me because you know he will fight for—"

My body sways, my head spins. The king is no longer on his throne but beside me. I don't even dare to face him; I can only place a cool hand on my burning cheek. While I want to straighten my shoulders and pretend his blow hasn't affected me, I can barely manage to reposition myself on my knees. No one moves or speaks. This silence amplifies the echo of the sob climbing up my throat. My despair is audible to everyone. The king recognizes my vulnerability, sighs with satisfaction, and then walks away.

As if nothing happened, the officiant resumes his speech. Still kneeling, I feel like I'm elsewhere. I see no one, hear nothing.

I recall a scene from three years ago. I witnessed a sentencing for mariticide. My father explained that, regardless of the reasons, a woman must endure and accept her condition. She should never take the life of a superior being to save her own. I don't know if he truly believed those words, but I found them unjust. As the king's daughter, I was forced to attend the ceremony. I wished I had the courage to rebel against the judgment, to disapprove of society, but I didn't. I watched as the woman was tied to a wooden post. That summer, the heat was scorching. Three days later, her body was sunk in Lake Emaìn. She was denied the flames that carry our dead to the afterlife. She is condemned to wander the world of the living, never finding peace.

Hands grab my arms, pulling me to my feet. I blink and follow the movement. My gaze meets Kaïs's, then drops to his fingers at his waist, ready to act. I lock eyes with him and shake my head, resigned. It's useless for him to play the gallant knight. Only Karel can save me. He starts to step toward me, but Amadeus's hand on his shoulder stops him. I look away as they drag me out of the room.

Even though I want to appear strong, not letting the king affect me, sobs shake my body. The injustice is painful, splitting my heart in two and stoning it. I don't hold back my tears, even as we leave the palace. I don't dare face the citizens gathered in the streets of the citadel. I want to scream my innocence, but I know it would be in vain, that no one would hear me. The world is deaf to women.

My feet struggle to keep up, so the guards eventually carry me. I wish I had the strength to look back at the palace, because despite everything, I still hope to see Karel appear. My tears itch and irritate my skin; they're acidic. My body tenses as we slow down. I look up at a hostile crowd.

"Why are you taking the princess?"

"The *Torment of Time*," answers the guard to my right.

This is enough for the woman who asked the question to understand the charges against me. She freezes before locking eyes with mine. "That's impossible; we all know what she has done for us."

Strangely enough, the hope I feel at seeing her doubt my guilt allows me to catch my breath. I stare at her, praying she won't condemn me. Suddenly, I feel this stranger's opinion matters more than any other. I whimper as she signals the citizens with her to let us pass. I focus my attention on the ground, unable to face the weight of their stares.

We finally arrive at the platform, where they release me at the base of the steps. My legs feel heavy as I climb the two steps that lead me to the post where they will tie me up. I turn around, my breath short, and let one of the men take my hands without resistance. My head rises along with my wrists, which are bound above my head. I scan the crowd and see the king has followed us, along with his subjects. He smiles, satisfied. So, I force myself to hold back any more tears. My heart beats so hard it makes my entire body tremble. When the guard steps away, my arms grow heavy, but the ropes are so tight they don't fall.

"I'll come at nightfall. We're going back to Viridia," murmurs the voice of the second guard in my ear.

I look up at Darkos, who turns away and leaves the platform before I have the chance to tell him that yes, I will leave with him. The king has given me a reason to fight. His desire to see me die is enough for me to want to live. And suddenly, I am terrified of what awaits me here.

The crowd is ordered to disperse, and I find myself alone. The sun begins its ascent in the sky and quickly reaches its zenith. My strength leaves me, and I fear I won't last until tonight.

"Open your mouth," a voice softly instructs.

My eyes, which were struggling to stay open, do so now with a surge of energy. The stranger from earlier is in front of me, holding out a container of water. I drink from it immediately, only to be seized by a fit of coughing. She looks at me with a sorrowful expression.

"I didn't—" I try to defend myself.

"It doesn't matter… Even if you had, it would certainly be justified. Most of us refuse to believe a woman willing to suffer for a kingdom that isn't her own would be capable of taking a man's life without a legitimate reason."

"Hey you!" a voice growls.

The Lapisian woman smiles at me before sighing and turning around.

"What were you doing?" ask the guard.

"I was just spitting in the face of the one who dared to go after our prince!" she lies. "Sorry," she whispers to me, then spits in my direction to match her words.

The guard who had left his post for a few moments looks me over. I wipe my forehead with my arm still held up in the air, and he nods.

As she descends from the platform, I feel a little less alone. If a handful of people believe in my innocence, isn't that all that matters? A final hope that the world can change one day?

As the hours pass, my throat becomes so dry it burns, and my body feels heavier. The dizziness makes me nauseous, and my mind sometimes slips away. It conjures visions, sounds—I start to drift. When it's not imagining things, it plunges me into a sleep that never lasts long. I faint only to regain consciousness moments later.

I feel guilty for no longer hoping for Karel's awakening, but instead for Darkos to come. Maybe it's because the first seems too cruel as it is impossible.

Karel will never come back. Darkos is my only hope.

Chapter 26

Karel

A sharp pain jolts me out of my sleep. My breath catches, and the pain is so intense it makes me nauseous. I turn my head and recognize him immediately: Hrim. The next moment, he moves away, hiding Kalliopee from my view. I struggle to sit up, holding my breath. A groan escapes me as I press my palm against my wound. A cold veil spreads from my head to my feet. In the other room, the sounds of fighting intensify, and I hear her scream. She screams as I fall to the ground. My hands break my fall, and I try to move on all fours.

Her voice fades. I collapse, too exhausted to fight against the pain spreading everywhere. I draw on my last reserves, praying to reach her, but the more I crawl, the farther away the door gets. Her face appears to me as she falls to the ground in the other room. I stop breathing, freeze, then force myself up to go to her. Her head turns toward me, revealing her lifeless eyes. I scream in turn. I reach out, but the distance between us keeps growing.

The room tilts, the floor slopes, and my body slides in the opposite direction. I grab onto my desk, but my feet dangle over the void. I look down at the window, just waiting for me to smash through it. My grip weakens, but despite the pain, I don't give up. I glance up at the door now above me and nearly lose my grip when I see Kalliopee, suspended in midair. Then gravity becomes stronger, and she falls. My fingers release the desk, and I fall, too. We both crash through the windows. I feel no pain, hear no sound.

When I reopen my eyes, I find myself suspended in the air, in the middle of a desert, my feet dangling over empty space. The heat is suffocating. I look around, kicking my legs, but the ground is out of reach. A tornado approaches. I can't escape. I can hardly believe this is real. Still, my instincts scream at me to flee. My heartbeat intensifies as the sand grains rise.

My body is pulled toward the sandy vortex. Despite my fierce struggle, I find myself caught in its whirl. The air, thick with particles, lashes my skin, and when I manage to open my eyes, I see her. In the eye of the tornado. Her hair hides her face, but I know it's her. I reach out toward her to grab hold, but every time I come close, she suddenly moves away. I scream and fight against the elements trying to keep us apart. When her face finally appears behind her hair, I feel a deep relief as my eyes meet hers, full of life once again.

"Lapisia will end up killing me," she says sadly.

The wind stops. The tornado disappears, and gravity reasserts itself. My body crashes heavily to the ground, but I feel no pain. Gasping for breath, I struggle to breathe again, my forehead against the earth. The smell is foul, and when I open my eyes, the texture of the ground seems strange. I grab a handful of soil and rise, crumbling it between my fingers. I realize it's soaked in blood.

"Son, remember," my father's voice echoes.

I ignore it and turn around, searching for Kalliopee. My worry grows, and all I see are ruins, flames, and ashes.

"What have you done!?" she screams from afar. "What have you done!?"

Despair grips me as I raise my hands to eye level and see they are covered in bright red blood. A groan catches my attention, and I step back when I notice a child's body bleeding out at my feet. I stumble over something and fall onto a soft surface. A lifeless face is next to me, and I struggle to swallow. Panic intensifies, and I lose my breath. The ground has been replaced by countless corpses. They cover the Viridian soil. I tremble.

Kalliopee's piercing scream presses so painfully against my chest that I curl up on the ground, gasping for air. My hands try to shield me until I completely stop breathing when I realize that the danger comes from me. From me alone. I am the only one responsible. I open my eyes, aware I can't escape. Then...

I implode.

I take a deep breath, overwhelmed by terror. Terror so powerful it prevents me from filling my lungs with air. I blink rapidly, desperately trying to remember where I am. As my vision clears, my breath, which had calmed down, quickens again. My last memories rush into my mind. A sharp pain in my side makes me wince when I try to sit up, and I force myself to lie back down.

"Karel!" Vàli's voice exclaims.

I turn my head and see him.

"I'll get the doctor," he tells me, rushing to the door.

"Vàli," I call out, my voice raspy. "Kalliopee…"

Even though I've just woken up, I don't miss the way his body tenses. I'm horrified at the thought that part of my nightmare comes from my memories.

"Vàli," I panic.

"She's been arrested."

He comes closer and tells me what happened—her capture, her imprisonment, then her trial. Nausea washes over me, and I feel myself pale, but I keep my eyes open.

"When is it?" I ask weakly, my anger rising.

I suddenly start coughing, and my friend hands me a glass of water, which I down in one gulp with his help.

"It was this morning," he says nervously.

My face turns toward the window, and my heart sinks when I see the sun is setting and it will soon be night. My body moves on its own, but the wound it sustained slows it down. I push the sheet off my legs, groaning in pain, but I refuse to give in. Kalliopee needs me.

"Karel, you're in no condition."

Impatience overwhelms me, mixing with terror and anger. "Then go get her for me!" I snap, my voice much too weak. "Bring my wife back to me!"

"These are the king's orders, Karel. I can't go against them."

"But you obey me," I say, grabbing his arm. "She's not guilty of anything. Do what you have to do. If they don't cooperate, kill them all."

He steps back, shaking his head. Realizing I'm on my own, I ignore the pain in my side and get out of bed. My feet wobble, but I don't let myself be defeated. I look around for my weapon, and as I move toward it, I have to hold on to the mattress to keep from falling. My body starts trembling when I realize with helplessness that I'll never make it to her.

"Vàli, I beg you."

My voice is barely a whisper. Never in my life have I pleaded for help from anyone, not even when I went after the Viridians who killed my mother and Maha.

"Karel, if she hasn't done anything, you need to take it to the king first so he can clear her name. But if I do this without his approval, he'll—"

"If my father needs to punish someone for what you're about to do, let him punish me. You'll only be following my orders. I'm willing to pay the price; I have nothing to lose."

Every word that leaves my mouth burns my throat, but I don't care. I'll feel the pain later. Right now, I don't allow myself that luxury.

"You do, her," he replies.

He couldn't be more wrong. If my father wants to punish me for defying one of his rulings, let him, but he'll never go after her. Not anymore.

"It's over. My wife won't pay for me or anyone else anymore. Hrim attacked me in my office. If she had been allowed to speak, she would have said so. If our world wasn't the way it is, she wouldn't have suffered so much unfairly. So go get her, because if you don't, I will, and I don't care if it costs me my life," I growl, trying to sit up, pressing my palm against my wound.

I swallow the grimace of pain that tries desperately to form on my face, but Vàli surprises me by silently nodding.

"We know about Hrim. Samael and Jonah have been searching the citadel since yesterday. Your father didn't want to listen to the princess, but we did," he tells me before leaving the room.

Relieved that he's agreed to go rescue her, I let myself fall back onto the bed. Shortly after, the doctor comes to check on me. He seems pleased to see me awake and tells me the worst is behind me. I don't tell him he's wrong and that it's not over yet. When he leaves, I'm alone again and growing impatient. I'm terrified at the thought that Vàli might fail and that neither of them will make it out.

Instead of thinking of the worst, I stare at the ceiling and let the guilt consume me. There's no way I'll let the world stay as it is, no way I'll let her endure it any longer. I knew this already, but I didn't act. Not once. I only ever promised to change it without ever trying.

I imagine her fear, her loneliness. I imagine her suffering and her sense of injustice. I feel the same things right now. Even though I'm here, safe, I feel like I'm with her and facing the same dangers she is.

Time drags on, and I watch the view out the window without blinking. How many hours has she spent, exposed like that to everyone's eyes and under the scorching desert heat? Unable to help it, I imagine the ordeal she's gone through. My stomach twists, the nausea grows stronger, and I know it has nothing to do with my painful awakening or my wounds. I'm here, in this bed, safe, unable to go free her. Forced to wait for someone else to do it for me.

A weight falls on my shoulders. I'm tired of this life, of her constant suffering. I wish I could take her place, endure for her the pain inflicted on her. The injustice of her situation eats away at my insides. My duty has always been to defend my kingdom, and I've never failed in that task. I've never backed down from an enemy; I've always come out victorious in my battles. I've killed so many men I've lost count. Over time, I came to believe I was invincible. And today, I'm paying for my arrogance. Regret consumes me. I'm unable to protect the woman I love. Worse, my actions keep putting her in danger.

I get lost in my thoughts, imagining the countless ways I could change things for her, but then I'm pulled from my reverie when the door hinges creak.

Kalliopee appears, carried by a man I recognize all too well. My heart falters, shattering on the floor, and with every step my father's guard takes, it feels like the scattered pieces are reduced to ashes. I move over, not caring about my wound, and Darkos lays her on the bed beside me. I order Vàli to go fetch Mira. I don't care that it's late. He looks at me cautiously before nodding to Zaïn, who had entered without me noticing.

"You, stay here," I growl at Darkos, unable to take my eyes off my wife.

Her lips are dry, and dark purple circles accentuate the pallor of her skin. With trembling fingers, I brush the strands of hair from her face. Her eyes flutter open slightly, and a distant smile appears on her lips. She seems to be somewhere else. Her eyelids flutter heavily, then she falls asleep again. I force myself to look away from her to face Darkos.

"You're the one I told to go get the doctor," I remind Vàli.

"I'd rather stay here."

"Why is he with you?" I ask, scrutinizing my father's soldier.

I stare at him while he gazes unwaveringly at my wife's body. I'm lost and suspicious. The jealousy that flows through my veins every time I catch Kalliopee talking with him intensifies. The way he looks at her, disregarding my presence, proves that whatever he feels for her is not insignificant. Either he has a forbidden affection for her, or he's deceiving her, playing on her need to be accepted. I'm not sure which option seems worse. However, because he helped rescue her, I decide to give him a chance to justify his actions. He better take it.

"I'm on the princess's side. Everything I do is to protect her from you, the king, and Lapisia," he defends himself.

My muscles tighten at his words. Protect her from me? I pull Kalliopee's sleeping body closer to me, ignoring the pain that assails me.

"You're under my father's orders, and you think I'm going to believe you?" I growl through clenched teeth.

I wait, but he doesn't say a word. A weary sigh escapes me when I get no response.

"Vàli… take care of him."

Darkos looks away from Kalliopee as soon as Vàli draws his weapon. The royal guard does the same.

There are too many mysteries surrounding this man. Even though I hate the attention he gives to Kalliopee, I've given him the benefit of the doubt. For her, only for her. Because, even if it kills me to admit it, I know she likes him and would have resented me for standing between her and one of the few people who have shown her kindness. For months, I swallowed my bitterness and jealousy, but that's over.

I don't know if this man is acting under my father's orders, if he was tasked with getting close to Kalliopee. I'm no longer sure of anything. There are too many shadows around him, and my passivity has already cost us far too much. I've increased the number of guards assigned to our protection, I've taken on mission after mission to finally get my hands on the enemy the pawnbroker's niece spoke of, all of this without arresting anyone, without brutalizing any suspects. Deep down, I wanted to deserve Kalliopee's kindness. It was foolish, and it put us both in danger. If I had acted as I always have, Hrim would have been caught before the worst happened, and Kalliopee and I would have been spared. That's why I refuse to let this Darkos get away. Because I don't know anything about him.

"Her father saved my life. I owed it to him," he finally defends himself, cornered, as Vàli approaches.

My eyebrows furrow at this statement. I'm not sure I understand.

"King Läven?" my former instructor asks, surprised, before I can react.

"I'm a mixed-blood," the cornered man continues, lowering his weapon slightly. "He saved my life, and in return, I was assigned to infiltrate your ranks. He wanted me to rise through the ranks until I became a royal guard. The idea of this marriage was something he had been considering for years, but he wanted someone inside the palace to ensure his daughter wasn't in any danger. I keep failing. I told him not to trust you."

I struggle to process his confession. I turn my attention back to my sleeping wife. I bitterly realize he's talking about Kalliopee, which means she likely knows his true condition.

"Does she know?" I ask, still hoping he'll deny it.

"Yes, I revealed my identity to her before you left for Aquaria."

I close my eyes, unable to sort through all the thoughts rushing through my mind. He should never have reached such a high rank. He should be scavenging for scraps at this very moment, not wearing the uniform of the royal guard.

"Vàli, sheath your weapon," I order reluctantly.

Though surprised, he doesn't argue with my order.

"You want to protect her?" I ask the mixed-blood, locking my gaze with his.

He completely lowers his sword and slides it back into its scabbard before nodding. Vàli doesn't seem to understand my change in attitude, but he hasn't realized Darkos could become an indispensable asset for me.

"Then, from now on, you will report to me every move my father makes. What he does, who he sees, but more importantly: what he plans. He'll want to go after her again. If we know his moves in advance, we can counter them."

"Why would I do that? The distrust you feel toward me is mutual, Your Highness." He spits out my title with a bitterness he doesn't even try to hide and adds, "You're responsible for every injury she has suffered so far."

I try to keep my cool and not order Vàli to execute him. This man is dangerously testing my patience.

"Because you don't have a choice. What do you think my father would do if he found out your true identity? If he discovers that King Läven sent a spy into his palace, the peace my wife cherishes so much will be over."

"I'm not here to spy on the king or even to gather intelligence," he counters, "but to protect the life of the princess."

"That's been a real success," I say sarcastically. He blames me for everything, but he's no more infallible than I am, no matter what he thinks. "We need to ally ourselves. We have no choice."

This is the last chance I'm giving him, the last time I'm extending my hand. If he refuses, he's done for. Of course, there's no way my father can find out that this man is a mixed-blood, or that he was sent by the Viridians, but I can't let him live; it would be too risky.

My new ally hesitates, then nods. He understands it's time for him to leave and heads for the door. Before he goes, I can't help but give him two final orders.

"She doesn't need to know about our arrangement, and it doesn't change my first directive. Stay away from her."

He sighs in frustration, shakes his head, and leaves the room. I resist the urge to remind him he must show respect when he's in my presence, but I'm too exhausted for that. Vàli is about to speak when a knock interrupts him. After I grant permission to enter, the door opens, and Mira appears. I don't miss the bruise coloring her cheek, despite her attempt to hide it behind a curtain of hair. When our eyes meet, I'm unsettled by what I see in hers. They show nothing but resignation. It's true I didn't care much about the fate of women before. All I lived for was war. But now, I can no longer turn a deaf ear to the injustices of our world. Not when I would be willing to give my life to save my wife's. I understand why Kalliopee is so determined to change people's attitudes.

I watch Mira as she checks on Kalliopee's condition. I don't know her husband, but I've observed her closely every time she cared for my wife. She always shows kindness and gentleness. The cruelty of her situation fills me with a rage I don't try to suppress. On the contrary, I feed on it, convinced it will be necessary for the battles we will have to fight. Maybe not tomorrow, or even in a month, but someday. When the time comes.

I signal to Vàli to leave the room, asking him to stand guard until Kalliopee's judgment is overturned.

For several long minutes, the young physician tends to my wife. She tells me Kalliopee is suffering from dehydration but seems confident she will recover. I help undress Kalliopee, and she hands me damp cloths, which I apply to her body. My eyes don't leave my wife's flushed face, her eyelids still closed.

"You need to give her something to drink regularly. Something sweet, if possible, but start with small amounts," she instructs me once we've cooled Kalliopee down.

I nod in thanks, and she asks if I need treatment for my wound. I decline abruptly. No woman, except my own, is allowed to touch me.

Mira slips away after telling me she'll return at dawn. Then I lie down on my uninjured side and drape an arm over Kalliopee's bare stomach. I stare at her profile until her breathing slows. I don't take my eyes off her, and an unpleasant sensation creeps into the depths of my being. An anxiety that weighs down my stomach and tightens my throat. My breathing becomes uneven. I let go of her face and shift my position on the bed, my back against the mattress. My eyes trace the ceiling.

I need to talk to my father.

I can't keep playing this charade.

CHAPTER 27

KAREL

It's late morning the next day when Kalliopee fully regains consciousness. Her lips are still cracked from dehydration, and her skin is still reddened from the sun, but her fever has gone down. I pulled the sheet up to cover her nakedness, but it slips off as soon as her body turns toward me. Her eyes study me with an emotion she doesn't even try to hide. She grimaces when her teeth bite down on her lower lip but doesn't stop doing it. I open my arms to her, and she immediately curls up in them. Her exhaustion makes her movements heavy and awkward, causing me to swear when she accidentally presses on my wound. She tries to pull away from me, but I place a hand on the back of her neck to keep her in place. Her fingers grip my shoulders as her forehead buries itself in my neck. She smells of sweat and dust, but I'm not bothered by it at all. All I want is to have her close to me.

Soon, her body trembles against mine. "I was so scared you were going to die," she manages to say through her sobs.

"I'm here," I reassure her in a whisper. "I told you everything would be okay."

She pulls back, and our breaths mingle. My eyes open, and I take in her face. She looks both relieved and desperate.

"I'm here," I repeat.

"I thought I'd never see you again," she says, her voice almost inaudible.

My hand clutches her neck fiercely, and I'll never admit it to her, but I was also afraid I'd never see her again. I remember her tears as the darkness overtook me, the fear I felt. I'm a warrior. I've known battles all my life, even though it displeased my father, who wanted me to be a politician, not a soldier. I've often found myself in tight spots, and I've come close to death many times, but I never feared not seeing another day; I think I even didn't care about dying in combat. I had nothing tying me to life. This time was different. I was terrified of never waking up again, of never being able to kiss her again, of never being able to love her again.

She pulls back slightly, searching my eyes. She often does this when I can't find the words, and while I usually prefer to look away, this time, I let her find what she's looking for without resisting. Her eyebrows furrow, and she moves her face a bit farther away. Does she realize how scared I was? Does she understand my life hangs by *her* thread now? That she's all that matters?

"I love you," I confirm.

She shakes her head, clearly frightened by those words. "Don't say that to me, not until you're completely out of danger. Your words sound too much like goodbyes or apologies."

This time, it's my eyebrows that furrow. "I'm not the only one who nearly died, Kalliopee. I thought I lost you. So don't stop me from—"

She shakes her head, then closes her eyes. She does it with such force that tiny wrinkles form on her eyelids.

"Please, don't say them anymore on days when the future is too uncertain."

"Every day is uncertain," I counter. "That's how our life is."

"Not as much as now. Please. Promise me."

"I promise," I concede.

She finally kisses me, and I can tell by its brevity and her awkwardness that her condition is making her uncomfortable. I don't push her and instead smile, caressing her cheek with my thumb.

I know for certain I won't be able to keep this promise. Because if our separation were imminent, there's no way I wouldn't tell her everything she means to me, how much I love her, and especially how much she has made Lapisian air breathable for me.

***

As Kalliopee falls asleep, a knock on the door pulls me from my thoughts. Vàli appears and announces the arrival of Amadeus and one of the royal judges, who enter immediately. The advisor gives me a relieved smile, while the man accompanying him, Judge Evon, looks at me sternly.

"Your Highness, you have taken the princess away from her punishment," he immediately accuses.

I stare at him, counting to ten in my head to keep my anger from getting the better of me, then respond as calmly as possible, "A punishment that was unnecessary. My wife had nothing to be blamed for, especially not for my injury. I'm sure you've heard this information, but you chose not to pay attention to it."

The man steps closer to the bed, forcing me to sit up, and glares at me defiantly. He's fully taking advantage of my condition, but there's no doubt that once I'm able to stand on my own two feet, he will be much less arrogant.

"You had no right to go against the orders of the Crown."

"The Crown's orders were rushed."

Amadeus, who has stayed in the background, tenses when the impatience in my voice bounces off the walls of the room.

Judge Evon continues, "The guards' testimonies were clear. The princess was near your body, dagger in hand."

"If you had listened to her, she would have told you what happened. You would have known there was an intruder in our palace. But you were quick to condemn her."

Judge Evon shakes his head. "We can't trust women. That's why the laws of the Union of the Five exist—to protect us from their treachery. How many judges would have been swayed by their pleas, their claims of innocence, their excuses? Don't question the world we've built, Your Highness."

I let out a disdainful sigh. The more days pass, the more my thinking evolves, and the more pronounced the disgust I have for our society becomes.

"The princess is innocent," Amadeus interrupts us. "The prince's testimony brings a new element to this case. There's no need to waste more time. And I'm certain His Highness understands the value of our laws."

Evon stares at me for a long moment before finally agreeing to release Kalliopee from her punishment. He reminds me, however, that my status doesn't exempt me from obedience, and then he leaves the room. When only Amadeus is left, I think about my father, and more than anger, it's a deep loneliness that overtakes me. I lower my eyes to Kalliopee, still asleep, and the question slips from my lips before I can stop it, "Where is my father?"

"In his office…"

"Did he come by?"

"While you were unconscious?"

I nod, but Amadeus shakes his head, and the answer twists my stomach. The advisor doesn't say anything more, gives me a sympathetic look, and then leaves as well, wishing us a speedy recovery. Once the door closes, I stare, a little dazed, at the wall in front of me. Then I look down at Kalliopee, who slowly opens her eyes. From the sad smile spreading across her lips, I can tell she was pretending to sleep and probably heard everything.

"I'm sorry for you," she whispers.

I kiss her forehead, grateful to have such a devoted wife, and tell her to rest.

No matter what my father puts her through, she doesn't judge the child still buried inside me, the one who just wants to be loved by him.

***

After a few days, we've both regained our strength. We've been able to leave the bed we were confined to and return to our rooms. Taking advantage of Kalliopee being with Amadeus in his library, I make my way to my father's quarters.

As I pass through the double doors under the watchful eyes of his guards, including Darkos, I head straight to his office. Quickly, one of his attendants steps up beside me. "Your Highness, His Majesty is busy."

I stop and turn my face toward her. "Do you value your position? Then change rooms and act as if you didn't see me. Because I assure you, I don't care if he's busy; I'm going in."

She glances nervously at the door in front of us, then steps aside. Once I'm finally alone, I close the distance between us. My hand grips the handle, and the door swings open.

My father lifts his head, looks at me for a brief moment, then returns to his correspondence. I'm torn between laughing and crying. His attitude doesn't surprise me. Yet, it hurts. Doesn't he know all that I've sacrificed for him and his thirst for vengeance? I've left a part of my soul behind for it.

"Was I not worth the trip?" I ask bitterly. "Is the palace so big you couldn't even bother to visit me?"

Not once, not even before I woke up, did he come to my bedside. Worse, he took advantage of my vulnerability to condemn Kalliopee.

"I'm working on an important matter," he says, meeting my gaze with his.

The hardness in his expression creates a chasm inside me. Not just because he's looking at me so coldly, but because that's what I see when I look in the mirror. Is this what Kalliopee sees when she looks at me? Emptiness and indifference?

"I'm trying to correct your mistakes. Aquaria," he clarifies.

I then realize that, despite his promises, Amadeus must not have intercepted Nokken's letter. There's no point in denying I turned down the deal my father proposed to the Aquarian king. Knowing he's likely planning to assure the king he'll still get Kalliopee in exchange for his help, I tell him my decision regarding my wife's status, "I'm going to summon the council."

"And for what?" he asks in a voice heavy with weariness.

"Kalliopee will remain my wife but will be freed from her constraints."

His burst of laughter twists my stomach and crushes my heart. It's filled with contempt. "And what right do you have to do that?"

"She is my wife; I have every right over her," I remind him.

He pauses before a triumphant smile spreads across his face. "Not the right to free her from her condition. Only the king can change the laws, not a prince."

I don't know how to respond to that. He's right, of course. But after everything that's happened, there's no way I'm going to let Kalliopee be in danger just because she's a woman. Because she's *my* wife. She was punished instead of me, condemned without the right to defend herself. What's next? My father seems determined to make her suffer. I thought he would calm down once our union was sealed, but I sense he's losing patience, and I won't be able to delay the inevitable much longer.

"Stop going after her. Kalliopee is my wife."

"None of this would've happened if you'd get her pregnant like I ordered. Don't forget what led us here, son."

"Father," I try, my anger rumbling inside me.

"You've strayed from your path," he spits out, disappointed.

"Which path?!" I snap. "The path of hatred and destruction?"

"The path of justice!"

My eyebrows furrow as his face contorts. For years, I lived through him and his emotions. I believed it was the only way, but it's now clear that his crusade has gone too far.

"This isn't justice," I try to reason with him.

"It's not what you thought a few months ago! She's manipulating you to the point you forget it's what you wanted! To the point you forget your mother and Maha!"

I raise my eyebrows, and a bitter laugh escapes my lips. "You're the one manipulating me. You're mad, convinced this will change something, but you're wrong. If you go through with this, you won't feel any better; you'll just be even more insane, because it won't bring them back! Don't go that far, Father. I beg you."

My muscles tense in the desperate hope that he'll relent.

"Get her pregnant, or she's useless. Whether you like it or not, we're going to see this project through."

My breath quickens, and I shake my head, looking into his crazed eyes. I search for a spark in him that might convince me all is not lost, but it's in vain. Realizing I won't get anything from him, I turn away and head for the door.

"I won't hesitate, Karel," he warns me. "And if you stand in the way of me and Viridia, you will no longer be my son."

My hand tightens around the doorknob, and I close my eyes, taking a deep breath. Hasn't he already lost enough? Doesn't he realize I'm still here? A thought, one that's been creeping into my mind for some time now, slips in again. "Haven't I stopped being your son since that day?"

Only silence answers me.

I open the door and leave his office.

When I was a child, my father was a joyful man. He was

strict, it's true, but he was also loving. However, when my mother and Maha were murdered, that part of him disappeared. Only his worst traits remained. Now, I know his heart died with them, and I'm not enough. Every step I take away from him fuels my anger. He doesn't understand what I've done for him, the rage that consumed me, that I couldn't shake on the day he ordered me to execute those men.

When I pass Amadeus, he looks at me and easily understands it's too late.

I walk down the long hallway that leads me out of my father's quarters and immediately spot Darkos. I give him a warning look, silently telling him not to betray me, and he subtly nods. I'm going to need to find a way for him to get information to me.

The farther my steps take me from my father, the closer they bring me to her, and the more I realize that while he always kept me by his side in the hopes of manipulating me, Kalliopee has tried to make me a better person.

I doubt she will ever succeed. I am what I am.

I act before I think.

I don't forgive; I condemn.

I hate more than I love.

But, despite everything, she stays. And, despite everything, I want to be worthy of the goodness of her soul. I don't desire the throne, but ascending to it would allow me to shape the world in her image.

CHAPTER 28

KAREL

It's only been two weeks since we returned to our rooms. Far too little time for another scandal to have overshadowed the recent events. Since then, Kalliopee has been on her guard. Whatever she does, she feels watched and judged. I've tried to reassure her, but it's been in vain. And yet, like her, I notice the heavy, suggestive looks the staff gives her. My testimony cleared her, but distrust remains. Only the attitude of my men hasn't changed, and that of Sienna, whom I caught scolding the maids under her command. I was relieved to know that, in my absence, someone ensures Kalliopee is respected. In any case, I won't tolerate any remarks or hostile looks within the walls of our quarters. In the rest of the palace, my father is the master, but here, it's our home.

Vàli has ordered me to rest. He has refused to let me back in the barracks until I've fully recovered. I'm almost there. My side no longer pulls, and the stitches can soon be removed. I'm pacing around, and being constantly within the palace walls only feeds my paranoia. I'm on high alert, ready to counter any attack. My only consolation is that at least this way, I can ensure Kalliopee's safety.

She has fully recovered, but I know it will take time for the inner wound to heal. Sometimes, I find myself watching her when she doesn't notice. Despite her injuries, her soul remains untarnished. She stays good and kind. She confessed to me one night, when insomnia kept us both awake, that she regretted having given up, even for a moment. She added that she thought herself weak. She's so far off the mark. How can she not see she has the aura of a true warrior? Nothing ever darkens her heart, and her determination is matched only by her courage.

Amadeus wasted no time joining me after my meeting with the king. He told me he had assured my father that my love for Kalliopee wouldn't distract me from my duties. I hated him for dismissing this truth I had finally managed to admit. He scolded me when I lost my temper, saying it was the only way to protect us. If I'm useless to my father, he won't hesitate to get rid of me, and then Kalliopee will be at his mercy. If I run away, he'll find me. I'm not afraid of living as a fugitive, spending my life in hiding, but Kalliopee deserves better. Her punishment was, after all, only meant to punish me. I refused Nokken's help, and she isn't getting pregnant. I'm delaying my father's plans, and he's proving his threats aren't just empty words. He didn't know what the consequences of this attack would be for me, but he hoped if I survived, it would bring me back to my senses when I woke up.

Kalliopee is in our bedroom when I leave my office. Tonight, the palace will host many guests to celebrate my birthday. But before that, we will have to parade through the streets of the citadel. While this tradition has always been a mere formality for me each year, today, it feels like I have a lead weight in my stomach. I have a feeling this first public appearance since her condemnation will be revealing. If my people despise her, I fear I'll harbor a hatred for them as deep as the one I feel for the Viridians.

As I'm about to head to our bedroom, a knock on the front door stops me in my tracks. I head over and, when I open it, find the hallway completely empty. My eyes fall on a piece of parchment on the floor. I bend down to pick it up and carefully unfold it once I'm in my office, away from prying eyes.

The tower.

I crumple the note and don't linger. I cross the living room and don't even stop when Kalliopee calls out to me from the doorway of our bedroom.

I walk calmly, though I want to run. I'm not naive; the guard wouldn't put us in danger unless the information he had to pass along was critical. No one tries to block my way; they're all far too busy preparing what needs to be prepared in the palace.

As I cross the small courtyard that leads to the tower, the heat stifles me, and my steps slow. I'm determined, but also scared. Kalliopee is changing my very nature. I've always been brave and confident, but now I'm more cautious. I reach the tower and head toward the staircase on my right.

Darkos is waiting for me there, standing rigid. He greets me with a nod, then briefly checks behind me before locking his gaze onto mine. I scrutinize him carefully, looking for differences I'd never noticed before. Now that I know his origins, I can see what marks him as a Viridian. His complexion is just a bit paler than mine, but his features are also finer. My eyebrows rise; I'm eager to learn the reasons for our meeting.

"We've found him. The king was also looking for him," he informs me.

I nod. I suspected my father was also trying to track down Hrim.

"He wants to offer him a reward in exchange for his disappearance," Darkos adds. "If he leaves the city, people will think you lied to protect your wife."

"Where is he?"

"At *Yel Naash*, a tavern near the east wall of the city. He hasn't left Lapisia; he must be afraid of getting caught."

I've heard of this place before. The name suits it, since, like a mirage, it always disappears and reappears elsewhere. When we were young, it was our game—finding it. Over time, that pastime lost its appeal. The customers are small-time crooks who don't really disrupt the city's life.

"Who knows about this?"

"Just me. I was about to inform the king."

"Very well. By the time you get there, it'll be too late. Lapisia will know Kalliopee is innocent and I'm not trying to cover for her."

I nod at him, still grateful to have him on our side. He's an invaluable ally, I have to admit. I decide to stifle my jealousy and trust him. If Kalliopee hasn't told me about this man's bloodline yet, there must be a reason. Maybe he made her promise to keep his secret. I laugh to myself, suddenly feeling pathetic for trying to come up with excuses for her silence.

I turn away without saying anything more and head to the barracks, hoping to find my brothers there. My hand stays firmly on the hilt of my sword as I walk through the streets. Unfortunately, when I get there, I see they're not around. I assume they're probably searching the city for Hrim. Impatience overtakes me. If I don't hurry, there's no doubt my father's guards will help the man who was once my friend leave the city, and he won't pay for the affront he's done to us.

I cross the citadel, on high alert. The sand that has settled on the cobblestones crunches under my feet, and a bead of sweat trickles down under my collar. The heat is stifling, and my agitation makes it harder to catch my breath. I finally reach the east wall and scan the street. It only takes me a moment to spot the tavern. It's not very big, but the noise coming from inside tells me it must be crowded with patrons.

I push open the door, and while the sounds grow louder, they gradually die down as the faces turn in my direction. Soon, the cheers turn into murmurs.

I survey the room, looking for the one who betrayed me, not once, but twice. Everyone stares at me, their hands moving to their belts, ready to draw their weapons. I smile, then regain my composure.

"Gentlemen, I'm looking for a man named Hrim. About this tall," I say, raising my hand to my eyebrows. "He's young, has a grudge against the Crown, and walks like a soldier."

A few coughs tell me they're waiting for more.

"A thousand gold pieces to anyone who gives me information."

Two patrons step aside, and a predatory grin spreads across my face as Hrim is revealed to me.

"Gentlemen," I add theatrically, "you will all receive a purse today, as I'm feeling generous."

I take a step forward as Hrim steps back. He reaches for his belt and pulls his sword from its sheath. Unfortunately for him, it seems the promised gold has bought the loyalty of the men here, as two of them push him toward me after forcing him to drop his weapon.

"You have so little honor that you won't even give a man a chance to defend himself against you?" he spits out when our faces are so close they're almost touching.

"Who said you're a man, Hrim?"

Hatred boils in my veins, but I force it back down. "You betray your brothers-in-arms for a woman, you stab me in my sleep, and you dare speak to me of honor?"

I study him closely; the boy I once knew is a far cry from the one facing me now. When we were young, I thought nothing could ever tarnish our friendship. Sure, I wasn't as close to him, but I still believed we were like family. A team. The hatred I feel for him now matches the affection I once had and the weight of his betrayal.

"You want a man-to-man fight?" I ask. "Is that what you want?"

He nods, not losing the darkness that consumes him. I should be worried, understanding he has nothing left to lose, but the opposite happens. I finally have a chance to put an end to the threat he poses, to make him pay for the suffering Kalliopee had to endure. I push him away and signal for him to leave the premises. When I'm facing his back, the urge to draw my blade and stab him like a traitor grips me, but I resist.

I am not him.

I have more honor.

We make it outside, and without delay, I shrug off my jacket before drawing my weapon from its sheath. I signal to the man holding Hrim's sword to give it back to him, and he complies. My former comrade takes it and smiles with an arrogance that will be his downfall, I'm sure of it. He faces me, and like two wild animals, we circle each other. Hrim is good in a fight, but I know I'm much better, even with a freshly healed wound. Besides, judging by his appearance, he's sleep-deprived and undernourished. He looks as frail as a child.

The men around us are already cheering, and this time, it's me who smiles arrogantly. They're chanting my name, not his. He's alone. He realizes it, and his shoulders slump.

Dying is terrible.

Dying alone is cruel.

I take advantage of this calm before the storm to gauge his state a bit more. His limbs are shaking, but I can't tell if it's from exhaustion or the tension between us. All I know for sure is that he's not holding his weapon firmly—a flaw he never corrected, despite my reprimands. I once swore to him one day it would cost him his life. I never imagined it would be me delivering the final blow. Because, yes, I'm confident, and I'm certain I'll come out victorious in our duel. Yet, rather than ending this moment quickly, I need to understand how he got to this point, how he could deceive us and want me dead. It's foolish; it won't lessen the feeling of betrayal, but I need to know his motivations. He was one of my brothers. I fought alongside him for many years. I need these answers.

"I spared you. When I found out you were involved with Xintia, I didn't say anything, Hrim. I thought she had manipulated you, and I chose to forgive you. So why?"

"What do you think? That I'm so naive I didn't realize she wanted to use the information she got from me? I knew, but I loved her."

"She didn't love you. Xintia only loved herself."

"With time, she would have loved me; I'm sure of it, but you took her from me."

He's wrong. Xintia would have discarded him as soon as he was no longer useful. She always acted that way, with everyone, for as long as I can remember. The only person she never lost interest in was me, but not because she had any affection for me. Only because she hoped to one day become the Princess of Lapisia.

"I knew what you put her through. Not content with finally getting rid of her, you had to humiliate her further by forcing her to kneel before that Viridian woman. All for what? To run her through with your blade and throw her body into the desert?"

There's no sadness in his voice. Just an immense rage. I then understand the depth of his grief. When anger consumes us, it's because the pain is unbearable.

"I dug a grave worthy of her with my own hands, but after that, all I had left was my pain. Pain I nurtured until I was given an opportunity for revenge."

The arrogant smile he gives me shows that he's not finished yet.

"But you're so naive. You didn't even think to ask me about what came of my investigation into the pawnbroker. I came back to tell you I'd found the girl, but you didn't give me the chance. She had the daggers, and no one knew the princess didn't have them anymore. You had told us often enough no one was to know. I had to act. Your death for Xintia's. And, as a bonus, that Viridian woman of yours."

The sound of boots pounding reaches us, and the crowd splits in two to reveal my father's men, along with Zaïn and Jonah.

"Your Highness, we're here to arrest him," the leader informs me.

Darkos, standing a little behind, plays his part perfectly.

"Alas, this man is mine," I counter.

The guard takes a step toward me, but I point my blade at his sternum. "Treason against the Crown. He wants a duel instead of a trial," I tell him. "He's mine."

"These are the king's orders," he defends himself.

"Then draw your sword; my men are eager to join a fight."

He scrutinizes me cautiously, probably wondering if my words are just meant to change his mind or if my threat is real. To support what I'm saying, Zaïn draws his weapon, quickly followed by Jonah.

"Samael went to find Vàli; they're on their way," Jonah whispers to me. "We ran into the mixed-blood while he was going to warn your father."

I glance at Darkos, who puts his hand on his weapon, just like the rest of the royal guards. I wonder whose side he would be on if the fight were to break out. Unfortunately, I won't get the chance to find out because their commander gives in, releasing the hilt of his sword and taking a step back.

"A duel?" he asks Hrim.

I look at Hrim, who nods before turning his attention back to me. Without warning, he lunges at me. I manage to block his strike by shifting to the right. The cheers have died down only to resume immediately, even louder.

Hrim charges at me again, but once more, our blades clash, and I move away. I let him wear himself out, let him get out of breath. He tires quickly, and I can tell he's on the edge, ready to fall. I'm just waiting for that moment, for him to go down. Despite the pull I feel at my side, I don't weaken. With a sweep of my sword, I stop him from reaching me, repeating the move each time. He's predictable, and with every strike he attempts, he puts more force into it, draining what little energy he has left.

As he raises his weapon above his head and lunges at me again, I counter his attack, and his blade falls to the ground. What did I say? It would be his undoing. Then, I shove him with a kick to the stomach. He crashes to the ground with a groan. I put more strength into it than I thought, and the impact seems to knock the wind out of him. I feel a sharp pain in my wound, but I hold back a curse. My hatred guides my actions, making me numb to the pain.

Still on his back, he coughs, growls, and rages. Then, he rolls onto his side to get on all fours and reaches out with his fingertips for his weapon on the ground. But he doesn't get up; instead, he starts laughing. Perplexed, I tense up. A madman is a dangerous man. I look at the crowd that has gathered, worried he might attack an innocent. My eyes meet Jonah's, who seems to share my fears.

It's at this moment that Vàli and Samael appear. I'm unpleasantly surprised to see Kalliopee with them. I shake my head in disapproval, and my wife immediately looks away.

Why did she have to join them? I remember all too well her reaction during the execution of her attackers. If she thinks she can stop me this time, she's mistaken.

Because of Hrim, Kalliopee nearly died. I won't forgive him for that.

CHAPTER 29

KALLIOPEE

As I make my way through the palace in search of Karel, I catch sight of Jonah and Zaïn hurrying across the entrance hall. We'll soon have to parade through the streets of the city, but without the main person involved, this procession would be pointless. In truth, having him close to me would help me feel less anxious about going out. Even though I've regained my strength, my spirits still haven't recovered from recent events. Some days, I pretend it doesn't affect me, and other days, it's harder to keep up the illusion. Anxiety twists my stomach—the fear he's still in danger, and the thought I might end up back in the dungeons, put on display like a criminal.

Samael appears a few moments later, apparently looking for Karel as well. "Princess," he greets me as he walks past, heading down the corridor I just came from.

"Have you seen Karel?" I ask him.

Samael stops but doesn't turn to face me. We're only a few steps apart. He seems stiff, tense, and without answering, he resumes his pace. His reaction worries me, and I catch up to him.

"What's going on?" I ask him.

He turns his head away, clearly eager to get away from me without giving any information. My hand rests on his forearm, hoping to stop him. He stops again, and although he only shows me his profile, I can see his eyelids slowly lower in resignation.

"I'm looking for Vàli."

"Why?"

He doesn't answer me.

"Where is Karel?" I ask.

Again, he remains silent.

"Where is my husband?" I repeat, impatience creeping into my voice.

"We found Hrim," he says simply, before continuing on his way.

Determined, I grab the hem of my dress and follow him quickly.

"You can't come with me," he tells me.

"Well, that's exactly what I'm doing," I counter.

"You should go back to your rooms," he insists.

I don't listen to him. Wherever Karel is and whatever he's doing, I don't want to be left out. Samael no longer insists I stay in my place, probably realizing it would be futile. With every step we take, my worry grows. I fear seeing the side of Karel that, at times, frightens me so much. When he lets madness take over, I'm always scared he'll remain in his darkness forever, that the storm won't calm down and he'll be lost to me for good. I've made him promise, every time. *Wherever you are, come back to me*. But what if one day he can't?

We make our way through the palace to the royal library. Samael stops there, and before I have the chance to ask him anything, he goes inside. I follow him and find Vàli and Kaïs in the middle of a discussion. My cousin by marriage straightens, all smiles, then puts on a serious expression.

"Vàli, we've got him. Karel is already there."

The older and probably the most experienced of my husband's men gets up immediately before joining us.

"Kalliopee," Kaïs calls out as I'm about to leave the room. "You should stay here."

I appreciate his concern, but unfortunately, I can't consider his advice. I give him a small smile before stepping through the doorway, Vàli and Samael on my heels. I let the latter go ahead of me, aware I don't even know where we're going.

"Kaïs is right, Your Highness," Vàli murmurs as we cross the small garden leading to the tower. "You should stay in the palace."

"Why? Because half the people of Lapisia still want me dead? Or because my husband is about to viciously execute the man who tried to kill him?"

Vàli glances at me in surprise before furrowing his brow as we enter the tower. "Because what you're about to see might damage what's left of your innocence."

"Vàli…" I sigh. "My innocence is gone. It was taken by Xintia, by my father, by King Xerios, by Aquaria. Even by Karel. Believe me, there's nothing left to damage."

Samael glances over his shoulder, and our eyes meet. I can't decipher the look in his eyes. I'm not sure if it's compassion or pity.

As we walk along the ramparts, cheers reach us. A crowd has gathered, and Samael forces them to let us through. No one protests. When Vàli stops, he steps aside. Karel's eyes land on me, but I look away immediately. I hadn't even thought about how he'd react to seeing me here. My attention shifts to a man on the ground, laughing like a madman. I don't need to see his face to recognize him. A quiet rage fills me as he stands. My throat tightens, my fists clench tightly as he rises to his full height. My breath quickens, and I've never felt such hatred for someone before. In my memory, I see Karel, lying motionless on the ground after Hrim's attack. I remember the chasm that took over my heart when I thought he was dead.

My body moves on its own. I only realize it when Samael blocks my path with his arm. Hrim turns toward me and seems to recognize me. The gleam in his eyes terrifies me so much that the air grows thin. He hates me as much as I hate him. He takes a step toward me, but before he can take a second, he falls heavily to the ground.

With a calmness that doesn't fool me, my husband stares down at the man who, not so long ago, was his friend. No matter what he says, his brother-in-arms' betrayal affected him deeply. It was evident in how his gaze clouded over whenever Hrim's name was mentioned. I stare at Hrim, motionless, still on the ground. Unlike Karel, I wasn't close to this man. So, what I feel for him isn't ambiguous.

A hint of euphoria runs through my veins at seeing him so at Karel's mercy. My own emotions frighten me. I've always felt the need to understand people, even the worst ones. Some were driven by nothing but boundless sadism, but today, for the first time, I don't care what pushed Hrim to do his worst. All I want, from the deepest part of my soul, is for him to suffer as much as Karel did. For him to beg. For him to agonize as much as I did.

Karel seems to read what's happening in my eyes, which have found his again, as he throws his sword aside, grabs the traitor by the hair, and exposes his throat to me. I break eye contact with the prince and easily recognize one of the daggers that caused us so much misery. Karel shows it to him, and Hrim's eyes widen.

"What a shame that it's you it finally kills, huh?"

Hrim takes his eyes off the blade and locks them onto mine. I don't care what I see in him; I don't give a damn about the fear that flashes through his eyes and radiates from his whole being. I drink it in, ravenous. The man's pupils dilate, then the light disappears. His face twists, turning pale, and I lower my eyes, drawn to the crimson river gushing from his throat with a gurgling sound. Inside me, it's an implosion. I feel so many things that I scare myself. Time seems to freeze, the cheers of the crowd have ceased, while the desert sweeps over the scene with a warm breath.

Karel lets go of the strands of hair he was holding, and Hrim's lifeless body falls to the ground. The prince's lips move, but I can't make out the words he's saying.

Hrim is dead. Karel is safe.

This realization twists my stomach, and I'm disgusted with myself for feeling a primal need to merge with my husband at the thought of this man's death. Seized by a jolt of remorse, I take a step back and turn away. I need to get away from here; I need to breathe. The sounds around me come back into focus, assaulting my ears.

I push through the crowd, and a glance behind me reassures me—Samael is close behind. I'm not suicidal, and I know leaving here alone could be dangerous. Without knowing why, I head toward the storage room that leads to the palace's underground passages. My steps become shorter, quicker. I'm running away from the satisfaction I feel, from the Kalliopee I'm becoming.

I finally reach the door, push it open with a swift movement, and lift the trapdoor to access the basement. The pounding of Samael's boots confirms he's escorting me. I descend and find myself in the dark. Now that I'm safe, I allow myself a moment to pause. My palm rests against the damp stone, and I take a breath.

"Kalliopee," Karel's voice growls from behind me.

I jump, surprised to find he's the one who followed me. His warm fingers grip my elbow, forcing me to face him. Before he can see the emotions overwhelming me, I grab his lips with mine, violently. I don't know which one of us I'm trying to distract. He stiffens, then pushes me away roughly. His hands hold my shoulders, pressing me against the cold stone wall.

"What are you—"

"Kiss me," I beg him, desperate.

I realize then the kiss was meant to distract me from my feelings.

He shakes his head, probably in confusion. I'm not used to begging him to give me an escape, but this time, I need it. I just want the noise in my head to quiet down, even if only for a moment.

"Kalliopee," he says with authority. "I told you, you can talk to me."

I face him again. For a brief moment, it feels like everything stops—my breathing, my heart, my thoughts. I'm motionless, unable to move or say a word. Then, it all comes flooding back. Hrim's death, my anger, my satisfaction, and the shame my own emotions provoke.

"About everything?" I ask, my voice dripping with bitterness.

He seems surprised by my tone, and my guilt only grows stronger. None of this is his fault—I'm angry at myself. I just don't know how to contain the rage that's boiling inside me. I was taught to choose my words carefully, to be kind, to behave like a princess. I was constantly told not to raise my voice, not to pass judgment, because that was my place. I was just supposed to watch and smile. I was never really able to do that, it's true, but now, this is different. I don't know how to express what I'm feeling, or even if I have the right to.

"Everything," he murmurs anyway.

I close my eyes, letting the emotions wash over me, knowing that if I don't, they'll destroy me. Then, without daring to look at him, I let out what I'm feeling.

"I'm relieved," I admit, "I feel a sick satisfaction at having watched the life drain out of his body. I feel a twisted pleasure knowing you were the one who took it from him. If you only knew how scared I was that day, how much I've hated him since then. I've never felt this way before, not until today. Not even Xintia—despite everything I went through because of her—made me hate her as much as I hate him. But now… now… What does that make me? What does—"

My eyes reopen, unable to finish my sentence, because I finally understand the way Karel reacts when someone hurts me. I finally understand the rage that consumes him whenever I'm in danger.

I drown in the depths of his eyes before he takes my lips. His kiss is possessive, hungry. I respond with an increased ferocity. I don't care that his men are right above us when I moan against his mouth, unbuckling his belt. I don't care if they can hear us when he growls into my neck, kneading my breast through the fabric. I taste him, devour him as he lifts the hem of my dress and removes my underwear. His fingers scorch my skin, then he bites my lip hard when I grab onto his hips. I notice then that he's trembling. Immediately, I pull away from him. He's in pain, but he doesn't dare say it. I can tell by the way he's looking at me.

"Don't push me away. I need this as much as you do," he says, his voice rough, only intensifying my desire.

I hesitate for a brief moment, then I lower his pants. Picking up the kiss where we left off, he lifts me, and my back slams against the wall.

"I need this," he growls against my lips as he thrusts into me, ripping a moan of relief from me.

With our foreheads pressed together, our mouths brushing, and our breaths mingling, there's no room for gentleness. There's no room for words, for apologies, for regrets or remorse. There's no room for rage anymore, for Hrim.

There's only room for him and me and our need to become one. With each of his thrusts, I feel whole, fulfilled. And I transform the hatred I felt for that dead man into love for the one facing me.

CHAPTER 30

KALLIOPEE

My breath catches with every hairpin that Sienna secures in my hair. With my little escapade, we've run out of time for my beauty preparations. As she places my crown, which is similar to Karel's, I look at myself in the mirror and catch my servant's reflection.

"You're stunning," she compliments me.

I give her a soft smile and take a deep breath. When we returned to the palace, the staff was rushing back and forth, busy preparing the ballroom. Karel walked me to our quarters before going to get his wound treated. The searing kiss he gave me needed no words. I often criticize him for not saying enough, but now that I understand what he felt when he wanted Xintia and the men who attacked me dead, I know words would be too much and still wouldn't convey enough. He loves me—I don't need a big speech when he offers me such meaningful actions.

I straighten, smooth the hem of my dress, and leave the room. Karel is already there, dressed in his immaculate uniform. Today, my outfit is devoid of color, just like his. Made of draped fabric, it has a V-neck that reveals the valley of my breasts, but it still doesn't seem indecent. It's fitted at the waist, giving the impression that my legs are long and my body is slender. From the way Karel looks me up and down, I can tell he likes it.

I walk over to him, drinking in the sight he offers me. A sash crosses his chest, and I adjust it when I stand in front of him. I do it carefully, removing the lint that's clung to the fabric, and I lock eyes with him as he places his warm palms on my bare arms. Even though he told me he's fine, I need him to confirm it to me out loud.

"It was just a few stitches," he reassures me immediately.

I exhale, relieved, then melt into his embrace. With my head nestled against his chest, I let serenity wash over me as I breathe in his raw scent. The beating of his heart soothes me while his calloused fingers stroke the bare skin of my neck. More than ever, I need to feel his warmth when I'm in his presence.

"Are you ready?" he asks, placing a kiss on my temple.

I nod briefly, probably without much enthusiasm, but he doesn't say anything and pulls away from me. His smile brushes my lips, and as soon as he captures them, I shiver. I wish we could stay here, safe and sheltered, but I know we can't miss the celebration where he's the guest of honor. So, I comfort myself by believing that no matter what happens outside our chambers, tonight I'll be in his arms, safe.

"Happy birthday again," I murmur.

Without saying a word, he brushes my cheek with his thumb. I truly think I could spend my life like this, sustained only by his presence. He gives me another kiss on my lips, then offers me his arm, and with a steady pace, we leave our quarters to head outside the palace.

As we pass, the murmurs stop and everyone bows. My fingers grip Karel's jacket tightly, as if that could keep me from fainting. I glance up at him. With his back straight, he walks with his head held high, his expression determined and confident. A smile appears on my face when I mimic his posture because that's what I did the day I arrived in Lapisia. It's what I do every time. I model my attitude after his. He always helps me, without even realizing it, to face the world.

We arrive in front of the tower and are quickly escorted by his men. Even though I try to hide it, my body is trembling so much that my muscles tense in effort to keep it hidden. I'm surprised not to see any citizens in the street we're walking along, but I realize access to the palace has been blocked when a line of soldiers appears. They step aside as soon as we reach them, and the city's clamor becomes audible. My grip on Karel's jacket tightens, which doesn't escape his notice. He places his hand over mine, frees it, and then intertwines our fingers. Surprised, I turn my head in his direction, but as always, he's looking straight ahead. I glance down at our joined hands and can't help but smile. This way of holding hands isn't exactly conventional, but it was necessary for me to keep going.

When we come across the first Lapisians, they cheer for their prince, wishing him a happy birthday. I'm surprised not to hear any insults or reproaches directed at me, and my heart skips a beat, then starts racing—not out of relief, but out of apprehension. As if this calm is only temporary. As if, at the next intersection, the Lapisians' hostility is going to erupt. When we finally emerge onto the main square, I notice it has been decorated everywhere. Music resonates here and there, and the rhythms sometimes blend into a cacophony of notes. Yet, I find it lively and enjoyable. There are days when I think being an ordinary citizen must be pleasant.

Without being able to help it, my gaze falls on the scaffold where I had to face my sentence, and I have to swallow the lump in my throat. It's not just sadness that overtakes me, but also anger. Anger at this unjust world that denies women the right to defend themselves, rendering our words useless. I want a fairer society, where our lives would matter. After all, it's mothers who help their sons grow into strong men; it's their love that helps them grow. They guide them, step by step, from the cradle until they take their last breath. They chase away the monsters lurking in the night. They drive away fears, dry tears, and show the way. Each one devotes her life to her children, praying to her ancestors that no harm comes to them, and cursing those who dare hurt them. They are solid and loyal allies. So why do the rulers want so badly to make us into slaves? My fingers grip Karel's more tightly. He does the same, and my heart feels lighter. I know I will never rule, but I believe he will support me in making the world fairer—for women, but also for the mixed-blood. I'm sure of it.

A little girl runs up to us and offers a bouquet of flowers to Karel, who releases my hand and immediately bends down to take it.

"Happy birthday, Your Majesty."

I'm touched as she curtsies. Her face is so serious I imagine she must have practiced all day in front of a mirror.

"Thank you, young lady," he says with a slight smile, which is unusual for him.

Karel doesn't correct her mistake in the title, and it moves me. The girl's eyes light up, and she blinks several times, as if surprised he spoke to her. She then turns her attention to me, staring at me with curiosity. I suddenly feel uncomfortable. Karel grabs me by the wrist, and my knees hit the ground as I cling to him to avoid falling flat. A little gentleness wouldn't hurt him.

"Do you know my wife?" he asks her.

Without taking her eyes off me, the little girl nods.

"What do you think of her?" he inquires.

I furrow my brows at him, silently scolding him.

"She's pretty," the girl whispers softly.

I blush immediately but quickly compose myself. "You're very pretty, too," I compliment her.

"Really?" she exclaims, her cheeks suddenly bright red.

I nod, keeping my smile as Karel straightens. He offers me his hand and helps me up, this time gently. I watch the young girl from Lapisia skip away.

"They're the ones you need to charm first," my husband murmurs. "The children are the future; they will all love you, and one day, you won't have to fight to be accepted."

I smile, not taking my eyes off the little girl. With a nod of his head, he asks if we can continue, and I nod in agreement. As we prepare to leave the square, a dozen men and women are standing curiously near the street we're heading toward. Their hesitant demeanor worries me, and I slow my pace. Karel, alerted by my change of speed, looks in the same direction and immediately tenses.

"Samael," he calls.

Samael appears beside us, and Karel points to the group not far from us. Samael seems to understand and signals behind him. He, accompanied by Zaïn, heads toward them. They talk for a moment, during which Vàli and Jonah stand in front of us.

"If anything happens, don't let go of my hand, okay?" Karel asks me.

I let out a faint "yes," reassured I'm not alone this time. When his men come back toward us, Karel grips my hand so tightly it feels like it wouldn't take much for my bones to be crushed in his grasp.

"They want to give a gift to the princess," Samael announces.

My brows knit together, and I move to observe the small group. I study them one by one, and relief replaces my apprehension when I recognize one of the women.

"All right," I say.

"No," Karel counters.

"Tell them to come," I insist.

"Have you lost your mind?" he asks me. He steps in front of me and looks at me as if a third eye had appeared on my forehead.

"That woman defied the rules to bring me water. So, no, I haven't lost my mind."

He doesn't seem to believe me, so I recount what happened, leaving nothing out. Our exchange had been brief, but it made me feel somewhat supported.

"She spat on you?"

I roll my eyes. I'm exasperated that this is all he remembers. "And what else could she have done? It was the only way for her to—"

"I don't want to hear it; she's not coming near you."

I sigh and get ready to approach them, ignoring Karel's orders, but he abruptly pulls me back. I'm about to snap back at him and tell him he's overreacting, but he surprises me by taking the lead. We reach the group, who takes a small step back when they see my husband's rigid stance.

"You wanted to speak to her?" he says without any preamble.

One thing's for sure, my husband is no diplomat.

"I recognize you," I say to the woman who had brought me water. "Thank you."

She smiles at me, a little embarrassed.

"She spat on you," my husband reminds me, never taking his eyes off the poor woman from Lapisia.

"Thank you," I repeat, digging my nails into Karel's hand.

"We didn't think you were guilty, Your Highness," a man says. "Most of us here didn't, for that matter. And even if it was true, it's probably because the prince deserved it."

I let out a hearty laugh as Karel stiffens at his words.

"Sorry, Your Highness," the man's wife jumps in, carefully choosing her words. "My husband is a supporter of the future queen."

"Look at that, you have something in common," I joke.

He doesn't relax and gives me a tight smile that's far from sincere as another woman offers us a pastry. Unfortunately, because of security protocols, I have to decline.

"Enjoy it for us," I say with a grateful smile.

They seem disappointed, but they still give me understanding smiles. I imagine the events of seven years ago are still etched in the collective memory. Life goes on, but some tragedies leave marks that never fade, like ever-present ghosts. They probably remember what they were doing that day, just like I remember what I was doing when my father, looking pale, told me, "It's war…"

Certain scenes are burned into our minds with surprising clarity. I can describe in detail the clothes I was wearing, the weather, my father's expression, and how I felt. I was terrified. That day, the calm of our lives was shattered, and I realized nothing would ever be the same again. I became certain fear would dominate our lives.

I pull myself out of my memories and watch my husband, who still doesn't seem to have regained his calm. Is he thinking about them? To chase away the shadows dancing in his eyes when he looks at me, I decide to steer his thoughts in a different direction.

"So, I have supporters now," I say, grinning widely.

I expect him to counter me, to take the bait of my provocation, but he surprises me. "I'm the first. The leader."

I burst out laughing when I realize he's jealous. We resume our walk in a pleasant silence. We circle the citadel and talk to several citizens. Although none mention the events of a few days ago, all speak to me with reverence and without hostility. I feel relieved, and my heart swells with hope.

"I was wrong," he suddenly says as the palace comes into view.

"About what?" I ask.

"You no longer need to fight to be accepted; you already are." His voice rings with pride.

Despite the knot that's taken up residence in my stomach since I started living in Lapisia, knowing the people outside appreciate me helps me walk through the ballroom doors with more ease. I'm ready to enjoy the evening ahead of us.

Chapter 31

Karel

After the speech opening the ball in my honor, I escort Kalliopee to the buffet, where we meet Amadeus and his brother Aesmé.

"Your Highness, I wish you a happy birthday," the latter greets me.

I thank him and don't miss the glance Kalliopee exchanges between Amadeus and his elder brother. The only things that differentiate them are their height and demeanor. The advisor's face shows his wisdom, while Aesmé's has a kind of hypocritical friendliness that, I'm sure, doesn't escape my wife. Otherwise, they look identical in every way.

"Your Highness, it's a pleasure to meet you."

"You were at our wedding," she suddenly remembers.

Aesmé smiles with a hint of arrogance. "I'm pleased you noticed me among the crowd of guests. My name is Aesmé. I'm Amadeus's brother and the supplier to the Lapisian armies."

My wife studies him closely, no doubt trying to figure out what he might be selling us. "Supplier?"

"Aesmé is an arms dealer," Amadeus replies. "He owns numerous mines and has his own manufacturing workshops."

The atmosphere immediately grows tense. Aesmé keeps his satisfied smile.

"Times must be tough for you."

I have to restrain myself from laughing at my wife's pointed provocation.

"You don't like war," he observes, amused.

"Like most people, I suppose," she answers.

"It's true my business will face a challenging period, but wars keep the world turning, so I'm sure my order book will be full again soon."

"Our world was doing just fine before the conflict between our two kingdoms."

I place a firm hand on Kalliopee's lower back, and she stiffens immediately, giving me a frosty look. I appreciate her standing by her convictions, but she doesn't always know the people she chooses to assert them to. Aesmé is a shark.

"Kingdoms, adversaries—there will always be buyers," he counters. "The Preen zul Lapisian will certainly keep me from going bankrupt."

This time, I'm the one on the verge of losing my temper. The *Lapisian Purity*... a faction founded shortly before our marriage. We don't know who's leading it or even how many supporters it has. However, we do know their demands, clearly written on leaflets circulating around the citadel: The annulment of our marriage and the refusal to see a mixed-blood become the future monarch of our kingdom.

"We're going to leave you now," Amadeus tells us, pulling his brother away, likely aware Aesmé's provocations could end badly for him.

Kalliopee exhales in frustration as we finally find ourselves alone. I grab a glass and drain it in one go. This ball is going to be long.

"I'd ask you not to try to silence me like that again," she says in a low voice as she faces me.

"You were rude to our guest."

She gives me a forced smile and grabs a glass herself, downing its contents immediately. Surprisingly, she doesn't argue further and turns to look at the room's decor. White is everywhere, accented with touches of red. The guests are dressed in their finest clothes, moving between the dance floor and the various buffets set up around the room. Kalliopee taps her foot nervously, her fingers clenched around her glass. Thankfully, Kaïs arrives, lightening the heavy atmosphere around us. With a few jokes, my wife regains her cheerfulness, at least outwardly, though she continues to ignore me, something Kaïs notices and finds amusing, pointing it out loudly. My cousin has no boundaries and doesn't understand some thoughts are better kept to himself.

"I thought spilling the blood of one of your enemies would

have put you in a better mood," he teases.

"Your cousin tends to—"

"I'll be right back," I cut her off.

I don't particularly want us to argue in front of Kaïs, and I've noticed my father. I couldn't miss Amadeus's insistent glances, silently urging me to speak with the king.

"Father," I greet him.

"Happy birthday," he says coldly without even turning to face me.

For what feels like a long time, neither of us speaks; we simply watch the guests as they wander around the room. A laugh catches my attention, and that of others in the room, and my lips spread into an uncontrollable smile. As much as she often annoys me, that sound always makes me forget how much she's capable of driving me mad.

"Do you love her enough to turn your back on your own family?"

My smile fades as I turn to my father, whose gaze is fixed on my wife. "She's my family now, too," I counter. "I just want to protect her. I'm still loyal to you, but there are some sacrifices I refuse to make."

His eyes meet mine. "What sacrifices are you talking about?"

"Her well-being. If you can assure me you won't harm her, I'll have no reason to oppose your plans. That's all I'm asking of you—to spare her."

"You want to regain my trust? Then give her a child."

With those words, he walks away. The weight that had lifted when I managed to voice my truth returned swiftly when Amadeus went to deny it. I hate the position he's put me in. But I also know I'm impulsive and he's much wiser than I am. If I had acted as I usually do, we would be far from here, but our enemies would be on our heels. At least here in the palace, I can keep an eye on my father and stay aware of his schemes.

I approach the advisor, who is now standing alone. "You're making me play a dangerous game," I accuse him right off the bat.

"Welcome to the world of politics."

I give him a sharp look, but it doesn't seem to affect him in the slightest.

"It's necessary to buy time," he adds. "Distract him."

"Buy time for what?"

"For power, Karel. Do what he expects of you, and when you're on equal footing, you'll be free to make your own choices. But for now, you are nothing. Just an heir."

"He won't hesitate to eliminate me," I assert confidently. "If I do what he asks, Kalliopee will be in danger. So will our child."

"She's *already* in danger. This is the only path that might bring you protection. Become king."

"He'll start a war."

"Isn't that better than what you had planned? You're the one who started all of this, so fix your mistakes."

I stare at him, pale.

"I'm not blaming you, Karel. Your decision was desperate, but you're the only one who can ensure the plan fails. Do what needs to be done. Lie. Cheat. Deceive. But if you're too transparent again…"

"He knows I love her, that I would do anything for her. I haven't denied it," I tell him.

"Good, that's a good thing," he says, surprising me. "He would have known you were lying. I told you not to be too transparent, but some things can't be hidden. I believe two mismatched eyes are fixed on us," he informs me, amused, bringing our conversation to an end.

My chest swells when I notice her, still with Kaïs. As soon as my eyes land on her, she looks away. Her expression seems irritated, but rather than making me angry, it makes me smile. This woman has a character that can withstand anything.

"You should go join her."

"She's mad at me; maybe I'm safer here with you."

"You command an army, you're on the front lines in battle, you have to play a double game to stay alive, and *she* scares you?"

"You don't know her that well?" I joke. "She's tougher than any soldier."

A distant smile stretches across Amadeus's lips, then I bid him farewell and head over to my wife, who pretends not to notice my presence when I'm next to her. She doesn't fool me; the goosebumps on her bare arms show she's putting on an act. As does the way her chest stills.

"A dance?" I offer.

She begrudgingly turns to face me and agrees, reluctantly. I only need one dance to shake off her bad mood. We take our place on the dance floor and prepare. She relaxes as soon as my palm presses against her back, pulling her closer to me. Her hand in mine feels so small. And yet, it gives me the sense she could protect me. She keeps my mind from going insane.

"Long day, isn't it?" I attempt, trying to divert my thoughts.

"An execution, a parade, a birthday party. Is your schedule always this packed?" she asks, an amused glint in her eyes.

"If I remember correctly, there was something else between the execution and the parade," I murmur, bringing my face closer to hers.

She can't suppress a nervous laugh as we continue our dance. The guests quickly join us as the melody sweeps us away.

"Amadeus's brother mentioned something called *Preen zul Lapisian*. What is that?"

"They're dissenters. Their name means *Lapisian Purity*. They're against this marriage and any future children we might have."

"The number of our supporters grows by the day," she says sarcastically. "Are we in danger?"

I pull back a bit and study her. Her face doesn't show any signs of worry. It's as if she's becoming accustomed to perpetual danger.

"They talk a lot but have no power, no means. So, I'd be inclined to say they're not our priority, but we're keeping an eye on them. Don't worry."

She nods, and I twirl her around before bringing her back into my arms.

"What do they want?"

I could tell her a ball isn't exactly the place to discuss our enemies, but I know I'm already keeping too many things from her. "To preserve Lapisian blood, not to let Viridian blood taint it."

"Our child isn't even conceived, and it already has enemies."

"He'll be a prince. He'll have enemies either way."

"*He*?" she retorts, a glint of challenge in her eyes.

I shrug, indicating I'm confident. Having a daughter might

protect us, but a son would more quickly put an end to the charade I'm forced to play.

"If we have a son and you had to choose between our two kingdoms, which one would you pick?" she suddenly asks, concerned.

Unable to answer her, I just shake my head. I have few options: tell her the truth or lie to her again. Instead, I choose a third option—I'd rather let her interpret my silence.

She gives me a half-hearted smile and then shifts her attention to my father. With her chest pressed against mine, I can't miss the quickening of her heartbeat, and I begin to wonder. What does she know? Does she suspect anything? I hate lying to her, but while I've managed to disappoint my father, I can't bear to disappoint her.

She locks her gaze with mine again. Her eyes are moist, and I can tell she's about to ask me something.

"What's going on?" I ask her.

"Are you still hiding things from me?" Her voice trembles. She tilts her head to the side, probably trying to access my deepest truths.

I look away for a few seconds, wondering how I should act. My gaze is drawn to Amadeus, who is watching me intently. Fear grips me. Guilt, too. But I can't do anything.

"Karel?"

So, because I'm a coward, I prevent her from reading me. Our gazes lock, but I conceal everything going on inside.

"When things calm down here, would you like to visit your father?"

"I'd love that."

She turns her head away as we continue our dance. She doesn't comment on the change of subject; she doesn't insist further. She just holds back her questions, keeping her doubts to herself. I wish I could dispel them, but I'm unable to. Instead, I press a kiss to her temple as I pull her closer. Her fingers tighten around my hand, and since we can't speak, we communicate through our movements. Mine was meant to convey my apologies; hers, a plea not to hurt her again.

Chapter 32

Karel

Two Months Later

"You're going to make me dizzy," complains Kaïs, watching me from the chair.

I stop pacing and glare at him, saying nothing. He raises his palms toward me, gesturing for me to continue my back-and-forth.

"It's taking too long… It shouldn't be taking this long," I say worriedly, staring once more at the door to our bedroom.

"She just got here. You should relax; it's probably nothing."

"Tell me again what happened," I demand.

My cousin sighs, then leans back more comfortably in his seat. "We were at the infirmary, and she got dizzy on the way back."

"You didn't eat or drink anything? Kalliopee has a hard time refusing anything…"

Since my birthday, two months ago, Kalliopee has been regularly visiting the citadel. Not satisfied with not being insulted, she wanted to strike while the iron was still hot. At first, I escorted her on every outing, but with Kalliopee, if you give her an inch, she takes a mile. Waiting for me no longer suited her, and she begged me to let her leave the palace, accompanied by Kaïs. As for me… if Kalliopee asks for an arm, I give her my entire body.

Until now, everything had gone smoothly, but today Kaïs came back, carrying my barely conscious wife. When he appeared in our apartments, I think my heart failed; I was overwhelmed by a fear I still can't shake.

I resume my pacing, wondering how much longer it will be until Mira comes out of our bedroom.

"We should go get some fresh air," Kaïs suggests in a tense voice.

"Go get some air if you want, but there's no way I'm leaving this room. I'm already holding myself back from breaking down the door that separates me from her."

He sighs but doesn't insist. He stands and walks over to a small sideboard, where he pulls out a bottle and two glasses. A few moments later, I accept the one he hands me and down it in one gulp. The burn of the alcohol at least helps clear my mind. Unfortunately, the effect is short-lived, and as soon as the warmth dissipates, doubts take hold of me again. I catch my cousin's worried look, and bile rises to my throat.

"I'm sure it's nothing serious," he tries to reassure me.

"The only person who can tell me that is currently making me wait. Are you sure you didn't eat or drink anything?"

"How can you ask me that again?" he snaps.

I'm surprised by the anger in his voice.

"I loved my aunt, just like I loved Maha. Do you think what happened to them didn't affect me? Do you honestly believe I would ever put Kalliopee in any kind of danger? You're not the only one who cares about her. She may be your wife, but she's also my friend! So please, don't ask me that again."

I don't get the chance to respond because the door to our bedroom opens. The doctor closes it before I can catch a glimpse of Kalliopee.

"She's fine," she announces immediately. "She'll need some rest, but you should go see her," she informs me, without saying more. "I'll be back tomorrow."

She gives us a small nod and leaves. I nervously watch my cousin as he downs the rest of his drink and stares at the door before looking away.

"You should go in…"

I want to apologize to him, to tell him I never doubted his sincerity and that I trust him completely, but I'm too eager to see my wife. I nod and head toward our bedroom.

I gently knock on the door and don't wait before entering the room. Kalliopee is sitting against the headboard, staring at a point in the distance, not noticing my presence. It's only when I sit down in front of her that her eyes finally meet mine. The paleness of her face worries me, but not as much as the fear I see in her eyes.

My breath quickens, and I suddenly realize the doctor might have downplayed her words. “Are you okay?”

She nods, but instead of reassuring me, the way her eyes fill with tears only increases my anxiety.

“What’s going on?”

“I’m scared,” she whispers.

“Scared of what?” I ask, alarmed.

She doesn’t answer and breaks eye contact, lowering her face. Now she’s staring at her clasped hands.

“Kalliopee,” I growl.

I see her swallow and take a deep breath. I realize she’s gathering her courage to tell me the truth.

“I’m pregnant,” she murmurs so softly that I’m not sure I heard her right.

“You’re—” I can’t even say the word.

“I’m pregnant,” she repeats, louder this time, locking her eyes with mine.

My gaze automatically shifts to her belly, and I understand that’s what she was looking at, not her hands. I can’t even begin to describe what I’m feeling; my emotions are all over the place. There’s the fear of not being enough, of not being strong enough to protect them both, and then there’s the overwhelming pride of realizing a part of us is growing inside her. But then it’s more than fear; it’s terror that grips me when I see my wife’s reaction.

“Do you feel sick? Is there something wrong with the baby?” I ask, worried.

“No,” she replies, a hint of surprise in her voice.

I tense, unable to read her expression. “What’s wrong?”

“I don’t know.”

I glance at her belly again, still flat. In a few months, it will be round. In a few months, she will give birth to our child. I’ve been waiting for this moment, anticipating it with fear. I even dreaded it. Maybe because I knew it would bring us closer to the end. I had considered everything—except the overwhelming emotions and their intensity. I feel a mix of joy, pride, and love. A happiness so intense it pushes back the remaining darkness that used to engulf me.

Unable to hold back, I grab the back of her neck and capture her lips with mine. I pour into her the intoxication this news has brought me. It's the sweetest elixir. When I finally pull away, I see she is exhausted and troubled. I'm not sure why, but I sense she needs space. I decide to hold back my desire to control everything and know all her thoughts. I'll give her a brief reprieve.

"I'm going to let you rest," I say softly.

She nods, giving me a weak smile. I hope she knows the discussion will resume tonight and there will be no secrets left by sunset.

"I'll ask Sienna to come join you," I tell her.

She lies down on the bed, turning her back to me, and I'm left alone with my questions and worries. I'm already shaken, so I can only imagine what she's feeling. After all, she's the one carrying this life inside her.

I leave the room and rub my face. I wish I could fully enjoy this news, but my father's shadow looms over me, darkening this moment. I decide to go look for Amadeus. I order one of the two guards posted outside our door to fetch Sienna, then walk through the corridors, hoping to find the advisor.

As expected, he's hiding in the library. Bent over a book, he seems lost in his reading. I clear my throat to announce my presence. His lips spread into a wide smile when he sees me.

"What's going on?" he asks when he notices my stiff demeanor.

"I need to talk to you. It's confidential."

"Let's go to the gardens."

I agree with his suggestion and wait for him to put the book back on its shelf before leaving the room. However, he leaves the rest piled up on the large, polished table and gestures for me to open the door once he's done. We walk toward the French door calmly. Though I'm eager to be out of earshot, I know hurrying wouldn't suit us and would only raise suspicions.

"I assume it's important," he begins as soon as we're outside.

"Kalliopee is pregnant," I tell him immediately.

The gravel crunches under our shoes as we approach a small grove. Amadeus is still deep in thought. I turn to him, and his serious expression doesn't reassure me. Suddenly, I'm worried about my father finding out. What if he doesn't hesitate to eliminate me to get what I promised to bring him: vengeance?

"He must not find out," I say nervously.

"He will find out, Karel. Staff talks, bodies change; it's not something we can easily hide..."

"Help me, Amadeus," I beg. I grab his elbow, forcing him to stop.

When his face turns toward me, he seems to read the helplessness in me, as he nods immediately. "Inform the king, he'll find out anyway. Everyone needs to know—it's the best way to protect her. If he were to discover the secret, no one would be able to protect the child. But if the news spreads, he won't do anything in plain sight. And as long as the child isn't born, you're safe. You're his only means to achieve his goal. He'll wait until you have a son to act."

"If it's a boy?"

"No need to anticipate. If it's a boy, we'll figure it out."

"We won't find out until the birth..."

"I know... If it's a boy, we'll take the necessary measures."

He doesn't need to say more. We've already discussed this recently, but I can't help being terrified by the thought.

"The only thing that matters is protecting the princess and your child. How is she?" he asks, concerned.

"She's scared."

"Have you talked to her about it?"

We continue walking, staying in the shade of the trees, out of the sun. Today, the weather is mild, and the heat is bearable.

"No, you've repeated enough times that I should keep quiet," I reply, irritated. "I don't know what's going on in her head. Sometimes, she can share even her smallest thoughts with me, scream her truths, no matter how much they might upset me. And other times, she shuts herself off."

"She reminds me of someone."

"It's the one thing she and I have in common."

"That's true. Kalliopee is—"

"She's honest, proud, but able to admit when she's wrong. She's diplomatic and thinks of others before herself. She—"

"She'd make a good queen." Amadeus chuckles. "She has far more qualities than all the kings I've ever met."

"She'd make an *excellent* queen," I affirm, supporting his statement.

"Too bad the world isn't ready for a woman to rule," he concludes with regret. "As for her fear, it's understandable. Her mother died in childbirth, and she grew up without a maternal figure. I imagine she's terrified at the thought of carrying a child who might never know her love."

His words make me thoughtful. I hadn't considered her past could be influencing her reactions in the present. I, of all people, should know sometimes ghosts have more power than the living.

"What should I do? Push her to talk? Confront her? Give her time?" I grumble, frustrated at not knowing how to support her.

"In case you've forgotten, I'm neither a husband nor a father."

I think I might have offended him, but I'm reassured by the teasing glint in his eyes.

"You just need to be yourself, Karel. I think it's worked so far."

We start walking again, and Amadeus glances briefly at one of my father's guards stationed in front of one of the French doors.

"Whatever the king asks of you, accept it, Karel. Don't betray yourself."

"I can't..."

"Don't raise suspicions. If he suspects anything, saving the princess will be impossible."

I nod, aware he's right and that any efforts would be in vain if I were to rebel against my father again. To anticipate his actions, I need to understand his plan. And for that, I have no choice but to keep playing this double game.

"He'll be hard to fool..."

"Not at all. The king is blinded by hatred. He thinks everyone must feel the same rage he does. He'll just believe his son has come to his senses. Just make sure your performance is convincing."

"This is all going to end badly."

I have this constant anxiety in the pit of my stomach, a persistent feeling that clings to me and fills my mind.

We turn around and retrace our steps. Amadeus ends the

serious conversation there, and we switch to talking about trivial things. I do my best to hide my impatience to return to my wife and enjoy this time with my mentor. As far back as I can remember, Amadeus has always been there, but after my mother and sister died, he took on a new role as my guide. How many times has he saved me from myself? I thought his loyalty to my father would remain, no matter what. I'm surprised to see how much he's defending Kalliopee, an *enemy* princess, instead of his king.

"Why are you doing all this?" I ask. "You could be accused of treason if this came out. You don't owe Kalliopee or me anything."

He stops when we reach the steps that lead us back inside the palace walls. "Because I've served your father for almost twenty years, Karel. I sacrificed the life I could have had. He could have done great things, but when the queen died, he… disappeared," he continues after hesitating. "There's nothing left to save, but you and Kalliopee, you are the future. You're the closest thing I have to a son, and I have a lot of affection for the princess. I think this family has already suffered too much. Your father is too lost in his pain to ever find even a little bit of happiness again, but you can."

He daydreams for a long time, and a sad smile slowly spreads across his face. "I'm sure Maha and the princess would have gotten along well," he finishes before opening the door.

Our paths separate when he returns to the library, while I head back to my wife.

I let my mind wander, imagining a life where Maha and Kalliopee would have gotten to know each other, and I realize that if the past could be changed, the princess with the heterochromatic eyes wouldn't be my wife. I would have loved for my mother and sister to have been spared, but I know if they hadn't lost their lives in that attack, our country wouldn't have gone to war. My father would have condemned the terrorists, and he would have accepted King Läven's words when he assured him the act was isolated and the kingdom of Viridia wasn't involved. We wouldn't have needed to forge an alliance, and I would likely be married to Xintia today.

Suddenly, I realize with regret that no matter how much I've suffered, the pain I've endured so far would seem small compared to the agony I'd feel if anything were to happen to Kalliopee.

Chapter 33

Kalliopee

Curled up in a ball, I stare endlessly at the lapis sky framed by the windowpanes. Today, there's no wind, just a breeze. No clouds, just blue as far as the eye can see. It's soothing. Yet, despite the calm outside, there's a storm raging inside me. I close my eyes, trying to push away the invasive thoughts whispering that I will never be able to protect my child. That I, too, will abandon them.

It's only been a few minutes since I realized why I've been so exhausted and so hungry these past few days. I was forced to eat; otherwise, the urge to vomit would only get stronger. My world has just been turned upside down, but I already feel like this little being means more than anything.

Only a few minutes… but a few minutes that have allowed doubts to crush me.

I place my palm on my belly, and my heart starts to beat a rhythm I've never known before. It's terrifying. It's chaotic and jarring, but also enchanting and full of hope.

"I don't think you're ill, Your Highness."

My breath catches, my stomach tightens.

"Congratulations!"

My eyes open again, and despite the warmth, a chill runs through me. I'm happy, but I'm also scared. I almost forbid myself from loving this being I fear I'll never meet. I almost wish it were all a mistake.

I swallow painfully, and against my will, my mind drifts. It picks apart my memories of growing up without a mother, all those moments when her absence was all too present. I'm not afraid of dying. I'm afraid of plunging a child into the same loneliness that was so familiar to me.

With my eyes closed, I let the past wash over me.

As Malo and I are having fun jumping on my big bed, the door opens. Enea, one of my nannies, appears, and I know from her furrowed brows that she's likely going to scold us. We stop bouncing immediately, and Malo kneels on the mattress while I stand still. Enea comes over to me and takes me in her arms to help me down.

"Kalliopee, that's not a proper way for a princess to behave," she complains as she sets me on the floor.

I look at her, my eyes wet, afraid I've made her angry. I don't like it when she's mad at me. She smiles at me gently before stroking my cheek with her thumb.

"I just wanted to have fun with Malo for her birthday," I admit, ashamed.

Enea turns her head toward her daughter. I mimic her and see Malo's mouth is curved into a shy smile. Then I shift my gaze back to this woman who isn't my mother but hers. Her lips curl affectionately.

"All right, I won't say anything this time. Malo, we need to go. Princess, be ready for dinner. I'll come to tuck you in when it's time, then Salvia will take care of you."

I nod as Malo climbs down from the bed to join her mother. They leave immediately, and I don't know why, but I make my way to the door. I open it just a crack and peek curiously into the hallway.

My nanny is kneeling in front of Malo, speaking so softly that I can't hear what she's saying. I'm worried she might be scolding her or telling her she can't come play with me anymore. But Malo nods enthusiastically, a big smile on her face, and her mother tenderly kisses her cheek. Seeing this, I don't feel relieved that she isn't getting in trouble; I feel jealous. I regret it instantly. Malo is my friend, and her family doesn't have much money. Her mom is all she has... But still, I wish she were mine.

I already know what cake she baked for her birthday and the dress she made for her. Malo was so proud to tell me everything planned for her little party. Meanwhile, I was resentful that she had so much to look forward to.

I love Enea. I love it when she holds me, when she tucks me in, even when she's angry with me. But at night, when nightmares wake me, she's not there to wipe away my tears. Salvia isn't affectionate;

she doesn't like me—I know that. Whenever I made her come to me, she scolded me for acting like a baby before leaving me alone with the monsters lurking in my closets. So now, I cry quietly and, in secret, envy Malo, whose every tear Enea wipes away.

I gently close the door and run back to my bed. I burrow under the covers, seeking refuge. It's a cocoon only I can enter. My fortress. Our *fortress.*

"You're beautiful..." I whisper.

Eyes just like mine gaze back at me with the same affection that fills Nanny's eyes when she looks at Malo.

Her long hair is tied in a braid. She smells good. Her scent is sweet, like the fruit cakes the cook makes for my birthday.

"So are you," she murmurs, a loving smile on her lips.

My lips curl into a smile in return, while my heart skips a beat with anticipation. I reach out my hand toward her. I want to touch that smile, to feel her breath and warmth. But my fingers meet nothing but empty air. My eyelids lower; I don't want her to see my disappointment.

When I open my eyes again, I'm alone. She's gone. I don't know why I love to reenact the conversations I overhear between Malo and her mother. Even though, every time, it's not enough. Every time, I want more. I try to snuggle into her arms, to brush against her, to plant a kiss on her cheek. And every time, she vanishes.

I push the blanket away and leave this refuge that always takes more from me than it gives, staring up at the canopy of my bed.

Papa always tells me that Mama was happy about having me, that she would have been proud of the little girl I've become. Sometimes, that comforts me. But not often. No, most of the time, it makes me feel even more alone.

I curl up in a ball and sob, letting the sadness wash over me.

A warm body presses against mine, pulling me out of my lonely memories, and suddenly, my lungs fill with air. His scent, though not sweet, calms me.

"Weren't you supposed to meet your men?" I whisper weakly, as if he might disappear, too.

"You need me… that's all that matters."

I inhale, then turn to face him. He props himself up on one elbow, and I look at him for a long moment, not knowing how to put into words the fear that's twisting inside me.

"Nothing will happen to you," he says, surprising me.

"How can you be so sure?"

"With everything you've been through so far, to drop will be a piece of cake."

"*To drop*?" I repeat, unable to hold back a laugh.

"I like that better," he murmurs softly.

I realize then that he chose those words just to make me smile, and immediately, the smile on my lips fades. My eyes fill with tears, and my heart starts to pound. "I'm scared he'll be like me," I confess.

He raises an eyebrow, and I know it's his way of asking me to explain.

"Alone."

His gaze drops, as if searching for the right words to say. It's not like him to hesitate, but I suppose this new situation must be changing him, too. He clears his throat before looking at me again. "He won't be alone, ever. Do you know why?"

I shake my head, eager to hear how he plans to reassure me. Karel isn't always great with words, but sometimes he surprises me. At times, I feel like his stoicism is just a front to hide the fact that, inside, he feels everything too intensely.

"Because everything will go well, and as soon as he's born, we'll start working on making him a little brother or sister," he says before pressing his lips to mine.

This time, the smile that forms doesn't disappear. He pulls back, his eyes roaming my face, studying every inch of my skin, and then the intensity with which he locks his gaze onto mine takes my breath away. His hands move into my hair, and he gives me a kiss quite different from the one before. This one makes my head spin, and all the dark thoughts vanish. Every doubt is erased by the touch of his fingers. Every fear is absorbed by his breaths. Every question is swallowed up by his lips as they travel over my body.

When he's above me, my legs part, ready to welcome him. But he delays the moment, his hands lingering on my skin, making it sensitive to his every caress. I feel like I'm drowning, like each of his movements creates a swell that pulls me to the surface only to drag me back into the depths again, so I cling to him to keep from disappearing.

He gently makes me sit up, and with a tenderness that isn't

typical of him, he slips off my dress. He lifts his arm and grabs his shirt by the collar to pull it off. Our skin meets, fusing together. The heat of his skin reignites mine, which had felt cold and lifeless. Then, when there's no more clothing left to remove, he enters me. His arms stretched out, he hovers over me. His dilated pupils add depth to the green of his eyes. Once again, I feel like I'm drowning, but this time, I never want to come up for air. He leans down to kiss me with a hunger that's not unfamiliar to me. His fingers grip my hair at the crown of my head as he starts slow, intense thrusts. Each one pulls a moan from me that I don't even try to stifle. My heels press against his back to match his rhythm, while my hands cling to his wrists.

My teeth sink into his lip as a wave crashes over my body. The torture is euphoric and addictive. I want more. A metallic taste fills my mouth, and I instantly regret losing control. He pulls away, surprised. One of his hands releases me, letting the cold seep back in. He touches his lips with his index finger, examining the blood that stains it. It's faint, almost imperceptible, but I'm afraid it's already too much. Time seems to stand still, and I don't dare move. His eyes seem to search mine, and just as I'm struggling for air, he gives me back my breath by resuming his slow, intense thrusts.

I forget everything, even my own name. I forget the reasons that brought me to Lapisia, the schemes meant to destroy us, the anxieties that sometimes make it hard to breathe. All I see is him. This impulsive man who can also be so gentle I feel like I could crumble. All I look at is him. This uncompromising prince who, nevertheless, gives my voice more weight.

I love him, and I believe him when he assures me that everything will be okay because it has to be. Because you can't suffer so much without happiness as a reward. Because I *refuse* to let it be any other way.

So, I confess everything to him. With my sighs, my kisses, my scratches. I tell him I don't want to disappear, that becoming a mother scares me, but I want to see this child grow up by his side.

He answers each of my fears with his growls, his lips devouring my neck, his fingers digging into my thighs. He promises me I won't disappear and I will see this child grow up by his side.

Because it has to be this way.

Because we *refuse* to let it be any other way.

CHAPTER 34

KALLIOPEE

"Are you sure it's this way?" Kaïs asks me.

I nod while reading the name of the store we just passed. "I have a great sense of direction," I add, noticing his doubtful expression.

He doesn't push, and we continue walking. The streets are packed with people, but now I blend in with the crowd. People treat me with respect. And while some still look at me with bitterness, most of the people of Lapisia seem to appreciate me. At least, I think they do.

"I still don't get why you're so set on going to see her…"

I stop and turn to face my friend. His height makes me tilt my head up. Ever since I mentioned our little outing, he hasn't hidden his disapproval.

"And you? Why are you so set on me not going?"

He stands in front of me, hands clenched at his hips. The stern aura he's giving off might be intimidating if I didn't know him so well. Seeing he's not saying anything, I finally answer. "Because yesterday, she seemed… different," I hesitated.

"Different how?"

"Desperate…"

I can't find a better word to describe how I felt when, just before she left, I asked if everything was okay.

"Something's not right…"

He sighs, rubbing the bridge of his nose, and I can do nothing but wait for him to signal that we can keep going.

For the past three weeks, Mira has been visiting regularly to make sure my pregnancy is going smoothly. Honestly, I'm not sure I need this much attention, but it calms Karel. Yesterday, though, she seemed lost in thought. I tried to get her to open up, but she's not one to share easily. And when I asked her that final question, the look she gave me made my throat tighten. I could feel that, no, she wasn't okay.

"What other directions did her father give us?" he finally asks.

A grateful smile spreads across my face when I realize this is his way of giving his approval. It's obvious I wouldn't have risked going without Kaïs. Sure, we're escorted by guards, but he's one of the few people I trust completely. Plus, he didn't take Karel's suspicions well when I fainted… and I don't want my husband blaming him again if I were to go without him. I invite him to follow me, still smiling, and I think I see him roll his eyes.

Since I have no idea where Mira lives, I had no choice but to ask her father at the dispensary. When we reach the intersection he pointed out, I recognize the house from his description. The blue shutters, with their chipped paint, are right there, along with the mold stains on the facade.

"Number four, is that right?" Kaïs asks me.

I nod but stop in my tracks, suddenly feeling uneasy. What if I'm being too intrusive?

"Are we going?"

Now that we're here, I'm not so sure anymore.

"Kalliopee?" he calls, forcing me to turn to him.

I don't have time to respond because the sound of breaking glass reaches us. Our heads turn toward the building in sync. There's no doubt the noise came from there. Immediately, a man's voice erupts, angry, sending a chill down my spine. The malice in it makes my neck stiffen.

But instead of listening to the warnings from my body, I rush toward the door. Before I can reach it, though, a hand wraps around my wrist, stopping me.

My heart is racing, pounding in my chest, while inside those walls, a struggle seems to unfold. The sounds overlap: yelling. *Her* yelling. Kaïs pulls me toward him, dragging me away from where Mira is trapped. He presses my body against his, forcing me to match his pace. I try to break free, to turn back, but he tightens his grip on my shoulders as we keep moving.

"What are you doing?" I ask him, my throat tight with

emotion.

He stops and turns me around, holding me by the arms. This time, I don't have to look up at him; he lowers himself to my level.

"We can't leave her…"

My throat tightens even more painfully as I hear sobbing from inside. My eyelids squeeze shut, a sharp pain spreading in my chest.

"We can't let her go through that," I continue.

"We don't have a choice, Kalliopee."

I open my eyes and search his for any sign his only motivation is to protect me, to get me out of here—that if it weren't for me, he'd already be kicking down that door. But no, all I see is acceptance. But I can't accept it. I won't. How can you just stand by when the law feels unjust? Do we have to accept it, or can we fight it?

"There's nothing we can do," he adds.

There's no way I'm staying passive. If I ignore Mira's distress, I won't be able to face myself.

"Yes, we can! We can choose to go in and stop her husband from hurting her."

"That's not how the world works."

I shake my head, disbelieving, and scan our surroundings. I see the guards who usually stay at a distance now forming a half-circle around us. More people have gathered near the house, but none of them seem willing to stop what's happening inside. Curiosity consumes them, but there's no trace of compassion or guilt. They seem to feed off the spectacle, indifferent to the woman suffering behind those walls. The screams stop, and so do the sobs. Everyone remains still, eyes fixed on the blue shutters.

How can people be so weak? How can they be so deaf to someone's pain?

"I can't…" I blurt out, my voice trembling.

"But you have to. Because that man is within his rights. Don't twist my words!" Kaïs adds as I open my mouth to argue. "I don't condone violence against women, but it's legal, no matter how cruel it is."

The acid burns my throat, and I know it has nothing to do with the new life growing inside me. It's the disgust rising up inside.

I step back, and Kaïs's gaze darkens. I can tell he's torn between stopping me and letting me go, but he doesn't move toward me. I see him surrender. I turn and march toward the small house, more determined than ever. I have to get her out of here. I have to get her away from him.

My heart pounds harder and harder, and I wonder how my chest doesn't burst. As I approach the door, I glance at the window. My body freezes, then begins to tremble uncontrollably. Terror paralyzes me. The dirty glass leaves little to the imagination. The urge to vomit rises again, and a cold wave washes over me. Despite the horror in front of me, I can't look away from the table where the woman who tended to my wounds so many times lies. Kaïs steps in front of me, blocking my view, but the image is already burned into my mind. Even when I squeeze my eyes shut, it's still there.

Mira. Her torn dress. Lying on the table.

And him. Her husband. Violently thrusting into her.

Taking what is his. Because he has the right. Because she belongs to him. Because the world is cruel.

"Let me go in, please," I beg him.

He doesn't answer. Instead, his arms wrap around me, holding me tight. I want to kick down that door, drag her out, but all I can do is cling to Kaïs's jacket as dizziness weakens my legs. How can her husband do this to her? How does she live with this every day, in plain sight? And how can these people witness what their neighbor endures and do nothing?

"Think of yourself, think of your baby," Kaïs murmurs, holding the back of my neck as I try to push him away. "What will happen if we go inside? Do you think my uncle would blame me if that man accused you of breaking into his home? No, he'd come after you."

His words sink in. How can I judge these people when I'm now considering walking away to protect myself? I stare at my stomach and realize Kaïs is only speaking the truth. If I intervene, if I step into that house, the king will make me pay. How far would he go? I don't know, and I don't want to find out.

"So, I just have to turn a blind eye?" I ask, my voice hollow.

"I'm sorry…"

"He's—" I can't finish the sentence.

"I know."

In a desperate attempt to keep myself together, I try to shut it all out. My emotions swirl—disgust, anger, helplessness. The same helplessness she seemed to feel yesterday. It feels unbearable, overwhelming, but I can only imagine how much worse it must be for Mira.

"I need to see Karel," I announce, a new energy surging through me as I pull away from Kaïs.

I can't give up without trying something. He's right—the king would come after me, and I can't act recklessly now that I'm carrying a child. I have to protect it, but maybe Karel can do something.

Kaïs shakes his head, and I know exactly what he's thinking, what he wants to say: Karel won't be able to do anything either.

I step back, turn, and quickly walk away. I try to hold back the tears, to stop them from spilling over. But with every step I take, it becomes harder. I navigate the streets without thinking, yet it seems my subconscious has mapped every corner of the citadel because, eventually, I find myself standing in front of the barracks.

"Let me talk to him," Kaïs asks.

"Why?"

"Because in your state, you'll probably bark orders at him, and I doubt he'll appreciate that in front of the new recruits."

I take a deep breath, staring at the doors that separate me from my husband, and nod. He's right—I wouldn't handle it tactfully. Kaïs steps past me, pushes the doors open, and motions for me to follow.

With his back to us, Karel is teaching defensive stances… to children.

"At what age do you recruit them?" I ask.

"Training starts at ten," Kaïs replies.

He gestures for me to wait, then walks over to Karel. When he reaches him, he taps Karel on the shoulder, and as soon as my husband turns to face his cousin, his eyes search for me. He's about to come to me, worry already creasing his brow, but something Kaïs says stops him in his tracks.

Karel stares at me without blinking as his cousin speaks. Unable to talk to him myself, I lock eyes with him, trying to silently plead for his help. I see him tense, then he breaks eye contact, turning fully toward Kaïs, leaving me with nothing to hold on to. They talk quietly, but when Karel shakes his head, I already know he won't do anything either.

I take a step back, my heart racing. I tilt my face toward the sky, trying to catch my breath, but even though we're outside, I feel like I'm suffocating. My body itches, my vision blurs. I suddenly feel the overwhelming need to escape these walls. My breathing becomes more erratic, my heart pounds louder, and the violent images from before flood my mind. I rush out of the barracks, and instead of heading back to the palace, I turn toward the massive gates—the ones that keep me trapped inside this citadel. I need to get out, just for a moment. It feels like I'm under a dome where there's no more air left to breathe.

"Open the gates," I order.

The two guards at the entrance stare at me, then exchange a confused look.

"Open them!" I repeat, more impatient this time.

"Kalliopee," Karel calls, catching up to me.

"I need to get out, please," I gasp, unable to face him. My whole body feels like it's crawling, and my chest tightens as if it's squeezing the air out of my lungs. "I just need to—"

"Okay," he interrupts me. "Open the gates!"

The creaking of the heavy gates echoes immediately, and as soon as there's enough space, I slip through, leaving the walls behind. My knees tremble as I take a few steps, inhaling deeply. My legs buckle under the weight of my pain, and with my hands flat on the scorching sand, I let the dusty air fill my lungs. Finally, I can breathe.

I'm out of breath but freezing. Nausea hits me, and without control, my body rejects my anger, spilling it onto the arid ground. The acid burns my throat, tears stinging my eyes. When the dizziness subsides and I feel steady enough to stand, I push myself up. I wipe my mouth with the back of my sleeve.

I close my eyes for a few seconds. Out here, beyond the walls, the wind moves freely. Just like the day I arrived, it sweeps through my hair, whipping it against my face. The sun's rays scorch my skin, but at least they warm me. It's true that inside the city, everything is designed to shield the people from the elements. But that protection feels like a prison. I'm sure that outside these walls, Lapisia wouldn't seem so suffocating.

I open my eyes again, squinting to keep the sand out. The view in front of me is bleak, offering no comfort. Emptiness. Nothing but emptiness.

I had forgotten just how barren Lapisian lands are. Suddenly, I don't feel better at all. In fact, I feel worse. Inside. Outside. No matter where I am, I feel like I'm suffocating.

Behind me, I hear footsteps. I know it's him. He doesn't say anything, doesn't try to offer meaningless words. Instead of turning toward him, blaming him for things he has no control over, I break. My throat loosens, and the sobs come in waves.

"Please, save her," I manage to say.

He forces me to face him, and my forehead meets his chest. My tears fall freely onto his jacket. I let the images flash before me, the ones I've been trying to block out ever since I left that house with the blue shutters, along with the ones my mind stubbornly insists on imagining.

One argument too many.

One hit too hard.

One death too soon.

I'm not stupid. I know it will happen. Whether it's tomorrow, in a few days, or in a month. Whether it's because he can't stop himself, because she takes a fatal fall, or even because she decides she's had enough, and her heart just can't take it anymore. I know it's inevitable. So I cling to him, repeating the same words over and over, "Please, save her."

Chapter 35

Karel

After escorting Kalliopee back to our room, I join Kaïs, who's sitting in one of the chairs in the living room. From the way he looks at me, I can sense all his worry.

"How is she?" he asks.

I simply shrug in response. "Thank you for stopping her from doing anything rash."

He shakes his head, then sighs. I know Kalliopee can be determined, but I have no idea what would have happened if she had entered that house.

"I regret it," he finally murmurs. "Not stopping her," he adds quickly, probably sensing I was about to protest. "But not acting myself…"

"You couldn't have done anything."

"No, that's true. We can't do anything. Because that's just how the world is, and it sickens me. I would never want that for Kahi, just like you wouldn't have wanted that for Maha."

I nod in agreement. Kaïs's older sister was lucky enough to marry a man who cherishes her more than anything in the world. He takes care of her and would never even raise his voice at her. But not all women are that fortunate.

Kaïs slumps in his chair with another sigh. He scratches his head nervously before sitting up straight, his expression determined. "What if we acted in secret… if we—"

I shake my head. "We can't."

"But you do it sometimes… in a dark alley, it could be quick and—"

It's true, I often take justice into my own hands, but I also know my father is always aware of everything. This time, I can't do anything. Supporting Kalliopee would cast doubt on my loyalty to the king. He already had a hard time believing me when I claimed to have come to my senses. Unfortunately, my hands are tied. Realizing I won't change my mind, Kaïs doesn't push further.

"All right, I'll head out then..." he says, standing.

"Don't you want a drink before you go?" I offer.

He shakes his head and turns his back to me.

Lately, our relationship has grown more distant. I think my reaction during Kalliopee's fainting spell disappointed him. Even my wife has noticed. She's subtly—or not so subtly—nudged me to reconnect with my cousin countless times: "*Did you talk to him today?*" or "*You two should have a conversation...*" She even resorted to lying, hoping I'd drop my indifference: *"He threw himself in front of me, acted as a shield, ready to give his life for me, can you believe it?"*

But I know that if someone had tried to hurt her, I would've found out. That so-called rescue was just her attempt to change my mind. But she's wrong. I don't resent Kaïs. I know full well that he would protect her with his life. It's just that I don't know how to apologize. It's not something I'm used to. I've always had a hard time admitting when I'm wrong, so saying it out loud is even harder.

But this time, facing Kaïs's disappointment and Kalliopee's sadness is especially difficult. Before he reaches the door, I call out to him. He turns around, eyebrows furrowed, as I walk toward him.

"I've never doubted you. I wanted you to know that."

He looks at me in silence. If he's surprised, he doesn't show it.

"And I know Kalliopee can be stubborn sometimes. It's hard to reason with her, and almost impossible to deny her anything."

"Especially when she gives us that look," he adds with a slight smile.

"The one that says, *I'm so disappointed in you, but with or without you, I'll see this through*?"

My cousin relaxes and smiles fully, nodding. Yes, I also struggle to face that look—the one that shows we're not living up to her expectations.

"It was unfair of me to suggest you didn't take every precaution to make sure nothing happened to her. I was worried, but I shouldn't have let my panic cloud my judgment. I'm sorry."

The corner of his mouth lifts, and I roll my eyes.

"Karel apologizing, then rolling his eyes… Who are you?" he teases.

I shake my head, frowning. He shouldn't push his luck.

"Dare I say you're—"

"I'm not weak," I cut him off before he can finish his sentence.

"Human. That's what I was going to say. Believe me, cousin, your *I'm going to fight the whole world* attitude can get exhausting."

He winks before walking out, leaving me alone.

I slowly turn and lean against the doorframe. Hands in my pockets, I stare at the door Kalliopee waits behind, wondering how I'm going to face her disappointment and those eyes that say so much. I search for the courage and strength not to give in. Not because I don't want to, but because I have no choice. I appreciate Mira and how tenderly she's cared for Kalliopee since her attack, but sadly, I can't change her fate. Not now.

Resolved, I push myself away from the wooden frame and cross the room. My shoes echo against the marble floor. Once I reach the door, I pause, take a deep breath, and push it open. I'm surprised to find that Kalliopee isn't in bed. I scan the room, but she's nowhere to be found. A sound from the bathroom catches my attention.

With my courage fading, I sit on the edge of the bed, searching for words that might soothe her. But there are none. Helplessness is one of the worst feelings a person can experience, and the only way to overcome it is to accept it—but Kalliopee never gives up.

The water runs, and I exhale loudly, preparing myself to face the storm. I know she's going to blame me for my inaction, and probably for the laws passed generations ago, but this time, I'll let her unleash her anger on me. I'll take it without protest because it's all I can do.

When I step inside, steam fills the room. She doesn't turn around, even though I've made my presence clear on purpose. I didn't want to startle her. Behind the fogged glass, she remains still. Instead of calling her name, I take off my shoes, remove my clothes, and join her. Her head bowed, she lets the water stream over her hair, which falls in a cascade in front of her face. She doesn't look at me, only offering me her back, but from the way her shoulders tremble, I know she's crying again.

My hand rests on her belly, and I pull her closer as my other arm wraps around her shoulders. She grips my biceps, and though her shaking intensifies, no sob escapes her. She quickly tries to push me away, and though it tightens my chest and knots my throat, I don't stop her. I loosen my hold, but instead of moving away, she surprises me by finally turning around. Her head bumps into my chest as her arms wrap around my waist. Kalliopee is small, yet I can feel the strength of her embrace. My fingers weave into her wet hair as I plant a kiss on the top of her head. That's all I do. I wait.

I could take her in an attempt to make her forget, but I know Kalliopee. The only way for her to find relief is by pouring out her pain. I stare at the tiled wall in front of me as she resumes her plea. "Save her."

But I won't.

Saving Mira would condemn Kalliopee. She'll blame me for it, but I hope that tomorrow, she'll understand. Mira will be saved when Kalliopee is no longer in danger. Until then, all I can do is comfort my wife.

Chapter 36

Kalliopee

When I realized that Karel wouldn't be able to help me, I didn't blame him… at least not as much as I thought I would. His position is complicated, and it's clear his father would never have approved his requests anyway. I don't want him to take any reckless risks. But that didn't stop me from searching for a solution on my own. Well… not completely on my own—thankfully, Kaïs helped me a lot. While I have the will, he has the means. The next day, I told him my plan. If we couldn't do anything to protect Mira from her husband, she needed to disappear. She had to leave the city.

When I revealed my idea to my friend, he called me crazy and reckless… I knew there was a good chance he would refuse to help, and I was prepared for that. I also knew it wouldn't make me back down, and no matter what, I'd find another solution.

At first, he refused, but the next day he changed his mind. He'd spent the whole night thinking about my plan, and by sunrise, he'd reached out to smugglers. They aren't the most trustworthy people when it comes to doing favors, but when a hefty sum is involved, they suddenly become reliable. Five thousand gold pieces to get Mira out of the city and head north, and another five thousand once she was safe. I promised Kaïs I'd pay him back one day, but he refused. He has no idea how grateful I am to have him by my side.

Convincing Mira, on the other hand, was more difficult. Two weeks had already passed when she finally whispered she needed my help. That day, her arms were covered in bruises. For the first time, she opened up about her life. I had thought her father had married her off to a violent man, but it turns out the reality was quite different. Mira and her husband fell in love when they were very young. He was kind, hardworking, and gentle. When she spoke about him, her eyes filled with tears. She still loved the boy who had disappeared long ago.

Her inability to have children and her desire to be useful by helping her father at the clinic were only small grains of sand in the beginning. But the gears jammed, and everything fell apart when her husband lost his job. A few months later, Karel offered Mira the chance to become my doctor. To her, it was a blessing, a way for them to recover financially. She also hoped once their financial troubles were eased, their marriage would regain its spark, and her husband would let go of his frustration. But instead, his impatience only grew. Everything quickly worsened. What had been occasional violence became daily beatings. The slaps turned into punches. Then… her inability to bear a child became a real issue. And a valid reason to force himself on her.

"If only you'd try harder…"

So, I told her my plan in more detail. She was relieved. So was I. But ever since then, I've had this knot of anxiety in my stomach. The fear Karel will find out everything before she can escape, or the smugglers will betray us.

Sitting on the chaise in my library, I continuously gaze at the shelves packed with books. My life here would make an excellent novel, I think, smiling to myself.

I'm waiting anxiously for Kaïs to come and tell me she's finally left the city. He warned me it might take a while, that the smugglers would contact him to avoid suspicion, but time seems to stretch endlessly, making it feel as if it's stopped altogether.

A knock on the door forces me to get up. After I give permission to enter, Sienna appears.

"Princess, the prince's cousin is here," she announces, blushing.

Her reaction surprises me, making me wonder if my maid might have a crush on Kaïs, but I quickly push aside such trivial thoughts, remembering the seriousness of his visit.

"Tell him to come in, and make sure no one disturbs us."

Sienna frowns, and I don't want her to get the wrong idea.

"It's important, Sienna. I'll explain later, but we can't be interrupted."

She nods immediately and closes the door behind her. A few

moments later, Kaïs enters the room. I rise, my heart pounding, eager to be freed from the anxiety that has been gnawing at me.

"Well?" I ask. "Did she leave?"

The way his lips press together causes my breath to hitch.

"Kaïs?" I beg.

"She never showed up at the meeting point," he informs me.

I freeze in complete confusion, then shift my focus back to the shelves, as if one of the books might hold some kind of answer.

"All right," I try to reason. "Maybe she got scared. I'll go visit her. If her husband is there, I'll pretend I felt unwell while out for a walk. Then—"

"Kalliopee," he interrupts. "She's not going to leave."

"You don't know that."

He rubs his neck, shaking his head. "She's not going to leave," he repeats.

"I'll convince her. Will you come with me?" I ask.

He closes his eyes, his body tensing. Kaïs is often carefree and lighthearted, but in moments like these, he strongly reminds me of Karel. He becomes imposing and almost intimidating.

"This is a bad idea."

"So you're not coming with me?"

"I didn't say that."

I nod, reassured he'll support me, and I don't linger. I leave the library, head to my room, and grab a scarf from my wardrobe. Lately, the wind has been blowing fiercely, and we're in the middle of a sandstorm that seems never-ending. The air is no longer clear—it's thick and ochre. I wrap the fabric around my head, leaving only my eyes exposed. When I meet up with Kaïs, I see he's adjusted his scarf as well.

"Let's go," I whisper.

He leads the way, and we leave my quarters. As we walk through the hallways, my steps grow heavier. I'm eager to reach Mira, but also terrified she'll refuse to leave Lapisia.

"Why do you think she won't go?" I can't help but ask Kaïs.

"Because it's not that simple. You told me her story, and I'm sure, deep down, she still has that irrational hope of finding the man she loves."

"Mira's smart. She must know that running away is her only option," I counter.

"Yes, but then what?" he asks, stopping in his tracks. He turns to me, pulling down the scarf that covers his mouth. "You're offering her a way out, but she has no idea what's waiting for her. Yes, she's living in a nightmare, but it's a nightmare she knows. What if what comes next is even worse?"

"It will always be better than what she's going through now," I say confidently.

He shakes his head, placing his hands on his hips and staring at me sternly. I nervously glance at the staircase ahead.

"And you? I know my cousin has changed a lot and is nothing like he used to be, but can you honestly tell me that, deep down, you don't wish to find the man you loved when we were younger? What makes you think she doesn't feel the same way?"

My throat tightens. Our situations are not the same.

"I love your cousin as he is. And he would never raise a hand against me."

"No, that's true," he concedes, "but you can understand that when someone loves, they're willing to endure, even when there's no hope. You cling to memories, and you suffer through it. That's probably what she's doing, too. There are likely moments when he becomes the man she once knew. And those moments, no matter how brief or rare, will always be enough to keep the illusion alive. No matter how much you want to save her, the decision is hers alone. The more you try to convince her, the more you push her, the stronger her husband's hold on her will become, and her loyalty will drive her to stand by his side."

He doesn't say anything more, and I remain silent as well. Yet in my mind, I'm analyzing his words. It's true that when I first arrived here, I had no idea what Karel was capable of. There were times he frightened me, but I'm certain if he had ever dared to hurt me, I would have given up all hope of finding the man I once knew.

Right?

Kaïs pulls his scarf back over his mouth, and we descend the stairs. A gust of wind greets us as soon as we step outside. The air is hot, suffocating. The wind is so strong it slows us down, making it hard to move forward. At times, it hits me so hard I can't keep moving. I'm already out of breath, and we haven't even reached the tower yet.

"We should turn back," Kaïs shouts, his voice barely audible over the howling wind.

"No!" I shout back, louder, determined.

I push forward, but almost stumble when another gust slams into us. We can't see anything more than a couple of feet ahead, and soon, Kaïs disappears from view. I'm completely blinded by the sand. I scream his name, but the wind's howl drowns me out. Even the beating of my heart is deafening.

Disoriented but resolved, I decide to keep going. The wind is against me, so I know I need to keep moving into it to reach the tower. I lean forward to brace myself against the gusts, my knees bent, moving slowly. With my hands shielding my eyes, I keep the sand from blinding me further. My gaze stays fixed on my feet, and when the ground beneath me feels smoother, I know I've reached the tower. I step inside, finally sheltered from the storm. The sound of the wind roaring between the walls is terrifying, but at least I'm no longer blinded by the dust. Kaïs is here, too, just as out of breath as I am.

"We can't go any further right now."

I nod, resigned. He's right. I should've listened to him. With this storm, we'll never be able to find our way.

"We'll try again when the wind dies down," he reassures me.

"I'm sorry," I whisper weakly.

His eyes meet mine, and his lips curve into a sympathetic smile, so I assume he heard me. I turn away, and we're about to head back when a group of men enter the tower. I recognize Karel by his jacket, and all I want is to lose myself in his arms. But my blood turns to ice when my eyes land on the person beside him—Mira. She seems distant, lost. She doesn't even notice me.

I take a step back. I should've known he would find out, but I never imagined he'd go so far as to thwart her rescue. His eyes narrow as my jaw clenches. He can't see it, hidden as I am behind my scarf, but I do my best to convey the hatred I feel for him in that moment. Without a word, he moves ahead of me, guiding Mira toward the palace, likely to have her taken to the dungeons. I have no idea what punishment awaits a woman who tries to escape her fate, but guilt crashes over me. In trying to save her, I've only brought her more suffering.

I'm about to follow them when Karel stops and, after leaving Mira in the care of one of his men, turns to Kaïs and me.

"Take her home," he orders his cousin.

I'm ready to protest when his hard gaze locks onto mine. He steps closer, lowering his head until, if it weren't for the scarves covering our faces, our lips would almost touch.

"Don't even think about visiting her. You'll go home and wait for me. Quietly."

"Quietly?" I snap, my voice sharp.

"I think that's the best thing you can do. This is all your fault, Kalliopee. You should've stayed in your place."

I grip the folds of my dress to keep from slapping him. My heart takes such a violent blow that it feels like it's trying to climb up into my throat. He turns his back on me, and I want to hurl something hurtful at him, make him feel the pain I'm enduring. But I can't. I'm too overwhelmed, frozen in place, unable to utter a single word. *What have I done?*

"Kalliopee," Kaïs calls gently, his hand resting on my elbow.

I can't bring myself to face him, torn between guilt and the deep disappointment of being betrayed by the man I love.

I leave the shelter of the tower, letting the wind carry me. The storm that had blinded me earlier now feels like a blessing, making me feel as though I'm nowhere, far from Lapisia. Far from him. I try to stop moving, but the wind seems to be against me; whenever I pause, it forces me forward.

When I finally step inside the palace walls, I untie the scarf and pull it off, letting it dangle from my fingertips.

"Kalliopee," Kaïs tries again as I reach the door to our room.

"What will happen to her?"

"Nothing serious."

His words make me laugh nervously, rather than comfort me. *Nothing serious*? Resting my forehead against the wooden door, I try to clear my mind, but Karel's betrayal keeps hitting me, each time with more pain.

"He…" I breathe, unable to find the words. "How could he do this? Why go so far?"

I don't cry. I can't. The anger is so overwhelming that it drowns out everything else. I don't wait for a response and head straight to my quarters.

I pass Sienna, who looks startled by my numbness. "Is everything all right, Princess?"

"I'm going to take a shower… Don't let anyone disturb me, not even the prince," I say, exhausted.

She stays frozen as I walk past, and even with my back to her, I can feel her gaze following me. I'll reassure her later. Right now, all I want is to wash away the dust clinging to my body. I just want to rid myself of this feeling of betrayal.

Would a physical wound have hurt more? I'm not sure, but I know one thing—I don't think I'll ever be able to forgive him for this wound he's left on my heart.

Chapter 37

Kalliopee

When I step out of the bathroom, I see Karel sitting on the bed, facing me, his jaw clenched. I look away, trying to contain the destructive energy surging through me, and head toward our closet. I have never been so angry with him before. This rage is beyond reason—it burns my skin, tightens my muscles. It torments my heart and churns in my stomach.

He clears his throat, and the sound makes my eyelids twitch. I clutch my towel tighter, focusing on the shelves as I search for clean clothes. I scan them, one by one, hoping it will help me forget he's there, but his presence feels heavier when he rises to come closer. It's suffocating.

"Don't come near me," I snap.

He lets out a laugh, but it's void of any joy, and my heart twists painfully at the sound.

"How could you?" I thunder, finally turning to face him.

He's so close I have to tilt my head up to meet his eyes. He's not expecting me to push him, so he stumbles back when my palms suddenly slam against his chest. I do it again, and again. Each time I push him, I feel the energy rise inside me, and suddenly I'm like a fire fueled by anger. The heat spreads, the flames rise, consuming everything. But then he grabs my wrists, stopping me. With one move, he smothers the blaze, leaving only embers.

My breathing is erratic, while his is controlled, though I can tell he's holding back from gripping my arms any tighter. I see it in the way his jaw is clenched, the way his neck is taut. But his restraint doesn't stop me. I don't care if I push him to his limit—nothing matters anymore. Because of him, Mira is in danger.

I try to free myself, spitting out the words that have been burning inside me since I realized what he did.

"I hate you. I hate you. I—"

He cuts me off, crushing his mouth against mine, but I hate even the taste of him. I cry against his lips because the pain of his betrayal is only made worse by the fact that my heart still belongs to him. What hurts the most is this love that consumes me, despite everything. I struggle against him again, and he finally lets me go.

"Are you done? Are you calm now?" he growls.

Infuriated he's blaming me for my anger, I push him again, and this time he throws me onto the bed. His body pins mine down, preventing me from escaping. He grabs my wrists again, leaving me no way to fight back.

"I'm just enforcing the law!" he yells, his rage boiling over.

"Enforcing the law?" I repeat, shocked. "You could've turned a blind eye, pretended that—"

"No," he cuts me off. "I couldn't. It's gone too far."

I close my eyes, trying to calm myself, but it's no use. "You betrayed me!"

My chest trembles, a sign tears are threatening to escape. I hear him sigh, then he releases me, and the weight pressing on me lifts as he stands up.

"Don't twist this around," he says coldly. "I'm not the one responsible for what happened. You are. *You* came up with this plan, *you* put her in danger, and now look at the outcome."

"I was trying to save her."

"Well, you failed," he says harshly. "So, if you're looking for someone to blame, take a good look in the mirror."

The look of hatred in his eyes stings my throat, but before I can respond, he's gone.

Instead of letting the pain consume me, I distract myself with simple tasks—getting dressed, fixing my hair. I know deep down I'm only delaying the inevitable, that moment when I'll finally break.

Sienna comes in a little later, telling me that Kaïs wants to speak with me. Unfortunately, I'm in no mood to see anyone.

My servant reappears.

"He says it's urgent, Princess."

I finally tear my gaze away from the mirror and look at her.

She nods to confirm the importance of the message. My fingers tremble as I set down the brush in my hand and head to the sitting room.

When I see Kaïs, he looks worried. Knowing this conversation needs to be private, I order the staff to leave us alone. Once everyone is gone, we sit down.

"How are you?" he asks.

That simple question is enough to reignite the bitterness I feel. "Just as well as earlier…" I say bitterly.

Kaïs grimaces, and I immediately regret my words. He's only ever helped me, and I'm being unfair to him.

"I'm sorry, it's just… I'm not doing well," I admit honestly.

He gives me a compassionate smile, and I force myself to ask the question that's been eating at me, even though I don't know if I can handle the answer.

"You haven't told me what she's facing."

"You and Karel haven't talked?" he asks, surprised.

I let out a bitter laugh and shake my head. "I said horrible things to him, and he said worse back…"

I try to say this lightly, to soften the blow it's dealt my already wounded heart, but Kaïs's expression remains grim. That's when I realize something's wrong.

"What's going on?" I ask.

"Karel didn't arrest her because she was trying to escape."

I freeze, my breath catching. If not for that, why would he have stopped her?

"But he—"

"She killed her husband," he tells me. "At dawn, he left the house but came back. He caught her while she was preparing to leave. He… he lost it, so she defended herself. She's going to be sentenced to the Torture of Time."

I stand, trying to process his words, desperately searching for a solution that won't come. I know all too well what they mean.

"She can be saved. Like me," I whisper, clinging to hope.

A wave of dizziness hits me when Kaïs shakes his head. He comes over, helping me to sit down. Everything spins around me as I replay what I thought, what I had imagined.

She's going to die.

Because of me.

He was right.

I feel the blood drain from my face. I hear Kaïs giving orders, but I can't make out the words. I don't know how long I remain in this daze, but I push my emotions down, holding them back from overwhelming me.

Then, when those familiar green eyes lock onto mine, I break.

When Karel comes to my side, I collapse. "It's my fault," I confess, feeling sick. "All my fault. I… I…"

I can't breathe, my chest tightening with every attempt. I sit up, ignoring the dizziness threatening to pull me down. My skin itches, as though guilt is eating me alive from the inside. I'm burning up—like a fire, but a fire that's consuming me.

I try to rip off my clothes, no longer caring if Kaïs or Sienna are still in the room. I need to get rid of these suffocating layers—this skin that burns, this flesh that's gnawing at my bones.

"Karel," I beg, gasping for air that won't come.

"Just breathe, Kalliopee, breathe."

I try, but I can't. The world tilts as Karel lifts me. Black spots dance before my eyes. Nothing in, nothing out. My body feels like it's forgotten how to function.

I don't realize where we are until Karel sets me down, and cold water crashes over my head. It's so icy I gasp, finally pulling air into my lungs. The breath is so sharp it makes me cough.

"Breathe," he orders, his voice stern as he kneels beside me.

Ignoring our soaked clothes, he moves closer, cupping my face in his hands. I inhale, exhale, inhale, exhale. At first, my breathing is erratic, but slowly it steadies. I focus on his sharp green eyes, their intensity grounding me, calming me.

"I didn't mean to yell at you," he mutters, half apologetic.

I shake my head, knowing his tone was only out of concern. As my breathing normalizes, reality crashes down on me.

"I condemned her," I say, my throat tight.

"Don't say that—"

"I condemned her, and I blamed you. I'm… I'm sorry," I sob.

Sometimes, I'm so unfair to him. I know how hard he tries to honor my beliefs. If I had just taken the time to understand, to think it through, I would have known he would never have done something like that. And the weight of my guilt only grows heavier.

He turns off the water and wraps me in a towel. Our clothes are soaked, and I'm shivering now—not from heat, but from cold, deep inside. Instead of letting me walk, he carries me to our bed. I'm too drained to move, so Karel gently removes my wet clothes. I expect him to bring me something dry to wear, but instead, he pulls back the blanket. He gestures for me to slip under it, then tucks it around my bare body. Without meeting my eyes, he stands.

My lip trembles as I realize how deeply I hurt him with my false accusations.

He heads back to the bathroom, and for a long time, I hear the water running. Then, the door opens, and he reappears. He comes over, a towel wrapped around his waist, and sits down, his back to me. I sit up, leaning against the headboard, waiting. He says nothing at first, and then his shoulders slump. My heart breaks. The wound is wide open.

"Despite all the secrets I've uncovered about you, I never blamed you for any of it."

His voice isn't angry, just wounded, and somehow, that hurts even more. I look down at my fingers, clasped around my stomach, feeling the weight of his words.

"Whether it was the fact that our relationship started with a lie or that you hid the true nature of Darkos. Yes, I know he's a half-blood, and I know you've known since we left for Aquaria."

I swallow, unable to respond.

"I always gave you the benefit of the doubt. I thought maybe I hadn't shown you enough that you could trust me. It's true I'm not always gentle, that I act on impulse, and that I don't forgive easily. I'm not perfect—far from it. But… I would never have stopped Mira because she wanted to run."

I look at his profile. He's sitting straight, staring at the wall in front of him, unblinking.

"I knew you and Kaïs were planning her escape. And even though my hands were tied, that didn't mean I agreed with her situation. That's why I let you act without interference. Because I knew you needed to save her, and I wasn't capable of doing it myself."

He pauses, giving me a moment to process everything. How could I have thought he betrayed me? I'm about to respond when his distant voice continues.

"No matter how hard I try to be worthy of you, I feel like it's never enough, like I'm not moving fast enough. I didn't make these laws, I'm not the king, I can't change the world, Kalliopee. You're asking too much of me."

"I'm sorry," I whisper.

"I feel like I'm constantly fighting against the wind. No matter how hard I struggle, it only blows stronger. I'm losing my mind."

His body shakes, and I can feel him on the verge of breaking down.

"Karel," I say, alarmed.

"I can't take it anymore, Kalliopee."

This time, I know his words aren't just about us. It feels like he's talking about much more than our relationship. And suddenly, my worry is no longer selfish. I'm not afraid for myself, but for him.

"What's happening?"

"Everyone expects too much from me." He murmurs the words like he's speaking to someone else, as if he's not really talking to me at all.

"That's what it means to be a prince, and when you become king—"

"And what about me?" His head turns toward me. The weight of his gaze eclipses everything else that's happened until now.

"You?"

He turns away, and no matter how long I wait, he doesn't respond. I watch his profile, trying to figure out what he can't bring himself to say. Karel has always seemed like he could overcome anything. Yet, in this moment, it's as if the weight of the world is on his shoulders.

I push the blanket aside and press my body against his back. His warmth envelops me instantly, but it doesn't ease the tightness in my throat. As my lips brush against his shoulder blades, he tenses, and that only deepens my fear. I hate feeling him so distant from me. I need him to tell me my words haven't damaged our bond, that I still belong to him, that his heart is still mine. I shift, reaching out to place my hand on his cheek, but he stops me.

A knot forms in my throat. His rejection stings, something I never thought I'd have to endure. I close my eyes when he moves, not wanting to witness him pulling away, not wanting to see him slip from my grasp. My eyes snap open when his warm fingers grip the back of my neck. His wounded gaze meets mine, and for the first time, I see Karel looking truly vulnerable.

"Never doubt me again, no matter what happens, no matter what anyone says, no matter what you imagine—always give me the benefit of the doubt."

He searches my eyes, but all he finds are tears.

"I won't do it again."

"Kalliopee…"

"I promise. Please forgive me."

I end up straddling him when his arms circle my hips. He holds me so tightly it's almost painful, but I don't care. Because when I thought I had hurt him enough to lose him, it felt like a part of me was dying.

CHAPTER 38

KAREL

Lying on my side, I watch Kalliopee's profile as she finally drifts off to sleep. We slid under the sheets, and I held her until sleep claimed her. Now, she seems more at peace. Surprisingly, I no longer feel any anger toward her—no bitterness. It's strange how she's the only one who can hurt me so deeply without leaving me with a thirst for revenge. How much would I be willing to endure from her? A lot…

When I realized she had misunderstood my intentions and Mira's arrest, I was too hurt to tell her the truth. The things she said were painful, but I didn't do anything to correct her. Deep down, I think I wanted to see how far she'd go out of resentment. Or maybe I needed her to blame me.

I was being honest when I told her I was going crazy. I'm exhausted by the expectations of my father, Amadeus, and my wife. I wish I could scream at the king that I no longer want his vengeance, tell Amadeus I don't want the throne, and tell Kalliopee I no longer want the crown.

But I'm too much of a coward. I'm drowning in my lies, and they're suffocating me.

Carefully, I pull away from her, trying not to wake her. She whimpers, rolls onto her side, and curls up into a ball. I wish I could stay beside her, but I need to find a way out of this situation before it destroys us both—I'm sure of it.

The sun is barely setting, and the storm that's been sweeping across Lapisia for two days shows no signs of calming. Quietly, I grab some clothes from the wardrobe, slipping into black pants and a short-sleeved shirt before leaving the bedroom.

The apartments are silent. I had dismissed the staff after I took Kalliopee to the bathroom. We needed to be alone. They brought us a snack, and we ate before she fell asleep.

I cross the living room and head into my study. Walking over to the bookshelf, I carefully scan the titles. I pull out a leather-bound book and take it to my desk. *The History of the Union of the Five*. If I'm not sure who I want to be, I can at least look for a loophole that will allow Kalliopee and the other women to be who they want.

I sit down and grab a notepad and pencil.

After hours of turning pages and reading chapters that taught me nothing, I look up when the door creaks. Kalliopee, in a pale pink nightgown, steps into the room. Her wavy hair cascades down her shoulders. Still half-asleep, she takes a step toward me but then stops.

"Everything okay?" I ask, noticing how she avoids my gaze.

"Yes… Aren't you coming to bed?"

Her heterochromatic eyes settle timidly on me. Despite the dim lighting, I can see the worry etched on her face.

"What are you doing?" she asks, curious.

I think for a moment, searching for the right words, and decide to tell her part of the truth. "I'm looking for a loophole, a way to free the women."

Even though she's not close to me, I can see her eyes begin to well with tears, and her body tenses. My explanation seems to convince her to come closer, as she quietly closes the door behind her and walks around the desk. I shift to make room for her to sit on my lap, which she does gently, and then I pull us closer to the desk. I inhale the scent of her skin as she studies the page I've paused on.

"Thank you," she whispers.

I don't reply, knowing words would be too much.

"It's in terrible shape," she remarks sadly, flipping through the pages.

I can't help but smile. Kalliopee has a deep love for books, treating them like priceless relics.

"It's very old. It's just a book," I say.

"No," she counters. "It's our past and our present. It's our history."

I lean back slightly and glance at the page where she's stopped. A history from three centuries ago that hasn't seen any significant change. It's as if everything has been frozen in time. Before the Union was formed, each kingdom lived more or less in isolation. Past events had taken their toll on our peoples, and out of distrust, they kept their doors closed to others. Then, just over three hundred years ago, our ancestors realized cooperation was necessary. We had to share our resources if we wanted to ensure the survival of our species. There were long negotiations on how to proceed. Some kingdoms were hostile toward those who didn't share their values. So it was decided differences would be erased. The five monarchs voted for common laws. If we wanted access to the Union's resources, we had to abide by its rules.

Since then, nothing has changed. Until the war. The Union wasn't dissolved, but it now exists in silence. Leaving it when I take the throne would allow us to make our own laws, but I know it would be a risky move, especially in this post-war era. Trade has only just resumed. Lapisia still hasn't recovered from those years of fighting, and it will likely take many more years for us to fully rebuild. We don't have enough farmland to feed the entire kingdom on our own. The Union is necessary to us. I hate this realization because I have yet to find a way around the laws that keep Kalliopee and women like her in chains.

"One day, all this will just be history. It won't be the present anymore," I say firmly.

She turns a page, some of the words faded beyond recognition.

"What would an ideal world look like for you?" I ask, curious.

I smile because it reminds me of the conversations we used to have in our clearing that summer. But back then, our concerns were much more childish. She takes a deep breath, likely considering how best to answer.

"My ideal world? It would be a world where Mira isn't locked up for defending her life. A world where Darkos doesn't have to hide his origins. A world where…" She trails off.

I wait for her to continue, but she sighs, as if giving up.

"A world where…?" I prompt her gently.

"Where I could sit on the Viridian throne."

I never considered the possibility that she'd want to rule, even though I've always been certain she would fit the role perfectly.

It doesn't take me long to find the right words. I believe we all have a reason for being alive. A quest to fulfill, whether it holds significance in history or not. No matter how small our mission, I'm convinced we all have one. Mine, I'm certain, is this: to shape the world into her vision. To mold it for her.

"One day, I'll give you that world."

She shakes her head, her hair brushing against my face, and then a soft laugh escapes her lips. One of those laughs that slips out when we desire something but know it's too idealistic to be real.

"You think the world is ready for that much change?"

"I don't know," I admit truthfully. "I can't say for sure, but I guess we'll only find out by trying."

Over her shoulder, I watch as she flips through the pages, some of them barely holding on. She eventually sets the book down gently and takes a deep breath. For a while, we sit there, savoring the silence, the calm after the storm of the afternoon's events. Outside, the tempest seems to have died down. It makes me smile again. As if the weather were in sync with our hearts.

"There's something I want to ask you," she says softly.

I trace my fingers along her arm, waiting for her request.

"I want to see her."

My hands freeze.

"Why?"

"Because all of this is my fault. Because I know what she's going through—I've been in her place. The only difference is, I had hope you'd wake up."

I kiss her shoulder as I think it over. The thought of her going there unsettles me, but I also know refusing her would hurt her deeply.

"All right," I murmur against her skin.

She pulls my arms tighter around her, and my hands rest on her stomach as I stare at the book. Those hours spent buried in its pages made me realize I don't want to be the son my father wants. I don't want to be the king Amadeus hopes I'll become. I just want to be the husband Kalliopee deserves. The one who can give her the world she dreams of. I have to find a way to free her and, in doing so, save us both. Because if I don't, our downfall is inevitable.

For both of us.

For all three of us.

***

"Are you sure?" I ask her.

Kalliopee stares at the door Mira is held behind. I hadn't waited for daybreak. At dawn, the judgment would be passed. She nods, and I kiss the top of her head before sliding the key into the lock. The door opens to a cell devoid of light. The condemned have no windows, no furniture. Just cold stone and darkness. The musty smell fills the air, assaulting our senses. That's when it hits me—this is where Kalliopee was held when Hrim wounded me.

A faint beam of light filters through the door, revealing Mira huddled in a corner of the room.

Kalliopee cautiously approaches her, while the young woman slowly lifts her head. Kalliopee kneels in front of her. Closing the door would give them privacy, but they would be left in darkness. I decide to step aside. At first, I only hear soft whispers, but soon their voices grow louder, echoing off the stone walls so I can make out their conversation.

"I shouldn't have… If I hadn't convinced you…"

"No, it would have happened sooner or later. Something would have eventually driven him mad, Your Highness. I'm sorry for causing you so much trouble."

My throat tightens, and I lower my gaze. The weight of helplessness is hard to bear. Mira is a skilled doctor, but more importantly, she has been an unwavering support for Kalliopee.

"I wish I could do something for you," Kalliopee says softly.

"There's nothing you can do. I'm just afraid. Were you afraid, too?

I don't hear her answer, but I imagine she nodded. I hear soft sniffles.

"I'm afraid the death will take too long, that the suffering will drag on for days."

Silence follows again. I risk a glance at the door. Kalliopee shifts, leans against the wall next to Mira, and takes her hand. I look away, trying to control my emotions.

"A friend came to visit me," my wife confesses to her. "He brought me food. I didn't touch it. I couldn't. Because I knew the energy from eating would just force me to endure longer."

I stare at the wall in front of me, imagining her loneliness that day, her helplessness, the injustice she suffered while I was kept alive a few floors above. What if I had died? The thought alone makes my chest feel like a void is opening inside it. I push the idea away.

For a long time, silence prevails again. I've taken the same position as them, sitting with my back to the wall. I guess a few hours pass because the first light of day filters through the window at the far end of the corridor. I'm about to tell Kalliopee that we need to leave when she clears her throat.

"I have poison."

My blood runs cold. Poison?

There's a long silence, followed by a barely stifled sob. I don't know what Mira says in response, but I know it's time to stand so we can return to our quarters.

Kalliopee lifts her head when I appear, understanding it's time to go. She nods softly, placing her free hand on Mira's arm.

"Thank you for not leaving me alone," Mira whispers to my wife.

Kalliopee gives her a faint smile and pulls away from her. Slowly, she stands and walks toward me without looking back. Her eyes lock with mine, and as I close the door, her face contorts with sadness, and she stifles a sob. We stand there for a few moments, just looking at each other. I don't know what to do to ease her pain; all I can do is bear witness to it.

"I'm sorry," I finally say.

She shakes her head before wiping away the few tears that have fallen. "Give me that world, one day."

I wrap my arms around her, silently promising myself I'll see it through. No matter the Union or whether the world is ready.

Kalliopee imagines the future, and I'll shape it. It's our mission together.

Chapter 39

Kalliopee

When we return to our rooms, Karel quickly heads to the shower. I sit down in front of my vanity. With a heavy heart, I retrieve the egg-shaped box. My fingers trembling, I lift the lid. Carefully, I take out the pendant holding the poison. I'm disgusted with myself for what I'm about to do, but if it can bring her peace, I'll accept staining my soul a little.

I inhale deeply, wondering how I can possibly give it to her. It will be difficult to hand it to her at the trial; they won't let me get close. Maybe if I give it to Darkos, he could deliver it to her… I sigh. I promised her a gentle way out, but it seems I can't keep my word.

I stare relentlessly at the liquid inside.

"What does it do?"

My heart leaps when I hear Karel's voice ask the question. I close my hand around the pendant, trying to steady my breath, but I'm too afraid to answer.

"I thought it was a joke, but it's really poison, isn't it?"

I hear him approach, and I finally dare to look at his reflection in the mirror in front of me. He's already dressed, with his scarf and crown. How long have I been staring at this vial? Hands in his pockets, he stares at his shoes, as if avoiding my gaze. Then he turns his head toward the door, his jaw clenched. I can tell my silence is testing his patience.

"Yes," I murmur.

His eyes close for a few seconds, and then he straightens his posture, still presenting me his profile.

"What are its effects?" he repeats.

I lower my gaze to my clenched fist, then take a breath before opening my hand again. If I'm not mistaken, it's oxyome—a poisonous plant whose sap is lethal.

"The heart simply stops beating."

Death is quick and nearly painless. It used to be what my people used to end the suffering of patients for whom all hope of recovery was lost. But now, these plants are rare—I don't even know if they still grow. All I know is the royal apothecary keeps a few vials.

"Were you planning to use it on me?"

I turn to him, worried he might think that. I don't know why I never got rid of it, but I never considered using it against him. I'm surprised to see that, this time, he's looking directly at me. Our eyes meet. In his, I see a deep, visceral fear, and I immediately decide to reassure him.

"Never."

I nod to reinforce my words. His shoulders relax, and I can see the relief wash over him. He comes closer to me, crouching down to my level. "I'm glad to hear that," he says lightly.

Despite his tone, I can tell he's being sincere and he truly feared this poison was once meant for him. I get lost in his eyes, which, if you pay close attention, reveal much more than you'd think. Karel has worked so hard to hide his emotions that it takes a lot of patience to learn how to read him. I can't say I always succeed, but I'm getting better at it.

"I love you. I would never hurt you in any way. Never intentionally," I add.

His brow furrows at my last words, but it would have been hypocritical not to say them. Because I have hurt him before, even if it was never on purpose, and it will likely happen again.

A shadow of sadness passes through his green eyes, which seem to be dulling day by day. Why is he losing his brightness? I want to know what's troubling him so deeply lately, but I'm too afraid of what his answers might do to me. He still has secrets; I can see that. He sleeps poorly, he disappears again at times. He often meets with his father or Amadeus… Sometimes I wish I had the courage to ask him what these matters are that seem to consume him, but I can't bring myself to do it.

My heart pounds. These are all the words I can't manage to say to him, fighting to get out. They scream inside me, but I don't let any of them escape. Because I believe his secret could destroy me. So I keep us trapped in this illusory bubble we've created. One day, it will all end. I'm more and more certain of that, but I hope it happens as late as possible.

Last night, he promised me a free world. I'm no longer naïve. Even if his oath was sincere, that will never be possible. Our future will be bloody. When I arrived here, I was convinced our marriage would end the war, but after meeting so many kings, I know one of them will find a new excuse to plunge our kingdoms back into chaos. All I hope for now is to protect our child from these schemes.

Karel moves closer to me, brushing his lips lightly against mine before tenderly caressing my belly. It's starting to round, though for now, it feels more like bloating than pregnancy. Still, I'm beginning to appreciate the changes in my body, and so does he. Sometimes, when I wake up in the middle of the night, I catch him gently stroking it, as if it holds the most precious treasure. Each time, it soothes my heart. If I don't survive this childbirth, I know he'll take care of our child.

"In seven months," he whispers thoughtfully.

In seven months, yes.

Once again, he locks eyes with me, and I try my best to hide the fear I feel as I see the seriousness in his gaze. I offer him a faint smile. There's this feeling that clings to me, this anxiety twisting my stomach. As if the birth of this child will destroy our worlds.

He asked me to trust him. Yet, I can't shake the sense he's hiding something far more serious than all the secrets he's kept from me until now. I fear for myself, for my baby, for us.

On his birthday, I asked him about his plans if we were to have a son. I'm not foolish; I know all too well giving birth to a boy would make him heir to the throne of Viridia, but it's a possibility I refuse to dwell on, as it terrifies me. I love him. He loves me. I have no doubt about that. But one day he told me that, sometimes, looking at me reminded him of all those he had lost. What did he mean when he asked me to forgive him for the pain he would cause me, even if he didn't mean to?

His hand rests on my arm, pulling me out of my thoughts as it slides down. He intertwines his fingers with mine, kissing me with less restraint than before. Then, as he pulls away, he takes the pendant with him. I realize then that his kiss was just a distraction to steal the poison.

"I can't let you do this, he whispers in my ear."

My breath catches, and I involuntarily close my eyes. I feel him straighten, and a coldness washes over me. I want to scream at him to give it back, to stop interfering, but I can't. I just clench my fists and turn away before opening my eyes again. He's standing there, only a few steps away. I rise on shaky legs and head toward my closet.

"I'll get ready," I tell him before retreating to the bathroom.

Only when I'm alone do I allow a few tears to escape. I understand… surprisingly, yes, I understand, but it doesn't stop the pain.

I stare at my reflection. I'm pale, and the dark circles under my eyes reveal my lack of sleep. Maybe I should be a bit more like him? Maybe if I were more like him, I wouldn't feel like I'm carrying the weight of the world on my shoulders. Lock my emotions away, learn to control them.

These past few days have drained all my energy. I can feel I'm no longer the same, and even though I'm suffering today, I'll come out of it changed tomorrow. I was right when I told him that Lapisia would end up killing me. Because that's what's happening. It's killing the person I once was. Slowly.

***

Seated beside the king, I watch Mira standing in the center of the room. I try my best to hide the pain I feel seeing her judged like this, for taking a life to save her own. The eyes of the woman who's healed every one of my wounds are downcast, lost. I remember feeling the same way once. There, but not really present.

"Mira, wife of Jorgen Ozan, son of Rugàn, you are accused of murdering your husband. As the law dictates, any woman who has attempted to take her husband's life is condemned to death. Mira, you will be exposed before the people, without water, without food. Time will take its course, and when you take your final breath, the desert will be your grave. Thus, you will not only atone for your sins in life but also in death. You will never find rest and will pay eternally for your crime."

My breath halts at these words, as a plaintive whimper escapes the lips of the woman I consider a friend.

Beside me, the king rises and descends the two steps that separate him from her.

"Karel, my son," he calls.

Immediately, my husband joins him, without so much as a glance in my direction.

"I entrust you to personally escort the murderer," he orders, turning toward me.

I understand this command is meant to hurt me. Ordering the man I love to escort my friend to her death. Though it pains me, I show nothing. Karel grabs Mira's arm, forcing her to turn back. I stand and follow the procession. As difficult as it is, I won't abandon her. I will stay by her side for as long as it takes, even if it means spending nights on the streets of the city. Karel passes Jonah and whispers something to him. I think I see him speaking to Mira while Jonah watches the monarch. The king doesn't notice this strange exchange because he's facing me, a smirk on his lips. But I'm intrigued, so much so I want to tell the king to step aside.

He steps forward, but I don't back down. It wouldn't help.

"You know, I had no respect for you when you arrived."

"And now you do?"

Kaïs joins me, likely worried I might do something regrettable in my current state.

"No, I still don't. But today, you're no longer free."

"My uncle," Kaïs interjects.

The king turns to him and shakes his head.

"Have I made you suffer?" he asks me. "You certainly haven't seen the end of your troubles. What I have in store for you now is beyond your imagination," he concludes before turning away.

His words cut deep, and though he constantly tries to provoke me, I know they are cruelly true, not just an idle threat. That foreboding feeling again, over and over.

"What does he mean? Do you know something?" I ask Kaïs, my voice hoarse.

He shakes his head, as lost as I am. Kaïs once told me his father was the king's brother, and while they tolerated each other, they were never close. Xerios had always feared his younger brother, more charismatic, would steal the throne. When the queen died, Kaïs's father left Lapisia, thinking his children would be safer away from the palace. The king doesn't hold much regard for his nephew either. I believe Kaïs when he says he knows nothing. There's no doubt the monarch would share nothing important with him, and if Kaïs did know anything, he would tell me.

We're about to rejoin the procession when panicked screams reach us. We rush out of the hall, and I freeze when we reach the doors. Mira is struggling, pushing the guards away. Karel's behavior, however, catches my attention. He stares at her, unblinking, as if waiting for something. Nervously, I turn my attention back to her. She's gasping for breath, then collapses to the ground. A cold wave shoots down my spine as I watch her curl into a ball, clutching her chest. A guard approaches her to force her to stand. A crowd gathers around my friend's motionless body, while my husband stands apart. Jonah pushes through the crowd, crouches beside her, and then rises again without drawing much attention. My gaze shifts from one person to another until it lands on Samael, who wipes a split lip. I look away from him to focus on Karel again. He stares at me, his expression unreadable.

I realize then the chaos was likely a distraction so that Mira could ingest the poison.

"What the—" Kaïs begins but doesn't finish his sentence.

"Well, what's going on?" the king shouts, furious.

The crowd disperses as the royal physician, a frail man, approaches the king. "Your Highness, the condemned has passed away."

"What did you do to her?" he demands, enraged, turning to me.

"Uncle, she was with you," Kaïs defends me. "We all saw her."

The sovereign stares at me, making no effort to hide the hatred he feels toward me.

"She'll still feed the jackals in the desert," he sneers, looking me up and down arrogantly before leaving.

I struggle to breathe, too shaken by the events that have just unfolded. Around us, people return to their tasks as if Mira's death were insignificant. Only Sienna stays by my side. After all, she knew her, too. I look at Mira's lifeless body, consoled by the fact she didn't have to endure a slow death or the humiliation of being put on display for all to see. Sienna takes my wrist and whispers I should rest, for the baby. Before turning away, I catch Karel's gaze.

Though the situation hardly seems appropriate, I try my best to convey my gratitude to him.

Because he didn't stop me from ending my friend's suffering.

No, he helped me.

CHAPTER 40

KAREL

Followed closely by Kaïs, I enter the palace. Ever since he joined the army, I've felt somewhat relieved. I know he won't leave, and although I often tell him he exhausts me and I'd prefer if he went home, his presence is important. For both Kalliopee and me.

"They'll need to toughen up," Kaïs comments.

I realize he's talking about our recruits. I don't respond, but he probably senses my opinion is even firmer. If they don't do it quickly, they'll be kicked out.

The young men who choose to become soldiers can do so as early as their tenth birthday. Usually, they're boys from families with few resources… Their families know if they join the army, they'll be fed and housed during their training. Of course, nothing forces them to continue this career once their education is complete. Just as nothing forces us to keep them. We'd be foolish to have men in our ranks who can't defend themselves. Unfortunately for us, this year's batch isn't the best…

Normally, I handle teaching them the basics during the first few weeks, then Vàli takes over. But he's been picky lately. He's asking me to test them even more and extend their integration. I think he's tired of seeing them quit as soon as things get tough.

Today, we left the safety of the walls, and I had them run through the desert, loaded down like pack mules. Naturally, they collapsed the moment we got back to the barracks, making it impossible to continue their training.

I open the door to my quarters and am surprised to find the place quiet. Kalliopee must be resting; sometimes she sends the staff away when she's too tired for company. I signal to Kaïs to wait. He's planning to take her out for a walk before dinner. I know it does her good, and she misses their outings, even if she never complains. I head to the library, where she likes to relax sometimes.

The room is empty, but my gaze falls on a box containing supplies. I immediately recognize the tools used to restore old books. When I was younger, this was how Amadeus taught me patience and precision. He also taught me to take special care of things that hold value—not necessarily monetary value. I was always amazed to see him handle what seemed to me to be just an ordinary book with such care. In many ways, Kalliopee is like him. She's wise, and although our past hasn't always been kind to women, she doesn't reject it. To her, ignoring it would be to forget, and forgetting would lead to repeating the same mistakes, over and over again.

Unconsciously, my mind drifts back to the condition of the book on the history of the Five Nations.

I leave the room, feeling like there's a weight of lead in my stomach. I don't know why, but a sudden sense of unease grips me, making my steps heavier as I head toward my study.

Kaïs has settled in the living room, waiting calmly, unaware of the rising panic inside me. With the flat of my hand, I slowly push open the door. Silence greets me. My chair is positioned in front of my bookshelf, and a few books are scattered on the desk. Nervously, my eyes lift to the highest shelf. I take a step back, my face going pale as anxiety floods me.

"Is everything okay?" Kaïs asks.

But I'm already rushing through the living room, heading straight for our bedroom. The door slams into the wall as I throw it open, unable to hold back my strength. I approach the bed and see the letters. With trembling hands, I pick one up, and the pain that grips my gut is so intense I wonder how I'm still standing. Alarmed, I scan the room. Where is she? Then a glint on the floor catches my eye—a puddle of water coming from the bathroom—and that's when I finally hear the sound of running water.

Kaïs, sensing my growing panic, has followed me.

"What's going on?"

I push him aside and race toward the bathroom door, trying to open it in vain.

"Kalliopee?" I shout, pounding on the wood.

If I had been scared of the words she might throw at me, or

the argument we could have had, now it's a different kind of fear that overwhelms me. The same fear I felt the day she was attacked. The same as in Aquaria. The same as when she was sentenced. That terror that never leaves me, not even in my dreams.

"Karel? What's happening?" my cousin asks, alarmed.

My throat is too tight to answer. I throw myself against the door, trying to break it down with my shoulder, but it won't budge! I shout her name, begging her to open up or at least talk to me.

"Karel?"

"Help me, Kaïs! Help me!" I plead, urgency lacing my voice.

Kaïs rushes to my side, and together we slam our shoulders against the door. On the second hit, we finally manage to break it down.

In the momentum, we both fall. Kaïs lands on the floor, but I manage to grab onto the sink. The reflection in the mirror shatters my heart. It disintegrates like desert sand, blown away by the wind. There's nothing left. I turn quickly, but slip on a puddle. I don't even feel the pain in my side. I just pull myself up by the edge of the bathtub and reach her. She looks as though she's simply sleeping, as if she just drifted off.

I plunge my hands into the warm, pink-tinted water and lift her from the tub, sloshing water over the sides with my movements. I collapse to the floor, cradling Kalliopee in my arms. That's when I notice the knife on the ground and, with horror, see the cuts on her wrists.

"*Shaadi*?" I call her, my voice hoarse. "*Shaadi*, answer me."

My throat is so tight it hurts. I have to blink several times to hold back the tears clouding my vision. A sob of relief escapes me when her eyes flutter open. She looks disoriented, but alive. For now, that's all that matters. Her eyelids flutter again, and then her gaze locks onto mine. I can already see the change that has taken place inside her. Weakly, she tries to push me away, but I tighten my hold, shaking my head.

I turn toward Kaïs, sitting in the water, his face pale as he watches the scene unfold. Guilt surges inside me again, along with fear. Fear he will hate me, too. Fear of losing the only family I have left because of my silence—her, for whom I would give my life, and him, whom I consider a brother.

"Go get Mira's father," I order him. "Hurry. Don't speak to anyone, and tell the guards to watch the door. No one is allowed in!"

He stares at me for a moment, nods, and stands up. He doesn't even seem to notice she's wearing nothing but her underwear. Neither do I, for that matter—it's the least of my worries.

Once he's finally gone, I look at her, reaching behind me for some towels. Her eyes, empty, lock onto mine. I see nothing in her gaze. No anger, no sadness. Just emptiness.

"I'll explain everything," I murmur.

I stand, my body weighed down by despair, and leave the bathroom with Kalliopee in my arms.

After laying her on the bed, I wrap two towels around her wrists, securing them, then dry her skin. I pull the covers over her and wait. I wait for her expression to change, for her to show anger, disappointment—anything but this void that seems to have consumed her. I've lost her, I know that, but I don't want her to lose herself, too.

Her eyes remain fixed on mine, but she's never seemed as lifeless as she does now. Despite all the times I've frightened her, despite all the times I've hurt her, she never lost her light.

"I'll explain, I promise," I plead, unable to stop myself.

She lets out a tired sigh and turns her head away. It's too late—she's asked me too many times to talk, and I've always refused because I knew all it would lead to was her hatred. I hid behind Amadeus's warnings because I didn't have the courage to face my mistakes. I wanted to push this moment away, to hold on to the love she still had for me. I imagined she would hate me, that she would never forgive me, but I never thought she'd make a decision like this. I underestimated the pain I caused her.

Her skin is a little pale, but she has enough color I'm not panicking to the point of losing my mind. I take her delicate hand in mine, but she weakly pulls away. This time, I don't insist—I let her go. I feel like I did that night, galloping through the desert, wondering if the gaping hole in my chest would ever heal, if the pain tearing me apart would eventually kill me.

"Say something," I murmur, my voice hoarse.

Again, she looks at me, but it's a Kalliopee I've never seen before.

"Hate me. Despise me," I beg, "but talk to me."

For the first time, I don't hide my tears from her.

Her gaze drifts into the distance, and she's so still that it feels like she's no longer here. Her lips part, and she exhales again. I watch her, impatient, hoping she'll finally say something.

I glance down at the letters that make me want to vomit. Why did I keep them? Why didn't I throw them away? At first, it was to stay focused on my goal, but after coming back from Aquaria, I'd made my decision. I would protect her heart instead of seeking revenge. I would save my soul. So why? Why didn't I get rid of them?

Because deep down, you wanted her to know! Those lies were suffocating you...

The door opens behind me. I stand, gather the letters, and leave the doctor to tend to her. I'd prefer to stay, to make sure everything's okay, but I know I no longer have a place by her side. Once in the living room, I turn away from Kaïs, who's out of breath from running through the city, and head out to the terrace. I never come here. It's always far too hot to enjoy. The sun is setting slowly on the horizon, painting the desert with an intense orange glow. I light one of the decorative candles, still brand new, and set it on the stone railing.

"Karel," Kaïs calls out.

I stay silent, unable to tell my cousin the truth. Before I can place one of the letters over the flame, Kaïs grabs the stack from my hands.

As he reads, I stare endlessly at the melting wax dripping onto the stone. Occasionally, a slight breeze makes the flame flicker, but it never goes out. When he's finished, he shoves the pile against my chest.

"I hope it was worth it. I hope your plan was worth this sacrifice."

He doesn't wait for a response before going back inside. I glance over my shoulder.

He sits down in a chair and buries his face in his hands.

One by one, I hold the letters over the flame. I watch the fire consume the words that just destroyed everything. The paper blackens, and I let the wind carry away what's left. Months of lies, of cowardice. But now, it's over. Everything is over.

Chapter 41

Kalliopee

That Morning

Sore all over, I wake up but find myself unable to move. A warm chest is pressed against my back, more like it's trapping me. While it's a pleasant sensation first thing in the morning, his weight quickly becomes overwhelming. Karel is a big man, and it feels like I'm caught in a tightening vise with every little movement I make. I try to slide out of bed, but his firm hand pulls me back against him, growling softly into my neck. I let out a quiet laugh, instantly relaxing and enjoying the moment.

It's been a month since Mira's death. A month during which Karel and I have grown even closer. His action was risky, and I'm grateful for it because I know Mira couldn't have been saved. At least she was granted a quick death. An autopsy was conducted, and the doctor concluded it was cardiac arrest. He speculated the recent events had weakened her heart. Of course, the king called for a second opinion. I was surprised to learn Mira's father had been summoned.

When I went to meet him, he asked if I had any idea who might have poisoned Mira. His conclusions were different—he found a natural death unlikely. After all, he knew Mira and her physical condition well. I couldn't lie to him. It might've been foolish, a huge risk on my part, but something about the way he questioned me convinced me. It was as if he was pleading with me to tell him a kind soul had wanted to help his daughter. So, I told him a half-truth, leaving out Karel's involvement.

Mira's father knew of my affection for his daughter, but I wasn't sure revealing my husband's role was the right choice. He thanked me, and just as I suspected, he falsified the report. As for my friend's body, there was nothing we could do, though I suspect Karel sent his men to retrieve it. The next day, her body was already gone.

He mumbles something unintelligible into my hair.

He loosens his grip, allowing me to turn around. When I face him, I can't help but soften at the sight of his sleepy expression.

"You're not sleeping?" he repeats more clearly.

"The sun's been up for a while."

He looks surprised, then props himself up slightly to glance at the window behind me. Lately, it hasn't been uncommon for me to wake up before him. Not because I get up earlier, but because his nights are restless, and sleep only comes to him much later.

His brow furrows, and he rolls onto his back. I study his profile for a long moment as he runs a hand through his hair.

"How's the recruit training going?" I ask, genuinely interested.

"They're still young, but they learn quickly."

"Then why do you seem so upset?"

He tilts his head in my direction, and instead of answering, he grabs me by the nape and kisses my forehead.

"You know you'll have to talk to me one day, right?"

"Just… not now."

"So when?"

I can feel him tense. I know I'm frustrating him.

When we wake up, I usually get to see a softer side of Karel, but it never lasts. As the hours pass, he becomes darker. By the evening, when we're at his father's table, he grows distant, and afterward, he can be either cold or possessive. I get lost in all his different sides. Naively, I thought catching him at his best moment would help me get some answers, but I realize now all I've done is accelerate the progression of his worsening moods for the day.

He buries his head in his pillow, and his hand instinctively comes to rest on my slightly swollen belly. It seems to calm him, and I feel the same soothing effect.

Sometimes, when we're like this, I close my eyes and imagine we're far away from here, in a little house nestled in the green forests of Viridia. A life where we would just be Karel and Kalliopee. No titles, no crowns, no responsibilities.

"What are you planning to do today?" he asks me.

"I don't know," I lie.

The truth is, I've managed to get the materials I need to restore some old books, and I'm eager to breathe new life into those in his library.

"I'll be gone all day," he sighs, sitting up.

He pushes the sheet aside, revealing his bare body, which immediately makes my stomach tighten. My desire has only been growing these past few days. It goes hand in hand with my moods, which have become erratic and often extreme. Kaïs takes great pleasure in testing my patience. It seems the hormones have stripped away all my usual restraint.

The king felt the brunt of it two days ago. While we were eating, he provoked me again. This time, I couldn't hold back and gave him a sharp retort. Karel ordered me to be silent, and I felt a lump in my throat. I couldn't even stop the tears from spilling. I hated him for siding with his father. When we returned to our quarters, I locked myself in the library and cried until I fell asleep on the chaise. I woke up in the middle of the night as he carried me to our bed. I wanted to push him away, tell him I would rather sleep in the desert than so close to him, but that would have been a lie. In truth, I was relieved he came for me. It wasn't much, but after being scolded in front of his father and Kaïs, even the smallest gesture felt like a healing balm.

I glance at him as he locks himself in the bathroom. I sit up, fluff my pillow for extra support, and settle against the headboard. I enjoy the apparent tranquility of the morning. As always, he quickly emerges from the adjoining room and begins dressing immediately. I can feel his tension, his avoidance. Maybe he's afraid I'll push him again; I don't know. To show him I won't, I shift my attention to the window. I hear him getting ready—the creak of the wardrobe door, the rustling of clothes, the clinking of his weapons. Karel always keeps them close by.

And then, silence.

Noticing it lasts longer than usual, I turn to him. His hands are clasped behind his neck, and his body has gone rigid.

"Is everything okay?" I ask, worried.

He bites his lip, then walks around the bed and sits down near my hips.

"Amadeus and I… we can't find anything," he confides.

I'm disappointed, but the fact he cares so much about it is almost enough for me. Of course, I dream of being as free as he is, but I'm still lucky to have him as my husband.

"Is that what's been weighing on your mind?" I ask, a soft smile spreading across my lips. I emphasize my words by tapping his temple, but neither my smile nor my words seem to ease his tension.

"You can just abolish those laws when you're king," I reassure him.

He nods, but still looks as tense as before.

"Is that all that's bothering you?"

He nods again, but I don't believe him. Something else is going on, something bigger than him, something stronger than his love for me.

He kisses me lightly on the lips, then heads for the door.

"I'll be home late. I'll see you at dinner," he tells me before slipping out.

When I'm finally alone, I barely have time to sigh before Sienna bursts into the room, exclaiming the day is perfect—the sun is shining, and the air is refreshing. I can't help but laugh at her cheerfulness.

"He won't be coming today," I admit to her.

Her smile fades instantly, but she shrugs it off like it doesn't matter. Mira's death had a direct impact on our relationship. Sienna has supported me a lot and comforted me, just as I've done for her. As we've shared more and more with each other, she's stopped calling me *princess* and now calls me *Kalliopee*. It's taken a little over a year and many tragedies, but here we are. We pretend to keep our distance when others are around, especially Karel, but otherwise, we act like good friends.

"You'll see him tomorrow," I reassure her.

"I don't know why you say that… He doesn't…" She shakes her head as she opens the windows.

Sienna finally confessed that she's attracted to Kaïs. I know it might seem hopeless at first, but after all, the world will change one day. Why couldn't a young woman from the people marry a member of the royal family? I've tried to get a sense of where Kaïs stands, but he hasn't picked up on any hints so far. He's focused on his return to Karel's unit. He's thrilled to be able to join the ranks of the army and put his time here to use. It could have bothered me since I no longer have anyone to escort me outside, but fortunately, Sienna's company is more than enough, and sometimes in the evening, after his workday, Kaïs comes to get me so we can take a walk before dinner.

When I get out of bed, I go straight to my bathroom, shower, and change. Under Sienna's disapproving gaze, I eat a simple piece of toast and head to Karel's office to gather half a dozen books.

And that's how I spend my day. As soon as I finish the repairs—simple enough, considering my skills in book restoration—on the books I take, I return them to their place and pick up six more.

Sienna even has to force me to leave the comfort of my library to eat a snack at noon. I try, but the persistent nausea holds me back somewhat.

I put away the last book I had in my possession, then turn to look at Karel's desk. It's meticulously organized, every pencil in its place—so much so that it's almost eerie how disciplined it is. For fun, I sit in his chair and imagine being in his shoes. Not that I want to steal my husband's role, but I indulge in pretending to be the one making decisions.

Realizing I've lingered too long, I leave the chair and drag it behind me. The noise alerts Sienna, who rushes into the room.

"Kalliopee! You shouldn't, in your condition!"

"It's not heavy," I reply, exasperated.

She holds the chair steady as I climb up. Of course, she tries to convince me to stop, but I'm stubborn and still capable of standing on my own two feet. There's no way I'm going to let anyone assist me more than they already do.

I hand her the first few books that come to hand, and she places them on Karel's desk. Then, I reach for the one at the top of the bookshelf. As I tilt it, a few papers flutter down and land at Sienna's feet. I offer her the book, but when I see she doesn't take it, I turn to her. Her face has gone pale, and she's picked up one of the fallen documents.

"Sienna?" I call out to her.

Her tear-filled eyes meet mine, and I climb down immediately. I take the parchment from her hands, and my world crumbles. A few words catch my eye. It feels like they're killing me.

I look away from the paper and stare at Sienna. A wave of nausea rises within me, but I show nothing. I grab her hand as she seems on the verge of fainting.

"Tell no one," I order her.

"But—"

I shake my head. She mustn't tell anyone, because deep down, I cling to the hope that I misread. Deep down, I pray it's all a lie.

I gather the documents and retreat to my room. One by one, I read the letters. Some are from the king, addressed to Karel. They date back to before I arrived. I might have believed these plans were abandoned, but a letter sent to King Nokken by Karel's father proves otherwise—they remain unchanged. I finally understand everything—his reactions, the moments when he seemed distant, and the real reasons he lashed out at the monarch of Aquaria. He didn't want to defend my honor; he wanted to protect his secret.

My stomach churns, and I immediately rush to the bathroom. I vomit the meager contents of my stomach as an icy coldness overtakes me. I glance down at my belly, and the pain washes over me. I hate him for deceiving me so deeply. Was everything a lie? Did he ever even love me? I replay each of our moments, and knowing it was all just an act devastates me. I collapse onto my knees. As I kneel, my mind struggles to refute the words I've just read. Sobs wrack my body as I try to hold back the tears.

So, none of it was real?

It hurts to have loved him, to still love him. It hurts to have been so naive, to have put the lives of so many innocents in danger.

With my gaze lost in the void, I search for a miracle solution. Run away? That wouldn't change anything. I'm already pregnant. It's too late.

Then, a horrifying decision crosses my mind. I wish there was another way, but I'm struggling to breathe. My thoughts collide. A sob escapes me when no alternative comes to mind. I hate him for pushing me to this point, for forcing me to commit the irreparable act that I will never forgive myself for.

To keep myself from getting carried away by my futile hopes,

I leave the bathroom and head to his office. I grab one of the daggers hanging on the wall. That day, while I joked about his complete lack of taste, I never imagined it would come to this.

I return to the bathroom, strip off my clothes, and stare at my bare belly. My breath hitches. My hands tremble and almost drop the weapon. The marks that bear witness to the punishment I've endured now take on an entirely different meaning. They were inflicted upon me because he feared they would jeopardize his horrific plan.

How can anyone do this? How?

I cry as the tip of the blade grazes my skin. I need to get rid of this child, the key to everything. My grip tightens, but I drop the dagger immediately. It hits the floor with a crash that nearly perforates my eardrums. I can't. Not this. I wrap my arms around my belly, unable to hold back my tears any longer. I'd rather die than separate from him. I could never recover from that.

I wanted him so much, imagining different features even though it's still too early. I can't pretend he's nothing, let alone get rid of him as if he doesn't matter. I can't think of him so detachedly.

My heart splits in two; it's never hurt so much. I realize I can't take any risks, and I have to choose between the thousands of Viridians and my child. The pain overwhelms me, and I release another sob, followed by a cry of agony. No, if my baby must die, then I will die, too. Because I've already sacrificed far too much, and I wouldn't survive it.

My vision blurs, my heartbeat slows. His father's written words surface in my head.

Son, the time for our vengeance has come.

On all fours, I make my way to the bathtub and fill it with water. My heart feels heavy, my chest like a prison as I sob.

Give her a son. We'll take care of the king. Viridia will be ours.

I don't know how, but I manage to get back on my feet, pick up the dagger, and immerse myself in the tub. I let my head rest against the ceramic. The heat of the bath suffocates me.

As we agreed, the female Viridian will be yours as soon as my son ascends to the throne. In return, your troops will help us exterminate these vermin.

My heart sinks.

A genocide.

My breath escapes me.

I knew his secret would kill me.

I look at the bracelets that symbolize my belonging and realize with disgust that on that day, I signed my own death warrant. I condemned my people.

The dagger cuts into my right wrist as my chest heaves from my sobs. The sting of the blade makes me feel nauseous, but I ignore it. I refuse to make it easy for them. Karel will never ascend to the throne. I switch arms, and the pain is so intense I feel dizzy. Yet, I don't back down and cut deeper into my flesh. I run my trembling fingers over the edge of the bathtub and let the weapon fall to the floor.

My hands move to my belly as the water continues to rise, and I silently ask for forgiveness from my baby. I pray he won't hold it against me.

I have no choice.

Karel's face materializes behind my closed eyelids. I recall his gestures toward me, the words he would whisper when he filled me with joy. Why did he manipulate me when I belonged to him by right? I would have preferred him to take my body by force rather than deceive my mind, rather than fool my feelings. I love him so much it hurts.

I push him from my thoughts, hoping it will stop the flow of tears streaming down my cheeks.

I focus on my child. My only solace is to disappear with him, to not remain in a world where he will not exist.

As the water level rises and blood escapes from my wrists, I begin to hum the lullaby my nurse used to sing to me as she rocked me to sleep.

"In Viridia, there was a creature with wooden legs…"

CHAPTER 42

KAREL

Heart pounding, I step into our bedroom. Three days. Three days she's refused to see anyone, refused to leave our bed, and the trays of food brought to her remain untouched. Three days Kaïs has left after being told she doesn't want any visitors. Since then, I've waited patiently for her to be ready to listen to me, but the longer I wait, the less I believe that day will come. I've destroyed the only thing that ever mattered in my life.

Unable to admit my mistakes, I went and blamed Amadeus. Now, I despise myself for it.

I push open the door to the library, nerves raw. The door slams against the wall, startling the advisor, who quickly stands.

"Karel," he says with concern.

"This is all your fault!" I shout. I rush toward him and grab him by the collar. His remorseful eyes lock on mine as I raise my fist.

"I never imagined it would have such consequences," he apologizes, his voice trembling.

"She wanted to die!" I accuse, my throat tightening. "She... she..." My eyes fill with tears, and my breath catches in the sobs that overwhelm me.

"She's fine," he murmurs, as my arm lowers.

I shake my head, rejecting his words. No, she's not fine. She never will be.

"I should have told her everything, should have never hidden anything from her. I should've done it, even if it meant losing her..."

I release his collar, step back, and stumble. My legs barely hold the weight of my despair. I catch myself on the table and turn away.

"Karel," he calls gently.

"Thank you, Amadeus, but now I—"

How do I tell him that despite his years of support, I'm going to face this alone? Since I can't find the words, I do what I always do—I run.

I push away the memories and look at Kalliopee. Lying on her back, eyes fixed on the window, she doesn't even glance at me as I close the door. It hurts. I feel empty. Her silence is killing me. I want to scream at her, force her to face me. I want to provoke her, push her to the edge, trigger her anger, even though I know it will be aimed at me. Because seeing her like this—apathetic—is more painful than anything she could ever shout at me.

Her arms rest on her stomach, and I can't miss the bandages covering her wounds. Mira's father told me she was lucky; that I'd found her in time, and she hadn't lost much blood. I couldn't even respond to him.

I walk around the bed and pull the chair closer to her.

"Leave," she commands coldly.

She didn't shout; she just spoke. Her voice isn't the same anymore, and neither is she. She's devoid of emotion.

"I can't," I simply reply, then sit down.

She stops staring out the window and turns her back to me. I want to move closer, to touch her, to place my hands beneath her shoulder blades and hold her so tightly she could never slip away from me again. I'm going mad from this absence, this distance, this coldness. But I know I have no right to blame her for it—it's my doing.

"I should have told you everything," I begin.

Her body shifts, and for a moment, I think she might get up, but she doesn't. Instead, she curls into a ball, unresponsive to my words.

"If I had confessed everything, none of this would have happened… I'm ready to talk to you now."

Still, she says nothing. I breathe, but it's labored. Three days it's been like this. I lost my breath when I found her, realizing my betrayal hurt her so much she would rather end her life than face me again. Since then, I haven't been able to breathe right. I know it won't return until she forgives me.

"*Shaadi*…" I murmur, hoping she'll look at me.

And she does. She sits up sharply, turning to face me. "Now you want to talk?" She laughs coldly. "Talk about what? What you've planned for my people?"

I no longer dare to speak, not even to move. I can see she's finally letting go, and I refuse to do anything that will drive her back into the isolation that separates her from me. I love her so much I'll take even her hatred over her indifference.

"Whether you like it or not, you'll never have Viridia," she spits. "I won't let you. No matter if I have a son and that makes you a contender for the throne. I'll kill you before I ever give you that chance. And after I've killed you, your father's next," she announces with venom.

Strangely, I believe her. There's nothing hidden in the hatred burning in her eyes.

"None of you will ever take the throne of Viridia," she adds in a whisper.

I want to reply, but no words come. I can't tell her I don't care about the throne anymore. That all I want is for her to look at me the way she used to, when, despite my mistakes, she would forgive me.

"What did you think? That because I feel guilty for what my people have done, I'd approve of your choices? Did you think I'd stand by and witness this massacre without trying to stop it? That out of love for you, I'd turn a blind eye?"

My throat tightens as I realize her words are coming out with more difficulty now. Her anger wounded me, but the tears welling in her eyes tear my soul apart.

"That's impossible. Do you want to know why? Because you're nothing to me now. I don't love you anymore. I don't even hate you. All you make me feel is disgust. I knew you were crazy, but now… now you're *a monster*. What was the plan, exactly? Huh? Tell me! Months and months of preparation. Long months of lies. It must have taken so much patience. What was the plan?" she repeats, screaming the words.

Silence follows. She says nothing more, breathing heavily. It's the only sound I hear. My heart, on the other hand, feels like it's gone silent. It's as if it refuses to beat, as if it no longer has the right to. I glance down at my clenched fists, trying to find the strength to tell her the truth. My throat tightens as I struggle to untangle my thoughts. All I want is to go to her, to beg her to believe me when I tell her that I love her and she's all that matters—but I know I can't. She only wants the truth…

"When your father came to propose this marriage, mine wanted to refuse," I begin. "He hated the Viridians, and there was no way he'd let his son marry one. It was unthinkable."

I remember that day clearly. Läven had sent us a letter proposing the union, saying he hoped it would bring peace between our peoples. My father was furious. I had grabbed the parchment from his desk while he paced, with Amadeus watching him in concern. I sat down and read the letter over and over, at least a dozen times, maybe more.

"It was your idea, wasn't it?" she guesses.

Now, I deeply regret it. I had been so excited, and years of hatred had made me ruthless. I thought we could finally avenge our people. I was exhausted from the endless war and saw this marriage as a double opportunity: a way to return home without straying from my path and a chance to regain my father's approval. Amadeus had gone pale, but the king smiled. I was proud.

"It was you?" she insists.

I can't bring myself to nod. I just stare at my hands, and a sob escapes her when she understands the meaning of my silence.

"I told him having a common descendant would be a good thing. Your father had no heir, and if I had a son with the Princess of Viridia, I'd become the next in line for the throne. The plan was to have your father killed as soon as we had a son, so I could take the throne as quickly as possible."

Though it's difficult, I turn my gaze back to her.

I stop, catching my breath. She stares at me without blinking. Her tears have stopped falling.

"And then?" she growls, while I remain silent.

"And then… I was supposed to start by weakening the army."

"How?" she demands through gritted teeth.

I avoid her again, unable to face the disgust I evoke in her with every word I speak, with every piece of the plan I reveal.

"King Nokken was to declare war on Viridia. I… I was supposed to give false information to the Viridian troops. Undervalue the number of enemies. The soldiers sent to the front would have been outnumbered, and over time, there would have been only a few left."

"Why? Why involve Aquaria?"

"By depriving a kingdom of its army, you deprive it of its defenses. And having King Nokken declare war was the best way to make sure the Viridians wouldn't suspect me. When the number of soldiers was too small, we would have opened the gates to my father's and Nokken's troops, and then…"

I can't bring myself to say what she already knows.

"Then? Finish your sentence! What then? You would've killed everyone? The civilians wouldn't have been able to defend themselves! They're innocent! How could you all be so insane? How could you—"

"I abandoned the plan!" I shout, locking eyes with hers.

"Abandoned the plan?" she retorts, incredulous. "These past weeks, you've been talking to your father more than ever since I got here, and you expect me to believe you've given up? You really want me to—"

"I had no choice but to pretend with him. It was the only way to protect you!"

"Protect me?" she repeats.

"I had to make it seem like I hadn't given up. If I'm crazy, my father is worse. If he finds out I won't help him get his revenge, what do you think will happen to me? Do you really think he'd choose me over the throne? Never! And then, I wouldn't be able to protect you."

She seems to be processing my words, piecing it all together, then shakes her head. "The only way to protect me would've been to tell me before you married me," she murmurs. "To…"

She pauses, and I see the pain wash over her.

"Don't tell me that when you married me, it was still for that reason. Don't tell me that at that time, you still wanted to—"

I close my eyes, and she understands that yes… My heart tightens, bile rises in my throat. The pain is so intense I want to smash every piece of furniture in this room.

"When did you change your mind?" she asks.

"When we were in Aquaria," I say, opening my eyes again.

She shakes her head, rejecting what I've said.

"I told King Nokken I'd never hand you over to him," I insist. "That's why he provoked me. He wanted to punish me."

"No," she counters, refusing to believe me. "You silenced him because you wanted to keep me in the dark. Because if I had known, I would never have let you touch me again, and I would never have given you a child."

A bitter laugh escapes her throat, and I tense.

"I'm so naive. I'm your wife; I have no rights. You would've taken me by force no matter what, wouldn't you?"

"I would never have done that," I assure her, gripping the arm of my chair to stop myself from rushing over to her.

We stare at each other for a long time, but I can see from her posture that she doesn't believe me. Though I don't have the right, I'm angry at the thought that she could believe such a thing.

"Never?" she asks, barely holding back a sob. "How am I supposed to—"

"I never would have done that!" I cut her off, harsher than I intended. "I begged you to give me the benefit of the doubt once, and you promised me you would."

"That was before I knew this, before I knew what you were planning!" she yells.

"I gave up the plan in Aquaria. When you were punished because of me, I swore if you ever had to suffer again, it would never be because of me. In any way," I emphasize.

I keep talking, my words boiling over in anger. Not because she doesn't believe me, but because I'm furious with myself for taking so long to make that decision. I should have abandoned the plan before our marriage and sent her back home. I tried—I knew it would've been for the best. The war would've dragged on, but at least she would've been safe. Yet, when relief flooded me after she refused to leave, I couldn't make her go, even though I knew I'd end up breaking her.

"I can't hurt you," I say, my breath more steady now. "Because… because if I'm capable of setting my own kingdom on fire for you, I'm also capable of sparing yours. Haven't I treated you well? I've tried to make up for my mistakes, even when you didn't know. Amadeus and I, we did everything we could to—"

"Amadeus knew?" she interrupts, bewildered.

"He's my father's advisor," I remind her.

She absorbs this confession, turning her gaze toward the window. Silence settles in once more. I wait for her next words, because I'm certain there will be more.

"Who else knows?"

"My men," I admit.

She inhales sharply.

"So, everyone's complicit?" she says bitterly.

"None of them approved of the plan," I try to reassure her.

"And Kaïs? Did he know, too?" This time, she faces me.

I shake my head, and I think I see a flicker of relief in her eyes.

"*Shaadi*…" I murmur.

"Don't call me that," she chokes out. "You no longer have that right. After everything I've endured for you, for your people, for peace… how could you?"

This time, she doesn't hold back her sobs, just as I can't hold back my tears. It feels like we're at an impasse. But I refuse to give up. I refuse to admit defeat. I love her so much that her happiness matters more than anything, even more than myself.

"Believe me," I beg her.

"How could I, Karel?"

"What do you want from me?"

I'll do whatever she asks. If she wants to leave, I'll help her go. Whatever her demands, I'll meet them. Even though, on the eve of our wedding, I told her this was her only chance.

"I want you to go. I want you to leave. I want you to disappear…"

We stare at each other for a long time. I stand, take an unconscious step toward her, but she turns her head away. So I grant her wish and leave. As soon as I close the door, I hear her sobs through the wall. They tear me apart inside—it's excruciating. I try to walk away, but the gut-wrenching cry that echoes from our room stops me.

I should leave, let her be. But I can't. I turn back, push the door open sharply, making it slam, causing her to jump. She angrily wipes her tears as I circle the bed. When I reach her, she throws off the blanket, sits up, and raises her arm to stop me from getting closer.

"Don't come near me."

I ignore her. I can't help it. She can hate me if she wants, but she can't ask me not to fight for her. She can't ask me to leave her like this, alone, consumed by grief and fear. I grip her face firmly so she can't pull away.

"I won't let anything happen to you or your people. I swear it."

"What's your word worth, tell me?" she asks through her tears. "What is it worth, Karel?"

"It's the truth. I'd rather die than hurt you. I swear it."

She closes her eyes, shutting me out from her gaze.

"Believe me," I whisper against her lips.

Her eyes finally open again.

"Then buy us some time. Die. Because you will hurt me. Again and again. Can you even do anything else? I thought… I thought I could save you from your demons, but they're far too strong. You destroy everything you touch. The only thing you leave behind is blood."

Her words tear me apart inside, but this is my punishment. I take it without a word.

"Even what you love, you destroy. You don't know how to do anything else," she whispers before she pulls my hands from her face and retreats into the bathroom.

The cold fills me when the door closes, leaving me alone. Unable to push her any further, or face another rejection, I leave the room, our quarters, and make my way through the palace. Once in the city, I walk through the narrow streets until I reach the barracks. I know my men will be there at this hour. What I hadn't expected, though, was to find Kaïs there. The heavy wooden door closes as I freeze. I've been avoiding him, too, for three days now.

He steps away from the group and approaches me, and before I can react, the tip of the spear in his hand grazes my neck. He glares at me with a hatred I've never seen from him.

"I've given up on the plan," I tell him.

I look at Jonah, who joins my cousin.

"You know me, Kaïs. We grew up together. Look at me, you'll know I'm not lying."

He hesitates, and then slowly pulls the weapon away from my throat.

"Even so, you once agreed to it. You weren't like this when we were kids. Yes, you were impulsive—you would've destroyed anyone who threatened Maha or Kahi—but this… we're talking about genocide, Karel."

What could I say? Nothing… I did agree to it. Worse, I came up with the plan. Six years of war, six years of watching my father suffer, six years watching him lose his mind—and his madness eventually infected me, too. I let the poison spread the night I killed the assassins of the women I loved most in the world. Then, with every Viridian soldier I killed on the battlefield, it consumed me more. And that day, I thought I had found the solution to all my problems, the way to unload all the hatred weighing on me. But then my Viridian princess appeared and shattered everything.

Was my vengeance worth the sacrifice of her heart?

No, absolutely not. And I realize now, it wasn't worth the sacrifice of mine either.

CHAPTER 43

KALLIOPEE

As I sit in the bathroom, sheltered from him, from his words, from my own heart begging me to believe him, the nausea grows stronger. Yet, I know nothing will come of it. It's been days since I've been able to eat. No matter how hard I try, every bite brings a wave of nausea that I can't overcome.

I miss him more and more each day. How is it possible to ache so much for his absence after what he did? Why, when I should be hating him with every fiber of my being? I try, with all my strength, each moment with more determination. I convince myself he's nothing but a monster, but my heart refuses to accept it. It clings to the idea of demonizing him, then to forgiving him, forcing me to relive memories that hurt because they were so beautiful.

I lean against the door, trying to catch my breath. I look around the room, and though I want to hold them back, the tears flow freely. My throat tightens. It's been like this for days—this constant feeling I can't breathe. My head pounds relentlessly. I place my hands on my stomach as I slide down against the wood. I blame myself for my desperate action. I blame myself for my weakness and the harm I've done to this child who isn't even born yet. Mira's father assured me the baby is fine, but that didn't wash away my guilt. I wish I'd taken more time to find another solution, but I couldn't. I couldn't think. Still, I believe that no matter what, my decision would have been the same… Escape was impossible. I can't see any other way that would have been better.

I don't know how many minutes pass, but I don't move. I just sit here, on the floor, exhausted from fighting with myself.

I know he won't come back tonight. Every night, he disappears. I'm grateful for it. Because at sunset, the barriers I desperately hold up during the day collapse. The loneliness of the dark could push me to go to him, but what he did is far too grave for me to trust him or forgive him. Will I ever be able to? I want to believe I won't, but I also know that in front of him, I'm far too weak. Despite the disgust his plan makes me feel, I'm desperate to believe him when he says he abandoned it right after our wedding.

"Princess," Sienna calls from the other side of the door.

I don't respond. I close my eyes and try to imagine I'm alone.

"Kaïs is here," she tells me.

"I don't want to see anyone…" I murmur, my voice hoarse.

That's all I can manage to say. I'm not even sure she hears me. I've been avoiding Kaïs for days, though I wish I could confide in him. But he looks too much like his cousin for me to face him without breaking.

I hear her footsteps fading as I keep my eyes closed. I imagine myself walking through a wheat field, the stalks tickling my palms while the breeze lifts my hair. Sunlight grazes my skin as I take a deep breath. There's no sound, except for the gentle rustling of the wildlife. No smell, except the fresh scent of greenery. I smile faintly, then open my eyes again. The bright white of the room stings my vision. Behind me, the voices are getting louder. The shouting grows more intense, so I get up, crack open the bathroom door, and see Sienna didn't fully close the one leading to the sitting room.

"Tell her it's urgent!"

"I can't… She's refusing all visitors. She's not ready…"

"I don't care if she refuses, Sienna! This is important! Tomorrow will be too late!"

The desperation in his voice freezes me. Too late? What is he talking about?

I don't have time to think before the door slams open, banging against the wall. Kaïs bursts in, disheveled. "Stop him from doing it!"

I shake my head, confused.

"He's going to kill the king!" he blurts out.

The breath is knocked from me, and a sudden panic grips me.

"He would never do that," I protest.

"I thought so, too, but he came to the barracks, and we argued. I told him there was a drastic way to save you, but I was too angry to think straight. If he goes through with this…"

"Where is he?" I ask, alarmed.

"He's still in the city. I ran here to get ahead of him. Samael and Jonah are trying to slow him down, but he'd be willing to kill them to reach the palace."

I push past him, my legs carrying me forward. I rush through the corridors, passing servants who are startled to see me running through the palace in my nightgown. My heart races as I fly down the stairs. Regicide? We both know what that means.

I burst through the door leading outside, and the warm air fills my lungs. It hits me so hard, I cough, but I keep moving.

The sounds of an argument catch my attention, and a sob escapes my throat. I'm terrified of what he might do, scared he'll hurt his friends in his desperate mission, and that he'll never forgive himself.

When I round the tower, I see him—his nose bloody. He doesn't even notice me he's so focused on reaching the palace. I rush toward him, feeling as though every step is vital, like time itself is stretching out. Our eyes meet, but I don't think he really sees me. His gaze is dark again, the same frightening blackness that used to fill his eyes, the darkness that scared me because I never knew if I could pull him back. I also feared it would eventually consume me.

My body crashes into his, and he grabs my hips, freezing, clearly surprised. I use his confusion to guide him aside, near the tower's staircase. On tiptoe, I pull him out of sight.

"Karel," I whisper against him.

He seems to come back to life, though his body still feels like stone. He tries to push me away, but I cling to him with all my strength. I close my eyes, inhaling his scent—the scent I want to hate but instead brings me a strange, life-saving warmth. Here, in Lapisia, where the air is stifling, his presence is the only thing that soothes me.

"Don't do this. You know what will happen," I murmur in his ear, tightening my grip.

"You won't pay for this crime. Kaïs will rule until his father takes the throne. He'll annul our marriage."

He pries my fingers loose and steps back. Does he really think I'm only worried about my own fate? I hate his father, I despise the plan that brought the last two members of this family together, but I would never want Karel to commit such a cruel act—not even for my own safety.

"Don't do this," I growl, hitting his chest despite my wrists still being held.

"Kaïs is right, it's the only way to make everything stop."

The determination in his voice makes my face go pale. I'm still angry at him for plotting such a plan, but I can't imagine a life without him. I can't fathom living without him by my side. It will take time for me to trust him again and to forgive him, but if he kills his father, he'll take away any chance we have to fix what's broken. He'll doom us.

"Don't do this," I repeat over and over.

I wish I could say something else, but I can't find the words to make him understand that all that awaits him is death.

"If you do this, he wins, Karel. If you go through with it—"

"It's the only way," he cuts me off, finally locking eyes with mine. "It's the only way for everything to end."

I shake my head, feeling as if my entire face is crumpling under the weight of the pain tearing me apart inside. "I refuse to let you die," I choke out, my throat tightening.

Every word feels like a battle, as if speaking is scorching my vocal cords. He releases my wrists, and though I beg him to stop, he averts his gaze.

"Karel," I cry out, clinging to his sleeves.

He stares intently at something behind me. Fearfully, I turn around, but relief floods me when I see it's just Jonah and Samael. They look just as beaten as Karel, proof they fought relentlessly to keep him from doing the unthinkable. My relief quickly turns to terror when I hear the sound of a sword being drawn.

"I won't hesitate to go through with this," Karel warns them firmly. "Don't waste your time trying to stop me. I won't back down. Don't make me hurt you—I beg you."

Samael and Jonah exchange a look, and my heart sinks as they step aside to let him pass. I grab onto his sleeve as he moves past me, but he continues on as if my grip means nothing.

Jonah holds me back as I struggle.

"Karel!" I scream.

Sobs shake me. I believe him when he says I won't suffer for this crime, but the thought of a life without him is unbearable. I'm furious at him for what he planned, but I can't bear to see him try to fix it this way. It's suicide. Every step he takes feels like agony to me.

"Don't leave me," I beg, unable to hide the raw pain it causes me.

As I realize he's about to disappear from the tower, I desperately search for the words that might make him turn back.

"I hate you for coming up with this plan, if only you knew! But I don't want you to die," I admit. "Please. Don't leave me. If you really regret this, I forbid you to go through with it. We need you—both of us," I remind him, no longer able to hold back my sobs.

Hope flickers as he slows down. Even though he can't see me, I watch him with pleading eyes. But that hope is shattered the moment he resumes walking and leaves the tower. I collapse onto the floor. I don't care about dignity; I don't care that others are witnessing my weakness, because right now, I feel like I'm dying.

"Princess," Jonah calls.

But I'm deaf to everything. All I hear is my heart shattering in my chest, his laughter echoing in my mind, our heated moments. All I hear are our memories. Does your life flash before your eyes only when you're about to die? No, it happens when the people you love are about to disappear, too. And every memory of him—our touches, our whispers, our arguments, our laughs—tears me apart.

I rise weakly, realizing I never told him the one thing that matters. Realizing that if he chooses to die, I want him to know how I feel.

I stand and break free from Jonah's hold, running after him. I reach the courtyard and feel relieved to see he hasn't reached the gate yet.

"I love you!" I scream after him. "Karel, I love you."

He stops, and I rush toward him. I grab his arm, forcing him to turn around, and the darkness in his eyes terrifies me. He looks at me with a despair I've never seen before.

"I'm so sorry, *Shaadi*."

"I know," I say honestly.

Because now, I understand the pain with which he revealed

his plans and his regrets. I refused to see it before, blinded by my hatred and disappointment. But as he looks at me like this, I can't believe he's lying, or that he's trying to manipulate me.

"I destroy everything. Everything that matters."

"Don't do this," I whisper weakly, my voice breaking as he steps back.

I regret the harsh words I've thrown at him. I spoke out of grief, out of pain. I was unfair. Because no matter how much I've suffered here, I've never been as happy as I've been with him.

His shoulders slump. I slowly approach him, forcing him to meet my gaze again. His eyes glisten with tears, and it makes the lump in my throat swell even more. I swallow again, my breath held. Standing on my toes, I let my lips brush against his. The soft sound he releases draws out another sob from me that I can't hold back. My right hand finds his, and with the tips of my fingers, I take hold of the hilt of his sword, which he releases without resistance. Jonah quickly grabs it as my husband's face tightens. I pull away, lowering my eyes to his chest, then to his fingers, which I entwine with mine, guiding him back toward home.

On the way, my heart feels alternately heavy and light. Though the original reasons for our marriage were cruel, I believe him when he says he'll do everything to ensure that never happens again.

Wiping my cheeks with the back of my hand, we reach our quarters. We enter, and I lead him to our room. He follows silently, and as I glance over my shoulder, I see a distant look in his eyes. When we finally reach the door, he lets go of my hand. The warmth I'd felt from him vanishes instantly.

Preferring not to pay attention to it, I place my palm on the doorknob.

"I don't think this is a good idea," he informs me, his voice breaking.

"Why?" I whisper.

"Because just a few hours ago, you hated me, Kalliopee. I thought I was losing you. I still think I am…"

I close my eyes, unsure how to respond.

"Did I lose you?"

My heart leaps.

"It will take time," I admit sincerely, "but… I can't stop

loving you. I try, but it's too hard. It's like every fiber of my being is meant to thrive in your presence; as soon as you disappear, a part of me dies. I wish I had the strength to hate you, but I don't. I love you so much it hurts."

I turn to face him. A few steps separate us, but it feels like the distance is far too great. I feel the need to close that gap, to feel the spark of life whenever I brush against him.

He closes the space by joining me. He looks at me intensely, his palms resting on my neck. The calluses of his fingers awaken the skin they touch, as if I were a frozen body and the ice melted away at his touch. His hands find my nape and gently tilt my face. His irises, which were fixed on his arms, reveal themselves to me in all their clarity. The darkness leaves them, and it's just the two of us left. The desire for him to kiss me intensifies. I hear my heart pounding, as if its beats were solely meant to propel me forward, to bring me closer to him.

My attention shifts to his lips, and that's when they land on mine. They brush against my lips slowly, as if trying to tame them. I hold onto his bent elbows, allowing him to infuse me with his warmth. It spreads through my chest with every kiss he gives me. Then, I can't hold back any longer; I stop being passive, and my fingers tangle in his hair. My mouth opens in a moan as his hands pull me closer to him. Our bodies touch. My barriers crumble. I kiss him with less restraint, letting fear, disappointment, and even anger guide my actions. I kiss him to punish him, to forgive him, to relieve myself. I kiss him in a thousand and one ways because that's how I feel with him. He always makes me experience a multitude of emotions, whether good or bad.

He freezes when my hands graze his neck, and I realize it's my bandages that triggered this reaction. So, this time, I kiss him to forget what I felt that day.

"Wait," he murmurs against my lips. He pushes my hips away, then releases me.

Without saying anything more, he leaves our quarters, leaving me alone, lost in the middle of our living room. Yet, I'm not afraid. I'm just full of questions. I replay the scene that just unfolded in my mind, trying to understand what could have prompted him to leave. I pace around the room until he finally returns. I quickly notice the tool he's holding and step back fearfully as he approaches me.

"Do you trust me?"

A flash of sadness crosses his eyes when I can't bring myself to nod. Still, I allow him to come closer.

"I might hurt you," he tells me as he takes my fingers to lead me to our room.

My heart races when I realize what he's about to do. He forces me to sit down, kneels before me, and places my wrists on my thighs. The pliers grip the first cuff, and after a fierce struggle, it gives in.

I know this won't change my situation. I'm fully aware I'll remain a wife like any other and this won't free me from my obligations, but the gesture carries such symbolic weight I can't stop new tears from flowing. For the first time in several days, these are tears of gratitude. He removes my second restraint and then places the pliers at his feet. His hands wrap around my wrists, caressing the insides.

"It may take time, I don't know, but I promise you will be free before our child is born. I will protect you, him, no matter the baby gender, and your people."

This time, I take the initiative to close the distance between us.

I want to believe him. I do believe him. I can't do otherwise; I love him. That's how it is. As brutal and relentless as he may be, I love him. And I refuse to imagine a life without him.

I don't think I would survive.

Epilogue

Kalliopee

Five Months Later

"Do you want to go back?" Karel asks me, concerned as he watches my round belly.

I smile at him, appreciating his worry, but I shake my head. Today is a big day for the citadel, which is celebrating its national holiday for the first time since the war began.

Euphoria reigns in the palace and outside its walls. For my part, I struggle to contain my excitement despite the fatigue that comes with my condition.

It has been several months since we've enjoyed this lull. Not a single event has darkened our lives or troubled our hearts. I know full well that danger is present, but I fully appreciate the reprieve it grants us. In the streets, citizens have put out their finest decorations and donned their best costumes. I thrill at every song that reaches my ears, at every smile directed my way by the Lapisians.

Karel, true to himself, spends his time scanning every corner, but I help him relax by putting a cookie in his mouth.

He immediately spits it out and looks at me with concern.

"They come from the palace," I reassure him.

His nostrils flare; I can easily tell he's a bit angry, but he surprises me by placing a kiss on my forehead.

After discovering his plans, we have timidly begun to rebuild our bond. Unconsciously, we've started anew. No more secrets, no more unspoken words. He no longer hides from me the nightmares that haunt him and sometimes wake him at night. Of course, he assured me he had no choice but to pretend to the king he hadn't given up on this macabre project. I could only accept; I didn't want him to be in danger, to have the monarch turn against him. When his father reproaches him for our closeness, Karel insists it's only to deceive me. Do I sometimes think he's lying to me rather than the king? Sometimes, yes… To claim otherwise would be a lie.

As for my restraints, I wear them in public but no longer at home. Not with *him*.

"Kalliopee, shall we dance?" Kaïs asks as we reach the main square.

I turn to my husband, who gestures for me to go ahead before holding me back by the elbow. "Not for too long; it's not good for you."

I shake my head with a smile and prepare to join Kaïs when Karel stops me again.

"Don't stray too far; stay within reach of—"

"Relax and go find the boys. Kaïs is a very good bodyguard, and I have my weapon."

He rolls his eyes but reluctantly agrees to let me go.

Even though I'm pregnant, I haven't given up my training. Who knows what might happen? Despite the affection the Lapisians now show me, I know some still don't approve, and now that I carry mixed blood within me, there's no doubt their animosity toward me has only increased. I find Kaïs, who is watching Karel with amusement.

"He should really relax."

"That's what I told him." I laugh.

Soon, a lively melody rises, and Kaïs teaches me the steps of the traditional dance. Unfortunately, my condition prevents me from jumping or twirling. Essentially, I can only sway from one foot to the other, but that doesn't stop me from having fun. I turn my head to Karel, who seems to be laughing at a joke from Samael, then I watch the one who has become my closest friend.

When I learned that Kaïs was unaware of anything, he was the only one I could speak freely to for a while. I felt betrayed by Amadeus, Jonah, and Samael, even though Samael and I had never been close. But just as I forgave Karel, I did the same for them.

To this day, my situation hasn't changed… I'm still a woman freed from her bonds but not from my duties.

Feeling a slight dizziness, I tell Kaïs I need to get out of this crowd. It parts for us, and everyone offers kind words. For several months, I've felt almost serene. *Almost*, because this baby will be born soon, and I don't know what will become of us. Darkos has suggested fleeing many times. I haven't hidden anything I've learned from him; he was unaware. Clearly, the king doesn't trust his own guards. It must be sad to doubt everyone all the time. This thought makes me smile slightly; it reminds me of his son.

We take refuge in a shaded alley, and I lean against one of the walls. The coolness of the stone eases the moisture of my skin a little. I rest my palms on it and look up to observe the azure sky. A gentle breeze sweeps through the calm area; we still hear a few sounds, but not enough to drown out my friend as he takes a few steps.

He soon stands beside me and lifts his nose to the sky. "Is the sky the same where you are from?" he suddenly asks.

"Sometimes, but it has many facets. Sometimes it's scattered with cotton clouds, and in winter, it hangs so low the snow falls from it."

"I've never seen snow," he says, surprising me.

"I'll take you there one day," I promise him.

Suddenly, screams are heard. Kaïs tenses and asks me to wait. Even though my movements aren't very fluid, I crouch down to retrieve the knife strapped to my thigh. Slowly, Kaïs advances and peeks around to see what is causing such commotion. His shoulders relax, and just as I expect him to return to my side, I see him leave the alley, waving his arms.

"She's here!" he shouts.

"Was it him?" I exclaim, surprised.

"Who else? He really should relax, *Shaadi*!"

"Don't call her that," my husband scolds, appearing and giving Kaïs a tap on the head.

I smile foolishly at Kaïs's expression. He never fails to call me that when his cousin is around. He loves to tease him. Karel closes the distance between us, and I'm certain he's going to lecture me.

"I was just over here," I interject, "with Kaïs. The only scare I had was when you created all that commotion," I lecture him.

"You should have told me!"

"You were having fun, and I'm fine… but I'd like to go home now," I confess to him.

"Then let's go home," he agrees, his expression softening.

As we lie on our bed with the window open, the wind sweeps through the room. Night has fallen for a while now. Karel unconsciously strokes my belly, just as he does every night before falling asleep. We don't talk and simply enjoy the end of the day. Sometimes, I think a whole life like this would be ideal. As he showers kisses along my neck, a bell tolls that I've never heard before, echoing through the palace.

Karel sits up abruptly, so suddenly he pushes me away. He jumps out of bed, grabs his pants, and hurriedly puts on a shirt he doesn't even bother to button. I sit up, my body trembling. I stare at him, my heart racing. Then I analyze his actions and demeanor. The Karel facing me is no longer the husband who dreamily caressed my belly just moments ago. No, the man pacing the room and searching for his gear is a formidable warrior. Despite the anxiety gripping me, I can't help but find him handsome.

I kneel and inch closer to the edge of the bed, hoping to catch his attention because I fear I won't be able to say a single word. The alarm continues to wail. Then, just as suddenly as it began, it falls silent. However, the calm that follows doesn't ease the anxiety.

"Karel?" I finally manage to call out to him.

He turns to me, then puts a finger to his lips, signaling me to be quiet, and retrieves his sword. Slowly, he approaches the door and quietly opens it. He shuts it immediately before rummaging through the wardrobe. I can only watch him; I'm unable to move. Fear has paralyzed my limbs. When he finally rejoins me, he grabs my wrist and places his dagger in the palm of my hand.

"Kill any stranger who comes near you," he whispers.

"What?" I panic.

"There's an intrusion," he tells me simply, in a calm voice. "I have to go."

"No, stay with me," I plead.

His hands cup my cheeks, not gently. He tries to maintain the confident mask on his face, but I can tell from his tensed muscles that his calmness is feigned. I search his irises, probing him as I drop the dagger to hold onto his arms. *Don't leave me*, is the silent plea I send him with this gesture. I don't want to be far from him.

His expression darkens, and I can see he's torn between his need to stay by my side and his duty to help those outside, but he eventually shakes his head.

"I'm sending Sienna to you. Don't leave this place, Kalliopee. Do you hear me? Don't leave this room and wait for me to come back," he commands, gripping my neck.

Knowing I won't be able to change his mind, I nod vigorously. Then his lips crash against mine. With an unimaginable violence, with an urgency that rattles my heart more than it soothes it.

"I l—"

"No, you can tell me when you get back," I cut him off.

It's silly, but I'm too afraid those words will bring us bad luck.

"Okay, I'll tell you later. And I'll even show you!"

His attempt at humor, meant only to ease my panic, does nothing to reassure me.

He places another kiss on me, gentler this time, and after a brief hesitation, slips out of our room. I want to follow him, but I force myself to wait here like he asked. Unable to stay idle, I leave the bed and rush to the wardrobe. I throw on a robe and grab the dagger left on the mattress. Moving silently, I approach the door and crack it open. Outside, I can hear shouts—some filled with fury, others with pain—and I realize that out there, a massacre is happening.

My grip tightens around the weapon as I place a protective hand on my belly. Time stretches unbearably, and I'm in agony. I hate how long he's been gone; it's torturing me. When the door finally opens, I step out of the room. Disappointment creeps in when I see that it's Sienna, but panic quickly overwhelms me when I notice her dress is stained with blood. She's crying as she comes to me.

"Are you okay? Are you hurt?"

She seems too shocked to speak; I'm not even sure she understands my words. I pull her back, checking her over, and breathe a sigh of relief when I realize it's not her blood.

"It's from one of the guards," she sobs.

I comfort her, pulling her into my arms again, still gripping Karel's dagger, my eyes never leaving the wooden door. I count the seconds. I hold my breath at every scream. I silently beg my ancestors to spare the innocents still inside the palace, pleading for them to protect my husband.

When the door opens again, hope rekindles. But it quickly fades when I see Darkos. I remind myself, like a mantra, that Karel is one of the kingdom's best warriors, that he'll return to me without a scratch. But with each passing moment, my fears gnaw at my insides.

Darkos closes the door behind him and walks toward me without meeting my eyes. "We have to go."

My heart pounds, and my mouth feels dry. He steps closer, and I step back.

"We need to move quickly."

"Absolutely not! Karel told me to stay here, to wait for him."

No sooner have I spoken than he looks away. Then, cautiously, he locks eyes with mine. I hate the pity I see in his gaze, the compassion. As if my reaction could change the course of events, I shake my head. I vehemently reject the truth he's about to reveal. This can't be real.

His pale face draws near, and my heart shatters. It's violent, painful, cutting. A sob chokes me.

"You're in more danger than ever."

I deny his words and the awful implication behind them with a barely audible "no."

Darkos turns to look at Sienna for a moment before facing me again, lips pressed together. I bring my hand to my mouth.

"We have to leave. Xerios will be free to do whatever he wants to you now."

"He told me to wait for him," I repeat, as if saying it could erase the deep pain I feel inside.

"He's not coming back. It's over. Kalliopee." Darkos shakes me by the shoulders, seeing I'm still refusing to accept his words. "Think of your child. We have to go!"

"You're lying!"

He promised he'd come back, that he would show me how

much he loves me. He swore he'd always return to me.

I stare at Darkos's shirt, unable to clear my thoughts. Everything is a blur, mixing together. It's chaos. Chaos so overwhelming I can't think or breathe. I feel like a part of me is dying tonight. Tears well at my lashes, and nausea washes over me. He promised he'd come back.

A cold chill sweeps through my body, clashing harshly with the damp heat of the night.

"Kalliopee!" Darkos barks sternly. "There are men everywhere! They're after your child!"

The purity of the Lapisian… I lower my gaze to my belly, torn between the need to protect my child and the desperate urge to find his father.

"What do you think they'll do if they find you?"

I don't know. I take a deep breath, and my tears stop. I wipe them away with the back of my hand and look up.

"Your husband would want you to be safe."

"I know," I murmur, my voice rough and low.

"Go change. It'll be a long journey."

It takes me a few seconds to gather my thoughts, to fully process the pain I'm feeling before forcing myself to lock my emotions away. Once we're safe, I can let them out. Once we're far from here, I can mourn him, even if it feels like it'll tear me apart. How will I go on without him? How will I survive? A fresh tear falls, but I wipe it away angrily. I'm furious at these intruders, at the positions we've held that have made us living targets, and at him for breaking the only promise that truly mattered to me.

Aware grief will consume me if I stay still, I force myself to move.

I return to my room, fleeing this living room and the news that's already killing me slowly. I strip off my nightclothes and grab some of Karel's clothing, then freeze. The tears come back harder, sobs shaking my chest, but I force myself to put them on. His clothes smell like him, so much so that it's like he's right here beside me. If it weren't for my child's life being at stake, I could almost let myself be lulled into that illusion, even if it meant perishing under the intruder's blade.

I focus on the clothes, avoiding the bed where we had been just moments ago. I refuse to give in to the urge to feel his warmth in the wrinkled sheets. I should have let him say those words; I should have said them, too.

Sienna joins me. She steps closer. With just a glance, I feel like my heart weighs a ton. There's so much I want to ask her, starting with words to assure me this is all just a nightmare, that I'll wake up soon. In her eyes, I see compassion that, instead of comforting me, pushes me further into shock. I don't want it to reach me. I look away, and then we join Darkos, who seems lost in thought.

"We'll need to be discreet. Once things settle down, the king will likely order a search of the citadel. With any luck, we'll be out of here by dawn tomorrow."

My head snaps up, causing the hood covering my hair to fall back. Amadeus's words come rushing back to me.

"There's another way out," I tell him.

"No, there's not—"

"Yes, there is," I cut him off. "In the back courtyard. There's a cavity that leads to underground tunnels. They go beyond the walls."

"How—"

"Amadeus told me about it a while after I got here," I interrupt again.

"And what if he lied to you?"

I could dwell on the bitterness in his tone or the way he suddenly looks at me. He thinks I'm naive. He's not wrong. I am, in many ways—but not this time.

"I've already gone to check if they exist."

He studies me for a moment, then simply nods.

His instructions come quickly after that: the order in which we'll leave, the path we'll take to get to the botanical garden, even how we should react if anyone tries to separate us. It's clear Sienna will be coming with us. I place a protective hand on my stomach as Darkos announces it's time to go. I take a deep breath and swallow with difficulty. For a moment, my head spins, but I force myself to ignore the growing dizziness. I have to get to safety first, for the sake of our child.

Darkos slowly opens the door, his cautious pace only increasing my anxiety. Immediately, we hear the sounds of a struggle—faint, but unmistakable. We make our way down the corridor and reach the stairs. I realize now that it's a full-on assault. Men I've never seen before, their faces covered in red scarves, are attacking the staff while others battle the guards. I hold onto my hood, staying close to the walls, unable to breathe. The savagery they display bodes ill for us. Darkos kills one assailant, then another, as we descend the stairs. Adrenaline floods my veins, propelling me forward with each step, dulling everything else, including the pounding of my heart.

Two intruders charge toward us as we pass down the hallway leading to the French doors. Darkos engages the first one, but the second lunges at me. His eyes flash with recognition the moment he sees me.

Every time I imagined myself in danger, I feared hesitation would be my downfall, that I would lose precious seconds, that my compassion would override my survival instinct. But that's not what happens. I don't hesitate for even a second. My swift action leaves him no chance. I drive the dagger into his neck with all the rage I can muster. I feel no remorse, no sorrow in my heart. On the contrary, I feel relieved.

The man freezes, surprised, and I pull the blade out. Blood spurts from the wound, splattering me with its warmth. I'm not disgusted. Strangely, this encounter with death fills me with a new energy. The need to leave this place grows more urgent. The assailant crumples at my feet, and Darkos watches me for a few seconds before resuming his lead.

The ground floor has become a battlefield. Some bodies appear lifeless, while others fight to survive.

As we near the exit, I can't stop myself from scanning the area. I'm looking for him. In the brave men defending the servants, in the boy who parries an intruder's blow before the enemy's blade slices his chest. Not among the corpses strewn across the floor. Because the thought of him being dead is too much to bear. I fear I wouldn't be able to keep going if I saw it with my own eyes.

"Princess," someone calls, pulling me back.

As Darkos guides me through the garden, I glance back at the palace we're leaving behind. The screams inside haven't stopped, and I notice part of the building is engulfed in flames. My eyes keep searching for him, desperately. And with every face that isn't his, I feel myself sinking deeper into a void that threatens to swallow me whole.

"Kalliopee, which way do we go?" Darkos snaps, growing impatient.

I tear my gaze away from the palace and take the lead. I focus on my steps like a machine, clenching my fists, gritting my teeth, doing everything I can to hold back my emotions. But the more time passes, the less certain I am that I can keep them at bay. I lead us through the woods, and after only a few minutes, we reach the tree Amadeus had told me about. It's a good thing I checked it for myself.

"I'll never fit," I say, alarmed.

"Yes, you will," Sienna reassures me, now more determined than I am.

Darkos slips in first to catch us as we follow. When he disappears, I sit on the ground and slide my legs through. I grip the roots tightly to lower myself, my legs dangling into the void before they are caught by the half-blood's firm grasp. I twist to the side to protect my stomach. I'd rather hurt my ribs than risk harm to my child. I stifle a groan as the wood scratches my skin through the fabric, then Darkos helps me down. He lifts me before setting me on the ground and quickly supports Sienna as she joins us.

She stands in front of me. The three of us stare at our feet, fully aware our lives will never be the same again.

"We should hurry. Let's put as much distance between the palace and us as we can," Darkos murmurs.

I rise without a word. We don't have to choose a direction since we're in a dead end. The tunnel is wider than the city's underground passages, but no light filters in. Feeling our way, I move forward. Each image of him that flashes in my mind is quickly pushed aside. I refuse to let myself be consumed by memories, not now. Not while I'm still within these walls. I scold myself, promising that in just a little while, I can collapse if I need to.

After a short walk, I realize we've reached another dead end. I alert Darkos, who joins me. I can't see him, but I can hear him. It's unsettling to be deprived of sight, as it leaves the mind free to conjure its own images. A blank canvas with nothing to focus on. I take a deep breath, my heart swollen with pain, sadness, and despair, and begin feeling the walls around us, searching for a way out.

"There," I hear him murmur.

He pulls open a trapdoor in the ceiling, and we're immediately bathed in light. The moon shines down on us. Darkos climbs out, disappears for a moment, then offers me his hands. I hesitate.

"Princess?"

Instinctively, I turn toward the other end of the tunnel, still shrouded in darkness, silently praying with all my heart for him to appear.

"Kalliopee, he's not coming."

Darkos's voice reaches me. It's painful, piercing my ears. I just want him to stop talking.

"He's—"

"No," I cut him off abruptly.

I refuse to let him say it.

Before his words can hurt me, I raise my arms, and despite the extra weight I must have gained, Darkos lifts me easily. He does the same with Sienna, and as I turn around, I see a massive rock that I move to go around. In the night, the flames from the palace light up the lapis sky.

Now, outside the walls, I allow myself to break down. Everything comes flooding back—I let the memories rush in. The most recent ones, our last kisses. The older ones, our first kiss. Everything blurs together, but the most painful remains the moment he walked out the door. If I had known I wouldn't see him again, would I have begged harder for him to stay? If we had known it was a final goodbye, would we have kissed more passionately?

A gut-wrenching sob tears from the depths of my soul. It's a cry of agony.

Just emptiness.

Only emptiness.

That's all I feel like I'm becoming.

The pain in my chest is so overwhelming it brings me to my knees.

"Where are we going?" I hear Sienna ask, worried.

"East," I manage to say. "We have to keep going east."

I feel dizzy, my eyes still locked on the city.

"Someone can help us. A friend of Amadeus," I explain

weakly.

"Kalliopee," Darkos tries to dissuade me.

"I trust him. We have to go east."

Then my body sways, quickly caught by a firm grip. I don't know if Darkos will follow my advice, but I can't fight anymore, and my eyelids grow heavy.

In the darkness, I find him. He's there, smiling, in his formal attire, and he steps toward me. He kisses me deeply. I breathe in his scent as he wraps me in his arms. The emptiness fades as he finally says the words I had forbidden him to speak.

"I love you, Shaadi."

To be continued...

Playlist

Calling Out – BOBBi (feat. Hannie)
Remembrance – Tommee Profitt & Fleurie
When It's All Over – RAIGN
We Have It All – Pim Stones
In The End – Tomme Profitt & Fleurie (Mellen Gi Remix)
Cradles – Sub Urban
Wolf – Boy Epic
Artistry – Jacob Lee
Make Me Believe – The EverLove
Zombie – Damn Anthem
Hate Me – Eurielle
Ghost Of You – Selena Gomez & The Scene
Innocence – Nathan Wagner
Shadow Preachers – Zella Day
Arcanine – Ursine Vulpine
Âme seule – Florina
NUMB – XXXTENTACION
Bottom Of The Deep Blue Sea (Stripped) – MISSIO
Can I Exist – MISSIO
Who Do I Think I Am – MISSIO
In Your Arms – Ryan Louder & Ashley Serena
Until Eternity (Orchestral Version) – Blackbriar
You Are A Memory – Message To Bears
Too Far Gone – Hidden Citizens & SVRCINA
Body – SYML
Immortalized – Hidden Citizens & Keeley Bumford
Runaway – AURORA
Fallout – UNSECRET & Neoni
Kill Everything – Skin (the one that makes this story started)

Spotify Link (Koko Nhan Profile)
YouTube Link (Koko Nhan Chanel)

Acknowledgements

As always, I'll start by thanking my little family. I know it's not always easy to share your wife or mom with the literary world, but you've never once held it against me. You accept that to live in this world, I need to escape to other universes that are uniquely mine. Thank you, Bao. You are an unwavering support, and I think I don't always show you just how much you mean to me. Thanks to you, I feel at home anywhere in the world. And thank you to my babies, L. and T. You were a true breath of fresh air whenever I left Lapisia to return to the real world.

Thank you to my dear friend, Kéké (the bookmark expert), and Gwen. You've heard about Kalliopee once, then again, without ever complaining. I promise, this is the last time!

Once again, I want to thank Sarah. You're a wonderful editor—available, kind, and reassuring. I've loved improving this book just as much as the first one. I'm proud of the work we've done together!

Thank you, Juliette, once again. Have I mentioned how much I love the covers? I couldn't have dreamed of anything better!

Thanks to Caroline and Pauline for your hard work and precision! They say the shoemaker's children go barefoot, so I sincerely hope the mistakes didn't shock you too much!

Thanks to the entire BI team. I'm really looking forward to meeting all of you. I feel so welcome among you!

Thank you to the bloggers, my beta readers, and everyone who encouraged me and helped this saga reach even the most reluctant readers.

Of course, I can't write acknowledgments without thanking you, the readers. For your feedback with each release, for your loyalty! And thank you to those discovering me through Kalliopee. I'll see you in a few weeks with the final book.

I hope you'll enjoy the conclusion!

ASLO BY KOKO NHAN

KALLIOPEE: A PRINCESS SACRIFICE

Other novels from
WARM PUBLISHING

Scan to easily acess all of Warm Publishing books:

Join also our Facebook Group, Book Warmers, to get the lastedt updates and talk about books and more!

Myrina Holmes Demons and Wonders
by ***Anna Triss***

I'm Myrina Holmes, the top Tracker of Infernum, tasked with neutralizing supernatural creatures who disobey our laws.

In my world, demons have legions. Fourteen to be precise: seven dedicated to the cardinal virtues and seven ruled by the deadly sins.

As a marginal hybrid, I belong to neither camp, which suits me just fine. I love my job and my life on Earth when I'm not on a mission. Except, of course, when mysterious corpses literally fall from the sky to torture my brain and when my succubus half-sister starts hanging out with the most detestable Hybresang there is, Kelen Wills.

A supremely powerful sinner, commander-in-chief of an elite army, he doesn't embody one deadly sin. No, he possesses all seven-with a penchant for lust, anger, pride, and gluttony. But keep that detail to yourself...

Anyway, this guy has made it his mission to seduce me, probably because I'm the only woman who can resist his dubious charms.

This Hybresang can go to hell, because I have other midnight demons to deal with.

My Hipster Next Door
by ***Mag Maury***

In Liverpool, the barbershop Hipster Maniac is an institution. Run by three bearded, tattooed friends, it is the place to listen to great rock, get a trim, and have a drink.

But for Line, it also spelled trouble. For starters, when she first got to the neighborhood, she rear-ended Jordan's car, who turned out to be one of the three barbers. Then she discovered that they were neighbors in business and residence! So no way can she escape this muscle-flaunting, smoldering man who is covered in tattoos and... completely insufferable!

He draws her near only to push her away. He toys with her shamelessly. But worst of all he hates Christmas whereas that is Line's very favorite time of year!

Beneath a backdrop of festive fairy lights, intoxicatingly passionate kisses, and blistering banter... It's on!

The Cocky Heir
by ***Ana K. Anderson***

She is about to get married. But not to him.

Quinn MacFayden, an accomplished expat businessman in New York, is set to return to Scotland in extremis to protect the precious family legacy. His 91-year-old grandfather is about to marry a perfect stranger sixty-six years his junior... And that is out of the question! Quinn swears it. Over his dead body will Dawn Fleming ever be part of the family!

But Dawn is not a future bride like the others. She is nowhere near the gold digger he imagined and, above all, she knows just how to stand up to him. And so a game of cat and mouse begins between them. A war with no holds barred and where surrender has never been so tempting...

My Stepbrother: A Sexual Revelation
by ***Sophie S. Pierucci***

Cassie is a highly intelligent young woman... Too much so for her own good!

And she is as daunting as she is intriguing. Carl, the son of his father's second wife, would hardly say otherwise!

Carl is the exact opposite of his steady father. He is a player and a slayer. Afraid of nothing and no one. Except for Cassie when she asks him to introduce her to the pleasures of the flesh.

And when the situation gets out of control, it is too late to turn back, and the two lovers find themselves ensnared in forbidden passion. Forbidden by everyone: society, their parents, their friends.

But how to resist the desire that consumes them?

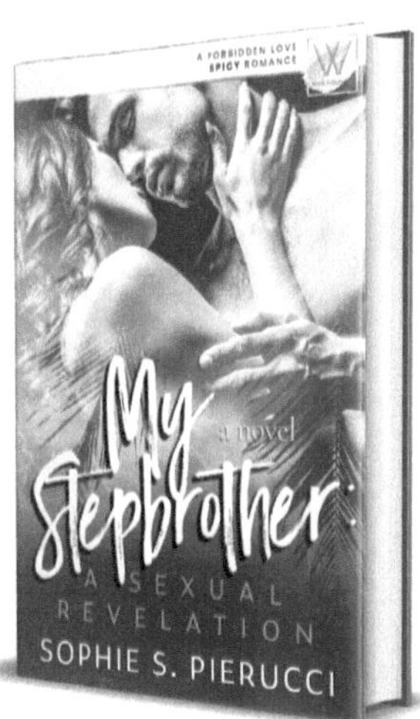

Roommate with my Boss
by ***Erin Graham***

Boss, roommate, fake fiancé... real lover?

Étienne is cold, charismatic, and he never shies away from a challenge.

He masters everything down to the smallest detail... until a little accountant with an unlikely look and flowers in her hair inserts herself into his daily life.

She is whimsical, full of life, laughs at the rules and gets around them, talks all the time except about her past... and she drives him crazy. Yet, it's impossible to fire her.

She needs a job and a roof over her head; he needs a fake fiancée...

Is it a deal?

Your Power Over me

by ***Missy Heart***

A family home heavy with secrets, a dangerously charismatic owner.

Will her arrival at Iron House be the end of her?

Ever since she was a teenager, Lovisa has known it: at Iron House, anything can happen, especially the worst.

However, when she is forced to return to the family home for her stepfather's funeral, her heart races: she is going to see him again, this "brother" who she never wanted and who yet turned her whole world upside down.

Now at the head of a drug cartel, authoritarian and brutal, Niklas is nothing like the teenager she knew nine years ago. At his side, Lovisa finds herself immersed in a harsh, ruthless—but fascinating—world.

Irremediably attracted to this man who wants her as much harm as good, will Lovisa manage to fight her unmentionable desires? Or will she give in to Niklas' magnetic darkness?

Touchdown
by ***Sonia Birdy***

She's a runner, but the campus star quaterback runs faster than she does!

Rocky has had a chaotic life from which she concluded three fundamental things: life is a succession of problems to be solved, men are assholes to be avoided and promises are only binding on fools who want to believe in them. So, unlike the other girls on campus, boys are not a priority for her. Worse, she sees them as an obstacle to her success!

But during a student party, she meets Jude. Freshly transferred from Harvard to play on Brown's soccer team, Jude is the new star on campus. Handsome and inaccessible, he is the type not to get attached: the perfect candidate for a one-night stand.

But the chemistry is too strong. And though Rocky is determined to run away from him, he is determined to conquer her heart.

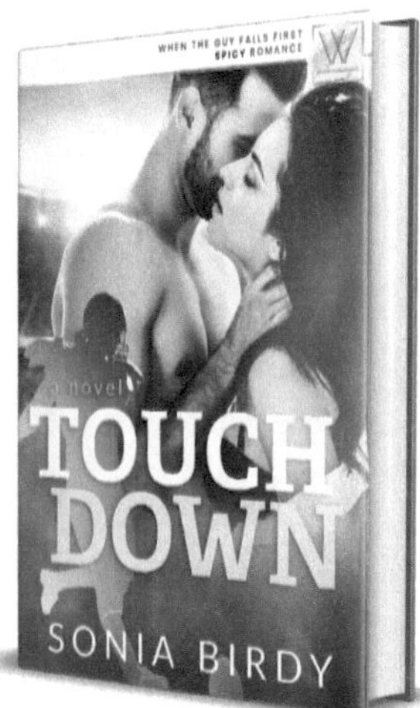

Kalliopee: A Princess's Sacrifice
by ***Koko Nhan***

After years of violent battles, Kalliopee agrees to sacrifice her freedom by marrying the prince of the enemy kingdom in order to bring peace.

In a world where women are treated as slaves rather than wives, she is still delighted to be reunited with her first love, Karel.

However, life is unpredictable, and the horrors of war have transformed Karel into a tough and ruthless heir to the throne, who despises the Viridians more than anything. While he has no qualms about mistreating Kalliopee, his determination wavers when confronted with her striking eyes. In the midst of desire and animosity, schemes and plots, dreams and disillusionment, will the princess's heart endure the price of her liberty?

The Private Garden
by ***Oly TL***

The most disturbing and transgressive of contracts...

Tiger Sexton seems to have it all. Charisma. Respect. Relentless business acumen. More fortune than he could spend in a life and a sublime wife, Sophia.

When Oceane is invited by Mrs. Sexton for a job interview in one of the restaurants that her husband gave her, the young French tourist knows nothing about this couple. Their name means

nothing to her, people are not her thing. She just wants a job, a place to live and to move on with her life... Sophia's proposal comes at the right time: the Sextons are looking for an *au pair.*

But by opening their doors to her, many other locks are likely to open. Is Oceane ready for this? And what about Sophia, and especially the Tiger lurking in this Secret Garden?

Keep in touch with Koko Nhan

Join her facebook reader group, Koko's ShaadiReaders, to get the lastedt updates and talk about books and more!

You can also find Koko here:

Website:

https://www.authorkokonhan.com

Instagram:

https://www.instagram.com/koko_nhan_author/

About the Author

Koko Nhan is a popular French romance author known for creating strong and relatable heroines in her stories. Whether it's a dystopian setting or a contemporary romance, she excels at bringing flawed and realistic characters to life.

Based in Montpellier, in the southern part of France, Koko Nhan crafts immersive worlds where women display courage and self-sacrifice. With each word, page, and novel, she has captured the hearts of numerous female readers.

Her debut volume, "Kalliopee: A Princess's Sacrifice," marks her entry into the United States, signaling her international presence.

When she's not writing or immersed in a good book, Koko Nhan spends her time taking care of her daughters, Tara and Lia (the best job ever!), relishing her husband's delicious meals, while also taking care of her two cute furry pets.